THE
FORGOTTEN
GODDESS

Rebekah Sinclair

Rebekah Sinclair

Rebekah Sinclair

Where to Begin

The Forgotten Goddess

The Unforgotten Flame (Novealla)
The Unforgotten Vow (Novelette)

Awakening
The Forgotten Goddess

Reclaiming
The Forgotten Goddess

Book 4: Title Pending
Anticipated Release: Fall, 2024

WARNING: THIS BOOK CONTAINS CONTENT THAT MAY BE TRIGGERING.

- Mentions and depicts mental health trauma responses such as anxiety, PTSD, and panic attack disorder.
- Mentions, but does not depict, non-descriptive reference to a prior sexual assault and human trafficking.
- Mentions and depicts child endangerment and death.
- Contains explicit language, sexual content, physical violence, abduction, and death.

To: Nanny
This one is for you.

Enjoy listening to The Forgotten Goddess playlist on Spotify!

A song has been added for each chapter to represent the tones or themes of the chapter.

1
Rhea

I wonder if dying feels like flying. I wonder if Icarus felt the difference between flying to the sun and falling to the ocean. If grasping a ray of sunlight felt the same as crashing into the brutal waves of the sea below. Was it worth it? Was Icarus' flight on wax-covered wings worth the short moment of warmth? Or did he regret risking eternal freedom from something so fleeting as a moment of wonder?

Running my fingers along the book, gold embossed words *Winged Grecians* sit on the surface of the pale blue cover. My mind travels to the clear waters of the Mediterranean—such a vivid fantasy. I can almost smell the salty wind rising off the sea, lifting the mythical beasts on their giant wings into the sky. A gentle tendril of wind caresses my cheek with a wisp of tenderness, interrupting the fantasy. My powers leak from the chasm inside me. I slam the book shut as I slam my magic back within me, snapping me out of my haze and bringing me back to the bookstore.

It's been ten years since the car accident, but every anniversary I spend my birthday thinking about death. Burning sulfur stinging my nostrils is a memory etched into my nightmares, as is being expelled from the vehicle and soaring through the air like Icarus crashing into the sea. But the twisted humor of fate kept me alive with the guilt of knowing I am a killer. Fate is so cruel.

When I'm stressed or stuck in the dark thoughts of my fatal car accident, I run to my favorite bookstore: Once Upon a Spine. Tucked between tall buildings in downtown Atlanta, the two-story brick building is my comfort spot. Running away to the pages of a book became my coping mechanism. Now it's my obsession to learn where my powers come from.

My Aunt Demi raised me after I lost my parents and brother. She is always teasing me about spending my time in libraries and bringing home stacks of books for the weekend instead of hanging out at the mall. Living simply, she sells her beeswax candles and fresh produce at the farmer's market; my memories are always of her bent over rows of crops and flowers on her quaint farm while the Pennsylvania sunshine streams through the canopy of trees, dappling the small, brown cabin where she raised me.

She was never one for marriage or kids. Living alone in her cabin in the Pennsylvania hills, she would look down her nose at children playing in the parks, calling them little harpies. But when the call came in, she rushed to the hospital and welcomed me to her home after the funeral.

Panic attacks became frequent after the accident. For the first few months I lived with my aunt, they assigned a social worker to monitor me and ordered me to see a therapist. I tried telling him about my powers, but he brushed it off as survivor's guilt and said I was looking for a way to blame myself for my family's death, which was ruled an accident.

Of course, how else can you explain suffocating your family to death with tentacles of black mist and smoke?

A few times, I almost asked Aunt Demi about my powers, wondering if she also had them or someone else in the family. But, like morning glories tucking away their petals when they see the moon, my anxiety keeps my secret bottled tightly within me. The guilt over the pain I caused acts as my prison, holding my mind hostage.

When I wanted to go to New York for college, Aunt Demi was sad but didn't pressure me to stay. Now that I live in Atlanta for my career as a publisher, she visits me every few months. Having her near always refreshes my broken heart, even only for a few days.

My cell phone vibrates as if my thoughts summoned her, and I add the book to the small collection building in the crook of my arm. My laughter escapes as she delivers her out-of-tune rendition of happy birthday.

"Thank you." I chuckle as she finishes.

"Any fun plans for today?"

"Yeah, some shopping, maybe a pedicure, and then dinner with a few friends." That answer is mostly true. No one has confirmed they can make it to dinner tonight, but I'm sure a few people from work will attend.

"Hey, when I'm down for my visit next month, it will be the Autumn Equinox. I'll bring homemade wine, and we'll dance naked under the moon."

"You're such a weird aunt."

"I'm your favorite aunt."

"You're my only aunt."

Our familiar joke is teased like always, but the truth is: our family is tiny. My grandparents died before I was born, and Aunt Demi was my dad's only sister. My mom was an only child, so after they died ten years ago, my aunt and I only had each other. I suppose she needed me as much as I needed her.

"All right honey, I've got to run to the farmers market. These tomatoes aren't going to sell themselves. Have a great birthday and call me in a few days."

It's a stormy Saturday morning—the perfect weather for book reading, so the bookstore is busy. Part of the blame for the crowd is the local author book signing event, the real reason for my visit today. Damien Lopez is an Atlanta resident and independent author. He specializes in werewolf mythology, but the subject of his latest release is the missing Library of Alexandria: *Burned or Hidden: The Disappearance of the Great Library*. Several chapters discuss the ancient libraries' collection of scrolls about people with elemental powers and shapeshifting abilities. I'm hoping to talk about his theories deeper and see if he will share some of the sources of his information.

Walking by the café's brewing cups of caffeine, the smell of freshly ground coffee beans and paper welcome me like an old friend. The worn, oversized seats with soft, brown leather invite me to sit and enjoy my books and my favorite caramel latte. Mrs. Clark operates the café and spots me with my usual stack of books shoved precariously in my arms after forgetting my reusable bags again. She offers me a friendly smile and a tote for today's treasures.

Chairs fill up a small section in the middle of the store, and I find a seat near the back, tucking my cloth hobo-style purse under the chair in front of me. My arm is thankful to be relieved of the books as I stuff them inside the tote and lean them against my hip, so they don't topple over. Raking my eyes over the other patrons waiting for the reading to begin, a remarkably handsome man a few seats down steals my attention.

Holy hell, that man is gorgeous.

Corded muscles sit tensely under his navy-colored shirt and light, faded jeans. He's tall with sun-kissed skin, chestnut hair, and bright blue eyes are fixed on mine. The stubble on his sharp jaw shows a few days of growth, and his long legs sit with one ankle crossed over his knee. His foot bounces up and down like mine.

A warm flush takes over my freckled cheeks and I know they are blazing bright red. I curse my pale complexion for giving my embarrassment away so easily. Living with the weird farmer woman in dirt-covered overalls didn't make me the most sought-after girl in school, especially with my nose always stuck in a book.

The only time guys really talked to me was because of a dare or to poke fun at me for turning bright shades of cherry red anytime attention was directed to me. Opening my mouth to defend myself would inevitably result in the red blush darkening with further embarrassment, so I learned to remain relatively quiet if I could. I would probably choke on my own words if someone as attractive as him tried to talk to me today.

A lock of my brown hair, muted and dull, twists around my finger while I bite the inside of my cheek. Heat rushes through my body, and I'm suddenly aware of my slouching posture and casual clothes choices for this morning's errands. My pale grey sneakers and plain black tights with an emerald top would do nothing to attract this supermodel of a man sitting at the end of my row.

I pull my gaze to the podium as Damien arrives from the back of the bookstore. He is in his late thirties; always wearing jeans and band t-shirts, he has a casual demeanor and takes time to talk with fans after his speaking events. We have had a few conversations after his appearances. He spoke passionately about his heritage traced to the ancient Mayans, and I loved hearing about his mother from Jamaica and his father from Pisté in Mexico. Colorful tattoos cover most of his arms with scenes like those of the Mayan carvings on the step pyramids of Mexico.

My stomach twists nervously as I review my plan at the close of the reading. I don't want others to hear my questions, so I'll hang back until the line dies down so I can join toward the end.

Damien begins his event smiling and looking over the audience with deep espresso-colored eyes. The effort to keep my attention trained on anything other than the beautiful man at the end of my row is immense. Using the start of the reading as a distraction, I decide I can't stand it any longer and peek at him again, but he's looking forward with a smirking grin.

Why is he smiling? Did Damien say something funny, and I missed it?

He'll know I'm not paying attention if I don't laugh. Or maybe he'll think I have no sense of humor. *I'm not sure which is worse.* I fidget with the seam of my shirt to hide my embarrassment. Thankful my hair is covering my hot ears, I do little to calm my fluttering heart which beats faster at the moments ticking by.

With a proud smile, Damien closes his newly released title. He retrieves the tattered Atlanta Falcons ballcap from his head, waving it overhead as a gentle clap from the handfuls of patrons signals the end of the reading. Snatching the tote at my side, I bolt toward the store's bathroom with a walk that quickens to a sprint as I near the door. Needing some distance between the people and myself, the approaching tailspin of a panic attack follows me into the bathroom.

With the edges of my vision darkening, a glossy stare threatens to take over my eyes. Refusing to let the panic overwhelm me, I lay my palms flat on the cool countertop of the bathroom, taking steadying breaths and rolling my head from side to side, slowly relaxing. After a moment of focus, my heart begins to slow its forceful pumping to a steady beat.

Seizing a brown paper towel from the nearby dispenser, I soak it with cool water and pat my face and neck. The refreshing chill helps soothe the rising panic until I've regained control of myself. Thankful for the small makeup pouch in my purse, I look at the tote bag full of books on the counter, and my heart leaps in my chest. Not only is it store policy to leave merchandise out of the bathroom, but I realize my purse must still be sitting unattended beneath the chair.

In my rush to create distance from the handsome man, the crowd in the bookstore, and my panic, I grabbed the wrong bag. Rubbing under my eyes to fix the smudges of brown mascara, I take the tote handles and prepare to exit the bathroom. With a plan to retrieve my purse, I'll hurry to the cashier for my purchase before I join the line for the book signing.

As I rush out of the bathroom, I run face-first into an immovable force with an unflattering "Oof!" The tote bag swings out of my hand and thumps on the ground, spewing the books from its confines.

"Sorry," I mumble to myself as I chase after the tumbling books.

A strong hand enters my view as the handsome man from the reading kneels to help me retrieve the last book. Hypnotized by the movement of his muscular forearms, I glance at him through my lashes, seeing a smirk still plastered on his face. Running my fingers through my hair, I fix a rogue lock behind my ear and snap my eyes to the gray commercial carpet of the bookstore.

"Don't worry about it." His deep voice rumbles in his chest like the thunder of today's storm.

He is well over six feet, towering over my five-foot, five-inch frame. My view darts around the space, looking everywhere but at him. His presence overwhelms my senses, and I push down the fluttering pulse I had calmed in the bathroom.

"Greek mythology fan?" he asks, offering the book to me, and widening his smile. With our closeness, the details of his handsome face strike me. Sparkling eyes with deep blue and aqua rivets reflect like the night sky on a calm ocean. Dimples dot his cheeks, and he smells of sandalwood and spices.

Of course. The hot ones always smell nice.

Rolling my eyes at my internal dialogue, I stand with a huff and situate the books back into my tote. "I was just looking for my purse."

"This purse?" He cocks an eyebrow, holding my cloth purse with its long strap and patchwork design. My lips thin in embarrassment as I reach out to take my bag. My fingers brushing his send shocks up my arm, raising the hairs on the back of my neck. My breath hitches in surprise as my powers nearly somersault under my skin. I relax my tight shoulders, trying desperately to calm my abilities and keep a straight face. The man's grin melts away as his blue eyes pierce me intently.

Tilting his head to one side, he squints with that look of familiarity like when you see someone and swear you have met them before.

"What is your name?" he asks. His chest rises and falls dramatically, as if he's out of breath. I force my eyes closed and pinch the bridge of my nose in concentration to dampen my trembling powers.

"Rhea Crenshaw."

"I'm Ethan." His buttery voice floats across the air, draping me in an intimate blanket of desire. I inhale a deep breath to relax, practically panting to regain strict control over the internal battle with my powers. Finally, I open my eyes again, and shock rattles me when I find I'm alone.

Searching across the bookstore with my forehead scrunched in confusion, I locate him walking toward the exit. He pauses, and our eyes meet. The adorable grin is back, and the boys from high school come rushing to my mind. Their teasing was always to lead me on for their enjoyment, and it seems little boys only grow up to be men who behave the same way. He winks as he pushes the double doors open with a dramatic flair. Clenching my jaw in annoyance, I respond with an obscene hand gesture. His laughter bounces across the store as the door closes behind him.

Jerk!

Looking back to the signing area for today's event, my shoulders drop when I see Damien is gone, with nothing more than a stack of signed books on the table. Abandoning my hopes of speaking with him about my questions, I resign to send a message to his social media account. Joining the long line of customers, I draft my message as I shuffle through the line to pay for the books crowding my new tote.

Outside the bookstore, the stormy day does nothing to damper the hot summer day in Georgia. A sticky heat clings to my skin as thunder rumbles in the distance. Despite the gloomy day, luck is on my side as I spot Damien across the street between two buildings. I may have a chance to ask about his sources of humans with powers after all.

Bouncing across the street before the light changes, I stall at the mouth of a dark alley, swallowing hard as I decide if this is a safe choice. My desire to seize time from Damien and aid my research to find more people like me—people with powers—drives me forward. I keep my footsteps light and clutch my two bags close to my side as I descend into the bowels of the alley.

The storm clouds bring wind gusts to the narrow channel between the tall buildings. Trash cans and garbage bags sitting along the brick walls cast long shadows and rattle in the breeze as they wait for collection. The storm throws a trash can lid against the dark asphalt, and it rings loudly in the alley. I jump, startled. The passage is a long L-shape corridor, and as I reach the end, I peek around the corner, careful not to show myself. As my stomach twists harshly, I pause. The rest of the alley continues to my right, and my eyes widen when I see Damien meeting Ethan from the bookstore.

Deep creases sit heavily on their foreheads as they talk closely in hushed tones. Damien reaches into his pocket and retrieves a small object, dropping it into Ethan's hand. A fresh gust of wind whips the hair around my face, and I retreat behind the building, hiding from their view. Hesitating, the sound of a door slamming causes me to look around the corner again, only to find it's empty. Ethan and Damien must have entered the adjacent building through the back door, and I find myself alone in the dark alley.

My senses return, and a flutter of panic makes my heart pound wildly in my chest. I spin on my heel and take large, hurried steps toward the open street, but the sight ahead freezes me in place. A huge man is stationed in the middle of the alley, leaning against the building with one foot against the brick. Smoke billows from the corners of his mouth as he takes a considerable drag of a cigarette before turning his head to me. Reflective eyes pierce me, and my very core constricts in terror.

"Don't move, and don't make a sound." His voice comes out as a low growl. My mouth is dry as I lick my lips and I curse my stupid decision to come down this alley in the first place.

"I don't want any trouble." My shaky voice is nearly a whisper and a knot lodges in my throat. I cough, trying to clear the obstruction and feign bravery as I stand taller, righting my posture and squaring my shoulders.

"Shame. That is exactly why I came here." His Italian accent is heavy as he flicks a cigarette to the ground and shifts his gaze behind me. A bottle rattles and I spin on my heel. A twin of the large man stands behind me.

"Our alpha wants a word with you, little lady."

Two men, identical in every way—even down to the matching scars running down their chins—block me from both sides of the alley. Their mouths are twisted in disgust as they regard me. The first twin flicks his spent cigarette at me, and tiny embers shower the dark pavement as it bounces at my feet.

My powers flare protectively within me as my pulse skyrockets to a painful speed. Sensing the threat, my magic pounds and begs for release, but I must keep it contained. I can't risk killing anyone else. I can't risk someone seeing me. What if a recording leaked online? How can I explain balls of fire rushing out of my palms or shadowed mist suffocating someone?

"I'll call the police if you don't stand aside and let me

leave." Angry tears well in my eyes at the direness of my situation, but I urge them back. Fixing my purse and tote from my
shoulder to my hand, I prepare to drop them as the tension
grows within the stifling alley. As if the storm above can sense
the danger, the alley darkens; shadows grow large around the
dumpsters and trashcans dotting the alley.

A surge of wind barrels from above, and I stumble sideways
into the brick wall at my side. My bags tumble to the ground
where I leave them. A flash of color shoots before me, too
quick to see. A woman around my age, but several inches
shorter, rightens herself from a crouched position as if she
dropped from the sky, but when I look, it is impossible to
know where she came from. Endless brick walls stretch ten
stories above us into the storm overhead.

Did she fall out of a rain cloud?

"Well, if it isn't dumb and dumber," she teases, her pale
blue eyes impale each of the twins as she stares up and down
the alley. The giant twins snarl. Taking a step closer, they stand
squarely in the center of the alley at both ends. My head pivots,
looking at both sides of the alley.

"Friends of yours?" I ask her.

"Not exactly." Her platinum hair, fixed in a high ponytail,
bounces with the movements of her head as she stands in the
center of the alley. Back to the street, she faces the twin at
the end.

"You pups should get back to your *master*. Quite a ways
away from home, aren't you?"

"It's nothing that concerns you, *Elemental*." The man spits
the last word back at her.

"Oh, I think it does concern me. I'm sure you recall that

abducting a poor mortal in broad daylight is frowned upon. You're breaking The Mortal Treaty."

Elemental. Mortal Treaty.

This woman clearly knows these men, but I don't understand what they are talking about. I keep my face stoic, determined not to show signs of confusion or distress. Remaining calm and in control may save our lives. With this woman here, I certainly can't use my powers. I already hate myself for what I did to my family. I can't relive that guilt again because of a stranger.

"You can tell as well as we can that she is no *mortal*. I don't think you want to start this fight today, Callie."

The petite woman doesn't answer. She stands firm, her shoulders set and eyes sparkling with an alert glare. A wind current wrestles against me, billowing the brown ribbons of my hair as the storm above us intensifies. Callie's long hair begins to blow and swirl as the wind increases; thunder rumbles softly in the distance and mirrors the tumbling fear rolling in my stomach. My shoulders are tense, and I bounce gently on the balls of my feet, poised toward the alley's exit.

Keeping her eyes on the threat before her, she turns her head to me. "When I tell you 'run', don't stop—just get out of here." She passes quiet instructions to me. I need to make it to the mouth of the alley so I can scream for help.

Resolved with this plan, an idea weaves into my mind. Keeping my back against the wall, I loosen the strict confines keeping my powers locked inside, and the tendrils of my power swirl within me in anticipation. Adding my winds to the stormy day could help me disable the imposing man towering over the mouth of the alley and give me the break I need to make it out.

Ready with my powers, I step into the middle and turn my back to hers, waiting for her signal. The storm builds around us. Sweat forms on my brow as I wrestle back my powers to avoid using too much. Within three heartbeats, the alley has become a wind tunnel as the storm's force increases.

"Run!" The girl's voice slams through me, and I sense her charge toward the twin positioned behind me. Without hesitation, I bolt to the street ahead. The unseen force of my wind power slams the twin's bald head into the brick wall. A crater of cracked brick shows the imprint of his head as he slides down. The bricks leave deep scratches and cuts on his skin.

I push hard off the asphalt and hurl down the street. Daring to glance behind me, Callie has charged the other twin. Propelling herself through the air in a forward flip, her leg crashes into the twin's face.

She's amazing!

My concern for the woman distracted me from my opponent, and the split-second look cost me a moment of speed. Righting my gaze, I push again with my feet against the ground, but my eyes widen, shocked to see the twin before me. A murderous expression rages in his bloodshot eyes as they bulge in their sockets. He moves unnaturally fast, closing the distance too quickly for my wind power. My inexperience is a detriment, and I lower my shoulder, preparing to use my wind to push myself past him.

My hunter lunges forward with a tremendous growl, wrapping his broad hands around my throat. Continuing his arm's path, he drives me by his grip on my neck and into the brick building behind—the dust from crumpled bricks sprinkle down my body. My head bounces against the wall, bringing spots and flashes of silver to my vision.

Still encasing my throat, my opponent whips me like a ragdoll to the floor and I land on my stomach with my hands flat against the ground. Pushing hard against the side of my face, the rocks and gravel of the asphalt dig into the soft flesh of my cheeks. As he twists my arm behind me painfully, my eye connects with the end of the alley to see Callie receive a punch to the face, and she falls to the ground, unmoving.

Hermes

If I never have another night shift babysitting werewolves, it'll be too soon. The Shifter holiday of the Autumn Equinox is in four weeks, and the pre-parties have been exhausting to monitor. The wolves always kick up a fuss during the equinox for the power boost they get from the moon, but this year is especially brutal.

News of sightings are on the rise, though the human news reports them as 'packs of coyotes' hunting outside their usual territories. Last night we had to break up a Lykaia ceremony. Thank the goddess the Shifters have stopped including human sacrifice as a part of it. A chill races down my spine thinking back to the Lykaia on Wolf Mountain two thousand years ago. If I didn't know if I was eating sausages or human intestines, I don't think I could ever recover for the rest of my immortal life.

Today's mission is at a typical human establishment, but one I especially enjoy. The aroma of the books, filled with their paper and ink, makes me think of my mother's bronze hands. She was a writer; a fantastic storyteller and books always surrounded her. I remember watching her hold her quills so tenderly as she dipped them into her inkwell. Two taps on the edge of the glass well to remove the excess ink before hearing the nib scratch across the paper as she wrote her poems and stories.

The closest thing I have to that memory now is the Commune library and it's the place I hide when I need to clear my mind. Of all the sites to have a mission, I suppose this is not so terrible.

Walking the aisles of Once Upon a Spine, I run my finger along the spines of the books, chuckling at the play-on-words of the store's name. I carefully observe the shoppers, noting how many mortals are here and checking for anything suspicious. I use my Light abilities to tell me who is here, human, or otherwise. My gift senses the particles of light that fill all living beings.

A Shifter sits in the back storeroom scrolling social media on his phone; that is Damien, the man I'm here to meet. Two dozen human shoppers are strolling around the first floor of the narrow brick building, picking up books and flipping through their pages before returning them to the shelves. Five humans are on the second-floor balcony sitting in a grouping of chairs, discussing a newly released autobiography of a famous British member of royalty. Eight humans dot the café, sipping their beverages, typing on laptops or reading magazines.

"Tell me again why we're staking out a bookstore instead of sleeping soundly in our beds?" Terra's complaints sound in our earpieces. Terra is not a powerful Earth Elemental, but she is unique with her ability of quicksand. Any element made from earth particles turns into a thick, swirling liquid with her touch.

I ignore the snide comments from the rest of the team. Of course, they don't know I volunteered us for this assignment.

Today's featured author, Damien Lopez, contacted me secretly two nights ago, wanting to meet. Kicked out of his pack ten years ago, he is a *Lone Wolf* and publishes books on werewolves and other mythology. He knows I'm hunting for the hidden location of the Underworld and promised to give me some information today if I would meet him and listen to his offer. Of course, I can't turn down this opportunity, even in the heat of Shifter-orgy season. *Gross.*

"Everyone quiet down and focus on your positions." Achilles, my best friend and second in command, gets the team back in order. Achilles, the best warrior of the Elementals, is a Flame Mage and fated mate to my sister, Calypso, a Wind Siren. Perfectly matched, Wind Sirens and Flames feed each other in their power charges, and the result of their incredible powers combined will leave you awestruck.

With my abilities, I continue to search the store, but a massive aura spike at one end of the bookstore freezes me.

"A powerful Elemental is here," I speak directly into Achilles and Callie's minds.

I make eye contact with my sister on the second level of the bookstore who is watching from the balcony. She feigns a crying face, mocking the team's complaints. Stifling a laugh, I continue my casual stroll through the bookstore to investigate the power spike. Tensions between the Elementals and Shifters have long been high and filled with prejudice, so we must ensure this meeting today is not a setup.

The Shifter population pledged their allegiance long ago to a rogue and powerful Elemental, Ares, the God of War. He thrives in turmoil and feeds off death. He manufactures conflicts and strife between human governments while selling off Immortals to the humans underground gladiator arenas for sport. Remaining long hidden inside the safety of his compound, the Underworld, he deserves death for his crimes.

My interest in capturing him is to avenge the deaths of my father, Apollo, my mother, Daphne, and my mate, Juliette. Ares has taken nearly everyone I love, and when the immortal ichor drips from his throat, it will be on the blade of my sword.

Evoking my powers of Mirage, I bend and refract the light that renders me invisible to humans. Masking my aura also makes me undetectable to Shifters with powerful senses, so now I'm free to investigate the anomaly.

Peering around the aisle, a young woman's laughter echoes inside my head, ensnaring my attention—honey-brown hair cascades between her shoulders in delicate waves with golden tendrils swaying near her face. Matching eyes, the color of honey, sparkle with flecks of gold as she laughs into her phone, and light freckles dot the rosy cheeks of her pale complexion. I track her meandering aimlessly through the aisles, making her way through the Greek Mythology section.

Ironic.

Her aura fascinates me. Like oil on water, silver starlight shines with hues of blues and purples swirling together. The forcefield of her energy is wild and chaotic, almost restless. It reminds me of Juliette, my fated mate who died four-hundred years ago. She also possessed a rare silver aura, beautiful to behold as it whipped around her. I shake my head to clear myself of Juliette's memories.

Vigilantly watching for suspicious activities is critical with the number of mortals present, and the team can't afford distractions today. It's nearly time for the author's reading, so I tear myself away from the beauty and find a seat at the rear of the audience with a view of nearly the entire bookstore.

Careful to remain cloaked, I track the beautiful woman as she meanders through the café, engaging with one of the mortal employees before she joins the reading, selecting a seat in the same back row. Her presence makes my skin hum with electricity; I feel pulled to her like the moon pulls on the earth's oceans, and I can't look away. Her sweet perfume of berries and vanilla wafts around me, filling my senses with her.

My spine stiffens, and every muscle of my body tenses when she turns and looks directly into my eyes. *She can see through my Mirage.* The gold-flecked eyes pierce me, and I swear my heart stops beating for the quickest moment. Paralyzed under her fleeting stare, she quickly looks away, a rush of embarrassment flooding her pale skin, and blazing her plump cheeks red. Even a powerful Sensory with their empathy and emotion detection abilities, should not be able to perceive someone with a potent Mirage like mine.

"Dude. I think she saw you," Achilles says over our earpieces from his position in the bookstore.

Heat rushes down my face to my stomach, filling me with uncertainty, and I don't answer.

"Man, what a shitty leader you turned out to be." Callie teases, lightening the mood so the rest of the team doesn't get antsy. My sister makes me snicker as I keep myself trained forward, watching Damien begin his reading. The strange woman fidgets through the event, stealing another glance in my direction. Her power is overwhelming to my senses as it wraps around me, rippling like an unsettled ocean in an approaching storm.

Thankfully Damien's reading doesn't last long, and with a wave of his ballcap, the beautiful mystery bolts to the bathroom. I have time to spare before meeting with Damien, and I need to get to the bottom of this anomaly quickly before I walk into a Werewolf trap.

Achilles approaches me as I stare at the bathroom door as if I can make her reappear at will. Being wrapped in her power, the absence of her presence feels like being dropped into a dark hole, and I long to feel her voltage on my skin again.

"How could she see you if you were cloaked?" Achilles says in hushed tones.

"No idea, but let's see what we can find out. Do you think that girl works with Ares? Gods, I hope not," I say, running my hand through my hair.

"And why would that be, Team Leader?" Achilles smirks. I knock him with my shoulder, rolling my eyes at his teasing.

Obviously, she is gorgeous. The type of woman that intimidates men by even speaking to them—but if she were found out to be working with the God of War, it would be a life sentence. She would spend eternity bound to the Labyrinth of Crete, enslaved in a Thaumium collar.

From the realm of Vulcan forged in the gods' fires, the ethereal metal can mute any Immortals' powers. It's a terrible sentence to live for eternity in the bowels of the Labyrinth, fighting the shadow creatures of Elysium and fallen angels from Hel with no more strength than a mortal. I can't imagine this beauty before me suffering for eternity in a place like that.

"Looks like she left her bag. Why don't you return it to her?" Achilles walks away, smirking over his shoulder at me after pushing a cloth bag in my hand. "I'm going to check the back."

I sense her shifting energy before she bursts through the door, face-first into my chest. The bag in her arms tumbles to the ground. Her nearness is like fire, and I rush to help her with the books, wanting to be near her warmth.

I'm suffocated by the power flowing off her in torrents, curious to know what her elemental power is and wondering if I would survive if I challenged her to battle. It may be worth my immortal life to see what she can do.

"I can hear your thoughts, brother. You may want to close that mind off before you think anything else. Please. For my sake." Callie interrupts, and the smirk on my face remains since first seeing this woman. I make no effort to conceal it, especially when her eyes shift quickly to my mouth before darting away.

"I was just looking for my purse." My eyes are fixated on her lips as they form the delicate words, and her melodic voice wraps itself around my senses. I nearly forget the reason I was waiting for her.

"This purse?" I dangle the bag by its straps, giving her access to retrieve it. Her frustration flares adorably, scrunching her brow.

As she takes the purse from me, I attempt to understand her elemental power with my Light ability. I bend the unseen particles of light around her, but her strong aura repels my probes with a light nearly blinding me from within. My lungs are heavy as I work on breathing at a normal pace.

"What's your name?" I wait for the answer as if I'm standing on the edge of a cliff, knowing it may send me plummeting below.

"H, it's time to go," Achilles speaks to my mind. The woman before me keeps her eyes closed, and her silvery aura flexes, enveloping me in a warm glow that feels like the last golden ray of sunlight at the end of a summer day.

"Rhea Crenshaw." The answer is a ripple across the atmosphere between us.

Before she can open her eyes, I cloak myself again and push the trigger of the portal wand in my pocket, sending me instantly to the bookshop entrance. Without her nearness, I'm plunged back into the arctic waters of reality.

Through telepathy, I project the fake name I use around mortals onto her thoughts. *"I'm Ethan."*

Rhea opens her beautiful honey eyes and searches for me, perplexed. Irritation flares causing her aura to expand when she finds me standing at the exit; the fire in her spirit only adds to her allure. I smile and wink at her, hoping to enflame her further and see the ripples of her power once more before I leave. Laughter rumbles from my chest when she flips her middle finger at me, and I pace after Achilles.

"Callie, keep an eye on her for me," I ask my sister, using telepathy. If this meeting is a trap and she comes to us for a confrontation, we're screwed. Achilles is waiting out of sight, ready to teleport Damien out should anything terrible go down. Being a Lone Wolf, he doesn't have the protection of a pack, and if he is caught by the Shifters working with Elementals, his death would be excruciating.

"Thank you for doing this. I understand the risks you take." I begin, taking his hand in a courteous greeting.

"I appreciate you taking my request for confidentiality seriously. Pack information is forbidden to be shared, even for a dispersed wolf." Damien shifts back and forth on his feet, and his eyes dart quickly between the rooftops as if a pack of Shifters will descend upon us at any moment.

"So, what is this meeting about?"

"I'm trying to save my species." My brows crinkle at his

answer. "The werewolves are dying. Growing populations of women can't shift, and neither can their pups. We call them Lycan."

"I've heard of Lycan before."

"Well, in each generation, there are more Lycan and fewer Shifters. I'm trying to find out why."

"Why is that something I should help with? If the Shifters die out, Ares loses his army, and the Elementals can fish him out of his trenches."

"You should know not all Shifters are loyal to Ares. Do you know what they do to Shifters who can't transform?" I keep my expression even, but my stomach knots. I've heard rumors of what happens to Shifters in the arenas of the mortals.

"They are sold to human markets," Damien continues. "By their packs. A woman with the aura of a predator and the ichor of immortality, but no protection from her pack, is better off dead than facing what happens in the gladiator arenas. Forced to fight animals, they suffer unending torture while they are healed, only to be tortured again and assaulted by unfathomable means. Anything is fair and available for a price."

"How can the packs do that to each other?" My face twists in disgust, thinking of someone selling off Callie to a fate like that, and my hands shake at the thought.

"I challenged Ares' orders once, and my Lycan wife suffered in those arenas for six weeks before the pieces of her body were returned to me."

"I'm sorry." My sympathy is sincere, but the sense we are being watched makes the hairs on the back of my neck stand on end, and I want to get out of this alley quickly. "Why do something now?"

I send out my aura, feeling for the presence of anyone else, but I sense nothing.

"There is a pattern of behavior which tells me Ares has something big in the works."

"What is he planning?"

"We can't talk about it here."

"So, what do you think I can do to help you? You're not giving me much—"

"—I need access to the Elementals' libraries. I have found clues that the Library of Alexandria was not destroyed."

"Everyone knows it was destroyed. Hell, half of us watched it burn."

"I don't think it was. I think it's still here and holds the secret to defeating Ares." Damien drops a small black storage device from his pocket into my hand. Unmarked and unassuming, I turn it over in my palm before tucking it into my pocket. "This is everything I have on my theories of where the Underworld is, and I'm giving it to you. Help me get access to your Commune records. That's it."

A shift in the winds blows the heavy scent of werewolves into the alleyway. Damien and I look toward the rooftops before turning to each other. I push him into an open door, and we trudge quickly to the center of the abandoned building.

"A pack is approaching," I speak to Achilles' mind, and he teleports into the building as planned.

"I'll be in touch with you in a few days. We have to be careful, or I'll meet the same fate as my wife." Damien says with his mouth tight with worry.

"Get him out of here, and I'll meet you with the rest of the team at the Commune," I instruct Achilles, who nods once in confirmation. He activates his teleportation device, and a large oval of pure light burns silently. "We'll be in touch." And with that, their doorway of light zaps out of existence.

"Everyone teleport back to the Commune now." I instruct the team through telepathy and use my teleportation device to snap home. Terra is the first back, and she quickly removes her protective vest, stretching her arms over her head and twisting her back.

Thinking about Rhea and her magnetic aura, I recall the book I retrieved for her. The title in white letters, sprawled across the red paperback, knots my stomach.

Eternal Hermes: From Greek God to Alchemical Magus

My ancient name scrawled on the book's cover make the corner of my mouth quiver in a smile—the messenger of the gods and escort of souls to the ferryman; the Herald. However, I haven't gone by that name in ages, but it makes me smile, nonetheless.

"Deliver our wolf safely home?" I ask Achilles as he emerges in our team's prep room, my hand toying with the storage device in my pocket.

"Yeah. I scoped out his building, and it was safe. No wolves around other than him. He wants to chill for a few days and will reach out for another meeting. Where is Callie?"

Damnit.

I told her to keep an eye on Rhea. "Terra, did you have eyes on Callie in the bookstore?"

"No, I was babysitting the mortals picking out their books," Terra answers sharply.

"Fuck!" Achilles curses through his teeth.

He stands beside me, pushing his teleportation trigger to snap us back to the bookstore stockroom. Heat floods my head as I rush to project my aura outward in all directions, sensing no trace of her within the bookstore. I expand it further to the streets outside. An odd void, like a bottomless hole, takes up an immense amount of space in the alley across the street.

What the fuck is that?

I've never felt anything like it before from any Elemental. A faint tendril of Callie's wind sways above the void briefly before it disappears.

"Achilles, the alleyway!" I blurt, the color draining from my face.

Another flash of light delivers us to the alley corner as a windowless white van shoots out and speeds down the street. Achilles and I both spring back on our heels to avoid being struck by the van until we realize it's full of wolves.

"Fucking Lupo's twins are driving that van," Achilles calls to me as we slide on the asphalt to quickly change directions and follow the path the van is blazing down the street. Lupo is the ruthless Alpha Wolf of the European packs and the second son of Ares. He's the second wolf ever created, and his packs are known for relishing in their gruesome bloodshed.

A large portal flashes, swallowing the van in bright light, and it's gone, Callie along with it.

T his is not the birthday I envisioned. Rocks and pebbles dig into my butt from the dirt floor of the hued cave. I fix my vision on a fly perched on the knuckle of my right hand and watch it dance in circles while I try to ignore the heavy metal collar locked around my neck. My right eye is swollen and hazy. Cuts and scrapes run down the left side of my face from being dragged down the asphalt by that ogre of a man in the alleyway. Beyond, Callie sits against the dirt wall of her cell as metal bars divide our two spaces.

One of her blue eyes is dark and swollen, and her lip is split in the corner of her mouth. The neat ponytail from earlier is now disheveled, and her bright blonde hair is tangled and stuck to her face from sweat and blood. Our clothes are torn and dirty, and they took our shoes. In the windowless van, one of the twins dumped the contents of my purse and slipped my driver's license into his pocket.

"Why did you help me?" I ask in a quiet voice, almost a whisper.

She doesn't answer but shifts her back against the hard dirt wall of the cell. The metal cuff is heavy against my collarbone, pinching the skin between the metal and my bones. I pull up on the collar, holding it above my skin, and sigh in relief.

"Yeah, these collars suck." Her voice is high pitched in the small space.

"Is this a tracking device?"

She cocks her head at me, narrowing her eyes before she answers.

"It's Thaumium. It mutes our powers."

My spine stiffens, and I square my shoulders at the mention of *powers*. The locked box containing my abilities stirs in excitement, thrumming against my chest. I knew I wasn't the only person who could do unique things. Deep in my soul, I knew there had to be others like me, and now I know it for sure.

As a child, I was always afraid to talk about my magic, scared to death to show my parents out of fear they would think I was a freak. But if I can find out where my powers come from and find others like me, I can learn to control them. I can make sure I never hurt innocent people again like I hurt my family.

I look at the palm of my hand resting on my leg. Dirt has etched itself into the lines and grooves of my sweaty palm. Loosening my internal hold on my powers, I feel the swirling mass of energy resting patiently beneath my skin. If this collar mutes them, should I still feel them? I flick my eyes at her. Sitting against the wall opposite, she stares with narrowed eyes.

"So, you have powers?" I try to keep hope from my voice, but inside I'm a raging storm, anticipating her answer.

"Of course I have powers. I'm a Wind Siren. What did you think was happening in the alley? What are your powers?"

I move my legs under me and sit on my knees. Turning my

head down, I attempt to hide my gaping mouth as my ragged breaths run in and out of my lungs. I hear her shuffle on her hands and knees as she nears the bars between our cells.

"What?"

I hesitate, unsure if I should reveal my secret. I've protected it for so long and hoped I would find others like me, others who have powers and can make things happen just by thinking about them. My abilities thrum and beat to be released, almost like they can sense a kindred spirit nearby. But the voice of my panic screams against it.

The collar around my neck is heavy and restricting, reminding me of my self-imprisonment. I keep myself isolated by holding my secrets inside me, being a loner and shutting people out. But hearing she has powers, I feel a sense of hope. Maybe there's a chance we can escape this place, and she can take me to others like us. I can finally learn to control my abilities. It's a long shot, but it's better than sitting in this cell, waiting for our captors to do who knows what to us.

Taking a steadying breath, I let go of the cell bars and relax the tight muscles of my shoulders. Carefully threading a sliver of power from their confines, I release a gentle breeze into our tiny prison. Mild at first, the current of air tickles the fine hairs falling around our faces in our disheveled states, like nothing more than a fan turning on inside a stuffy room. Fanning the beads of sweat coating our foreheads, the tendrils of air dance around us, encircling our wrists playfully, like a child, as the currents grow in strength.

Recognition rocks Callie's expression as her eyebrows shoot to the ceiling and her glassy blue eyes shine brightly, feeling the power twirl around the room in a cool gust. Our hair whips around us, the torn and ragged shirts billowing in the breeze. Her knuckles turn white as she clutches the metal bars separating us, tethering her to the earth as I pull my powers inside, bringing the winds with me.

"How can you still use your powers?" Excitement rings in her high-pitched voice, and color flashes to her face with hope.

"So, you can do this?" I quickly ask. "Is this what you can do, too?" I match her excitement, desperate to hear her say yes, so I know this is not a dream. Perhaps this would be a nightmare, teased with the hope of finally belonging, only to have it wrenched away when I awaken.

"You're a Wind Siren too? I don't understand how you can use your powers with the collar around your neck. It should keep you from using them." She looks away, casting her eyes downward, before shooting up with renewed eagerness. "You can get us out of here before they come back to kill us. Can you get this collar off me?"

A sound trickles in underneath the metal door. I freeze, straining to hear if the sounds are nearing. Callie shifts in her cell, hearing it too. Her breathing rises as we both listen to the footsteps of multiple people drawing near.

"Listen to me." Her tight grip on the metal bars intensifies as she pulls herself closer, lowering her tone. "Whatever happens, don't let them know you can use your powers inside this cuff. They will torture you. You will be sent to gladiator arenas where the foulest things you can imagine will happen. Just survive whatever comes next. Do you understand?"

Footsteps in the hallway grow louder and stop outside the door. As keys jingle and rattle against metal, we prepare for the interruption. *Just survive.* Callie's words ring in my mind as chills run up my body. The light extinguishes as the room plunges into a cavern of darkness.

My pulse races against my neck, and my heart threatens to beat out of my chest. I put as much space between myself and the cell door as possible and give myself a second longer to compose my powers. Squeezing my eyes shut, I swallow my fear and bring every ounce of bravery I can muster to the surface.

The door to the room opens, and the twins from the alley rush into the small space. Their size was large before, but inside this dirt room, they are suffocating. A shadow lurking in the hallway blankets me in an all-consuming fear that coats my body in waves of freezing chills. Like being dunked into a tank of icy water, my throat collapses in on itself, and I stifle a scream.

A gargantuan wolf, impossibly large with a fanged muzzle, snarls a warning. Unnatural orange eyes glow like fire embers and are locked onto me. All black fur melts into the shadows, caressing the beasts imposing frame. The twins unlock my cell and fling the cage open. My fingers claw at the dirt wall behind me as if I can quickly dig a hole for escape, but there is nowhere to go.

Hands with a crushing grip capture my legs and drag me out of the cell. I thrash like a captured animal, spasming and screaming for my release while the twins march out of the small room. Looking back at Callie, she nods once at me, her brow furrowed in seriousness as if passing the tacit encouragement again. *Just survive.* I hope I convey my promise back to her as the thick metal door slams shut, leaving her locked inside the cell alone. *I will.*

The corridor leads to a maze of roughly carved tunnels. Following our route is impossible because of the twists and turns, but I watch attentively. Closed doors have a single window in the center with dark rooms on the other side, devoid of light. Are they perhaps empty?

I fight back, hoping they'll drop me so I can run into one of the darkened rooms. Maybe I can lock myself in one and think of a way to escape. One of the twins squeezes my wrist so hard I think my bones will snap. I look up at him and feel tremors of terror as his reflective eyes darken with anger; he releases a growl from deep within his chest. I stop fighting and hang within their grasp as they march down the corridor, breathing heavily from my pointless struggle.

If Callie has powers like me, these men must also have magic. Their eyes reflect an ethereal glow no normal person can possess. I need to find out their powers so we can plan a fight against them when we escape.

Reaching our destination, I'm heaved into a room and thrust to the floor. The heat of my fear consumes me in sweat as they bind my hands over my head. Pulling me to my feet, the twin I fought in the alley hangs my tied hands on a hook suspended from metal rafters in the cave's ceiling.

The wolf's presence is like the long cloak of death wafting in the night while its skeleton hand wraps around the deadly sickle, coming to take my life. The imposing shadows warn of its approach before it enters the room. Violent tremors overtake my body in anticipation of seeing the beast again as the hallway darkens. Its large frame blocks out the light while it descends toward us.

The beast slowly pads into the room. Each massive paw thuds on the dirt floor as it stalks to me. A growl shudders through the room, and long, white fangs gleam inside the wolf's jaws. Halting in front of me, the great muzzle of the animal is mere inches from my face, glaring into my eyes with a knowing expression. A whimper escapes my trembling lips, waiting for the jaws to open and engulf me.

But it never comes.

I've never seen a wolf in real life. I know they are larger than domesticated dogs, but this monster stands six feet tall on all four paws. Nothing natural causes a wolf to grow that large. My mind races through the pages of all the mythology books I've researched, and only one beast comes to mind.

Werewolf.

I open my eyes again, and the beast is still transfixed on me. Hot breath hits my face as orange eyes attempt to cut my resolve. An electrifying sensation fills the room, almost like the weight of gravity increases. A thousand pounds pull on my bound wrists, and my knees buckle under the pressure. An unseen force, like two rough hands, snaps my head down. My eyes fixate on the dirt floor, unable to move.

This unearthly stir suffocates the room, and my breathing is stifled. My lungs force short gasps of air in and out in an exhaustive effort. The faintest tether of my power seeps out of the pretend box, and my gentle wind coils around me to help fill my lungs with air. Unable to keep them locked away with this force around me, a cooling breeze so soft and minuscule wafts affectionately around me. It's so subtle; I'm confident no one can sense it, and I allow it to wrap around my ankles, spiraling up my body in an assuring caress.

This is a battle of will—an attempt to make me submit. *Just survive.* I have to win this. This wolf wants to feed off my pride and make me grovel at its massive paws. Giving in will weaken me to whatever it wants next, possibly my powers. So, I'll starve him.

As I inhale the refreshing currents of my magic, it reassures me I can do this. Using all my might, I push against the force filling the room. Imagining my power is like a balloon, I fill the room with it, carefully pushing my magic into every corner. It works. As my power fills the space, it pushes the oppressive feeling out.

My eyes travel the length of the wolf's body until I lock eyes with it, unmoving. With my jaw set and brow furrowed, I hold the beastly eyes with my own. Pressure builds against my wrists strung above my head, as blood drains from my fingers. Tingles shoot down my arms as the battle of our determination wages.

The moment stretches uncomfortably long until the great wolf steps back into the hall and sits on its hindquarters. A chill cascades from the crown of my head down my body as a twisted grin forms on the wolf's face at my rebellion, almost like the beast is happy I'm not complying. The suffocation of the room dissipates with the wolf's distance, and a breath of relief escapes my chest.

A resounding crack reverberates through the hall, and the wolf's body contorts violently. Its back bends unnaturally as if its spine has broken into two pieces. The beast's head shoots upward with a crunch as its neck follows, bending impossibly at a sharp angle. Were my hands not bound, I would grasp my mouth to suffocate a scream. Under the onyx fur, bones break and slide, moving freely like a live animal running beneath a blanket.

I can't look away, though I beg my eyes to free themselves from the prison of this scene before me. The wolf collapses to the floor in a heap, and its dark fur slides and roils with the movement of the bones. The pelt covering the animal's flesh seemingly recedes into the wolf's body as if being skinned alive;

a viscous, clear slime discharges, mixing with the blood of the exposed skin, and the fur's needles retreat inward.

It's a repulsing sight to watch, and my face can't help but crumble and twist as the transformation from animal to human takes place. When the beast's hind legs shoot outward, popping from their hip sockets, my stomach threatens to spill its contents on the floor. I'm finally released to avert my gaze.

Looking away from the horror, one of the twins stands static in the corner with his hands crossed in front of his chest, a sneer plastered on his face as he looks down his crooked nose at me satisfied with my reaction. Steeling myself, I turn back to the spectacle. I won the first battle of wills a moment ago and will also win this one. They want me to be horrified. They want to watch my disgust. *Just survive.*

As the transformation ends, tanned flesh is coated in sweat and dirt. Black hair shines in the yellow light of the dull cave, and the beastly eyes, still smoldering orange, remain locked on me. Naked, the imposing man rises and stands squarely facing me. Six feet in height, as the wolf was, the man before me is still daunting with his muscular frame and broad shoulders. His lips curl upward in a menacing grin, exposing retreating fangs.

He chuckles as a bundle of clothes is delivered to him. Once dressed, the wolf-turned-man strides toward me, deliberately slow in his movements. His finger tucks under my chin, lifting my head forward. His lip twitches, and I hold my expression steady.

"You would challenge me, little one?" His deep voice, heavy Italian, spills out like tar. "My name is Lupo. Who are you?"

I feign disinterest as I hold his gaze, forcing boredom to

wash over my eyes. "Your goons looked at my driver's license, so you should know."

"It doesn't matter if you want to play hard-to-get, little one. I *love* to hunt and will hurt you either way." He savors the flavor of his words as he draws them out. The threat catches in my throat, and I swallow a cough. A chuckle tumbles from his mouth, satisfied with my reaction. Scolding myself for giving it to him, I straighten my spine, and stand taller.

Silence engulfs the room while he circles me like a shark. I track him as he ambles around me, puffing his chest with arrogance. He stops in front of me and grasps my jaw and cheeks, yanking my head upward to look at him. The force pushes my lips into a pout as he turns my head from side to side, looking at me.

Lupo lowers his face to the level of my eyes. His own gaze is a dark abyss attempting to bore into me with his glowing irises. He brings his face to my collarbone, his lips brushing against my skin. Inhaling, he drags his nose up the length of my neck. Nausea rocks through my body from the intrusion, and I fight against the restraints holding me in place.

"You smell different than the other Elemental, little one. Curious... don't you agree, boys?" Lupo doesn't wait for an answer from the twins; he pushes his jet-black hair away from his eyes. "There is old magic in your blood."

He lowers his mouth directly beside my ear and whispers, "You *reek* of it."

"I don't understand what you are saying." I lie. My magic boils, wanting to escape and lash out at the man before me, but I fight against its force and push it deep within.

Finally, he releases my chin and turns away from me. My shoulders relax in relief, and I shift in my restraints. Turning,

Lupo charges his arm toward me, crunching his fist into my cheek. The force of his punch across my face yanks tears from my eyes.

White flashes dance in my vision, and I blink to clear them. Lupo pulls his other hand back, launching toward my other cheek. This one caught my left eye. My head jerks suddenly, and the static in my ears has become a high-pitched bell clamoring throughout my head. I swallow hard, pushing my powers further down and willing them to remain inside while I attempt to breathe and blink.

"Let's see your power, little one." He rears back and hits me again. This time it was with his fist, and the taste of metal fills my mouth. Over and over, until I lose count, he slaps and punches me. My left eye swells shut, and a gash oozes blood down my face. Saliva drips from my mouth as my head hangs low, swinging lazily from side to side.

"I don't have any powers." My defenses stammer each time Lupo takes a moment's pause between assaults, hoping each time will be the last. But he continues. The metal collar pinches my shoulders; my arms cut into the metal as my head flings around from the assault of his fists on my face.

Lupo is sweating when he finally stops, walking a lap around the room, and taking large swigs of water from a bottle. My mouth dries as I watch him. Licking my lips, the cut stings, and I wince against the pain. A string of spit hangs from his mouth like a feral dog, and a deep rumble emanates from his chest, pleased with his work as he looks me over.

Lupo drops the empty water bottle and grabs a wooden broomstick, leaning against the dirt wall. The end is fractured and jagged. He says nothing, and I prepare for another round of assaults. Air comes through my nose quickly as I repeat Callie's mantra. *Stay alive.*

"I can taste your magic oozing from you. Show it to me, and this is all over, little one." Lupo whispers the promise so close to my ear his breath hits against my skin. I recoil, spitting what little saliva I can collect into his face.

The sensation of Lupo's arm charging back, preparing to burst forward and strike me, fills the room with anticipation before it snaps. The walls seem to tremor with the impact. A soundless cry of agony rips out of my throat as my spine stiffens.

This new round of assault seems like a never-ending parade. My body twists as Lupo strikes me across my ribs, back, and thighs. I turn uncontrollably on the hook until I think my arms will pop from their sockets, but he continues. Panting and spitting, sweat flings off him, spraying me as he continues the beating. The final blow arrives with a blinding white surge of pain exploding up my torso, extending my spine. I gape at the ceiling with my mouth open in silent agony. Tears warm my cheeks as if to apologize for my pain.

The spectacle of my flailing body burns Lupo's expression as he tracks the blood flowing from my cut lip. Satisfied, he retrieves a knife behind his back, cuts the rope suspending me off the ground, and I drop in a heap. Dirt clings to my body and fills my mouth as I flounder on the ground, gasping for air.

Lupo lowers his knee and wraps his large hand around the metal collar, pulling my torso off the ground and digging the metal into my skin.

"I promise you this; I'm breaking your spirit during the next round. You *will* show me your power." He quickly retreats with a breeze brushing against me, flinging the door open with a bang.

The metal door screams into the tunnels, and one of the twins throws me back into the cell. Every inhale attempted burns my throat, and my lungs cry in agony. It's impossible to take a complete breath, no matter how hard I struggle. The burning in my side is all-consuming, blocking my vision and voice. My battered body doesn't cooperate, and I lay at an odd angle as I wait for my limbs to decide to work again.

I survived. I did it.

My mind repeats the truth as it fights against the pain in my side. Sweat mixes with blood and tears until I no longer care who hears my cries of pain. My powers swirl, calming me and offering reassurance. I finally find Callie staring at me wide-eyed on her side of the divided cell.

"He's a Werewolf." My tiny voice says out loud with a hiccup.

"I know."

I ease into a sitting position and wince as every movement sends a new surge of pain rocking through my body. Callie watches me closely, never moving her eyes from me.

Leaning up against the dirt wall, I lift my shirt to inspect my side. A sizeable piece of the wooden broom is splintered, sticking out of me, and impaled between my ribs. Callie gasps when she sees the wound, but I can only stare. Placing quivering fingers around the protruding wood, I pull to dislodge it. My torso spasms, and I cry while blood fills my mouth. Throwing the bloodied chunk of a broomstick to the ground, I clutch at my side, sobbing.

Callie reaches her arms through the metal bars, trying to

pull at me, but I'm out of reach. "We need to stop the bleeding. Scoot closer. I think your lung is punctured."

"I can do it." I cough at her as I choke on the pain.

Black mist seeps from my quivering hands as I place them over the wound. Instantly, my healing water element stitches the wound together and closes the injury. I gasp, devouring the first rush of clear air in several minutes.

"Holy shit," Callie says, eyes wide. Her large blue eyes shift from my face to my hands, watching the blood stop running from the wound as the skin seals shut. Collapsing against the dirt wall, I let my head rest against it as my shaking hands slow their tremors. "Wind and Water Siren?"

I shake my head, keeping my eyes closed. "I–I can control fire and earth too." I croak out of my dry mouth. Callie's frozen expression is a mix of horror and amazement as her mouth slowly forms unspoken words; her eyes look off as if she is lost in thought.

"I've never heard of an Elemental so powerful." Her answer rings the bell of uncertainty that flared in my mind as I watched her process my confession. *That can't possibly be true.* I hide my powers and cower at them. I've locked them away for a decade, afraid to hurt anyone. I'm sure plenty of others have more power, and I'm desperate to find and learn from them.

"We can talk about that later." I push down the thoughts so we can escape before Lupo comes for the next round of punishment. "Let's get out of here." The break has given me a moment to catch my breath, and we need a plan.

I inspect Callie's collar, looking for a clasp while telling her about the tunnels outside our cell. The collar is a solid metal ring, and Callie takes a turn inspecting mine. Trying to use my wind power, I attempt to create a spinning wind current around the collar to break the metal, but it's impenetrable.

"You can't take on Lupo and the twins on your own. He's the second most powerful Shifter there is. We won't make it ten feet if we try to take them on directly with me in a collar, and yo–"

Another distant rattle of keys rings down the hall, and Callie pauses, listening. Dread burns tight in my chest, and I work to withdraw my powers again, pulling the fronds of magic inside me into a tight coil and shoving them inside their cage. We've only had a few minutes and no time to devise anything.

"How was your lunch, ladies?" Lupo smacks on the last of a sandwich, wiping his hands together and smiling at us. An arrogant smile stretches across his face as he wears the white shirt, still stained with my blood. "Boys!" he calls to the twins behind him, and they ascend on us both.

Grabbing us by our hair and collars, they drag us out of our cells and down the halls. Yanking us up, we struggle to find our footing as the twins drive us forward. Lupo strolls ahead, whistling an easy tune as we return to the room I just left.

I push back against my captor when I see our destination. He pulls back on the fistful of hair in his sweaty, fat hand and yanks my collar, choking me before he pushes his body against mine, forcing me into the room. The twins remind me of Pain and Panic, serving as Lupo's mindless imp demons.

The twin I have named Pain holds Callie in the center of the room while Panic pushes me to the farthest end. He turns me to face her. Lupo leans his shoulder against the dirt wall, picking my dried blood from under his fingernails.

Pain places a pair of metal cuffs, connected with a chain,

around Callie's wrists and attaches it to a hook in the ceiling. Lowering it further to accommodate her short stature, the bright metal gleams at me in the dim lighting.

They spin her to face me, and her clear blue eyes find me immediately. With thinned lips, she gives me a single nod again, and her message is clear. *Just survive.* She knows it's her turn to be beaten, and I'm meant to watch.

"I promise you this; I'm breaking your spirit during the next round." Lupo's words dance behind my closed eyelids as I ready myself. Resolving to endure my beating was one thing. Knowing I have to endure someone else's sends a pang across my chest like I've been struck in the heart.

Lupo pushes off the wall with his shoulder and strolls over to me. One side of his mouth is turned into a smile, enjoying drawing out the dramatics. He gently rubs a hand down my bloodied and swollen cheek. I sneer, jerking away from him, which makes him smile more.

Looking over his head, I motion discretely upward to Callie, pointing my eyes to the silver chain. She steals a glance quickly as Lupo walks behind her. It looks shiny, unlike the matte metal of the cuffs around our necks. If it's not a strong metal, that could be our escape. She nods once at me, understanding.

Squaring her shoulders and widening her stance, she visibly readies herself.

"The great Calypso." Lupo taunts her. "Your little tornados are always so annoying, ruining my pack's fun."

"Maybe if your packs didn't have a moron for an alph–" He slaps her with the back of his hand before she can finish. Lupo blows out his cheeks as he releases a large puff of air.

"Still a bitch, I see."

She spits blood on the dirt floor, barely missing his shoes. "That makes two of us."

Walking behind her, he pulls back on her collar, choking her as he fixes his hot amber eyes on me. "Let me know when you are ready to show your powers, little one. I'll be happy to see them." He lunges his knee into Callie's back with a grunt of exertion. She winces and jolts, pulling on the chain.

The assault Lupo wages on Callie's petite frame pulls tears from my eyes. With each hit or kick, she pulls or yanks on the chained cuffs at her wrists, weakening the glinting links of metal that hold her fixed to the ceiling. She keeps her eyes locked on mine, reassuring me she is okay.

She is already bruised, with the left side of her face red and swollen. Her lip splits and drips blood. I beg the links of the chain to break with each assault, but they hold firm.

Lupo removes his dirty shirt, now covered in brown dried blood from me and fresh red from Callie. He takes the neck of her tattered flannel shirt and rips it off her in a single pull, leaving her in a thin grey tank top. Her nostrils flare as her breathing hitches, but her eyes remain locked on mine.

"Cuff her now." Lupo directs, and Pain jumps at his command, bringing a pair of chained cuffs and locking them around my wrists. My hands positioned in front of me, I feel for my powers and can still sense them there. They seem distant but swirling deep inside me as they wait to pounce. I'm ready with my plan as soon as Callie can break the glinting chain in the ceiling. "You're going to love this, little one. This is payback for spitting in my face."

Lupo holds a leather whip in his hand and circles Callie, letting the whip uncoil like a snake around her feet. He rubs the whip's handle along her jaw like a caress. Jerking her head away from him, she glares with the one eye that is not swollen shut.

My face reddens, and I jerk against Panic's hold on my collar. He's going to whip her. *Over my dead body.* Callie's eyes widen in silent warning. She holds one of her cuffed hands, splaying her fingers wide, urging me to wait. Callie gives me one more nod, and I drop my shoulders, conceding to wait if that's what she wants.

Stepping back, Lupo holds his position opposite me on the other side of the room. The whip cracks across Callie's back. She tenses and bows her spine but doesn't make a sound. She pulls again on the chain, but it holds. One link is stretched and weakened; it will soon snap.

She watches me as I study the chain above her before I find her eyes again, relaying our silent communication of the plan we didn't have time to discuss. Two lashes crack across the room back-to-back. The double-hit rips a yelp from Callie's throat as she squeezes her eyes against the pain, giving another pull on the chain. I'm on the brink of releasing myself and flooding the room with my magic to save her as soon as the chain gives way.

Callie holds my gaze fiercely through it all, but I grunt and pull against Panic's hold on my collar. *Just a bit more, Callie.* I try to relay the encouragement with my eyes, but a person can only take so much. Ten lashings have torn her back to ribbons, and Lupo releases another double strike, up and down with fast flicks of his wrist powered by his muscular arm.

The chain snaps, and Callie crumples to the ground. I ram my head backward into Panic, knocking him into the wall as I blast a fireball at Pain. A blinding flash of dark hair and tanned skin rushes me. A clawed hand, enlarged with razor talons and patchy black fur, wraps around my neck, lifting me three feet off the ground by my throat.

With blurring vision and a burning throat, I grasp with both hands at Lupo's wrist. He opens a fanged mouth and throws his head back in laughter.

"There she is!" he roars. Lowering me to the level of his face, my feet dangle a foot off the ground. The corners of my vision darken as I suffocate in his grasp. He runs his nose along me, inhaling my scent like he's feasting on it. "And with two sets of cuffs. We've been looking for you, goddess. Welcome back." His hot tongue lays flat against my bloodied and scraped cheek as he slowly licks the side of my face. He releases a bellowing growl, savoring the taste of my blood as he smacks his lips.

Dropping me in a crumpled mass on top of Panics' body, he pushes me off while recovering from the assault my skull took on his face. I roll to the dirt, gasping as air floods my lungs. Panic is ready with a third set of cuffs for my ankles.

"Bring the bitch." Lupo wraps the clawed hand in a partial transition around the cuff of my neck and drags me out of the room. I can't get my chained feet under me as Lupo stalks further down the recesses of the halls. My throat burns from the choke hold, and my eyes work to focus. Pulling on my powers, they struggle within as though they are miles away in a dark abyss.

The new room is blinding; hot lights and intense heat ripples off the dirt walls like an oven. Lupo roughly drops me into a metal box that sears my legs and exposed skin. There is no escaping when a loud click echoes within the chamber, locking me inside the box. I push on the lid, burning my hands to no avail. It's nothing more than a small metal coffin baking under the intense heat of the lamps.

"Don't worry, goddess; you performed perfectly. Sit tight while the cavalry comes to save you. I'll see you around, little one." Lupo bangs on the top of my box twice.

"Are you sure this is the plan, Alpha? We're supposed to release her?" One of the twins speaks for the first time since the alleyway. The sound of a hand hitting flesh snaps around the room.

"You have a problem with the plan, then take it up with Ares yourself." Lupo snarls. "We got what we came for, and we're going home. Their saviors will pick them up soon."

I can't see outside the small holes of the box because of the bright lights, but I hear shuffling, and the locking of another box before the large door of the room slams harshly and I am left alone. My voice reverberates around the small coffin as I call for Callie. A flash flood of relief washes over my body when she weakly answers me against the hum of powerful lights.

I was so stupid. Of course, the chain was put there on purpose. It was planned from the beginning to put a weak chain there and give us hope of escape; knowing we couldn't resist trying to take it, I would use my powers to get us out. I feel like a fool, and I turn my head into my hands as tears flow freely from my eyes.

Alone in the room with Callie, the sands of time pass slowly under the heat of the lamps. I hum a slow, melancholy tune while my heart thumps like a loud bass drum. It's a song my mom sang to me when I was little during bedtime. When I have a panic attack, I play it in my mind as I remember her soft touch on my hair, stroking my head until I finally slept.

Thoughts of my mom and nighttime stories flood my

memories and send an incredible rush of ease over my body—fairytales of pixies and Greek gods. I would always let my imagination continue as I dreamed; my favorite were the stories of Hermes. Traveler between realms and messenger of the gods, I always envied Hermes for his freedom. The ability to stand on the threshold of any world and travel into it, to explore its beauties, was so fascinating.

I think of Hermes escorting souls to the ferryman and wonder if he reassured them. I send a silent wish into the universe that Hermes will come for us now and replace this insufferable heat with the cool River Styx.

As if on their own, the faintest sliver of my wind power spreads within the little coffin in a torrent of comfort. A cool breeze swarms around Callie and me, giving us a small semblance of relief from the suffocating heat. The three cuffs around me, and the heat from these lamps, pull the remaining strength from my body. I'm so weak that within a minute, my powers withdraw from me; a final wisp of wind caresses my cheek as it fades.

Hermes

It's been six hours since Calypso went missing, and I've been snapping at everyone in the tactical room as we search for her. After losing the van, we found a tote of books in the alleyway. Squeezing the cloth straps of the bag in my hands, I realize these were the books I helped Rhea retrieve from the floor. *This was a setup.*

I'm Head of Security for the Commune, and I allowed my distraction to get in the way of the team, and now my sister is in danger. The events of the bookshop play on a loop in my memory, and pain blooms in my chest for asking Callie to keep an eye on Rhea. It's my fault I let the aura and power rolling off the strange Elemental distract me.

Achilles tries to connect with Callie in the alleyway using their fated mate connection. Being soul-bound, they have a constant tether to each other to communicate, send power boosts or locate each other. Using their bond, he should have known where she was, but the invisible tie between their souls is blocked. *She is in Thaumium bindings*—the only thing that can dull the connection of fated mates; aside from the bond being severed completely. If Patroclus were still alive, perhaps he and Achilles could have located her together.

Fated mates are rare, a fated mate group even more so. Achilles and Patroclus met long before Callie came into the picture. Both Flames, the men were already a deadly combination to be paired as mates. When they met Callie, she became the balance they desperately needed. She was an expert at tamping down the fire of their power when they got too hotheaded or propelling them higher by feeding their flames with her winds.

Losing Patroclus all those years ago was a big blow for our Commune, but nothing compared to Callie and Achilles having to learn to live without a piece of themselves, constantly off-balance. We have all lost a lot in the fight against Ares, yet the pain of our suffering fuels us to keep fighting.

Returning to the Commune, I called all the security teams to the war room to help search for Callie. Achilles took a group of Sensory Elementals back to the alley. Like soundwaves traveling between objects, the residual energy left behind from someone's emotions lingers in the space, and the Sensory Elementals can see and interpret them. They quickly pinpointed the two werewolves and Callie but noticed two other Elementals in the alley.

"One of the Elementals fought against one of the twins while Callie took on the other twin." Achilles reported.

"Maybe that was Rhea." I offer. The flash of her chaotic silver aura in the bookstore hits my memory, and a fresh wave of guilt washes away my curiosity about her. I should have asked Terra to back up Callie. I was so thoughtless. But I can't help but wonder why she was in the alley; maybe she was spying on me or there to spy on Damien.

"There was someone else, however. A Dark Mage was sitting behind one of the dumpsters. Sensors can't pick up much on Dark Mages, but I think that was the void you picked up on."

Atlas joins us in the war room, where everyone searches for Callie. Holding his gold-rimmed glasses in one hand, he pinches the bridge of his nose with the other. His sandy brown hair is especially disheveled today, though it's typically shaggy and unkempt. Atlas is a powerful Mind Mage that can hear thoughts, see memories, and project illusions.

I saw him take over the minds of a thousand Shifters during the Battle of Thermopylae, making them believe they had already been bound and captured. Thinking they were tied up, a thousand Shifters lay on the ground for hours while we worked to process them. It takes a lot to hold that many minds under your control for so long.

"Something happened that you're not telling me." Atlas accuses. "Achilles is not saying anything either, but if I don't know the extent of what happened, how can I fully help, Hermes?"

Only Achilles, Callie, and I know about my secret meeting with Damien, and we're experts shielding ourselves against Mind Mages after what happened to Patroclus.

Directly engaging with Ares is forbidden because of the retaliation he is known for. Brutal in his warfare, there are no depths Ares won't go to ensure he remains hidden. If the Commune's Head Mistress, Eris, found out I met with Damian secretly, she would have the authority to expel me from the Commune and my position as Head of Security.

There are too many people in the war room for me to confess the real reason my team was scouting the bookstore today.

"Hermes, we need a break here, and we can't waste valuable

time arguing with each other. You know as well as I do that Ares rarely keeps prisoners beyond a day. Callie will die before sunrise if we don't find her tonight." He waits for me to answer, but I only stare back at him coolly.

"Let's step into the hall." I finally resign as I nod to Achilles across the war room, and he turns to follow us. Standing in the hall, I confess the secret meeting with Damien to Atlas and the interaction with Rhea inside the bookstore. Atlas is a Commune Council member, and technically, he outranks me. But I lead Security, and while I don't need his stamp of approval on the missions I send my teams on, I usually take his advice. He and my father were great friends, nearly brothers, until Ares killed my father. Since then, Atlas has looked over Calypso and me.

"Gods, Herm. What were you thinking?"

"I'm tired of playing Ares' cat-and-mouse game. You know as well as I do we waste our time babysitting his watchdogs and chasing dead-ends. It's time to work together and bring him to an end." Achilles raises his eyebrows at me in a silent signal to calm down. Inhaling a soothing breath, I continue. "This author wants to help and has good information to share. If we work together, we may finally find Ares and bring the war to him."

"Can you contact him? See if he can tell us anything about where Callie may have been taken." Atlas suggests.

I walk down the hall and call Damien even though he wanted to cool off for a few days to avoid suspicion of the Shifter packs. Still, after explaining my sister being taken, Damien suggests looking in the Mitchell Mountains of California. Several packs often meet during moon cycles, and rumors about a hidden complex within the caves circulate.

With new information, Achilles talks to the Sonus and Sensory Elementals to focus on that area, listening and looking for signs of activity to narrow down a large search field. Atlas sits in the war room and rests his head on the back of the chair. His eyes glaze over with a milky white film, deep in a trance as he attempts to locate Callie through Astral Projection.

Every second Callie is gone raises the level of unease. The wolves have an extensive network of packhouses and intense loyalty to each other as well as Ares. It's possible they will move her to a new location or take her directly to him, if they allow her to live. It's impossible to predict the God of War and his latest plans.

Within five minutes, Atlas picks up a faint trace of Callie's aura, but he can't pinpoint her exact location. The facility seems to be within the mountains and must be constructed with enchantments to dispel Elementals.

Achilles rushes to Atlas' side. "Is she okay? Is she being hurt?"

Atlas' body flinches, but he can't hear us when he's Astral Projecting. He continues to deliver information on what he senses, remaining homed in on Callie's aura. I can tell he is sparing Achilles the details of what is happening. My blood boils under the surface of my skin, thinking of what could be happening that Atlas is shielding us from. A glow of my power radiates off my skin as my emotion rises.

"Take a walk. I'll keep watch over him," Achilles says, worried eyes looking at my skin, emitting a faint blue glow of my Light power.

"Hey," I call to him. "She's strong and smart." Achilles doesn't answer, and I know it offers no solace in helping the situation.

I need some air.

Shoving my hands deep into my pants pockets, I walk through the Commune. My head feels like a vise, with thousands of thoughts racing through me simultaneously. Like cars stuck in a traffic jam, more arrive each second but have nowhere to go.

The first time Achilles met Callie was the last time Ares took her from our camp at Troy. He tagged along when I staged a rescue mission. Once Achilles laid eyes on her, that was it. Their fated-mate connection was made with him and Patroclus. The rest is history.

Juliette pops into my mind. A knot forms in my throat even four hundred years after her death. Sometimes I feel like I died along with her: merely half a being, existing in a hollow and dull world without my mate, reduced to only a memory by the God of War. I can still see the life leave her eyes as his spear, tipped with Stygian Iron, ran through her. The ethereal metal absorbed her immortal powers until nothing was left of her.

Having found my way to the empty portico off the kitchens and communal eating areas, I rest my shoulder against one of the white columns stretching two stories above me. Emulating our ancient Grecian Commune set over the Mediterranean, the Atlanta Commune overlooks a large lake of sparkling blue waters, clear as topaz.

Playing back to this morning's events, my mind pictures honey-brown eyes, so round, looking at me. Deep golden hair with soft waves flows around me and cocoons my senses with her sweet fragrance. A gentle wind ushers in a soft melodic humming that dances around the portico, swirling around me like an invitation. It has a beautiful, haunting melody and makes me think of

Water Sirens calling sailors to their happy deaths. The song pulls at a knot in my stomach that's been festering since the bookstore. But the atmosphere around me shifts, and the euphoria fades.

It's hot.

I can't breathe.

The cafeteria is suddenly dank and stale.

I feel claustrophobic and afraid.

The vision is hazy, but I see a dark interior with bright lights surrounding all sides. There is nowhere to move, as it seems I'm buried alive. The wind whips around me, and the knot in my stomach snaps to a hard line, and I tightly hold on to the plaster banister surrounding the portico to stabilize myself.

I know where Callie is.

Adrenaline fuels me so intensely that I run down the halls and rush through the doors of the war room with lightning running through my veins.

"I found her," I gruff, punching in the coordinates into our portal, and without question, the entire room surges to life to prepare our vehicles for the extraction.

"How?" Achilles says with an intense stare.

"I don't know, but she's alive." Relief washes over him, and he quickly steels himself to prepare the tasks with the rest of the team. I bark orders and give an overview of what I gathered in that flash of connection. Sparing a glance at Atlas, he's still in a trance with Callie, so we assign someone to monitor him while we prepare.

Flashes of tunnels and dirt floors are playing in the background of my mind while we hurry to the three black vehicles, armored against Elemental and Shifter powers, sitting on large portals. The heat from the location where Callie is kept makes me sweat.

Anticipation pulls tightly on the assembled tactical team but they move with expert precision. Twelve Elementals are geared up in our all-black uniforms with nerves on edge for the mission. We're all anxious to return Callie to safety but none more than her mate, Achilles. While I'm eager to see my sister safe, my curiosity can't stop wondering about Rhea. The vision of the hot, dark caves keeps flashing in my mind and I hear a voice I recognize.

"The calvary is coming." I hear Lupo say.

"Lupo. We need to hurry."

I send Achilles the message through our minds. While we have encountered some peaceful packs of wolves, the majority are faithful armies of Ares and none more devoted than the packs of Europe under Lupo's domain. With his orders, wolves have decimated villages of defenseless women and children while their mortal men are off at wars created by Ares.

"I'm skinning that wolf alive." My friend says out loud.

Few weapons help against a Werewolf. Decapitation by Adamantine Steele or Elemental Fire are the most effective means. Armed with Thaumium cuffs and Oleander darts, as well as our Elemental powers, we leave.

The portal zaps us to the California mountain range, and the orange glow of twilight burns as the sun sets. The Sensors work on the area and detect two Werewolf guards near a cave entrance. Earth enchantments disguise the door, and my well-trained team moves forward, silent as Achilles and I charge ahead.

Terra creates a quicksand vortex under the feet of the guards, and the ground soundlessly consumes them. We press forward through the entrance and descend metal stairs into the belly of the mountain.

I quickly extend the essence of my Light ability through the twist and turns of the caves, creating a map in my mind, but the tug on my stomach guides me like a rope. The underground network of roughly constructed rooms is nothing more than a bunker. Seeing the images in my mind and now with my eyes, the accuracy of the vision is astounding. I've never encountered such a strong visual connection like this before.

"No one is here," I announce to Achilles and the rest of the team. Recalling the Sensors that found evidence of a Dark Mage, I instruct them to remain vigilant. The Mage could be concealing an ambush within its shadows.

At a cross in the halls, the essence of my core vibrates with the need and longing to find the end of this tether pulling me from within. The force is irresistible to fight against. Even if I use the power of all the stars in the universe, I cannot go any other direction but where this rope leads me.

Arriving at a closed door, the etchings of runes along the doorframe let me know why we couldn't pinpoint their location. The wolves are working with Witches. Despite the protective rune, I know what we seek will be on the other side.

Achilles blasts the hinges and lock of the metal door with his fire element. The door crashes into the room before clattering to the floor. Without hesitating, we move inside. The rest of the team guards the hall in case we're ambushed.

Ultraviolet lamps burning as bright as the sun's surface have turned the dirt walls into the infernal burning pits of Vulcan. Stretching my power to the lights, I quickly diminish most of their intensity, leaving enough light to see. A sheen of sweat instantly forms on our bodies from the stifling temperatures soaked into the walls.

Achilles blasts the locks to two metal boxes, at most, four feet long. A growl escapes my chest and white-hot rage roars within me at the thought of Callie being shoved inside. Simultaneously, Achilles and I thrust the lids open. The sight before me freezes me deep in my bones.

Rhea.

Beaten and almost unrecognizable, every exposed piece of skin is coated in sweat, blood, and dirt. Her lips, pink and plump a few hours ago, are thinned and split with the wounds she sustained during the short captivity. Unconscious, tiny groans from her throat let me know she's still alive. Her eyes are swollen shut, and her head bobs uncontrollably as I carefully lift her into my arms. My eyebrows shoot into my hairline when I see three Thaumium cuffs around her.

What kind of power could someone have that requires three cuffs to mute them?

My hesitation clears as Achilles retrieves Callie from the metal box. Looking at her, she is in no better shape than Rhea, and judging by the blood showing on Achilles' hands, she has other wounds somewhere I can't see.

Rhea's satchel of books in the alley and the Sensor's interpretation of the energy discharge made us assume she played a role in things. We need to get them back to the Commune to be healed and find out what that role was.

"Packages are in hand," I order the teams over our earpieces. "Clear back to the portal."

Achilles comes to my side and says quietly, "Can we even bring her with us?" His eyes linger on Rhea sympathetically.

"Try and stop me," I reply firmly, climbing the stairs and

exiting the caves. I know Achilles is not challenging me; he is only reminding me that the Head Mistress will have some choice words for me once we return with a stranger.

I know two things for sure. Rhea will keep these three cuffs on until we understand her part in Callie's abduction, and no power in this universe can stop me from bringing her with me. While I hold her body, some deep recess within me—that has been long, cold, and empty—rouses from a long slumber.

"You're going to be okay," I breathe as we run toward the vehicles. I stare at her, my eyes begging to see any sign that she can hear me. My pulse leaps when I hear a tiny word pass across her lips—my name.

"Hermes?"

Rhea

Blinking my eyes against the room's brightness, the memory of my imprisonment's stale, dirt-filled air slams into me, and I bolt upright with a start, choking on my saliva. Instinctively, I pull my arms into my body, but the biting metal cuffs still hold my wrists. Secured to a chain in the center of a cold metal table, it scrapes along, echoing in the grey room. Jerking my legs, my ankles are suffocated by cuffs, shackled to a large bolt in the center of the floor. The room is sterile. Cinderblock walls stand like silent guards in a windowless room with a single metal door.

"Hello?" I call out to no one.

Bending to inspect the chains around my ankles, I notice my shoes are still dirty with dust and brown spots of dried blood. It turns my mouth into a grimace. The ache in my side from my impalement is gone. As I focus on the feeling of my injuries, my brow crinkles in confusion. *I feel... fine.* My eye is no longer swollen, and I can see clearly. My lip is no longer cut, and even my muscles, sore from straining and being suspended in the air, feel normal.

My hands are clean. The dirt compacted under my nails and smashed into the lines of my palms has been washed away.

My torn and bloodied clothes have been changed into grey sweatpants and a matching shirt. My hair falls around my face, wafting a clean shampoo scent, and I wonder who bathed me while I was unconscious. Knowing I'm clean does little to wash away the grime of my captivity from my mind or skin, especially with these cuffs still digging into me.

"Ah! So lovely to see you awake, Rhea." A slender woman smiles warmly at me. "I'm Athena Li. I'm the primary healer here." She tips her head towards me in a slight bow. "Please, relax. You're safe now."

Her fine black hair is styled in a neat bun with jade hairpins. Each has a small, carved snake coiled around the end. She has long, elegant features like a ballerina and stands poised by the door.

"Where am I? Where is Callie?"

"You were seriously injured when you arrived last night, but I'm sure you'll feel quite recovered now. I reset the laceration on your side and your broken ribs and took care of the smaller facial injuries. We gave you some fluids because you were both quite dehydrated. You did a great job healing the punctured lung." Her smile extends to her eyes.

"Where am I?"

"Back in Georgia."

"Where is Callie?"

"Calypso is fine. She will be here momentarily."

In relief, my stomach releases a long, low rumble of hunger pains, making Athena chuckle. I shift uncomfortably in the chair, darting my eyes away to avoid her gaze. "I'll have some food delivered just after Atlas evaluates you."

"Am I a prisoner here?"

"No." The woman answers, but her smile falters before she picks it back up.

"So, am I free to leave?"

Her eyes darken briefly before she lifts her chin to answer. "No."

Knuckles wrap on the door, and it swings open. A thin man in his mid-forties enters the room with gold-rimmed glasses hanging low on his nose. His physique tells me he is apt to sit behind a desk with his nose buried in a book. He has soft brown eyes that crinkle at the corners. Shoving his hands into his creamed-colored trousers, his brown loafers tap on the concrete floor as he approaches the table.

"My name is Atlas. How are you feeling, Rhea?"

"Like I need to be released from these metal cuffs." I keep my expression even as I search inside for the wisps of my power, but it's as if they have been buried beneath ten feet of concrete, far out of my reach.

"We'd love to get these off you, but I need some information about yesterday." Atlas looks at me sternly as if he believes I am somehow responsible for the abduction. Instantly, my body tenses in defense, and I square my shoulders before answering.

"I'm not telling you anything until I see Callie." I shift my gaze to the table with my jaw set firm. I'll wait them out. They want something from me, and I'll act like I'm ready to sit in these cuffs all day until I get what I want. Each second these cuffs hug my skin, it seems they constrict around me tighter and tighter. The cold biting of metal grates on me from within like fingernails skimming a chalkboard. I hold back a shudder and remain unchanged as they observe me.

"I don't actually need you to *tell* me anything. I'll only be a moment if you remain still for me."

Like ice-cold water poured directly onto my brain, thin fingers spread through my mind. Blinding white light replaces my vision, and my head is yanked toward the ceiling with a gasp.

"Show me your life." A voice echoes inside my head as flashes of memories play behind my eyes like someone is flicking through a stack of photographs. Christmases, birthdays, and family vacations blend with laughter, tears, and love as I see my parents and younger brother, Jason, play through my mind; the frigid claws rake through the memories of my childhood.

Tears well in my eyes of their own accord as hundreds of recollections play. Some, I don't even remember. Falling in a silent parade, the tears roll freely down my cheeks as I clutch onto the table. The sensation of someone's touch grasping my mind is jarring and dizzying. The room spins on all axis, tumbling into nothingness. Scared of floating into outer space, the table becomes my lifeline to stay fastened to earth.

Jason was only six years old when I killed him, and the last memory I have flashes brightly in my mind. His hand, so little in mine, pulled away from me when I tried to reassure him that everything would be okay. But it was a lie. Nothing would be all right ever again.

"What are you?" These are the last words he said to me as my black mist filled the car and ripped him away from me. Ripped them all away from me forever.

Pushing back on the table, I can't hold on anymore. The blinding light sears my eyelids from the inside. This man is seeing my most intimate and personal secrets. He's invading my terrors and grief for his gains.

Images of teasing boys at school, pushing me down, and spilling the contents of my bookbag over my head jolt my body; standing alone in my aunt's living room, dressed in my evening-wear, and waiting for a prom date that never came, brings me to my knees.

The searing pain turns to boiling anger as I reach within myself to the chamber where I lock my powers away in their prison. So far away from me, I stretch and yearn to feel their familiar presence inside me.

The dark alleyway's deep shadows reach over my head, pulling me further into my mind as the clammy ribbons of Atlas' power swirls within my skull. Lupo's sickening transformation from a wolf into a man constricts my throat. I don't want to think about the pained look in Callie's eyes as she endures her torture. *It was my fault she followed me to the alley.* I put the whip in Lupo's hand when I spit in his face, and each of the slashes that ripped at her back should have been mine.

Finally, finding the crevasse beyond the deepest recesses of my soul, I find my powers. The swirling mass of silver sits wait-ing. Yanking them out of their confinement, my magic careens out of me in a protective swirl around my body.

The three cuffs are expelled from me, and icy tentacles of the mind invasion blast out of my head. Shooting the chair away from me, I jump farther into the room and stand with a wide footing at Athena and Atlas.

Athena is pressed against the wall. Pieces of her hair are blown out of their neat placement and billow around her face as she looks at me, breathless. Atlas has been knocked onto his bottom. Sitting on the floor with his knees bent and hands holding himself up, the gold glasses rest crooked on his nose as he looks at me with wide eyes and a gaping mouth.

"Don't touch me again." I hold my hand out in front of me protectively. My mist shadowed in darkness, swirls from my palm in a warning to them both.

With the exertion, my breath comes to me quickly in large gulps, but the relief of having the three sets of cuffs off me is like having my first taste of moonlight after a decade in the sun. My powers return to me fully, swirling inside like whirlpools of starlight. After years of pushing my magic away, the suppression of the metal cuffs make me realize I missed them. As much as I have been scared of them, they are a part of me that I can't keep running from.

"O–okay." Atlas stammers. "We'll do this your way. No cuffs."

The door is thrust open, and I aim my palm, ready to strike. Callie rushes into the room, looking as she did the first time I met her in the alley. No bloody and swollen face or dirt-coated skin can be seen. She bounds toward me, healed and clean, with fresh clothes and her ponytail sitting high on her head. Relief floods me as a waterfall of chills dances along my body, happy she is okay.

"Atlas, what did you do?" she demands, and she rushes to me with worried eyes.

"Callie!" I exclaim as we close the distance and wrap our arms around each other's necks. The tears fall in a rush, seeing her whole. "Are you okay?"

I pull away from her and attempt to push her behind me. Putting myself between her and Atlas. My last memory of her back in bloody shreds curls my stomach and constricts my throat. The sound of a whip cracking snaps in my ear, making me flinch. The familiar tingle of my panic grabs hold of my hand and slowly crawls up my arm. My fingers tremor as spots form in my vision, reaching out protectively before me.

"Rhea, it's okay." Callie moves in front of me. My consciousness is aware she is speaking to me, but my glassy eyes look through her, unseeing. Behind my vision is the memory of her torture. The crack of another whip stings my memory. "Rhea?"

"Get me out of this room." My choke echoes around me in the haze of my panic attack. Callie takes my wrist, freed from its prison, and pulls me toward the door. Atlas takes a step to the side, moving in her path. She stops abruptly and puts her hand out.

"Don't," she commands, and a rising wind blows her platinum hair.

"Atlas," Athena says with a tone of warning. "She is not well. Callie, let's get her to my office." Without waiting for an answer, the ladies march me out of the room as the walls close in on me.

Still pulling firmly on my wrist, Callie guides me, and my feet follow obediently without thought. I'm sat in a chair, and Athena hands me a glass of cool water. Rolling the glass carefully along my forehead, the cold chill fights away the panic, trying to immerse me in its suffocating darkness. As my constricting throat relaxes, I take large gulps of the refreshing water and feel it run through to the ends of my limbs.

"Rhea, I apologize for being abrasive." Atlas defends himself from the doorway. I am not yet ready to meet his eyes, so I focus on the surrounding space.

White marble covers the floor, and tall walls are trimmed with a thick border of gold foil, casting a warm glow on the ceiling. A ruffling noise in the corner pulls my head, and my mouth gapes, seeing a large white owl in a gold cage. Arched windows are open, and sheer white curtains billow against the wind. The refreshing breeze cools the beads of sweat that collect on my head as I continue the tour.

A large expanse of bookshelves holds a collection of artifacts that seem straight from a museum. The most significant item is a perfectly polished bronze helmet on a stand, gleaming under a bright penlight. Reminiscent of a Trojan helmet, it would cover the face of the warrior with almond-shaped openings for the eyes and mouth, while the plumes making up the helmet's crest are a deep crimson. Next to the shelves is a disheveled wooden rack holding half a dozen spears. Each is decorated with different shape tips of varying metals. Leather straps adorn the sharp ends and display beads, white feathers, and bronze coins.

The faint trickle of water turns my head to the wall behind me. An impressive mosaic of tiny tiles makes up an image that runs the height of the wall and must be six feet in width. Ferns and colorful flowers line a tile basin, collecting the water in a small pool. The fountain is calming as the water gently flows from the top of the wall and glides over the uneven tiles. The centerpiece is a large, circular shield edged in yellow tiles; it holds a large, round face with bulging eyes and an exposed tongue and twists of hair around the edges of the circle.

The symbology seems familiar in my memory. My beloved Greek mythology books and studying the representations of the gods and goddesses within them sparks a thought too irrational to be true but no other explanation makes sense.

"You're the goddess Athena, aren't you?" I grasp the arms

of the chair with white knuckles, looking at her expectantly with bulging eyes that match the mosaic.

She smiles warmly and dips her head in another polite bow as she answers. "I am."

My head is tilted to the side, and my mouth hangs open in disbelief. "That's impossible."

"But you just said it, so how can it be impossible?"

"And Atlas?" My mind fits together the pieces of their names. "Calypso?" They look at me expectantly. "The gods are real?"

Hermes
6

Headmistress Eris' quarters starkly contrast the rest of the mansion. Frigid modern designs cover the warm, classic interiors of our Commune, matching her cold demeanor. I knock on her door and enter when she replies.

White marble covers every surface, from her desks to the floors and walls, stripping away the Grecian craftsmanship in the rest of the mansion. I find this the coldest area of the Commune. Of course, the Mistress is seated at her desk, reading glasses on the end of her pointy nose, head down while she reviews reports on goddess knows what. Her thin hair, leeched of color, is pulled into a tight bun. I stand, waiting for her to acknowledge me, knowing she'll spitefully make me wait.

"You may take a seat, Hermes." She finally instructs me.

"I'd rather stand."

"Very well. Report."

Retelling the sequence of events that occurred when we arrived at the location in the mountains, I paused as I recalled finding Rhea's battered body inside the small metal coffin. Renewed anger stirs in my chest and pulls tight across my shoulders.

Returning my thoughts to the marbled room, I continue my recollection.

"We found that both women had been beaten and tortured. We rallied with the beta team and returned to the vehicle. The trip back to the portal was without incident."

I finished summarizing the mission's events in the manner I knew the Mistress preferred. Of course, she doesn't look up from her papers, but I know heard every word. She prefers to make me wait for the response she will give in her own time. It's a pitiful power-play she likes to do. She's a Headmistress but a weak one, and she knows it. She can only keep her position through cold and cruel treatment of others, imposing harsh punishments for offending her to keep order through fear.

"Why did you bring the unknown girl?"

I knew the risk of bringing Rhea, but Eris' question still grates against my nerves, and I roughly respond. "Was I supposed to leave her there?"

"You did not have approval to bring her here nor the authority to make such a decision. A human healer could have attended to her."

"She's not human. She is an Elemental."

"Yes, Athena has confirmed that but whose side does she belong? She could be one of Ares. Atlas is interviewing her now, so we will soon know. It was an irresponsible decision made without rationale."

"Would he stage Callie's abduction to plant a spy? He already has spies infiltrating our Communes, sending him intel and helping him stay out of our grasp."

"This is not something for me to converse with you and nothing for you to consider. Your mission was to retrieve your sister, which you did. However, you returned with an unknown being whose allegiance is a mystery. I will suspend your rank as Head of Security for thirty days, during which time Achilles will take command. Do you have any questions?" She finally makes eye contact. Her dark eyes are like voids with no soul resting within them.

"No, Mistress. No questions." I respond coldly. Usually, this would send me into a fury, but with Callie recovered and the storage drive of information from Damien, I'm anxious to see what is on it. Leading Security for the Commune is a full-time job, more so with the Autumn Equinox looming in a month. I'm not happy to push Mabon off onto Achilles, but Eris doesn't realize she secretly did me a favor.

"Thank you. Leave."

"**S**he's being such a bitch and all because I saved someone's life. How did she even become Headmistress anyway?" I yell at Achilles as I search the kitchen for breakfast. Repeatedly opening and slamming the same cabinets in frustration, I abandon my search for food and start pacing the kitchen as Achilles sits with his feet propped up on the table, sipping his double espresso and eyeing me with a smirk.

"Are you going to pick something or shall I make us some breakfast?" Achilles replies coolly.

Running my fingers through my dark trusses, I blow out my cheeks, releasing a defeated sigh into my hands. Achilles grabs two bowls and dishes us a hearty serving of porridge. Drizzled with warm honey and sprinkled with yellow raisins, Achilles passes me the spices as he sets the table. Dashing hearty amounts of cinnamon and nutmeg, the warm porridge works its charm, relaxing the tense muscles of my shoulders.

Setting a plate of fruits, cheeses, and cold meats in front of both our spots, Achilles joins me and begins dressing his porridge.

"Let's talk about what is on that drive from Damien." Achilles begins. "Have you had a chance to look at it yet?"

The drive includes scanned documents of handwritten memos, emails about meeting times, and locations from old communications with a hand-drawn map of the underground levels. Ares remains out of our reach because he lives some-where in the belly of the earth in a well-hidden and heavily enchanted compound he calls The Underworld. I have searched for the entrance for centuries with no success.

"They have flowing water, so they must be near under-ground springs," I tell him with my mouth full of porridge.

"Unless he has Water Elementals."

"Eh, for this many people? He must have a thousand Immortals living underground."

Achilles picks up a fig, dipping it in honey. He pauses. "They have to have some Life Elementals growing their food down there." He shoves the fig in his mouth, the wheels of his mind moving in all directions, thinking of the systems and teams of Elementals keeping an underground city running.

"We need to talk to Damien as soon as possible. Can you contact him and set something up?"

Achilles nods his head in agreement, taking another fig. "Atlas wants us to meet at his studio and assess Rhea." he says. "What do you think?"

"I think I want to challenge her to a fight so I can see her powers." I raise an eyebrow and flash him a crooked smile. The power rolling off Rhea yesterday was more than I've ever felt.

Tens of thousands of years in this realm, and life can get mundane. We yearn for the times of peace when Ares is resetting his armies and staging new strife for the governing mortals. We search for him and work to build alliances with those who are—or were—loyal to him.

And in these times, humanity becomes restless. So accustomed to the discord that Ares injects them with, they invent their own conflicts from time to time. If he doesn't have a plan, he sits and watches their demise, relishing in the mistrust and corruption he plants within the governments of the mortal countries.

Playing this endless chess game with human pawns, you become aware of the impending cataclysm that will launch us into another great war. I can smell it on the horizon: the sun is about to crack over the plains of the earth, propelling them toward the masked face of death, all working up to his eventual rule.

Becoming the Titan that rules over the realm of Gaea has been his only focus, age after age. He lines up his complicated streams of dominoes and waits for the perfect moment to tip the first one. And as sure as I know my shadow will stand beside me on a sunny day, I know the first domino is about to topple over any day. One day soon, when the sun rises, it will be the last day of true peace this realm will know for years, perhaps decades.

So, if we can work to stop him first, prevent the suffering and bloodshed, and finally end his tyranny of this realm, we must put everything we can into it. If Rhea has a fraction of the power I suspect she does, she could tip the scales in our favor.

Touring the Commune is like taking a step into ancient Greece. Roman columns run as high as the sky, with plaster depictions of deities and scenes memorialized into history. The former glory of the ancient Parthenon and Acropolis can be seen in the architecture of this grand place. The main structure of the Commune is a huge white building lined with columns and proudly displaying a large gold dome in the center. Tall bronze doors etched with the peaceful symbols of Greece's famed olive trees open, and the interior of the building swells as if taking a big breath of air and welcoming me inside. The opulence and grandeur are overwhelming to my senses, like walking the long corridors of the Vatican and trying to take in all the works of art at once.

A large fresco painting with a thick gold gilded frame hangs on the wall of the large building. Stretching fifteen feet high and twenty feet wide, the familiarity with the infamous Renaissance painting *The School of Athens* is nearly uncanny. Instead of the old men dressed in their robes, different figures crowd the steps and chambers of the painting. Slowing down to allow me to gaze, Callie stands with me, her hands folded patiently. I recognize Atlas in the center; he stands beside an older woman, whose mouth is turned down in a sour expression; the hollows of her dark eyes are unnerving.

To one side, the bright blonde hair of my companion is depicted in the scene, standing among others. She holds the arm of a tall man with light brown hair.

"Is that you?" I ask in awe. Smiling at my amazement, she agrees. "And your husband?"

"My partner." she corrects, a sly smile on her face.

My heart falters when I take in the details of another man standing beside her partner within the fresco. Dark brown hair and tanned skin stand out against the white robes the figure wears, but the bright blue eyes sear into my memory. *Ethan.* The man from the bookstore.

Clearing my throat, I step back from the painting, and Callie motions for me to follow with her hand. Watching her walk ahead, her dress reminds me of a Greek stola with a modern style. Brown sandals wrap around her ankles and up her calves. The short, white dress is cinched at her narrow waist with a thin gold belt and has one strap that crosses her shoulder.

Looking down at my borrowed clothes, I suddenly feel the stare of a dozen people as my dirty sneakers thump on the large marble tiles of the floor, echoing to the tall ceilings high above our heads.

Callie walks me through a maze of halls and corridors, pausing at large picture windows to point out other buildings across the grounds until I'm utterly lost. The extensive estate is hundreds of years old, with antique furnishings that look as fresh as newly cut flowers. Centuries-old frescos and plaster artistry depict scenes of Greek gods and goddesses in iconic imagery as if they were crafted yesterday.

Walking past another long fresco, a sea of Trojan soldiers steals my attention. Standing on a mountain, Athena leads them, dressed in gold armor and carrying a long spear; she points down to an imposing army of man and beast. Following the lines of the image, a man faces her as her opponent. Tall in stature, he wears red and brown leather and a helmet with the two curling horns of a ram. He holds a wooden staff, lit with fire at the tip. Both opponents are depicted with mouths open as if shouting their commands to their massive armies. Athena leads droves of Trojan warriors while men and giant wolves back her opposition. *Werewolves.*

The gold plate in the center of the fresco tells me its title: "Athena battles the God of War."

Callie explains that a preservation spell over their Communes helps keep the artifacts in pristine condition through the ages, and my mind has a hard time processing the fantastic scenery of this place. It's like stepping back to the day these lavish paintings were crafted, and I'm amazed such magic exists.

The heat of the stares from everyone we pass on our route feels like an inferno, but Callie seems unaware of them as she rambles at me through the hallways. A tall woman with legs that stretch forever descends a set of stairs. Her deep red dress drapes around her figure with an exaggerated split, showcasing her lean legs with each step. Dark hair falls around her face in ringlets, and the weight of her stare drives my gaze to the ground.

She is the type of woman I could never be—beautiful, confident in her body and poised for the attention of everyone who looks upon her. That would never be me. I remain invisible, plain to the eye and only hold the attention of others when

I'm doing something that benefits them or when I'm the object of their joke. At the thought, the grey pantsuit I've been gifted begins to scratch against my flesh.

"Would it be possible for me to get some different clothes?" I ask Callie, biting the inside of my mouth as I count my footsteps, following her down a corridor.

"Sure. We can do that now." She smiles.

Passing through two enormous doors to the right, another expansive space opens up before me. Its modern features starkly contrast the ancient designs of the main corridor we left. Turning my gaze upward and looking around, I realize it's like a shopping mall with shops and storefronts displaying all kinds of things: from clothes to food to even furniture. It's so unexpected and takes my breath away.

"You have a mall?" I gasp, and Callie chuckles. This self-contained community has everything it needs to exist, completely free from the outside world—no wonder the gods have been able to hide all this time. I would never leave this place if I lived here.

Following Callie's lead, she heads toward a clothing store, and we begin browsing the selections. More styles from ancient Greece hang on the walls and racks alongside modern options like blue jeans and stretch yoga pants. Talking with Callie is easy, and it's almost like we've done this a million times before; it surprises me how comfortable I am around her. My awkwardness at the interim silence is brief before we launch a new question or topic.

She has such a bright personality. A true beauty, her features are gentle and delicate as the fragile petals of a white lily flower. Blue eyes gleam and sparkle as she talks and laughs, carefree as if no harm has ever existed in her world. She doesn't glance behind her shoulder for the glares of others or pick at herself from the nervousness of her powers. I find myself wondering about the life she has lived to be so happy. Has she ever known the loss or pain of a loved one?

As I contemplate the differences in her joyful spirit, she throws outfits at me without regard to what she is piling in my hands. I've never been good at dressing my hourglass frame, but my arms fill with options. Content with what she's gathered for me, Callie pulls me toward a dressing room, and I try them on.

I look at my reflection: the plum-colored stola Callie picked is stunning—a perfect tone against my brown hair and fair skin. A smile threatens my lips. Replacing my dirty shoes with brown sandals, I'm at least thankful for my recent pedicure. Feeling less itchy than in the jumpsuit, I exit the changing room with a bundle of grey clothes and dirty shoes.

"Let's just toss these in the garbage," Callie suggests, showing me a large trashcan.

"Where do I pay for these?" I ask quietly, even though we are alone in the store. Darting my eyes around, I notice that there are no other customers and no one working either.

"Oh, we don't use money here. Everyone needs clothes, so we just come here and take what we need." She smiles, heading to the door. The feeling of leaving without paying is strange, but I continue with her.

"Where are we going now?" I ask.

"We're going to Atlas's place, and I'll introduce you to my partner!" She beams at me. "I'm going to assume you have never used a portal before?"

"I'm sorry, a portal?" My eyebrows shoot up in surprise, and Callie giggles.

"We travel a lot by teleportation, by light. It's instant from one place to the next." Callie snaps her fingers. "It's harmless. I'll show you."

She motions for me to follow her and enters something similar to an elevator. Closing the door behind us, a small digital screen glows blue on the wall. Holding her hand to the panel, a signal dings, and Callie opens the door, revealing an entirely new space than the clothing store we visited.

"Come on." She enters the apartment, giggling at my gaping mouth and I hesitantly follow.

The busy shopping mall has transformed into an intimate setting of a private residence. Atlas's home is what I would have expected, full of overstuffed bookcases and worn leather armchairs. We arrive at an office with a brown wooden desk under a large picture window showcasing a lake. A sitting room features couches, large pillows on the floor, and a brick fireplace. Three of the walls are lined with shelves bursting with more books. The home's ambiance is warm and easygoing, where time passes slowly and is to be spent lounging within the pages of a book. Atlas sits at the desk, squinting over papers, and a younger man stands behind him, looking over his shoulder.

"Hey, Attie," Callie announces our arrival. "Rhea, this is my partner, Achilles."

Oh my god.

He stands upright and waves pleasantly while I stand frozen on the floor.

Achilles, the tall man I saw in the fresco, stands several inches over six feet tall. His toned arms are a canvas for colorful tattoos that disappear under his sleeves and emerge again around his neck, likely covering his shoulders and chest. His hair is stiff atop his head, swirling to one side, and a faded shave cuts to his sharp jaw. Chestnut eyes match the brown color of his jeans, and his white t-shirt contrasts his tan skin. A scar covers his left eye, healed long ago.

He wraps his long arm around Callie's waist as she smiles at him brightly. You can understand what people mean when they say a couple "looks good together." They fit perfectly around each other, and Achilles' reserved temperament seems to be the perfect tether to Callie's bubbly personality.

"Oh! Apologies. I lost track of time." Atlas says, slamming papers into a desk drawer. "Right this way, ladies."

Atlas leads us to a dining area, and a wall of shock slams through me when I see Ethan setting covered plates around one end of a long dining table. His ocean eyes are locked firmly on mine for too long to be polite. My face burns, and I force myself to break the trance, swallowing hard. The force of Ethan's gaze remains on me as I continue into the room.

"Rhea, this is my brother, H–" Callie begins, but Ethan quickly cuts her off.

"—Ethan. We met yesterday."

Awkwardness hangs in the air at the interruption, but Atlas rushes in, and it quickly clears.

"Please, sit," Atlas says, holding a chair out for me while Achilles helps Callie with her chair. Ethan sits across the table from me, carrying the presence of a giant. He is as tall as Achilles, but his demeanor commands every light in the room to shine on him. My chest is tight, like he's pulling all the air out of the atmosphere, and my cheeks flush as I adjust nervously in the chair.

Everyone removes the domes off their plates, and my stomach can hardly contain its excitement to see it filled with food. I haven't eaten since breakfast yesterday, and while Athena gave me an IV, my hands and knees lightly shake from hunger.

A steamed fish is perched on the plate, seasoned and glistening. Under is a pool of pale-yellow lemon sauce, leaking into a healthy mound of brown lentils and several spears of grilled asparagus. My mouth waters at the sight of the offering, and I quickly grab my fork and knife to dig in, almost forgetting Ethan is still eyeing me. I don't hesitate to enjoy the food, as does Callie. Atlas takes his utensils but pauses before taking a bite.

"Well, I'll just come out and say it. Rhea, you're an immortal goddess."

"**H**onestly, Atlas?" I bark, keeping my eyes on Rhea as she nearly gouges herself with her fork, shocked by his comment.

"Atlas!" Callie exclaims with me, clanging her utensils onto her plate.

"I'm sorry?" Rhea sputters, struggling with the food in her mouth. The silver aura that hypnotized me yesterday is more chaotic now than when I first saw her in the bookstore. Knowing her powers cannot be contained with even three sets of Thaumium cuffs is fascinating—and alarming. Achilles and I are the two fastest beings in this realm, and Atlas is the most powerful Mind Mage ever.

We don't know her allegiance yet because she kicked him out of her memories before he was finished scanning them, so he wants to try to do it again *with* her permission this time. Achilles and I may need to restrain her quickly if things don't go well while Atlas puts her mind to sleep.

"You said it in Athena's office. The gods are real. And we are. We are very much alive. And you are one of us," he answers. "Each of my guests here has abilities, as you do. You know Calypso is a Wind Siren. Achilles is a Flame Mage."

My friend holds his hand out; a flame dances off his palm, extinguishing it when he closes his fist with a sizzle.

"And I'm a Light Bearer," I interrupt before Atlas can reveal my true name to Rhea. Knowing the book she was looking at yesterday, I want to know more about her interest in the mythology surrounding me before I let her in on my true identity. I hold my palm to show off a ball of brilliant blue light while the home's lights fluctuate at my power.

She stares at each of us, transfixed at what is happening. It's as if the trauma of yesterday's abduction and the cruel beatings she faced at the hands of werewolves is no comparison to the news she is hearing right now.

"Let me start from the beginning. Please eat, and I'll talk." Atlas launches into the account of our history. "In the universe's early days, twelve Titans guarded twelve realms. Each with a different ability. Earth, Wind, Water, Fire, Light, Dark, Shifting, Mind, Sonus, Sensory, Life, and Death. The realms were filled with beings that could wield the powers of their Titan. Over time, people explored and visited each other. Falling in love with new realms, the people relocated, and the realms were strengthened by the sharing and blending of power, except one—The Void.

"Ruled by Chaos, the Titan of Death, The Void, has no living being as it is the Realm of Souls. Driven mad in solitude and envious of the other realms, Chaos set out, seeking to rule the realms or consume those who fought against him.

"As he arrived at a new realm, he would consume the power of the Titan that presided over it and demand loyalty from its inhabitants. Any that didn't comply had their souls ripped from their bodies and sent to his realm of The Void. Those forced into allegiance joined his army and set off with him to the next realm."

Rhea's mind must be spinning with the information. I watch her as Atlas tells the account, careful to watch her hands for sudden movements or a change in position that she may try to flee. She keeps her wide eyes fixed sharply as Atlas's story continues, and she slowly eats her food as if on autopilot.

"Chaos arrived in Tartarus."

"The abyss that imprisons the Titans?" she asks. Her incorrect knowledge of the mortal studies of Greek mythology shows what she thinks she knows of our history, but it's so much different than the carvings and depictions have shown over the centuries.

"It's a beautiful realm of sunlight and fire. Not at all an abyss." he corrects before continuing. "Hyperion was the Titan god of Tartarus and fought bravely against Chaos, giving time for his people to flee the realm. The closest neighbor and ally was the realm of Gaea, which you now call Earth. Gaea was protected by the Titan god of Water, Oceanus. When refugees teleported here to save as many evacuees as possible, Oceanus came to the aid of Hyperion and joined him in battling Chaos. I was one of the last to flee before the realm was broken into pieces by the scale of their great powers."

Rhea gasps into her mouth. The idea of the power required to break a planet into pieces must be unfathomable. Even for me, it's difficult to imagine, and I was there.

"We were fearful Chaos would follow us here, to Gaea–Earth. We destroyed the teleportation platforms, and many great Elementals combined their powers to place protective enchantments around the realm. Chaos never came, but a new conflict for control took over.

"Already a God of War on Tartarus, Ares believed we should prepare for Chaos's arrival and be ready with an army large enough to overpower him. The mortals lacked our powers and had short lifespans, but they reproduced quickly and became obsessed with our immortality. So easily misguided by Ares, he promised them strength and to share his immortality for their obedience."

"How can he share his immortality?" she asks.

"When the realms began to migrate between each other, the offspring of Immortals from two realms sometimes were blessed with more than one ability. Ares is a mighty Flame

Elemental with some Shifting ability. He shared the essence of his power and created a Wolf-Shifter named Lucas. Lucas then created other wolves, like Lupo, the man responsible for your injuries."

Rhea flinches at the name, and her knuckles drain of color as her grip on the armchair tightens. Callie places her hand on top of Rhea's in comfort.

"Athena, the Goddess of War over Gaea, took her legions of Immortals against Ares. He threw a misguided army of Immortals, humans, and Shifters into the battle, uncaring how many souls were fed to The Void that day. More than either side could afford to lose. Ares retreated into the underbelly of Gaea with his remaining forces. He's remained hidden ever since, plotting and raising more forces and spending his immortal days creating discord among the humans purely for the sport of watching them slaughter each other."

"So, who am I in all of this?" Rhea's chest rises quickly, and a flush of pink swallows her cheeks. Her power fluxes as I watch her aura pulse and her emotions rise. Glancing at Achilles, he has also been watching Rhea intently and flicks his eyes to me, worried. The others cannot see her aura as I can, but it doesn't require my skills to know she is becoming distressed.

"I'd love to help find that out with you." Atlas answers. "Rhea, I suspect your memories have been altered."

"What?"

"When I looked into your mind–"

"When you invaded me, you mean?"

Atlas holds his hands out in surrender. "Again, I apologize. You must understand–"

"I understand you violated the most private memories of my life without permission."

"I'm sorry. There is no justifiable reason. However, I will help protect the people of this Commune, and we had to know if you are an agent of Ares."

"And what did you find when you imposed on the memories of my life?"

"Magic." he blurts out, making her recoil. "The glimmer of intentional tampering lays like a thick blanket on all your memories, Rhea. They aren't yours."

Every eye in the room is focused on her. Rising from her seat, she paces in front of the picture window. Her silver aura pulses like a beacon, spreading outward from her body—the shiny tendrils of her aura wisp behind her as she paces. Sweat beads on her forehead, and she fans herself with her hands to cool herself.

"My family–" The words catch in her throat.

Atlas closes his eyes and shakes his head back and forth.

"Rhea? Are you okay?" Callie asks, rising from her seat and approaching slowly. Rhea doesn't answer as she stops near the table and rests both hands on it. Her head hangs, and her breaths come in short, shallow puffs as her aura bursts brightly.

"Rhea, you are going into shock. We need you to focus on your breathing." Atlas has both hands on the table, standing opposite Rhea. "Achilles, get Athena. I'm going to try to calm her mind." Atlas focuses his stare on Rhea and concentrates with his brow furrowed—the emerald haze of his aura shimmers gently around him as he harnesses more power.

Stumbling back, he falters, releasing a large puff of air in defeat.

"She is blocking me. I can't get past her."

"Let me help you," I tell him.

Her knees buckle, and with quick reflexes, I catch her

before she hits her head against the table. Unable to calm down, she desperately gasps for air, but her throat constricts with each breath.

"Quickly."

I set her on my lap, and she clutches my shirt in desperation, squeezing her eyes shut. Holding her against me, the intensity of her distress wraps around me. She tries to push away from me, but I hold her firmly. "Shhhhhh," I soothe her. "Breathe with me," I whisper in her ear.

Placing two fingers at the temple of her head, a beam of obscuring light enters her mind, and I project an image of safety. Closing my eyes to the mirage that forms, I let it surround her.

Her chest rises and falls quickly, and she pulls in a shaky breath, trying to match my slower breathing. Inhaling deeply through her nose in the crook of my neck, I ignore the goosebumps rolling down the entire side of my body.

Taking steadying breaths, the long pulls of her scent enter my nose, and I relish her fragrance of sweet vanilla.

"Show me where you feel the safest." My power floods us like a rushing wind. As if standing at a subway station, waiting on the approaching train, it builds to a significant force threatening to burst our ears before suddenly stopping as we're engulfed in silence.

"Rhea, open your eyes," I gently coax her. My voice echoes around us, bouncing endlessly as if we are in a vast cavern.

Still trembling and afraid to open her eyes, she squeezes me tighter with her pale hands. I rest my cheek on her head, and we both spend a few pulses steadying ourselves.

"Rhea, you're safe here. Open your eyes and look around."

Slowly she does, lifting her head and taking in the space. A twin-size bed is next to us, with a single nightstand. A small collection of books fills shelves on each side of a bay window, and a picture of a happy family hangs on a wall with a single candle sitting cold on a shelf. A younger Rhea sits in the photo with a mom, dad, and little brother, smiling happily at the camera. Years ago, those honey eyes with bits of mahogany and amber smiled in the picture, looking less sad.

It must be her old bedroom. I lean over and grab a quilt off the bed next to us, wrapping it around her shoulders.

"Feel this, Rhea? Look at it and tell me what it is." I tell her; her fingers holding my shirt still tremble. She takes one of her shaking hands and pulls a part of the blanket up to her face, inhaling the scent and closing her eyes. She releases her breath and relaxes.

"This is the blanket my mother made me," she says quietly before taking another deep breath and relaxing back into me, laying her head on my chest.

"That's it," I encourage her. My voice is a whisper, so close to her neck I can see a shiver spread across her exposed skin. She takes in another breath, steadier this time.

"All right, keep breathing. That was pretty intense." My breath is labored by the exertion of holding this mirage. Pulling the blanket around her and letting her feel it envelop her skin, her sobs calm. I extend my aura around her in comfort but also to get a sense of understanding of this memory. My aura stretches endlessly as if there is no boundary. Using this power, I have to be careful to keep a grip on the edge of the memory, or else I can lose myself within the vision.

"I don't understand any of this." she whispers. Like my voice, it bounces around this vast cavern.

"I know. It's a lot." I reply, distracted. Still expanding the reach of my abilities into the void of her mind, I find nothing.

"You don't know anything."

"It's a lot to absorb to think your life might be a lie. I can only imagine how hard that would be to hear. You'd be a freak if you didn't have a nervous breakdown." I reply with an awkward chuckle. She looks at me sharply to find humor on my face, and I can't help but grin at the flash of irritation in her eyes.

Stiffening against me, she attempts to stand.

"Oh no you don't. I can't let you go. I'm inside your mind right now, but something is not right, so let's stay like this." I explain, shifting my hold of her.

"What do you mean something is not right? Can we leave?" she huffs, looking around her room with fondness in her eyes.

"I'm working on it." My answer is more to myself than Rhea's. A framed poster of Angel Falls hangs on the walls. I've always thought they were so beautiful. The falls are so tall that the bottom half of the mountain is usually shrouded in mist. "Have you ever been there?" I ask her, nodding my head at the poster.

She turns to match where I'm looking. "No. I had to do a Geography project on South America and picked Venezuela. I thought the falls were amazing, and I told my aunt everything I had learned about them for days. She got me that poster after." She smiles slightly.

"You know it takes twenty seconds of free fall to reach the bottom?"

"How would anyone know that?"

"I've jumped off the top before." I boast. The falls are one of my most cherished locations in this realm. They are where I retreat when I need to get away from everything.

"You have not!" Rhea exclaims.

"It's true. We put on some wingsuits, and off we went." I move my hand in a sweeping gesture as if I'm mimicking the flight path.

"That would be terrifying." she says, looking like she is imagining what it would be like to stand at the top and have the mist and wind whip around her. My stomach warms, seeing the flecks of gold in her eyes dance in the soft yellow light of the room.

"Nah. I like flying. I have dreams that I can fly sometimes." I don't know why I confess this to her. "Those are always fun. But that felt just like my dreams. It was awesome." I smile, recollecting the experience.

"So then, how do we get back to... reality?" she asks, finally looking back at me.

I hold her gaze for a moment before replying. "I'm not sure."

She bites her lip and looks around her room curiously as if trying to figure out how to solve this riddle.

"Close your eyes and take some deep breaths." she says.

"Excuse me? Let's remember you're the one having trouble with the whole breathing thing," I reply mockingly.

She drops her shoulders in irritation, and it makes me chuckle.

"Just close your eyes." she demands while her cheeks betray her, showing her embarrassment.

I draw a sly smile, but close my eyes as she instructs.

"Listen to your breathing, to the sound of it." she says in a low voice, mere inches from my face. I can feel her eyes on me. I shift her around my lap again, knowing she is studying me.

Trying to focus on my senses, she continues, moving closer to my ear. "Think of a closed doorway; on one side is us, and the other is Atlas's home." Her voice is like warm honey dripping down my neck, and I pull her closer to me, wanting more of it. I hear the faint sound of rushing wind approaching.

"Think of us walking through that door, back to ourselves in Atlas's house, and closing the door."

The rushing is growing louder. I expect to feel my hair move with the coming wind, but it's surprisingly still. The wind grows louder as the room around us fades away to blackness. It's like falling through a hole: the darker it gets, the louder the sound of the wind around us.

I tighten my arms around her waist, and she hugs my neck firmly, afraid this invisible force will pull us apart. And then again, like the first time, the noise of the wind abruptly ends in deafening nothingness. We loosen our holds, leaning back and looking into each other's eyes, breathing heavily.

"Oh, thank the goddess, you're back!" Callie yells, throwing herself on her knees and hugging us both.

Constantly aware of the light, I feel the warm golden power of the sun has been replaced with the cool blue light of the moon. I observe the empty table, cleared of our lunch dishes.

"How long have we been in the Mirage?" I ask, with my brow pulled tightly to the center.

S even hours we were gone. Athena had been waiting with Atlas and rushes to me, grabbing my hands and helping me stand.

"Are you okay?" she asks with strained eyes.

I nod my head. The entirety of my face burns with embarrassment from the eyes that fell upon us as soon as Ethan made the vision end.

Atlas looks at Ethan with a worried expression. "You disappeared. You *physically* disappeared. I couldn't connect with you at all. What happened?"

He looks at me in disbelief before simply answering, "I don't know."

Achilles stands next to Callie, who puts her arms around Ethan's waist, hugging him tightly. Atlas stands from his kneeling position and places his hands on his narrow hips.

"I just connected like always and thought about taking Rhea to a place where she feels safe. We landed in a dream; at least, I thought it was a dream. It seemed okay to me." Ethan shrugged.

"Interesting," Atlas says, looking Ethan and me up and

down as if some clues to answer his questions are stuck on our clothes. "How did you get back?"

Ethan glances at me and sends my cheeks into a brighter shade of crimson.

"Focus." he says, still watching me.

I clear my throat and shift uncomfortably, looking around to see if anyone else notices how bright red I am.

"Promise me you won't scare me like that again, H?" Callie says, holding on to his arm, and looking at him desperately. The initial "H" strikes me oddly, but Ethan takes her head in his hand and rests his cheek on top of it. "I promise, little Calla-Lilly." he whispers.

It's an endearing sentiment that immediately brings a hollow feeling to my core. Perhaps my little brother Jason and I could have been this close if only I had better control over my powers when he was little.

The door to Atlas's apartment bursts open without warning, making me jump. A tall man with red hair enters the room, pushing a large cart with platters of food that releases a loud grumble from my stomach. The lunch was terrific, but I couldn't finish it before I lost control of my panic. I'm ravaged now since we missed the rest of lunch and dinner.

"If we can all have a seat again, please?" Atlas motions for us to move to his sitting room. "I want to continue our conversation. I asked Flint to bring us some dinner." Atlas motions to the newcomer, who tips his head at me in greeting.

"Rhea, how are you feeling now?" Atlas stands next to the fireplace, his eyes trained on me intently.

"I'm better, thanks. I think that was a little too much to absorb all at once."

"I'm sorry for dumping all that on you," Atlas says.

Flint places platters and bowls of food around the large rectangular coffee table. Skewers of still-sizzling beef and shrimp call to me, and my mouth waters at the sight. Toasted slices of flat bread are smeared with soft white cheese and sit on a platter around a bowl of chopped olives.

"It's olive and honey relish. Spread it over the goat cheese flatbread." Athena says quietly as she hands me a beef skewer and a glass of red wine. "It's delicious." Her eyes dance as she takes a piece of bread for herself.

My stomach praises me for finally giving in to its demands for food, and I quickly finish the first skewer of tender beef, then reach for another before indulging in the flatbread. Everyone takes seats around the comfortable furniture and floor, digging into the assortment of foods. Dishes filled with cheeses, fruits, roasted vegetables, and bread cover the table. Without plates, the small group takes forks and their hands, eating directly from the platters.

Taking a small bowl of sliced apple and pomegranate seeds, I toss one of the pink fruits into my mouth. Its tart flavor pops on my tongue as it bursts against my teeth.

"The pomegranates are my favorite, too," Flint says with a wink. Shifting uncomfortably in my seat, I flick my eyes at Ethan and catch a fleeting glare as he turns his eyes down from Flint's and back to the food in his hand.

"Thank you, Flint; that will be enough for now." Atlas releases Flint, and he departs with a brief smile at me, rushing blood to my face and making me bite the inside of my cheek.

"I have some questions for you, Atlas," I interject before any more conversation begins. He nods at me, so I continue. "I have never known where my powers come from, and I've recently started trying to... *learn* about them. Would I have gotten these from my parents?"

"No," Atlas answers. "I don't believe those people in your memories are your family." His eyes are covered with sympathy as he clarifies.

I'm speechless again. Is it possible that everything I know is a lie? My entire childhood, my family? It can't all be fake. *Can it?*

"Does your community have recorded history? Any books that could help me understand?"

"We do. We have a large library. I'd be happy to help you explore it."

This prospect turns my knotted stomach to hope, and excitement rings through me. Learning the truth through the lens of beings with power brings a smile of joy to my face, and I calm myself.

"Do you know where magic came from? How did it start?" I ask my next question.

"That, we don't know. The Great Library at Alexandria was the first structure that ever existed in this realm. It was enchanted by the aura of a great Mind Mage and automatically kept written accounts of all events in the realm. Every event, every birth and death; everything."

"What happened to it?" I think back to Damien's book, *Burned or Hidden: The Disappearance of the Great Library.* The book talks about the accounts of the library being burned, but whether it was destroyed or badly damaged is the point of his argument. His theory states that perhaps it contained such damning information of history that it was intentionally hidden, or the records moved, and the library destroyed.

"We lost it long ago. Along with the collections of works

inside." He presses his lips into a thin line, revealing a dimple on each side of his cheeks. "It was a terrible loss. I am a big book enthusiast." He chuckles and gestures his arms around his home. "As you can see."

"Me too." It makes me smile, looking around the room and all the spines of books crammed into every possible nook and cranny. Imagining all the truths and things I could learn about myself being within my reach excites me. For so many years, I've hated myself for having these powers—for being different. I resented what I did, for losing control of myself so quickly.

But if Atlas is correct, maybe I didn't kill my family. Perhaps they never existed, and I'm not a murderer. My throat tightens as the memories try to come to the surface. If I can somehow fix my memories, restore them, and know what happened, perhaps I can get some peace from my anxiety.

"Atlas, if my memories were tampered with, can you fix them?" I can't hide the hope in my voice at the prospect of knowing that maybe my family's deaths are not because of my doing.

"It would be worth a try." He agrees, a gentle smile on his face. I smile and nod in kind. "May I ask you a question?" His gaze turns serious, and I take a steadying breath before I nod. "What did Lupo want from you?"

The room quiets immediately, and all eyes turn to me except for Callie's. She keeps her eyes on the platters of food, nearly empty now from everyone's grazing.

"He wanted to see my powers." I shift in my seat and cut my eyes to Callie, who looks up at me, encouraging me to continue. "I tried to save us at the end. But Lupo was ready for it. I overheard him talking. They were instructed to put us in those boxes and leave. That someone would come to rescue us."

"I don't remember hearing that," Callie says with a small voice.

"You weren't there yet." I give her a small, sad smile, and she returns it. We hold each other's gaze momentarily before Atlas adds his thoughts.

"So, they wanted you to be found? Curious."

"No," Ethan speaks up for the first time since we began eating. "She said they *knew* someone would come for them. How long between Lupo saying that until we arrived?"

"I wasn't exactly wearing a watch," I reply blandly to the ridiculous question. Like either of us was in a coherent state or watching the passage of time. Ethan looks at me, disapproving of my sarcasm, then turns to Atlas.

"We have a rat in our midst."

"We shouldn't jump to conclusions." Atlas says, looking at the floor in thought.

"Does that mean Lupo will come back for me?" The thought of being at Lupo's mercy terrifies me. Remembering his face near mine and seeing his glowing eyes pierce me is enough to chill my entire body. Athena places her hand on my knee, and warmth radiates from her, calming me.

"That would be my guess. I'm sorry, but I fear you may still be in danger. We need to learn why they were looking for you, but knowing Ares, he has something else in store for you."

"Do you have any family you can visit and lie low while we look into this?" Achilles suggests. My heart begins to beat quickly, and I feel my cheeks burn red at the thought of endangering my aunt. She is the only family I have. Imagining glowing eyes reflecting in the dark Pennsylvania forest surrounding my aunt's property sends a shiver up my back. I can't put her in that kind of danger.

"No, I can't bring my family into this. No matter if my Aunt Demi is my real family or not, she raised me, and she's all I have left. I won't put her in harm's way, defenseless. I'll stay on my own and keep my head down."

"You'll last about five minutes out there," Ethan scoffs. "With your aura having a field day constantly, the wolves will pick you out in a crowd, just like that." He snaps his fingers at me.

"What is an *aura*?"

"The field of energy your powers emit. And yours is like a fucking homing beacon." Ethan answers. I furrow my brow, offended. I have hidden my powers for this long and stayed out of anyone's detection until now. I can keep them locked away again.

"It's not like I'm doing anything on purpose." I huffed back at him.

"I can teach you how to mask your aura," Athena offers, then looks at Atlas. "We have to help her. We cannot abandon her, knowing Ares is hunting her."

"You're right," Atlas says. "Of course. We will help keep you safe, Rhea. The Commune defenses protect us from Ares and his armies and keep us hidden from the mortals. No one can get in or out of our territories, so you'll be safe here. If you care to stay with us."

I live in an apartment building near downtown and work in a skyrise in the city. Both places are too crowded for me to consider getting caught by the wolves again. I exhale a deep sigh of relief, closing my eyes. "Thank you."

Callie and Achilles walk me to a studio across the hall from their apartment. Showing me a tour of the space and how to use the intercom to page them, Achilles walks me through using the *portlet* system. Like the portal machines, the smaller portlet transports goods like food and purchases from their mall into the homes.

The technology here is impressive, and to think of all this existing while the mortals are ages behind makes me shake my head in disbelief. If only humans could access these things and live in such self-sufficient communities where money has no value, and everyone works collectively together; it would be a utopia.

A moment after they leave, there's a knock at the door. The pad at the entryway shows a video of the hall and Ethan standing at the door, waiting. Reluctantly, I open it. Nervous around him, I chew the inside of my cheek.

"We found this in the alley. I thought you would want it back." He holds out my tote, heavy with yesterday's books. Looking at the bag, a strange appreciation fills my heart. I'm happy to have the books, but it brings me to the moment I dropped them in the alley as Callie dropped in from the sky, and everything changed.

"Thanks," I answer, taking the bag from his hand and feeling that same jolt of anticipation when my fingers gently brush against his. "Goodnight."

I close the door and plop on the large king-size bed. Looking at the clock, it's just after midnight. The studio is modern, with exposed brick and a view of the large lake behind the main building. Double sliding doors close off the bedroom and bathroom, but I can't close my eyes for thoughts of yesterday blinding my mind. So, I take out my books, including my copy of Damien's new book, and flip through the pages, finally resting the book on my chest when my eyes refuse to stay open.

I t's a grey and stormy day like it always is on my birthday.

Riding in the car, the dream I always have haunts me again tonight. I hate knowing it's a dream and that I can't do anything to stop what is to happen.

I'm about to kill them all.

I steal one last look at Jason, still so young. His face is round with baby fat that hasn't fully grown into his six-year-old 'big boy' face. My heart breaks for the millionth time.

I look away when it happens.

Closing my eyes, it's burned into my vision, and I'm forced to relive it with every blink.

Then, I hear the sound I've been waiting for, which marks the moment I can't get past. The flapping wings of a bird coming toward me.

I lay down on the pavement like I'm supposed to, and I keep my eyes closed, listening.

I can feel her. I feel her change from a bird to a woman. She feels cold, not warm like a person should. She is cold like a shadow.

I lift one of my eyelids open ever so slightly and see her—the blurry faceless woman with raven hair. Like every time I look upon her in my nightmare, I fall into the abyss of her black eyes.

I bolt awake, trembling and shaking. My eyes dart across the room, jumping from shadow to shadow. They seem to move in the edges of my vision as my brain interprets what my eyes are taking in. My heart is racing faster than a purebred at the Kentucky Derby and it takes a few moments for my mind to catch up with the understanding that I'm awake and the long shadows of the room are not people here to harm me. Checking the clock next to the bed, it's only four o'clock in the morning.

Opening my book about Hermes, I lose myself in the pages and think of riding in the ferryman's boat with Ethan sitting by me on the bench, telling me jokes and laughing over a picnic as Charon paddles down the River Styx.

Hermes

I **knew visiting Rhea at her studio was a bad idea.**
Delivering the tote of books was supposed to be a quick
and friendly gesture. Turning my back to the door after she
closed it, I find Achilles standing in the open doorway of his
apartment, arms folded over his chest, and leaning his shoulder
against the frame. One ankle crossed over the other, he casually
watches the interaction with a crooked grin.

"What are you doing here?" he asks me, cocking an
eyebrow.

"Don't start with me."

"She's pretty."

"Good for her." I gruff and turn to retreat down the hall. I
know where this is headed, and I don't feel like entertaining a
gripe session about my love life. Achilles shuts the door and
jogs after me.

Achilles and I have been best friends for thousands of years,
evenly matched in height and strength of our power; we're
both competitive and arrogant. We grate on each other's nerves
sometimes, but we both know it comes from a good place.
Since my mate died, I know I've been a brooding, grumpy
mess, but that happens when part of your soul is ripped away

from you. No one knows more about what that is like than Callie and Achilles, losing Patroclus in the Trojan War nearly four thousand years ago.

"Hermes," He grabs my arm, turning me to face him and stop my withdrawal. "No one will question your loyalty to Juliette if you decide to move on."

"I don't think tonight is a good time for this conversation."

"I'm just saying she would want you to be happy for the rest of your immortal life. You've punished yourself long enough." He knows not to press anything further and returns to his apartment, sparing a last glance before nodding goodnight. I stare at his closed door and then look back at Rhea's.

Even behind the walls of her studio, I feel her power radiating and filling the space. It's suffocating and intoxicating all at once.

I need to go for a run.

Running is second nature to me, and having the power to move at the speed of light, it is the best way to blow off steam when I'm stressed. Heading out for a night run around the Commune, I start near the lake at the center of the property. I pick up speed as I run around its banks to the trails on the wooded side of the property; the faint glow of my power illuminates the darkness, guiding me. The running path takes me through the meadows and forests around the Commune, and the hills and dips of the terrain force me to focus on the ground before me.

A million thoughts of the past twenty-four hours race through my mind, and each one brings me back to thoughts of Rhea and her aura of starlight. It's unfathomable to me how she has remained hidden for so long, with so much power thrumming through her. At least in our Communes, we have others to teach us about our abilities. Training facilities designed to withstand our elements so we can practice using them in new ways.

Rhea is like a nuclear reactor with a million warning lights flashing. She desperately needs to learn to use and control her powers, or, one day, she'll detonate—or worse. In the hands of someone like Ares, she could be unleashed and unable to control the havoc she could cause.

Stopping at the farthest end of the Commune, my running always leads me here with thoughts of Juliette. The topmost part of our property looks down to an expanse of pasture land for hundreds of acres; the gibbous moon is high in the sky and nearly full, so it's a bright night, even without the glow of my abilities. She always loved nighttime and the blanket of darkness draping over the landscape.

Being a Dark Mage, the nighttime called to her, just as the daytime calls me. The irony of a Light Bearer and a Dark Mage being fated mates was always comical to her. Our powers canceled each other out.

As I look across the sky and the bright stars, movement catches my attention on the farthest side of the pasture.

Werewolves.

A mile away at the edge of the treeline, five werewolves saunter into the woods, and melt into the shadows. It's no coincidence they are here tonight. Whether they are here observing or meeting with someone inside the Commune, Rhea is drawing them here.

One of them stops walking into the trees and pauses. This wolf is enormous—an Alpha. Black fur blows in the wind, and I know my scent has reached him. The Alpha stiffens and turns his neck slightly in my direction at the hilltop.

While lower-rank wolves can look similar in size and coat, the Onyx Alpha is unmistakable. Lupo has come himself. After a pause, he disappears into the tree line with the rest of his pack. I hold my place at the top of the hill a moment longer, projecting my aura to be sure they are leaving the Commune.

The morning sun invades my closed eyes, and I turn over on Atlas's couch, away from the intruding light. After I spotted the wolves, there was no way I would sleep anytime soon, so I stopped by the tactical team on the night shift and had them call in a few extras to watch the perimeter. Terra scolded me for pushing orders and being grounded, but I didn't care, nor did the team. They'll follow the orders because they know it's the right thing to do and don't give a shit about the Headmistress's demands.

Atlas kicks the couch, and I respond with a grunt. He's such a morning person, it's annoying.

"Morning sunshine," he says in an overly cheery voice for such an early morning. "You going to head over to Rhea's to start her training or sleep all day?"

"What time is it?" I ask, my voice husky from sleep.

"Time to get up." he says, walking away with his steaming mug of coffee.

With a sigh, I heave myself up and rest my elbows on my knees. I rub the sleep away from my eyes. After a giant yawn, I stretch and head to the bathroom to freshen up.

I'm here so often that I have clothes and other belongings. Dressing quickly, I head to the portal and punch in a code that will bring me to the hallway and close to Rhea's guest suite to pick her up for aura training. Being suspended for thirty days, Atlas thought I would have nothing better to do than babysitting the 'new girl', as Flint called her. I listen to her door for a moment and hear signs of life behind it, so I knock.

"Boy, that was fast." she says, opening the door; she jolts back, her eyes shooting into her hairline, not expecting to see me back at her door this morning. She has dark circles under her eyes that tell me she slept as poorly as I did.

"Couldn't sleep either?" I gruff at her, pushing past her and into the studio.

"Well, come on in, why don't you." she says smugly, pushing the door closed and crossing her arms over her chest. "Is there something I can help you with?"

"Yeah, you got any coffee?" I ask, finding juice and fruit in an otherwise empty refrigerator. "Oh, and good morning." I smile sleepily at her.

"How did that get there?" Rhea asks, perplexed while pointing to the fridge.

"Did you order it using the touchpad?" I ask, helping myself to the decanter of juice.

"Well, yes, but I just did that. Like a minute ago. No one's been here to deliver it."

"Portlets. It gives us instant service and makes us spoiled brats. The kitchen's computer system delivers the groceries directly into your refrigerator or pantry. Want some breakfast?" I ask, scrolling through the room service menu. Our teleportation is an extension of my light power—not mine specifically, but the power of Light Bearers like me. Harnessing Light through our technology, we can travel anywhere in the realm, but my favorite is the instant access to room service.

"I already ordered some. How long does that take to get here?"

I smile, pointing at the portal in her studio. I open the door and find a service cart filled with covered platters of steaming food and a pitcher of coffee. "Is there someone else here with you?" I ask, looking from the enormous cart of food to the living room and finally back at Rhea. "Flint hasn't made a move on you yet? Surprising."

"I think you should leave now if you have no business here but to taunt me." she snaps.

"Okay, okay." I laugh, holding my hands up in surrender. "I promise I'll behave myself." I resign while I help myself to a plate and start piling food on it. I put on my best innocent face, but I know my smile betrays me, and I hand her the food as a peace offering.

Rhea furrows her brow, but she takes it from me.

Flint is a creepy bastard, and he grates under my skin. Atlas keeps trying to talk me into giving him a spot on the tactical teams, but Flint always fails our Elemental Test, so he can't qualify. And he makes Callie uncomfortable. He always stands too close when he talks; he doesn't understand boundaries and personal space when it comes to the ladies in the Commune. I think he wants to weasel his way into Callie and Achilles' partnership and replace their lost third mate, but no way in hell will someone like Flint ever hold a candle to Patroclus. And the fated mate connection doesn't work like that. It can't be replaced by someone else stepping in.

"Why are you here, eating my food and being rude?" she asks, pouring us both a cup of coffee.

"Sorry, there's enough food here for four people, so it seems you need some help to tackle it." I tease her again, gesturing to all the food she ordered. "And... I'm here to start your training. After my little stunt saving your life, being noble and whatnot," I pause for dramatic effect, "The Headmistress grounded me from my position as the Head of Security. I get to use my downtime to whip you into shape."

"Why do you think I need your help?" she asks with a mouth full of food.

"You are no lady, miss," I mockingly throw her a cloth napkin. "Aura training first, then Atlas will hack into your memories. And then I will get you into the blast chamber and see if you can melt the walls."

"But I wanted to go to the library today and start my research." she interjects.

"Such a nerd." I joke and chuckle as she tosses the napkin back at my face. "Okay, wall melting tomorrow then."

"Can I ask you a question?"

"You can ask; it doesn't mean I'll answer." I'm not a morning person, and today is no exception. Having little sleep last night will worsen my gruff morning demeanor, so I lighten my expression and try again. "Sorry, yes. Please ask your question."

"Why were you meeting with Damien Lopez in the alleyway?"

"So, you were spying on me?" I accuse but keep my tone lighthearted. With the beating she suffered and her attempts to rescue Callie, we at least know she is not part of Ares' army, but I don't know how trustworthy she is yet.

"He wanted to trade information, so we were meeting."

"Why the alley?"

"He's a Werewolf, so it's perilous for him to be seen meeting with Elementals."

"Oh, my god," she exclaims. Her gaze drifts to the corner of the room, in thought, before she shakes her head and looks back at me. "Well, you ruined my plans. I was going to talk to him about some of his research. Are you going to be meeting him again? I want to come if you do."

"I don't know if that's a good idea."

"Either take me with you, or I'll find my own way to meet him. I have to talk to him about what he knows about people with powers."

Releasing a huff of air, I agree. My fork scrapes the remaining food off my plate, and gulp the last of my coffee. "Ready?" I ask, bouncing off the couch. I feel much more awake now.

"Not really." she murmurs, finishing her breakfast.

"Oh, don't be a wimp. Come on."

Walking to the portal, I open the door for her. Entering after she does, I select an exit to deliver us outside to the lake.

I love the weather in Georgia, but the summer humidity is unbearable. It's hardly eight in the morning, and we'll be coated in a sheen of sweat in five minutes. The sun is already bright in the blue, cloudless sky as the Commune wakes up and people start making their way to their daily assignments.

Athena is waiting for us by the door, always punctual. Her billowing pants and crop top flutter in the gentle breeze, and her hair is fixed in a braid down the center of her back. Greeting Rhea, Athena guides her to the lake as she explains the morning's exercise.

"Rhea, please stand here to the side while I give a demonstration." Turning to me, she asks, "Will you be so kind as to offer some explanations?"

Athena steps toward the lake. The Commune is busy with

members going to their assignments and tasks for the day. Athena doesn't often meditate on the lake; when she does, the spectacle pulls an audience. Even now, passersby can guess she is about to put on a water show, and they pause their morning commutes to watch.

Placing her sandals off to the side, she steps her first foot into the water and begins her trek to the lake's center. Rhea gasps when she processes what she sees.

"Is she... walking on water?"

I laugh at her surprise. "She is. Athena is a Water Siren."

Athena stops in the lake's center, and the entire surface calms to a standstill, looking like a dark sheet of glass. She stands momentarily, breathing, and then lunges into a martial art pose. She moves her arms and legs through a practiced routine with the lake's surface remaining solid. Athena arches her leg slowly with grace and points her dancer's foot to the water—a great ripple bounds across the lake towards the shore.

"Athena is unique among Elementals. Most Water Sirens will control the water around them. They will summon water nearby, from a stream or within the ground, and then command it to obey them. But Athena can make water, as well as control it. Water will flow from her like a raging river out of her hands."

"That is amazing," Rhea exclaims, staring wide-eyed at the show Athena is putting on display.

Lowering her back and sweeping her arm, Athena bows before raising herself entirely, a stream of water shooting upward in time with her movements. She moves through her repetition, gliding across the body of water. The elegant poses guide the water to flow in a coordinated dance mimicking the movements of her limbs. Her pace quickens, and the lake's water moves in streams, columns, waves, and bubbles as if she is wielding it as an extension of her body.

"Most Water Sirens are healers. Since our bodies are mostly water, they can manipulate it to heal us, as she did with you on your arrival. Callie as well."

Athena releases the golden hue of her aura, glistening in the sun—its brilliant against the lake water. It grows, and the appearance of wings almost seems to shine within the glow of translucent light emanating from her.

"What is that?" Rhea asks. "That light around her."

Surprised she can see the aura, I snap my head at her. Not every Elemental can detect auras. Made up of light and power, Light Bearers and Sensors are usually the only elements that can see auras. I make a mental note to talk to Atlas later, letting him know.

"That is her aura. Beautiful, right?" My fondness for her shows as I watch her dance on the lake. Athena and her partner are very close friends of mine, and we've been through a lot together. Neither of them deserved what Ares did to them. But Athena and her pure heart took it with grace. Hanging up her helmet and resigning as Gaea's Goddess of War, she devoted the rest of her immortal life to healing.

As we continue watching, I explain more about auras to Rhea. "It's an energy field, and when she commands her element like this, she calls upon more energy, and her aura grows. Not everyone sees them; we mask them when we are within the mortal population."

"Does everyone have an aura?"

"Yes, yours is especially unique."

"How so?"

"It's a rare silver aura. Pure starlight from the center of

creation. Not many Immortals in history have an aura like yours."

Her eyebrows crinkle inward as she thinks about my answer for a moment before asking another question. "Did you know anyone with one like that before?"

I look at her, and my fated mate's face floods my vision. As if I can see her standing at the edge of the lake, the memory of Juliette pulls at my broken heart. Without answering her question, I gesture back to the lake, where Athena ends her dance on the water with a respectful bow.

"Come on."

The golden glow of her aura fades as Athena walks back to the shore, turning to Rhea with a smile.

"That was amazing!" The smile on her face is genuine, and her eagerness draws out a laugh from Athena.

"Thank you. It's my morning exercise. I usually do it in my office without the water, but I thought you might like to join me. The routine will be a good warmup for your training, and we can practice your aura control."

"Rhea, I'm leaving you in skillful hands. Athena will take you to Atlas' office later."

Walking away, I'm reminded of Achilles' words from last night.

"You've punished yourself long enough."

But that's not true. I wasn't fast enough that day, and Ares leeched Juliette of her power. I watched her turn ashen and grey as he stole her ichor, and then before I could reach him, he vanished. I fell to my knees while my soul mate turned to dust and blew away. So, I'll punish myself daily in this mortal realm until I find Ares and drain him of everything he has.

Joining Achilles in the tactical room, I get a report on the wolves from last night.

"They just sat there, near the spot where you saw them."

"What were they doing before I got there?"

"Just looking at the Commune, like they were waiting," Achilles explains while the team members play the surveillance footage. As Achilles said, five large wolves are sitting in a line, looking directly at the Commune.

"Look here." Achilles points to another monitor, and the bright flash of my power moves quickly across the monitors, showing my evening run. I'm too fast for the recordings, so it shows up as a streak of light. "They saw your aura, and that's when they started walking toward the tree line."

"Weird. Did the Sensors find anything?"

"Yeah, that dark void again. The same one from the alleyway."

"I would bet you a decade of night shifts... the Dark Mage is our spy."

Rhea

Aura training with Athena is remarkable and exhausting. She holds my hand as I cautiously step into the water, ready to sink under the surface. Walking on water feels like walking on Jell-O, and my stomach remains in knots as we step into the middle of the lake.

Athena is patient, but her smile tells me she is holding back her amusement. I have to agree that I look ridiculous walking with my back hunched over, my arms splayed low, staring intently at the water as I wait to fall below the surface.

"Rhea, stand up straight. I promise I've got you and won't let you fall." Athena has such a warming presence about her, her deep brown eyes full of patience and kindness. My shoulders drop, and the grimace on my face melts away as I relax.

Working for hours, Athena explains the movements of her poses and the intention behind the meditation. Instead of trying to push my powers into a box and keep them hidden, total control is my overall goal. It will be more effective to shield them in protection versus concealing them in fear. As I move through the dance, she wants me to focus on freeing my powers; with it, my aura will respond.

My arms ache and my legs scream as we repeatedly move

through the routine, but after two hours, I finally progress. Keeping my eyes closed, I've memorized the pattern of the movements, and a memory of my mom floats into my mind. At least it's the woman I believe is my mom.

Celebrating my tenth birthday—Jason was two—my parents took us on a family picnic. As Jason wobbled on his chubby legs, Mom took me to the center of a field full of spring flowers. Growing wild in a clearing, we were surrounded by yellow daffodils. Holding my hands, we spun in circles as the floating white seeds of thousands of dandelions tickled my nose.

"Sometimes, little Rhea, nature can be astonishing." She told me as she plucked a young dandelion and showed me its bright yellow petals. "Like the dandelion, when the flower first blooms, its yellow petals are pretty and seem to die as it closes. But it's not dead, only sleeping, because when it opens again, a hundred seeds are ready to dance on the wind, creating more flowers everywhere they land." She took the flower to her lips and blew. The tiny seeds danced like little ballerinas, carried away by the wind.

I think about our enchanted picnic with the feathery dandelion seeds as I spin in the lake's center with Athena, and warmth fills my core. Behind closed eyes, a bright light burns white against the golden glow of Athena's aura. Opening my eyes, my face blooms with happiness as a wild shimmer reflects off the surface of my skin.

Shining like the Aurora Borealis high in the night sky, the translucent ribbons of light are pure silver and sparkle with the glitter of a thousand rainbows. It gleams and pulses with the rhythm of my heart, and Athena encourages me to keep flowing through the movements of the dance.

"Would you look at that," Athena gleams at me with pride.

"Never have I seen such a beautiful aura. Well done, Rhea." Finishing the dance, my aura still shines, and the water beneath my feet begins to ripple. Scared of messing up and falling into the lake, I cast worried looks at Athena.

Not seeing the ripples, she continues the movements until she is done, turning to me with a bow. My heart spikes as the waves continue, but soon I notice they dissipate as we close the dance. Relaxing again, I blot the sweat on my forehead, and Athena places her hand on my shoulder.

"Amazing progress for one day. Let's meet here each morning and keep practicing." Athena escorts me to the cafeteria, where we grab lunch. My nerves are building as the minutes tick by until my session with Atlas.

I can still feel the icy fingers of his power crawling along my mind, leaving a haunting residue on my nerves. Athena tries to distract me, filling the meal with a conversation about the world of the Immortals. She explains the difference in tracking years for Immortals, which fascinates me.

Just like we celebrate twelve months in a year, the realms commemorate the passing of time but on a much longer scale. As the realms travel through the universe, they pass through the twelve houses of the Titans. Taking 2,500 Earth years to pass through a house, the Immortals refer to this as an *Age*. Once a realm has passed through all twelve houses, it's called *The Great Year*.

"In about fifty Earth years, we will enter the Age of Oceanus while passing through the house of our own Titan," Athena tells me as we walk through the Commune to Atlas's office. "All the realms would send gifts to the people of Gaea in honor of Oceanus. It would be a time of many festivals and celebrations." The light in Athena's eyes darkens as she continues. "But ten Great Years have passed since the portals to the other realms were in operation, and I find the celebrations quite lonely now, and the Immortals have turned them into a time of grieving those we have lost in the battles with Chaos and Ares.

Arriving at Atlas's home, Athena presses a button on the door, and it opens for us.

"Sorry, Atlas, for being tardy. We decided to take a long way and lost track of time."

"No harm at all." Atlas is calm as he closes a huge, antique book on his desk with a thump. His respect for Athena is evident in how he addresses her, and I think back to my hostile tone yesterday at our first meeting. Granted, I had just woken up from the most traumatizing event of my life and was shackled like a prisoner. But getting to know Athena today, she is a lovely person. It comforts me that she will be here to monitor Atlas's attempt to look into my memories.

"Rhea, are you ready?" Atlas asks.

"Not really, but let's do it," I mumble.

Preparing myself to learn hard truths makes my anxious mind race with the prospects of a dozen outcomes. What if my family never existed, or I suddenly remember thousands of memories at once? Can a mind even handle that kind of thing without completely breaking? The closer I walk to his couch, the more my stomach twists like a pile of thorns and vines scraping my insides.

"You don't have any questions?" Athena asks.

"I don't think any question can prepare me for this, so let's do it."

Atlas directs me to his couch, where I lie down. Athena sits in a chair beside my head and places a small, round sticker on my temple to monitor the session. Atlas pulls up a second chair at the other end of the couch and sits near my feet. His eyes are closed in concentration. I take a deep breath and prepare for the icy crawl of Atlas's power on my mind.

As his power spreads over me, the feeling of cool liquid metal pouring over my brain causes me to shiver. The white light that blinds my closed eyes approaches like the lights of a car, coming at you head-on in the dark of night. As the light reaches its pinnacle, the searing pain slams into me, and my back bows in a dramatic arc. Atlas grasps my calf firmly with his hand, and the pain dissipates. I collapse into the couch, my chest rising quickly with the racing pulse of my heart.

Like yesterday, the images flash behind my closed eyelids at dizzying speeds. Memories of riding my bike without training wheels or showing my mom the poorly frosted chocolate cake I baked race like high-speed trains. It is impossible to grasp and savor the sweet moments with my family before they flutter into the darkness.

The memory I dread most starts like it always does in my nightmares: large raindrops bounce off the top of the car with a plop, and next, I become a murderer.

No. Not this. I don't want Atlas to see this. I don't want to see this.

The billow of my powers surprises me as it careens from within, taking over the vision and fighting against Atlas's powers. Like the shockwave of a bomb, my dark, shadowed mist surges in all directions, casting him out of my mind.

I ignore the knock on my door, wanting to lay here like a puddle of mush. I don't think Atlas was prepared to be ejected, and the force of my power knocked him unconscious.

I certainly wasn't prepared for it.

Crying for most of the afternoon, I'm lying in the middle of the king-size bed with the white comforter pulled around my chin. Hiccupping each time I breathe, the sound of the door opening forces me to wipe my eyes.

"Rhea? You in here?" Calypso calls from the kitchen. Her light footsteps bring her to the bedroom doorway, and her shoulders drop when she sees me lying on the bed in my state of self-pity. "Atlas is fine. Athena sent me to let you know." She sits on the edge of the bed, bending her knee and turning to face me. "Are you okay?"

"Not really." I huff my pouty reply. Seeing Atlas blown out of his chair with his body sprawled on the wooden floor was jarring as a flash of my family's faces, choking to death on my powers, made me clasp my hands over my mouth to avoid screaming. Then, I rushed out and ran to the other side of the Commune into my tiny studio.

"Hey, it was an accident. And he's immortal, so he's okay." She dons a sympathetic smile as her light blue eyes take me in. "Come on! I have something that will cheer you up! But first, we need to get you some new clothes!"

Callie operates the touchpad in the closet as she takes in my small inventory of clothes from yesterday's short trip to the clothing store. Pausing periodically to look me up and down, she looks back at the device with a furrowed brow as she works. Satisfied with her efforts of ordering more clothes that will be delivered through the portlet, she returns the touchpad to its home and shuts the closet door.

"You will feel better after a shower, so get to it!" Rushing me into the bathroom, she's right. The shower is excellent, and the hot water loosens my tense muscles as the steam clears, the guilty thoughts colliding in my mind.

Exiting the bathroom, Callie has placed a pair of jeans, a casual top on the bed, and a pair of ankle boots. Dressing and drying my hair, I exit my bedroom, greeted by Callie as she jumps up and down, squealing as she rushes to my side.

"You're going to love this!" Her smile is infectious, and while she's not letting me in on the surprise, I can't help but smile, too. We enter the studio's private portal, and she jams her thumb on the touchpad.

Allowing me to exit the portal ahead of her, my mouth gapes at the sight before me. A massive two-story library welcomes me, brightly lit and proudly holding thousands of books.

Greek columns line each side of the long, rectangular building as it stretches before me. The center of the building opens up higher with a glass dome adding sparkling light from the sun into the space. Below the dome is the recognizable bronze sculpture of a muscled figure crouched over and holding the world on his shoulders—the mythological representation of Atlas. Seeing the statue, my heart burns with regret at how things played out today.

"Callie, it's wonderful," I say, still gawking at the rows of shelves on both floors, stretching fifteen feet high and crammed with the spines of books and rolled-up ends of parchment. My fingers flex, wanting to explore the pages of the books and dive into their words.

"Come on. There are some people I want you to meet." The excited smile is back on her face, and I eagerly twist my fingers.

Callie walks us deeper into the building, and I spot Achilles standing with a couple near a sitting area tucked off into an alcove. They are both very tan with dark hair. The man has short curls that sit close to his head, and the woman has much longer hair, resting in tight curls by the middle of her back. Wearing a traditional white stola, the woman's brown skin is accentuated by the olive sash draped around one shoulder and crossing her body.

The pair pauses their conversation when they spot Callie, and the dark-haired woman approaches her with arms spread wide, embracing Callie in a hug.

"My dear, we're so glad you have returned safely." she says to Callie before they turn in acknowledgment to me.

"Rhea, this is Penelope." Callie introduces me, and I extend my hand with a warm smile.

"Nice to meet you."

"And this is her partner, Odysseus."

12
Hermes

"So, how was it meeting Odysseus and Penelope?" I ask Rhea as we make our way to the training rooms. She and Callie were up until the early hours of the morning, chatting with our aunt and uncle; Callie even dug books out of the archives for Rhea. Penelope and Odysseus are not our blood relatives but are close friends of our father. They took over the Commune in Delphi, Greece, as Head Minister and Headmistress after my father's death.

"It was so amazing." Her eyes grow wide with excitement, and she tells me of the questions she asked and how amazed she was hearing the truth of Odysseus' infamous quest around the Grecian Isles.

Odysseus is an Earth Mage, and Penelope is a Water Siren, like Athena. The couple traveled the oceans looking for one of the lost portals, thought to still be in operation but under a heavy enchantment. Callie traveled with them for a few decades. They never found it and eventually gave up the search, but Ares was a torment to them and their ships the entire time. Odysseus always suspected it was because their hunch was true, and Ares was trying to keep them from finding the lost portal.

We arrive at the training rooms, and I watch Rhea's amazement while she observes the new space. Fighting gear and weapons of all sorts hang along the tall walls of the training facility. Swords and daggers catch her eye, and she tracks them as we walk along. Her interest in them makes me want to show her my blades hanging on my wall.

The sounds of two men sparring steal her observation, and she stops to watch them. I approach the room and stand near the floor-to-ceiling protective glass for a better view of the Flames practicing their fighting. Rhea watches alongside me. Even in their gear, I know the fighters are Flint and Achilles.

This should be entertaining.

"Have you ever seen Elementals fight with their powers before?" I ask her, thinking this may be the first time she'll ever see these kinds of powers from Elementals other than herself. Confirming my suspicion, she shakes her head and keeps her large honey color eyes on them.

Achilles and Flint are fully covered in protective gear and locked in a fighting stance. Flint allows himself to be distracted by our arrival and turns his head when he notices Rhea. It's the faintest movement but more than enough for a fighter of Achilles' skill and speed.

He launches a fierce assault of flames and fireballs with precision timing, taking advantage of Flint's distraction. Flint fights back with misplaced blasts that sizzle as they hit the walls behind Achilles. I know how this fight will end, so I watch Rhea as she takes in the spectacle with eyes full of wonder.

Living in this Commune for the last few hundred years, we all fall into a rhythm, and everyone knows everyone. No one has any secrets, and new gossip spreads like wildfire. The excitement of a new member of the Elemental community is one we rarely experience. Unlike the werewolves and vampires,

Elementals do not reproduce here in Gaea—something that is difficult for couples wanting children, but is also alarming with each battle we face against Ares. If we keep this up, there won't be any Elementals left to go against him, and he'll finally take over the realm.

The fire dances in Rhea's eyes, turning into a swirling inferno as she watches the Flames fight. Her face lights up with the golden glow of the fire as it blasts between the fighters and reflects off the honey highlights of her hair. She has a natural beauty about her, the kind that intimidates men and keeps them from approaching as they'd be certain someone like her would have a long list of suitors. My eyes wander, taking in her narrow waist that curves into the small of her back and ample bottom. My hand burns to slide along her skin, and my body warms in response to her. Realizing I'm practically gawking, I turn my attention to the fight just as it's ending.

Achilles is a master at close combat and better controls his fire element than Flint. He throws fire blasts around the training room floor, guiding Flint exactly where he wants him. Achilles feigns an attack to the left, but his foot placement pivots him to the right at the last moment. The maneuvers confuse Flint as he shoots a fireball in the wrong direction.

Ending the match, Achilles lands a fireball on Flint's calf, and the room lights up green, showing him as the victor. Achilles pats Flint's shoulder and tells him 'good job.' Flint, with his leg still smoking and looking unabashed, smiles at Rhea as they exit the fighting room and meet us in the observation area.

"That was amazing! Are you okay?" Rhea asks Flint, looking at his singed suit.

"Ah, it's fine. The suits protect us." he says, looking coldly at me. "So, how are you liking the Commune?"

Speaking in low tones, I ask Achilles about Damien and our next meeting.

"I got in touch with him last night. He says the tension among the wolfpacks is picking up, and he wants to lay low a little more," Achilles whispers. I look at Flint and Rhea as he's telling her about his Fire Element. I roll my eyes as he spits the same lame pickup lines he's tried on every woman at the Commune. "He thinks something big is going down at the Autumn Equinox."

"Does he know what?"

"Not yet, but he's trying to figure it out. I pressed him for a meeting tomorrow morning. He agreed, but only if we come to his place. Nothing in public."

"Good job." I grasp my friend's shoulder and check back on Rhea. Like a stranger is talking her ear off, she's trying to be polite; she listens and nods her head at the right moments.

"I'm going to scout the building for some observation points," Achilles adds, but my ears pick up on Flint's conversation when he invites Rhea to *The Coat*.

The forcefield surrounding our Commune is like a giant dome covering our property. We call it The Coat. It's an electromagnetic forcefield keeping out unauthorized guests and acts like a Mirage to mortals. They only see a vast expanse of rolling hills and Georgia pine trees. Meanwhile, if they were to wander close to it, the enchantments and wards would gently expel them away, and they would be none the wiser.

Flint habitually tries to lure women to the top of the antenna tower to fool around. He's played his cards with everyone here, so I assumed it would only be a matter of time before he made his moves on Rhea.

"Isn't that your make-out spot where you took Lexi the other day? Weird you're inviting Rhea there, too." Teasing him is easy. He gets angry at the most minor comments. "Sloppy seconds." I mouth to Rhea, and she holds back a smile and smacks my arm.

"If you find your training lacks Rhea, come find me." Flint winks at her and turns to leave. I usually don't use my powers without provocation, but he's begging for it by even pretending he can outfight me. Using Mirage on him, I make the long bench in the observation area invisible, and he runs into it with both shins. Cursing and stumbling over the bench, he catches himself before totally wiping out.

"Oh, no. Be careful," I say in a nonchalant tone, dripping with sarcasm. Rhea gasps but covers her mouth to hide her laughter. I can't stifle my grin as I turn and walk into the training room he and Achilles just vacated.

"Was that necessary?" Rhea says, placing her hands on her glorious hips, but her smile gives her away. "Making fun of him when he trips?"

"Yes. I can't stand that kid. Let's get started." I walk to the middle of the room. "Let me see your powers."

Her shoulders tighten, and the color in her face drains. Rhea shakes her head back and forth anxiously while she backs away from me. Her hands clasp together, and she wrings her fingers nervously. Regret washes over me for not being more sensitive and easing her into a demonstration. I heard from Callie how upset Rhea was when she knocked Atlas out.

"I'm sorry. That was a dick thing to say." My apology

relaxes her slightly. An idea strikes me. "Let me show you something."

Exiting the room, I open the door for her. Rhea's mouth presses tightly in a thin line, but she follows, still fidgeting with her hands.

There are several training rooms on this floor, and I reserved one of the smaller ones for a more private lesson. A teacher calls out instructions to their class, so I walk up to the wall and lean my shoulder against it. Rhea peers through the square window of the door. There's a class of lower Elementals practicing aura control. It's like the exercises Athena puts Rhea through, but on a much smaller level. The students, who appear to be teenagers in mortal years, stand in rows and lines, all moving through the fluid motions together as the teacher calls out the movements.

"Is this supposed to explain something to me?" she asks.

"Just watch," I tell her. After hesitating, Rhea observes the training class from the window as they run through their practiced routine. I extend my hand to her. "Now, come over here by me and close your eyes."

Rhea hesitates near the door, but I keep my eyes fixed on her, patient for her to accept my offer. I'll wait while she opens up to her training. She must be very powerful to overcome three sets of Thaumium cuffs. One could argue it was purely from her distress, but I believe it's her strength.

Finally, she steps toward me, and a jolt of heat spikes through my arm when she accepts my hand in hers. Her soft skin glides against my callused palm, threatening to take my breath away.

"Close your eyes," I repeat. Rhea huffs but follows my direction, and I smile slightly at her stubbornness. With my shoulder on the wall, I use my abilities to *see* into the training room and extend my vision to Rhea. She audibly gasps when the image of a dozen forms dressed in white uniforms move through their dance with punches and kicks in unison. The power of my Mirage allows her to see the events of the other room and hear the instructors' directions as if she were inside the room herself. Her eyes fly open with amazement.

"Is that real?" she exclaims, which makes me laugh.

"Of course, it's real. You just saw it for yourself."

"Do it again!" she demands and I smile wider, entertained by her eagerness while I open the vision to her again. She mirrors my smile and closes her eyes again. This time, she holds my hand firmly with both of hers and takes a step closer to me; the scent of her honey hair wraps around me like a heavenly cloud of berries and vanilla.

Juliette's hazel-green eyes flash in my mind.

"What was that?" Rhea startles and drops my hand. I accidentally allowed her to glimpse my late partner, and guilt washes over me. Careful to keep others at bay, I've never even entertained a thought of another relationship since Juliette. She was the perfect completion to the missing part of my soul, and any other romantic relationship would be a barren wasteland, starved of emotion. No one deserves to love a person incapable of loving them back. And so, remorse has overruled my heart each time someone attempts to get near.

"Nothing." Pulling away from the wall, I walk back to our training room, and she follows. "Can I ask you a question?"

A sly grin creeps along her face before she answers. "You can ask; it doesn't mean I'll answer." She jabs, throwing my grumpy demeanor back in my face from yesterday morning. I escort us back to the middle of the training room and sit down on the floor, and Rhea follows as I do.

"Back at the bookstore, why were you looking at a book about Hermes?" I attempt to hide the anguish in my tone as I pose the innocent question. I've been desperate to know ever since she walked out of the bookstore, and the thought has burned with curiosity since she mumbled my name as I carried her out of the caves. I hold my breath, waiting for her answer.

"I studied Greek mythology and literature in college. I've always been obsessed with the subject, but Hermes has always been a favorite."

I can't help but grin bashfully at her confession, and she takes note of the change in my expression, pausing.

"Why are you looking at me like that?" she asks, raising one of her eyebrows suspiciously. Rubbing the stubble on my chin with my hands, I try to hide my smile. The gleam in my eyes only worsens as I try to figure out how to introduce myself properly.

"Well, we can't go by our real names among mortals. Can you imagine the looks Achilles would get if he used his real name?"

"I suppose," Her voice gets higher, and she's becoming suspicious about where this conversation is going. Her cheeks are flushing, a light pink indicating her nervousness.

"So, Ethan is not... *exactly* my name." With a dramatic pause to draw out the confession, I continue. "My real name is Hermes Ethanus Itus. I go by Ethan in front of mortals."

Realization takes hold, and Rhea's face turns exceptionally red before she places her face in her hands. It's impossible to hold back my smile now.

"So, you are *Hermes*?" she mumbles, still covering her face.

"Yes," I answer matter-of-factly, an amused grin refusing to leave my face. Rhea peeks at me through her fingers.

"Oh, my god. This is why Callie called you "H" right?" She drops her hands, looking at me with eyes wide and accusatory. My smile bursts into laughter, and I nod my head. "This is so embarrassing."

"It shouldn't be embarrassing," I tell her. And I mean it, but I can't help how amusing this is.

"You're a liar." She's feigning irritation. "And I'm never trusting you again, by the way."

"Eh, sure you will. You're Immortal. You can't stay mad forever." I wink at her, standing up and holding my hand out to her to stand as well. "Okay, show-and-tell time. I showed you my powers; now, it's time to see yours."

Rhea keeps her gaze fixed on her lap, but after a moment, she takes my hand and stands. Wiping her hands on her pants, she quickly shifts her eyes around the room to ensure no one is around and watching. Callie told me Rhea has more than one power. I nearly didn't believe her until she said Rhea used both wind and water elements while they were held captive. Callie said she may have used fire but Callie was unable to recall for sure. A primary and secondary power is not unheard of—just rare. But three elements, impossible.

Her shoulders straighten, and she lifts her head as if steeling herself. Raising one of her hands so her palm is facing upright, black mist seemingly filled with smoke or shadow billows from her hand. Appearing out of nothing, a small black rock appears in her palm. The rock levitates under her focused power, and she ignites it with a super-heated flame.

Holy shit.

The fire burns from yellow and red to white and blue.

Knowing Achilles and Patroclus so well, I know a Flame that can generate white-hot fire is nearly unheard of. Not even Ares is that strong, and he is the most powerful Flame in this realm. The black rock vibrates and jolts within its floating space with heat from the intense fire under Rhea's power.

Her roiling mist floats upward, forming a small rain cloud over her hand. Tiny grumbles of thunder roll as lightning strikes the rock, and rain sizzles on the fire, extinguishing it. With her brow furrowed in concentration, the black rain cloud spins until a small tornado, no larger than a foot tall, swirls in her palm.

Lifting the stone with her winds, she finally raises her eyes to my gasping face, eyes wide in shock and mouth gaping.

"Catch," she says as the tornado disappears and the rock flings at me, still warm from her fire.

Fuck.

"You have four elements," It comes out more like a statement than a question, and she nods her head up and down. Caution is etched in the worry lines around her eyes as she squints.

"Is that bad?" Her tiny voice is almost a whisper.

"Are you kidding me? It's amazing!" I exclaim truthfully. She visibly relaxes and exhales a big breath of air. "But I can see why the werewolves—why Ares is drawn to you. I—" Stuttering over my words, I pause before finishing my sentence. "You are the most powerful Elemental I have ever met."

13 Rhea

I will sleep like a baby tonight. I collapse into my soft bed and hug my pillow with a deep sigh. The past three days have been exhausting. Thank my lucky stars that *Hermes* took his first session with me slowly. *I still can't believe he gave me a fake name.* I once gave a fake phone number to a stranger in a bar. He was sleazy and thirty years older than me, but I felt terrible—not for the creep but for the poor person who would get a call or text from him because of me. I can't imagine pretending to have a whole different name for *days*.

Rolling my eyes, it's quickly replaced by a smirk as I think about the boyish look of excitement on his face when I showed him my powers. I hear his voice, sending waves of satisfaction through me, and bringing butterflies to dance in my stomach.

"You are the most powerful Elemental I have ever met."

What does that even mean? Achilles practicing with Flint was amazing. They weren't even trying to hurt each other and were in a confined training room. What would be possible in an open field? And if I am more powerful than what I saw today, I wonder how long it will take me to learn my powers well enough to stop being afraid of them finally and to stop having anxiety attacks every time I think of using them.

The rest of the day, Hermes wanted to see my four elemental powers again and again in different ways, like using fire and wind together to make a vortex of flames. I never considered using them together, and my mind races with the other possibilities. Using my powers so much was more draining than I expected. I'm not complaining, though, because it gave me an excuse to avoid Atlas and the shame of looking him in the eye after I knocked him out yesterday.

Planning to do more research, I grabbed an armful of books from the Commune library, but they are sitting on the wooden nightstand next to my bed like the Leaning Tower of Pisa, about to topple over any second. My eyes drop as Hermes' cologne lingers on my skin and sleep drifts over me quickly.

A loud clank from my closet shoots up my spine, and my eyes fling open. An immediate heat spreads across my chest and my pulse spikes. *I'm not alone.* Behind me, the heat of another's presence burns against my back, and I freeze, straining to hear another noise. Hoping I imagined it, I squeeze my eyes shut when another clang rings from the closet as if someone is looking around. My heart thumps loudly in my chest, and I'm confident anyone here could hear it.

Pausing momentarily, I consider rushing to the studio door and across the hall to Achilles and Callie's apartment. But the intruder could run away without knowing who broke in. I reach within myself for my powers and call my wind ability to me. Taking a silent but deep breath, I extend my aura outward as Athena taught me. If I can do it like Hermes does, I may be able to feel the energy of the person, but my aura is happy to keep itself hidden from me when I need it most.

With no other option, I quietly untangle myself from the

blankets and ease toward the closet. Pressed firmly to the wall, I hesitate before turning the light on, revealing an empty closet, aside for my few possessions and empty hangers. One swings wildly on the bar as if just disturbed.

I quickly exit the closet, running for the apartment door. My racing heart is no longer fearful but determined to see who is taunting me. Standing in the middle of an empty hall, I quiet my breathing again and listen attentively. Two voices bounce through the hall as they draw closer. Looking around, I see a portal door and decide to hide inside, waiting to see who is coming down the hall. I open the door and spin into it, hitting hard against someone's chest.

"What in the hell...?" Flint's shocked voice rings out from inside the portal. I close the door and cover his mouth with my hand.

"Shhhh! Someone is coming!" As the door shuts, the room goes dark. My mind returns to the metal coffin in the dusty caves, and ice runs down my back.

"Who are we hiding from?" Flint grins against my hand and mumbles as I keep his mouth covered.

"I don't know," I whisper, "just listen."

The knots in my stomach are replaced with a familiar sensation of longing. The feeling I get when I'm around Hermes. It's like a signal that alerts me when he is nearby. The voices get closer, and as they pass by the portal, Achilles' voice talks over Hermes' laughter.

Relief floods me, and I pull my hand down from Flint's mouth, feeling ridiculous. I'm thankful for the dark space; it's serving me well and hides my burning cheeks. Looking up at him, I realize this room is much smaller than I expected—more like a closet. His tall, lean frame looms uncomfortably close to me.

"Sorry, I got spooked is all." I turn to the door, but Flint holds my upper arm, pulling me back gently toward him.

"Hey, what's the rush? This is nice and cozy." He has a satisfied smirk on his face and steps closer to me. Chills crawl along my skin at the lure he attempts to lace in his tone.

"I should get back." My voice is steady, and I pull away towards the door again. Flint grabs my hand, pulling me back to him. My heart spikes, and I push against his chest to make room between us.

"I'm just trying to ask you out on a date, Rhea." Flint's cologne is suffocating in this small space. Glancing for something to help me, I realize there are crates of store goods and items. This must be the delivery system to shepherd things to the Commune members. He puts his arm around my waist, pulling me flush to his body.

"Flint, stop." I push against him, and he releases me. Before I can reach for the door handle, the closet door flies open, and Hermes wears a look of pure rage. His glare alone seems enough to rip Flint's head off, and my relief is flooded by shame for being caught in here, alone with Flint.

Hermes stands aside, and I exit the closet, flustered and casting my eyes to the ground. My cheeks blaze, and I'm embarrassed that I even ran into the closet, getting myself into this situation.

"Rhea." Hermes nods to me as I dash past him.

Hermes steps toward Flint, blocking the door. He's fuming, and his eyes seem to have a brighter blue color about them, as if they are glowing almost.

"Let me make something clear to you, Flint. If I ever catch

your hands on her again, I'll rip them off your body and shove them down your throat. And I'll enjoy every second of it."

My mouth falls open, but I quickly close it when Hermes turns to me, placing his hand on the small of my back and guiding me back to my apartment. I bolt through the door, wanting to bury my face in my pillow, and scream.

"Hey," Hermes says softly as he closes the apartment door behind him. "What happened?" Concerned eyes roam over my face, inspecting me.

"It was nothing, really. I just scared myself, I think. Then I thought that was a portal, but Flint was in there, and it got... weird. But it's fine. It was my fault."

"I heard you yell *stop*. It didn't sound fine." Hermes' face is serious, and some of the anger from before is faintly showing again. "I've been looking for a good reason to murder Flint for decades, so just say the word." His tone lightens slightly, and his mischievous grin reveals the dimples on his cheeks that draw my eyes to his mouth.

I raise one of my eyebrows. "Jealous?" My stomach flutters when I hope he answers yes.

"Of Flint? No." Hermes approaches me, and I step back, hitting the apartment door. "Jealous of how he was looking down at you? Maybe." His voice drops, becoming deeper. His eyes dip to my mouth; then, he meets my gaze again. My breathing hitches, and I part my lips surprised. Hermes places one hand on the door above my head, leaning closer. I crane my neck to keep eye contact, and my skin buzzes excitedly at his proximity. "Jealous that he had his hands on you? Absolutely." he whispers the last word in my ear. His breath against my skin sends goosebumps careening down my neck. I close my eyes, anticipating the touch of his lips on me.

Intoxicated by his closeness and the warmth of his body, my hands burn wanting to touch him. Ready to push off the door and run my palms up his chest, I'm taken back when he pulls himself back two steps. Straightening myself and clearing my throat, I tighten my jaw, looking at the floor. Of course, it was just a joke. Like so many others, I'm only good for a tease.

"Well, thanks for your help." I open the door and stand aside, looking anywhere but at Hermes. He hesitates for a moment; the weight of invisible words hangs in the air between us a moment before he leaves.

I collapse into my cold bed and squeeze my pillow with a deep gruff. I am going to sleep like shit tonight.

*T**he gentle vibration of the earth quaking grabs my attention, and I sit up in my cage.** A great crack echoes between the mountains. I search the valley below for the source of the noise, and all heads of the soldiers are pointed at the opposite embankment.*

It's an ambush, and my sight is drawn to the source. A deep rumble escapes the earth as it quakes, and guards run to their weapons, unsure of what is occurring.

A single attacker stands at the ready with a sword glowing with brilliant blue light as the bands of Ares' soldiers sprint toward him. My hands turn white as I clutch the bars of the enchanted cage that serves as both my home and prison. Spells prevent me from using my abilities and for good reason. I would leech the lives from Ares and his packs of dogs for holding me prisoner.

This man, the lone warrior, who is he? My gaze pulls to him uncontrollably as if I am the moon and he is my earth. I know him, though this is the first my eyes have seen him.

Mate.

The word slams into me and roots deep within my mind. It's not a question or a possibility. It's a matter of absolute, universal truth.

"Why doesn't he feel me here?" I speak the thought out loud, expecting no answer in return.

Watching the hillside with my life, the warrior's sword slices through the onslaught, never faltering, never slowing. I can feel a connection to him, but something else is tethered between the lines of our souls.

I long to run to him and push my aura down the bond. He should feel it. He should feel me. Something is latched on to the invisible link, not allowing me to connect with my mate. Turning my head, I meet my captor's soulless, dark eyes as he sits on a throne of his construction, smoking a pipe. A smile of accomplishment spreads across his face as he watches me.

A growl from within the caverns of my heart rumbles in my chest. If I were free from this confinement, Ares would be the first to die. His dog of a servant, the great onyx wolf, bares his teeth at me in warning.

The decoys emerge from the hillside on the other side of the valley. A woman, one of the captives, stands. Defiance burning in her eyes can be seen where I'm huddled in my tiny cage.

She raises her arms and hurls her power across the oncoming soldiers. To my delight, her rage spawns a tornado that streams down the hillside and swallows Ares' men, hungry to exact her vengeance.

"Oh, I like her," I comment to my jailors, who offer no reply.

The convoy flees up the hill, having retrieved their women.

My mate turns to face our tent, perched part of the way up the opposing mountain, and he stares. Anticipation gleams in my chest. I pray to the Titans that he can sense me here. But as he turns and leaves with his party, my heart breaks as the distance between us grows as big as this mountain range.

I lay back down in my cell and close my eyes. Fat tears roll out of the corners of my eyes, and my body trembles as my partner retreats, the distance growing cold between us.

I feel Ares approach behind me with his decrepit son.

"It worked, Father. He didn't sense her. His connection is removed."

"Find me; please find me." I send my hopeful prayer into the void of the universe.

T he gentle vibration of the earth-shaking grabs my attention as a great crack echoes between the **mountains.** The earth shifts under our feet, and we tumble down the hillside, along with the dirt and rocks of the embankment. I snap my attention to the valley below as hundreds of soldiers spot us.

"Really, Odysseus?"

"Sorry! This soil is a lot sandier than I expected."

Odysseus' quake was only supposed to expose the entrance to the underground bunker, but the whole side of the hill crumbled beneath our feet. We're at least twenty meters away from the opening of the tunnels where my sister is held captive.

Shouting and metal clashing resounds off the valley walls as a massive hoard of soldiers race up the mountainside.

"The passage will choke them and slow them down. I'll hold them off. You guys run back up to the bunker and get the girls." I extract my sword, and the metal shrieks delightfully as it scrapes the scabbard. With its enchanted runes, the Sword of Truth gleams its brilliant blue light as my hands fix around the hilt. The power of starlight surges up my arms, bonding with my power and ready for the onslaught of warriors approaching.

Amid the rumbling of the earth and the power from my sword, there is something else. A sensation trying to pull my attention to the valley's far side. Ready for the soldiers, I turn to the cliffs on the opposite side of the valley, spotting a heavily guarded tent.

Ares is here.

There is no time to dwell on The God of War now as his battalion advances through the pass. The first soldiers reach me, and I dance through their masses with my light-emblazoned sword. As we sway through the maze of flesh, the blade is an extension of me, and never falters or slows. The natural funnel of the mountainous terrain squeezes the troops through a small pass, and my enchanted sword cuts quickly, faster than they can replenish a fresh soldier in front of me.

Even still, we need to hurry and get out of here. Ares loves to toy with his enemies, and the rest of the valley is flooded with waiting soldiers, ready to ascend upon us at his command.

As the thought leaves my mind, Achilles exits the hillside, holding Calypso. Penelope limps at their side as Odysseus carries another woman, also stolen by Ares and his Shifters. She seems unconscious but alive.

Damn it! We hadn't planned on another being here.

"Hermes." Calypso's voice rings in my mind. She's angry. "I would hold on to something if I were you."

Callie pushes against Achilles until she is standing upright. With a mighty surge of her aura, all the clouds of the mountains converge above her, instantly forming a great vortex of rage. I drive the shining blue blade of my sword deep into the earth and cement my hands around the hilt. The roar of a tornado rips just above my head, slamming into the ground beyond me and sucking up the soldiers approaching from the valley.

Odysseus slides down the slick hillside, joining me, pulling me upward as the funnel threatens to rip me into its gluttonous belly. His mouth moves, shouting for me to get up, but the deafening winds carry away his voice. Using his Earth element, he moves the dirt below us, creating a blockade to shield us from the wind and allowing us a step to push ourselves uphill. Together, we climb the embankment and join the others.

Watching the vengeance of the Wind Siren, Calypso, the screams and shrieks of brave warriors are the only things escaping my sister's anger.

"Let's go," I order as the last soldiers who survived the vortex retreat to the valley below. They'll quickly regroup and send another battalion after us.

Watching my friends and family flee, I pause at the top of the hill and observe the valley of Ares' warriors. The tent pulses at me like a beacon, and the desire to run to it nearly suffocates me. That sensation from a moment ago pulls at me again, like a rope is affixed to my stomach, wanting to pull me across the valley. But there is no time for Ares today, not with Penelope and the others injured.

"I'll find you." I cast my threat into the void of the universe.

The dream always wakes me at this point, with the image of the tent haunting my memory. The regret at walking away and not confronting Ares when he was so close has faded over the years, but a stain of remorse remains.

My feet hit the cold wood floor as morning light pours in through the open curtains of my studio. I rub the remnants of last night from my eyes and stand with a stretch, elongating my back and waking up my sore muscles. I can't believe I almost kissed Rhea last night. Since my mate died, I haven't so much as looked at another woman. No woman could hold a candle to *my* Juliette and the energy that radiated from her. But Rhea makes me wonder; she makes me want to try. I almost want to allow myself to hope that maybe the Fates are being kind to me and placing a goddess like Rhea in my life on purpose.

But why would the Fates do that for me? I'm like a plague who curses those I love to a torturous death. First my father, then my mother, and my mate. They didn't deserve death at the hands of Ares. I can't curse Rhea to that fate.

Hues of silver and gold light reflect on the ceiling of my studio like a kaleidoscope as Rhea and Athena practice aura training on the lake. Rhea's aura shines bright and silver from my picture window, and it's enchanting to watch. I think back to seeing her for the first time in the bookstore and the chaotic swirls of her power snapping around her. She's already learned so much control as it gleams with a steady pulse. Athena's golden aura radiates next to Rhea, and the combination is magnificent to behold.

The Commune, usually in a hurry each morning, shows up to watch from the lakeside. Spectators line the bank to watch the spectacle of the water dance; some have even started following along the shoreline with their small shimmers of aura.

The spirals and towers of water shoot up around them as the moves and stances evoke the elemental water power within them. Rhea's columns are demure and hesitant compared to Athena's. She remains patient as she coaxes Rhea to harness her control over the water. At the end of the routine, facing each other, Rhea concentrates on lowering her aura, and it quivers as it shrinks inward. As they finish, Athena smiles and places an encouraging arm around Rhea's shoulders. The gesture is warming; even from my view at my window, I can sense the happiness in Rhea.

I know what it means to have a mentor to stand by your side and help guide you. After our father died, Calypso and I were lucky to have Atlas.

Readying myself for the day, I meet everyone in the tactical room. Atlas and Achilles talk in hushed voices while Callie and Rhea laugh together at one of the tables. Rhea's gaze flicks to me as she holds a look of indifference in her eyes, and it stabs the pit of my stomach. Pushing the sensation down, I give her a polite nod and join Atlas, standing beside Achilles.

"Why can't we teleport directly into his home?" she asks Callie, turning her attention back to their conversation.

"He has wards and enchantments around his home for protection." Callie answers.

Last night, after leaving Rhea like the dumb ass I am, Atlas wanted to have a healthy debate about bringing Rhea today. Atlas argued she is not ready to be off Commune property yet leaving her behind doesn't feel right.

"She's not a prisoner here, Atlas. Rhea has every right to chase after the truth about her life, and you promised to help her do that."

"I agree, but she can wield four elemental powers, it's unheard of and exactly why Ares would want to claim her for his army. I'm just looking out for her safety."

"No, you're looking out for your own curiosities and wanting to keep her on a leash. Work it out with the Headmistress because she is coming with us." I ended the evening storming out of his office and slamming the door behind me.

Walking up to Atlas and Achilles this morning, Atlas gives me a tense greeting, still irritated. "You know I disagree with you, but trying to keep her here could push her away and into more danger. So, be careful today, and don't let her out of your sight."

"I'm offended you would even need to say that." I place my hand over my heart, and the sarcasm lightens Atlas's mood. Dropping his chin, he looks at me with raised eyebrows over his wired glasses.

"I mean it. She's not ready yet, H. Don't get reckless just because you're catching feelings."

"Careful."

"You know I'm right, even if you don't like hearing it." Atlas turns on his heel and leaves the training room.

Rhea stands beside Callie, dressed in tactical gear and a small bookbag on her back. A crease between her eyes and the way she sways side to side tells me she is nervous, perhaps excited. The black ensemble she's wearing for the meeting is bulky but still hugs her curves perfectly.

I never thought laced boots and tactical pants with a tucked-fitting shirt could look sexy, but I was wrong. Biting my bottom lip to prevent myself from dropping my jaw open at the sight of her, I scorch a trail down the length of her body with my eyes, knowing she is aware and trying to ignore me. As I move my eyes up her legs, she clenches her thighs together and pinches her fingers nervously. Finally, she locks eyes with me, and I'm pleased to see her cherry-red cheeks flaming excitedly.

Shifting her weight to one leg, she juts her hip out and crosses her arms over her chest. Shooting one arched eyebrow, she cocks her head, challenging me to keep gazing at her. The flare of her cheeks gives her away and a predatory mask slips over my demeanor. My mouth waters at the thought of tasting her and seeing how far I can push that stubbornness before it turns to begging. We only break our battle of wills when Callie steps between us, oblivious to the moment.

"Here. I want you to have this." Callie bounces in place as she hands Rhea a small box wrapped in beautiful pink paper and a fluffy bow.

"Oh, I can't accept this."

"What are you talking about? You don't even know what it is!" Callie looks at Achilles and me as we watch, amused. "It's a gift of my friendship. You would turn that down?" Callie fakes a pouting face, and Rhea laughs.

Callie is always happy, a ray of sunshine on a cloudy day, but she doesn't trust quickly. Friends can be hard to come by during immortality because there is so much time for backstabbing and betrayal for power plays. Rhea and Callie have taken to each other quickly, and I know Callie is thankful for their friendship.

Rhea seems more protective of herself; perhaps she's too accustomed to being on her own. Maybe she was forced to depend on herself in her seclusion out of fear for her powers. But something in her lights up when she is around Callie, and their conversations are full of laughter and whispers.

She opens the box, smiling but reluctant. Inside is a silver necklace with a sword charm. Callie and I received a matching set from our father before he was killed. Callie never cared for hers because it is not gold, but I wear mine daily. They are tiny replicas of my swords, one with blue topaz and the other with black onyx on the hilts. Callie talked about gifting hers to Rhea, and I agreed.

"If you ever feel scared or alone, hold it and remember you're not," Callie repeats our father's words when he gave us the gifts years ago. She slips the necklace over Rhea's head, holding the charm. "We're friends now, forever."

"Thank you." Rhea hugs Callie and then looks down at the charm with a black stone hilt as if it's the most beautiful thing she's ever seen.

"I thought today might be a good time to give it to you before we head out." Callie beams at Rhea.

"Time to go," Achilles directs us to the portal. "Penelope and Odysseus are already at the location and have been for the past two hours. Rhea, you stick to Hermes like glue. Got it?"

She nods quickly in agreement with strained eyes that fail to hide her nervousness and stands beside me on the large portal platform. I want to apologize to her for last night. I let the intoxication of her nearness cloud me and it was inappropriate right after her encounter with Flint. But now is not the time. We need to focus and be alert as we head to Damiens apartment. The biggest concern is a pack of Shifters that may pick up our scent and try to abduct Rhea again. As the portal flashes us to the location, I shield our presence using my Mirage powers to avoid being seen by mortals.

We planned our arrival in a densely covered park surrounded by dogwood trees draped with vines to help conceal us. Directly across the street from Damien's apartment building, it makes a quick entry and exit point for teleporting. It's a bright day out, full of sun and humidity. It's nearly August in Atlanta, and you can see the heat rippling off the ground like an oven.

Damien lives above a coffee shop in a busy neighborhood on the edge of Atlanta's downtown district. Narrow streets are

lined with four and five-story buildings with commercial shops
on the ground floors and residential apartments and homes on
the upper floors. Cars and city buses race on the streets,
blowing horns at each other as pedestrians rush along the
sidewalks.

We check in with Odysseus and Penelope with our
earpieces and get the signal that everything is clear. Staking out
the building for the last two hours, they have been able to
monitor any suspicious activity, like a wolf scout lingering by
the building and waiting for our arrival. Callie and Achilles
leave our side and walk the perimeter of Damien's residential
building before taking their position on the roof. While Rhea
and I wait, we sit on a park bench under the shade of the tall
pine trees.

"You doing okay? Nervous?" I break the tension that is still
pulled tight from last night. Rhea sets the bookbag down on
the ground next to the bench.

"A little." She releases a puff of air and bounces her knee
rapidly as we sit. Her aura begins to fluctuate and pulse. The
surges of her power tingle against the hairs on my arms sitting
so close to each other on the park bench.

"Are you able to mask your aura?" I ask through clenched
teeth.

"I'm trying." She leans forward, resting her elbows on her
knees and holding her forehead.

"You've kept your powers hidden for years before meeting
us; how do you calm yourself when upset?"

"I imagine this little box locked away in a cave."

"Close your eyes and tell me about it."

She follows the instructions, her long eyelashes brushing
her flushed cheeks. Turning her chin to the sky, the light

passing through the tree canopy dapples her face with sunlight.

"Can I hold your hand and see the vision in your mind?" She nods her head at me, pinching her brow together. Taking her hand in mine, a wave of chills radiates up my arm, and I swallow hard, closing my eyes to focus on the vision.

"It's a dark cave with an inlet from the sea. The moon fills the cave with white moonlight." Rhea's aura pulses as she talks. The image in her mind is a grey and rocky cave with choppy waters beating up the rocks. The full moon is a pale yellow and abnormally large. Twinkling stars are a kaleidoscope of colors burning in the velvety night sky.

"What do your powers look like?" My tone is deep and breathy, drunk by the feel of her power pulsating around me through our connecting hands.

"A black mist. It rolls into the box, and I shut it, locking it away with a key. Then I place it in a hole within the cave walls." The Mirage we share is precisely as she describes. The same dark misting fog, shrouded in shadow from her training yesterday, billows low to the rocky flat floor of the cave, lit by moonlight with long dancing shadows.

"That's good, Rhea. Think about that, but pretend the moon's white light is your aura. You need to pull it to you and into the box. Does that make sense?" She squeezes her closed eyes tighter as she concentrates on my words. Keeping my tone low and soothing, I coach her. "Don't force it; imagine the light is tangible like your mist. Something you can direct."

In her mind, she imagines reaching up, and the moonlight ripples as she faces her palms out to it. The moonlight moves like a blanket draped over a bed. The pale-yellow moonlight sinks into the box like a thin silk scarf.

Opening my eyes, I watch her again. Rhea's aura tremors, but slowly, it shrinks and fades. Happy to see her relax and visibly shake off the tension between her shoulders, Rhea opens her eyes with joy; her aura is only a faint halo now shimmering dully off her skin.

Under control, the tampered powers are barely a thrum beside me, and it feels cold without them. Curiosity rolls through my mind, wondering if she feels the incredible sense of loss as her powers sleep inside her.

"Let's go meet this author."

W e pass **Odysseus and Penelope sitting on a bench at the park.** Rhea adjusts the bag on her shoulder and quickly cuts her eyes at them, not accustomed to being secretive. It pulls a grin to my mouth.

The scent of ground coffee beans from the first-floor café is a welcome assault as I open the residential door of the two-story brick building where Damien lives. At the top of the narrow stairs is a platform with two apartment doors on each side.

"I wonder what those are." I rub my hands down the carved symbols etched into the wood around the doorframe of Damien's apartment. Rhea peers around me, taking in the carved shapes of animal heads.

"I know what these are," Rhea says proudly. "Damien wrote about these in one of his books on his Mayan ancestors. His family uses the jaguar as their totem for protection." She points at the carved head of a jaguar, looking outward as if watching for visitors who may approach the door. "Funny since he's a Werewolf, don't you think?" She chuckles.

I extend my aura outward to check the space inside as I knock on the door three times. A dark void rests behind the door like a limitless expanse of space rests beyond it. My aura can't penetrate it. Chills run up my spine, remembering the Dark Mage detected in the alley and at the Commune. I can sense something waiting for us on the other side of the door, but the power of darkness obscures it. Putting my arm behind me, I slide Rhea into the corner of the small space between the apartment doors and shield her with my body.

"Something is wrong," I tell her. "Achilles, come to the stairwell," I instruct through our earpieces.

Rhea shifts uncomfortably behind me, wrapping both of her fragile hands around the backs of my arms. With her touch I feel like a super-charged battery, ready to burst. Achilles arrives at the base of the stairwell and climbs it quickly, two steps at a time.

"My power isn't working inside, but something is *wrong* inside."

"Stand by," Achilles says flatly into the earpiece to alert the others outside. Nodding at Rhea, he adjusts her position to the corner farthest from the door and stands in front of her. She fidgets with her fingers and picks at her nails as her large golden eyes dart chaotically around the narrow stairwell.

I ram into the door with my shoulder, and it shudders against its locks and enchantments. Bracing myself more firmly and powered by my Light aura, I propel my shoulder into it again, blasting through the charms. The door splinters into the room, carried on a wave of blue light.

My power clears the darkness filling the space, and the

smell of decay hits us like a foul bog of rotting vegetation. Rhea releases a horrified gasp behind me. Damien's body lays on the floor, half-shifted into wolf form with sporadic tufts of fur spotting his human skin. His hands are clawed with long talons at the tips of his fingers. His face is frozen in a twisted and tortured expression. His throat has been torn away, and his flesh is white as a sheet, drained of all blood.

I grab Rhea and turn her into me, wrapping her in my arms and shielding her from looking at Damien's corpse further. The rest of the apartment has been trashed, with shelves of books and hundreds of pieces of paper thrown about the floor. The shades and curtains have been drawn on all the windows. A single yellow bulb burns in the corner of the living room, casting ominous shadows across his strained face.

"You have company," Callie announces over the earpiece. Extending my aura beyond the building, a wolf takes a seat at an outside table at the coffee shop below. Further down the street, about two blocks away, an Alpha and two Beta wolfs are walking in this direction.

In my arms, Rhea is sobbing, and she is losing the grasp on her aura control as her power begins to thrum against me. I wrap her fully in warm light, compressing it around her like the heavy quilt I wrapped around her shoulders as we sat together in that projection of her childhood room.

"We can't take her out the front," I tell Achilles. Extracting the portal wand from my pocket, I press the button to take us to a nearby rooftop, but it doesn't flash.

The enchantments.

We need a plan quickly. Rhea is slipping into a state of panic.

"This way!" The whisper of a woman hisses behind us from the other apartment door across the landing.

At once, we spin to look at her. "They're coming back to clean up. Come in here. It's safe." Achilles and I look at each other, but Rhea breaks free from me and runs into the woman's apartment, eager to be anywhere away from this scene.

The woman lives directly across the hall, and Achilles follows Rhea into the woman's home. She pushes past me, her sight lingering on Damien's dead body before closing the broken door. Holding her hands to the space in front of her, she closes her eyes, and I hear her whispering incantations.

A deep purple cloud of her power causes the door to repair itself, and the damage is gone in a matter of seconds. I hear the clicking locks behind the door slide into place.

"Let's go." She nods firmly to me, and I enter her home.

Rhea is sitting on the woman's couch, her head in her hands while her body convulses with sobs as she rocks back and forth. Her aura is shimmering wickedly, and with wolves nearing the building, we need her to calm down. I start towards her, but the woman steps before me and walks to Rhea, crouching in front of her.

"My name is Bridget, and I'm a Witch. Damien is dead, and Shifters are on their way here. You need to get yourself under control, or even the great Hermes won't be able to hide you from them." The woman is blunt and looks intently at Rhea with her dark brown eyes. Rhea looks up, her face soggy with her tears. "Turn it off."

Rhea takes a deep breath inward as she steadies herself.

"Turn. It. Off." The woman commands, calm but firm.

Rhea's aura dissipates like a flipped switch, and she no

longer cries. Bridget smiles at her slyly, and Rhea returns it with a small smile. "Good girl."

Bridget stands and hurries to a cupboard, quickly throwing herbs and oils into a small cauldron. Rhea and I lock eyes, and she nods slightly, letting me know she is okay. I release the tension I've been holding in my shoulders but worry still holds me as I see a glazed film slide over Rhea's vision.

Witches are the nomads of the Immortals and take no sides for the most part. In a realm of mortals, the Witches are a mystery. Most of the Elementals came to Gaea as refugees from Tartarus. Ares shared his powers of transformation with the Shifters, and their population has grown over the eons. But the Witches are their own breed and keep to their covens, neutral to the conflicts with Ares.

Watching her cautiously, Bridget approaches her apartment door with the smoking cauldron, having lit the ingredients on fire. She places the pot on the floor and lifts her head to the ceiling; incantations in a strange language flow from her mouth in hushed tones as she fans the smoke around the closed door of her home.

I speak dozens of ancient languages; many of them have been lost to time, but I recognize the language as Rapa Nui. The language of "The Watchers"; said to be the first inhabitants of this realm.

Achilles peers carefully through delicate floral curtains hanging closed around the windows. He looks at me and nods, letting me know the Shifters have reached the building. Keeping my stance near the door, with my eyes locked on Rhea. Her gaze is fixed, staring across the room where the floor meets the wall. The unseeing film over her eyes keeps them unfocused, but her aura remains controlled.

Loud footsteps ascend the stairs upward as multiple heavy boots approach. I place my hand on Bridget's wall and see the two Beta's arriving on the landing of the stairs and their Alpha following behind them. *The twins and their Onyx Alpha.* One of the twins, with charred scars on the left side of his face, makes quick work of Damien's locked door, kicking it open and entering the apartment.

Lupo, the Onyx Alpha, pauses before entering and turns his head of dark hair toward Bridget's door as if considering investigating it. He sniffs the air loudly, and the sound carries through the walls, and I snap my head to Rhea. Her body tenses and tremors shake her limbs as she clutches the sword charm from Callie tightly in her hand. Her glazed honey-colored eyes widen. Even though her mind is a thousand miles away, she still hears the wolf on the other side of the wall.

If it weren't for these enchantments, Bridget and the mortals on the street can be damned, I would teleport her out of here in a fraction of a heartbeat to get her away from harm. My body fights between wanting to rush to her and wrap her in my arms and remaining still to keep our presence hidden. Watching her struggle while knowing Lupo is on the other side of the wall tears at my resolve.

Her aura flickers above her skin, and carefully, I coat her again in my aura. Pushing around her, my blue power warms Rhea like an embrace, and the flickering of her muted powers dampen. Bridget remains kneeling on the floor, silent incantations flowing from her mouth rapidly as sweat forms on her brow.

Frozen, we wait as the seconds tick on like hours.

"*There is old magic in your blood. You reek of it.*"
Lupo's words still stain my memory. Sitting in the Witch's living room, I feel his hot breath on my neck and see the piercing of his orange eyes. I strain against the pull of my magic, against the tight confines I have them wrapped in. Hearing that sniff outside the door brought me back to that moment in the caves, when Lupo shifted into his human form and smelled my neck.

As I feel a soft caress of Hermes' warm light wrapping around me, my mind flashes to our moment in my apartment last night. The feel of his mouth was so close to mine, so full of promise; even now, my skin turns to gooseflesh thinking about him. The warmth keeps my mind tethered to this apartment and stops it from floating away in the breeze of my nightmares.

But he pulled away so quickly, and the rejection was like being slapped in the face.

I'm never the one chosen, and it always stings, no matter how many times I pretend it doesn't hurt me. Then, when it does happen, I hate myself for being so gullible to think someone could genuinely want me for something other than sex. Any show of attention and I sacrifice my wants and desires for theirs. They love how I love them, but I never receive that same love in return.

Eventually, I see it. Color returns to my vision, and the red flags are everywhere. I punish myself for being ignorant of them, but it's hard when you don't feel worthy to receive your true desires. In my romance novels, the heroine gets the guy of her dreams, and he would go to the ends of the earth for her.

But that could never be real for me. It will only exist within the pages of books and live in my imagination. So, as I sit on a stranger's couch, wrapped in the warm caress of a man who will never want me, I push away his aura and surround myself from the inside with the companionship of my powers. Closed off to the world, my thoughts whisper too loudly to hear what is happening around me.

"Drink." Bridget holds a steaming mug in front of my face. I unlatch my shaky hand from the sword necklace, and I reach for it with a tremor in my fingertips. The hot herbal tea brings life back to my body. The trembles still, and my muscles relax. My back is sore from holding myself firmly for a long time while the Shifters were across the hall. Hermes is sitting next to me, attentively watching in case I lose control of my powers. The only visible sign of his unease is his knee quickly bouncing.

"I'm okay." I think the words are more for me than Hermes.

Bridget is a lovely woman with delicate features. Her long, dark hair is wild and wiry. A few tiny braids dot her head and hold small charms and stones, wrapped with leather ties and thin ribbons. Her brown hair, warm copper skin, and matching eyes offset the brightly colored skirt that kisses the floorboards of the old residence and billows as she moves around her home. Faded tattoos swirl around her hands and up her arms. The dark line of a tattoo runs from her bottom lip, down her chin, and meets a larger tattoo on her neck.

The apartment is small and packed with warm furniture, small items on every surface, and pictures dotting the walls. An impressive antique buffet with cabinets on the bottom, a work surface in the center, and shelves overhead is the focal point of the living space. It must be the altar Bridget uses for her witchcraft based on the number of herb jars and the residue of a dozen candles dripping off the edges. Suspended from the ceiling around the apartment are bundles of dried flowers and skeleton heads of birds swaying in the gentle breeze of air conditioning.

"They left several minutes ago. Achilles is back outside with Callie and the others keeping watch." Hermes reassures me.

"You all were here for Damien? They killed him last night." Bridget says coolly.

"That body didn't smell like it died last night," I blurt out before realizing the insensitivity of my comment to his neighbor. "I'm sorry. I didn't mean to be rude."

My renewed hopes of talking to Damien about where to find the origins of my powers have been pulled away again. Searching the library at the Commune and accessing ancient documents is fantastic, but we're searching for a needle in a haystack. I hoped Damien would have some information to set me on a more defined course or have some magic piece of paper with the exact answer I'm seeking. Shaking away the ridiculous and selfish thoughts, I focus on Bridget.

She brushes the comment off with a wave of her hand. "It was a venom in the bite causing the decay."

"Who are you?" Hermes' tone is laced with skepticism.

"Damien's neighbor," Bridget pauses, raising an eyebrow at Hermes. "And lover." She retrieves a beat-up shoe box held together with tape and rubber bands from the cabinet of her altar. "He suspected he was unsafe and left these things with me."

Hermes takes the offering from her, setting it on the table for inspection. Removing the lid, the box holds an array of damaged pictures and folded papers, yellowing due to age. Hermes pulls out a voice recorder and presses play.

I recognize Damien's voice from his book signings and social media videos. The sound rings through the small home as his message plays.

"Hermes, it's Damien."

Bridget walks to the window, folding her arms over her flat stomach, and watching the commuter's street. I nudge Hermes with my elbow and nod toward her.

"How did you know who we were?" Hermes turns off the recorder and puts it back in the old shoebox.

"I'm a Witch; I know things." Hermes drops his shoulders in irritation, and Bridget chuckles.

"When you were casting your incantations, you spoke Rapa Nui... The language of The Watchers."

"Very perceptive, Hermes."

"Are you Rapa Nui or is that another thing you just know because you're *a Witch*?" The mocking tone in his voice makes Bridget chuckle again, satisfied she is getting under his skin.

"Rapa Nui?" I ask, curious. "What is that?"

"You may know it as Easter Island, my young goddess. My ancestors serve as the Watchers of this Realm. But that is a story for another time, perhaps."

"What happened to Damien?" Hermes asks as he hands me the beaten-up shoebox. I stuff it inside the bookbag, zipping it up tightly.

"He was doing dangerous work, but several months ago, Lupo arrived in the States, and things became a pressure cooker."

"Did Lupo and his pack kill Damien?"

"No. It was a man; I didn't see his face. My wards would have kept the wolves and your kind from getting to him. This was someone else—someone *different*." Bridget sits at the table, turning her head to me. "He was a lot like you, my goddess."

"What do you mean?" My voice is breathy as my heart rate increases.

"Ancient." She studies me, moving her eyes up and down my body, a spark of knowledge in them as if she is aware of something I am not.

"Lupo said something similar to me when he captured me. He said I smelled of *old magic*." I cross my arms over my chest and a heat wave pebbles up my arms. "What does that mean?"

Bridget lays her hand on the tabletop, palm facing upward, inviting me to take hold. Her rings, piled on top of each of her fingers, bang on the table, and a dozen bracelets on her slender wrists clink as she moves. I extend my hand, placing it within hers. She closes her eyes and encases her hands around mine. A deep purple aura swirls around my hand and wrist, emanating from Bridget. I didn't realize Witches would also have auras, and my shoulders jolt in surprise as the cool vapers of her power wrap around me curiously.

"You have a powerful spell holding you in limbo, ancient one." Bridget releases my hand and stands. The purple aura dissipates instantly. "The Oracle is waiting to meet you when you are ready."

Hermes scoffs in response.

"Who–" I begin to ask more about the Oracle, hope blooming in my chest at the prospect of someone else who can help search for my powers. But Bridget quickly stands and interrupts me with a quick dismissal.

"You came for Damien's information, and you have it. Please leave now. I need to cleanse the building and replenish my wards." Crossing the apartment, she reaches her door and holds it open expectantly.

The trek back to the Commune is tense. When we first arrived, the afternoon sun was high in the sky, and now it's setting low on the horizon. Meeting the two couples back at our location in the park, Odysseus, Achilles, and Hermes huddle together for a fast summary of what Bridget told us. Callie and Penelope check on me to make sure I'm okay. I smile with genuine appreciation when Callie takes me in her arms and hugs me. The group is tense and defeated as we teleport back to the Commune.

Atlas is waiting for us on the portal platform, looking relieved to see our return. "How did it go?"

"Not great." Hermes takes long strides out of the room and down the hall, not pausing for Atlas to explain.

"Hermes, what happened? Do I need to call Athena?"

Hermes stops in the hall and faces Atlas. "Our source was murdered, and Lupo showed up as the cleaning crew. We waited while they left, and now we're back."

I desperately want to shower. Since I heard Lupo in the stairwell, I feel stained, tainted by his nearness. I want to dive into the box of artifacts in my book bag, but I won't be able to mentally process anything until I get today's grime off me.

Penelope and Odysseus head to the cafeteria for dinner. Achilles and Callie walk with me in silence to the hall leading to our apartments, and Hermes trails behind us, deep in thought, as he stares at the marble tiles. About three doors down, I stop abruptly, pulling everyone's attention as I stare at the door to my apartment.

It's open.

A gasp escapes my throat as I think about the noise in my closet last night. I forgot to mention it with the encounter with Flint and the confusing rejection by Hermes. It's not like the past few days have been a cakewalk. I seem to be jumping from one trauma to the next, and it's hard to keep everything from taking me over like a tsunami. Closing my eyes so I don't have to see the disappointment on their faces, I tell them about last night and the scare in my closet.

Hermes stands with a wide stance, with one hand on his hip and the other pinching the bridge of his nose. "You said you got scared," he sighs, "I should have asked why. I'm sorry; this is my fault."

"How is this your fault?" I argue; shame crawls up my arms, and I wrap them around my stomach.

"I'm Head of Security; it's my job."

Of course, that's the connection. He only concerns himself with me because I'm a security risk. Because it's his job and no other reason. Steeling my jaw, I swallow down the knot in my throat and force back the burn in my eyes.

Achilles and Hermes spring ahead of us and stand on each

side of the door, their tactical training has them moving like predators. A cool surge rushes past me, and the rippling waves of blue light from Hermes' aura drifts out of him. This is the first time I've been able to perceive his aura, and it's hypnotizing as they pulse like ripples in a still lake. It runs ahead of him, entering the apartment and I see it expand, illuminating the entirety of the apartment.

"No one is in there, but it's a mess." he says, pushing the door open and waiting for me to enter first.

The beautiful apartment looks like the aftermath of an earthquake. The furniture has been overturned, and the drawers and shelves are empty. Aside from the clothing and toiletries Callie helped me acquire, I had no personal belongings here, so I can't help them figure out what they might have been looking for. The invasion of my private space is upsetting, mainly because someone was able to gain access while we were away. Looking at the room now, it feels slimy and exposed.

Atlas arrives within two minutes with a few tactical team members. They use their Sensory powers upon Hermes' orders but detect no lingering aura.

"So, what does that mean?" I ask as we wait for them to finish their search in the hall.

"It was either someone skilled in masking or a Dark Mage. Sensors have a difficult time picking them up. It's the nature of the Dark Mage to hide in the shadows and have an aura that is challenging to detect."

"How is the security footage of the hall and the parameter?" Hermes asks Achilles, who has just returned from the tactical team's war room.

"Nothing on either." he answers.

"So, someone could have gotten into the Commune, or it

could be someone here now?" I ask, disbelief etched on my face as the reality of the violation begins to sink in. This place felt impenetrable, surrounded by this massive dome of protection and gods from the pages of my mythology books.

"Rhea, we'll figure this out." Hermes' tone is determined, but it's laced with uncertainty.

"You don't know that for sure. You can't say I'm better off here than anywhere else." The disgust from Lupo's nearness collides with the violation of someone breaking into my studio, and I want nothing more than to run home to my aunt in Pennsylvania. But I can't do that.

Rubbing the tension from my tight brow, the hallway is suddenly suffocating. "Is there another empty place I can stay? I can't go back there knowing someone was inside."

"Come stay with Achilles and me tonight. We'll figure out the rest tomorrow."

Within minutes, my few belongings are moved to the spare room in Callie and Achilles' apartment across the hall.

Standing in their guest bathroom, I stare at myself in the mirror. Images of Damien's dead body flashes in my mind each time I blink and I hear a cracking whip before Lupo's clawed hand squeezes my neck. My hands on the sides of the sink keep me steady, and I hang my head, taking a few deep breaths to make it all stop, praying for quiet.

Ready to face myself, I raise my head and meet the reflection in the mirror. A haunting image stares back at me. The bruised and bloodied version of myself pulled out of the caves four days ago looks at me with disappointed, hollow eyes and sunken cheeks. My mind stumbles forward into the vision and in a flash, the twisted and pulled face of Damien's corpse is watching me. The beautiful and modern bathroom with sleek white tiles and clean surfaces is replaced with the rough walls of the cave and dim lighting. The shadows in the crevasse of the hand-hewn walls grab me as I stumble between flashes of the bathroom where I'm currently standing and the caves of my captivity. Feeling with my hands along the bathroom wall and counter, I desperately fumble to find the shower, turning the water as hot as possible.

My body lurches forward into the tub, slamming my shoulder against the wall as I tumble into the vortex of a panic attack. Clawing at the collar of my shirt, it wraps tightly around my neck like the clawed hand of Lupo is squeezing me tightly and sneering with saliva dripping like acid off his fanged teeth. My throat is a vice, collapsing, blocking fresh air from entering my lungs. *I need my powers.* I need my mist and wind, but I can't find them. Usually thrumming below the surface of my skin, my powers would be begging for release. Now, when I'm desperately pleading for them, they are gone.

My vision is turning dark at the corners of my sight, and I work myself into a sweat, begging my lungs for air. I search, desperate to find that space within my mind where I lock my abilities away, but it's just a black limitless void of nothing. My mouth flounders open, and only small gulps of air make it in before the vice closes around my throat.

A shadow with a solid mass bumps into the side of me, and platinum blonde hair swings in front of my face tickling my cheek. *Callie.* Pulling me upright, the shower drenching her clothed body, her bright blue eyes, dark with worry, grab hold of me. The dark cave zooms out, and the brightly lit bathroom and its gleaming white tiles return. The spin of the room slows as Callie moves, her mouth forming words I can't hear. Static rings in my ears with the intense thumping of my heart racing through my chest.

A rush of gentle wind swirls around me. Like my mist, its revitalizing chill jolts my body back to awareness, and I take a big breath of air into my dirt-coated lungs. Choking and coughing, my burning throat is cooled by the currents of Callie's power. My body slumps deeper into her hold, and she wraps me tightly in her arms, resting her cheek on the top of my head.

The speed at which the panic overtook me was so fast and intense. Like I swallowed a gallon of dirt, my stomach recoils, and I lunge for the toilet. The few contents of my stomach surge into the bowl, and I rest my head on my forearm as sweat trickles down my face. Callie doesn't shy away but holds my wet hair and whispers reassurances as her other hand rubs circles on my back.

I collapse into the smooth bathtub, and Callie grasps my hand firmly in hers. Sobs break free from my chest, and I clutch at her, terrified that I'll fly off into the void of space again if I let go. At some point, the shower was turned off, and Callie filled the tub for a bath. Bubbles and oils scent the air, and I remain numb as she undresses me, guiding me into the steaming water. Callie sits beside me on the tub's edge in silence, patient, while my body slowly returns to reality. My melted mind reforms back into a solid mass, and tears sneak out of the corners of my eyes.

Realization of my fit slams into me, and a wave of humiliation washes over me. I sit up, drawing my knees to my chest and hiding my face in my hands as my shoulders shake with my sobs.

"I'm so sorry," I repeat. She comforts me, excusing every-thing away and telling me I'm ridiculous for apologizing.

"Rhea, you have been through an extraordinary few days. Achilles told me what you saw today. That would not be easy for anyone to handle." Callie keeps me company, periodically refreshing the hot water several times to keep me from getting cold as she tells me stories of their past exploits.

Callie laughs about Hermes and Achilles' never-ending wagers about who can run faster. She recounted the race where a thorn, sticking out of the ground, pierced Achilles' heel. He was running so fast when he stumbled and fell; he slid for a hundred feet across the ground until he crashed face-first into a stream of water. The story brings a weary smile to me as my sore muscles sit weak and shaky in the bath. When she feels it's safe to leave, she exits and returns with towels and a fluffy robe before helping me from the tub.

"Thank you for helping me." My voice is mousy, and my mouth is dry as I form the words. Never has anyone seen me have a large attack like this. When I feel the dizzying vortex begin to spin, I lock myself away using any means possible—usually running to my car or shutting myself in a closet. The vulnerability of her eyes on me makes me feel like my chest has been cracked open with an axe, open for her to peer directly inside and see the monster that killed their family.

"I couldn't make my powers come out." I hang my head down, unsure why I feel ashamed for admitting it.

"Rhea, you are not in this alone. We're all here for you. Have you ever talked to someone about your past? About your panic attacks?"

"A little bit after my family died. They said I made up my

powers as a coping mechanism, so I stopped going." Maybe I should talk to someone. Being fourteen and seeing your family die while you survive is a cataclysm most people don't have to suffer through, but it was made worse knowing they died by my powers. I had desperately wanted someone to know the truth of what happened, but everyone dismissed me.

And so, I closed the memories and my powers up in the prison within my mind and tried so hard to ignore the emotions. But they refuse to go away and let me have peace. The reminders of the blood on my hands surge from within me, and my body becomes overwhelmed with panic.

"I think Atlas could help if you feel comfortable talking to him. He's helped me greatly after losing my other partner, Patroclus, and after my father's death."

"I didn't realize there was someone else before Achilles."

"Actually, Achilles and Patroclus were paired first." She giggles as my shock is painted across my face. "I came along a few decades later. We were all fated with each other. Me to them and them to me."

"What happened?"

Callie looks as if she is a million miles away and thousands of years in the past before she turns back to me with a small smile that doesn't reach her eyes.

"Something terrible."

I nod, understanding, as I look at my hands in my lap, sores around the edges of my nails burn from my picking. Thinking back four days ago, it was hard to imagine Callie feeling the loss of someone close to her because she has such a bubbly outlook on everything. Unblemished by the pain of her past, I realize no one can escape the heartache that attaches itself to us as we live our lives. Perhaps the difference is in how we each deal with things.

I push my pain down and lock it away. It builds until it busts out of me, and I lose control over everything. Maybe she is right; having someone to talk to can help me. I'm not sure I forgive Atlas for invading my mind when he first met me, but I'll give it a shot. If he can help me look into my memories and find the truth, it can be the start of learning how to move forward from my past and into a new life.

"You need some rest. It's been a long and terrible day." Callie strokes my damp hair and holds my head in a motherly hug against her chest. "Do you feel like coming into the living room, or would you rather be alone?"

"I think I'd like to be alone in my room if that's okay?"

Callie smiles gently at me. "Of course. I'll get you some dinner and something to help you sleep from Athena."

Left alone to dress out of the robe and into my silky sleeping pajamas, I comb through my hair. Rubbing my puffy eyes and blowing my sore nose, it tingles from the time spent crying. I feel like a puddle of mush.

After eating the hearty dinner Callie delivered, I drink a tonic of poppy flowers from Athena, and it immediately sends me into a deep sleep.

Thunder growls in the distance, and a cool breeze rustles the trees. It's hot and humid. A layer of sweat coats me, and I look down at my hands, turning them over. The awareness of the dream is clear because my skin is a rich terracotta instead of its milky complexion.

Turquoise bangles clamor up my wrists, and the short grass tickles my bare feet. A deep red shawl is tied around my breasts, and my dress is thick and heavy. The symbols of the revered Mayan animals of the jaguar, eagle, and snake pattern the dress with beautiful designs in a golden yellow thread.

People surround me, all looking at me in similar clothing. Some with headdresses covering their raven dark hair as they glare at me expectantly. Behind me, an imposing pyramid stands tall, coated in total shadow.

"Are you ready?" a man asks, holding his hand out to me. "Today is Mabon. The great serpent will descend the temple." It's Ares. I'm not sure how I know, but I do.

But I'm not scared because I know it's a dream and I'll soon wake up.

"Where am I?" I ask, looking up at the man, his hand still extended while waiting for me to take it.

"You are home. As I always remind you." he says with a sad smile.

"This doesn't feel like home," I reply.

Sadness covers his face with a dark veil as black as the shadows covering the pyramid.

"Maybe it will feel like home after the Equinox. Come. Let's find out." He waits for me to take his hand.

I take it, and we turn to ascend the stairs.

Where are we? Chichen Itza? But that is its new name. Before, it was called the Temple of Kukulcán.

I live here? No, I was brought here.

Stolen.

I look at Ares observantly. He looks back at me and smiles sadly again.

"Almost there," he says.

At the top, we turn and face the crowd gathered at the base, where others are waiting around a stone table. Four giant wolves sit at each corner of the platform like guardians. The two wolves at the front look back at me. One with fur as black as obsidian and glowing orange eyes. The other, with burnt red fur and hazel eyes. They're so big, and I look like a child next to them.

"Lie down." Ares instructs me. "I've already promised; it won't hurt."

"What is going to happen?"

"You're going to remember that this is your home. I am your home. You'll be our queen; we'll rule this world together."

"I don't want to rule." I only want to rest, to stop running.

"You will," he says coldly.

Men approach and take my arms. I try to pull away, but they are firm. I kick, but they hold me. They lift me to the stone table and tie me down. They chant while keeping me in place. Ares rests his hands on my shoulders and lifts his head to the skies.

An old woman, ancient and wrinkled, holds a black stone blade. She approaches the table.

She smiles at me with tar oozing from her teeth, weeping down her chin. Her eyes are blinded white, but she stares at me still. Her scalp is visible beneath what once was thick, curly hair. She puts a finger to her mouth in silence and then laughs with a loud cackle, her head falling back to the skies before thunder erupts, closer this time.

I've never seen her before and wish never to see her again.

The screech of her laugh spills over me like sludge, cold and disgusting.

I tremble as fear overtakes me, and the rain beats down my face.

The woman raises the blade above her head as lightning strikes close by. Her eyes blacken, and she brings the blade down swiftly to pierce my chest.

16

"**Hermes, it's Damien.** I gave my box of research to Bridget in case something happened to me. So, I'm guessing we both know what this means if you have the box and are listening to this recording. When we first met, I told you the werewolves are dying. Female Shifters can't transform, and neither can their pups.

"This upcoming Autumn Equinox will take place during a rare celestial event. The Orion Constellation houses the Fae Realm of Avalon and will be aligned to Gaea during the Equinox. The alignment will quadruple the lunar power of the moon, giving the Shifters a massive boost in strength. They'll be faster, more resilient, and stronger for the month the two realms are aligned.

"Something else is happening with the Alphas. The Zeta King, Lucas Weylyn, has been missing on a mission ordered directly from Ares for weeks. Lupo has moved into the packs in America and is leading in the absence of the Zeta. Lucas would never leave the packs in Lupo's charge unless it were a matter of life or death. Lupo is directing the packs to search for a woman: an Elemental with tremendous power."

At once, our heads snap to Rhea. Sitting around the table in

Callie and Achilles' apartment as we listen to the recording from
Damien. Her face flushes in that recognizable blush—a trademark reaction of her fair skin burning with emotion. The
recording continues, and I focus on the patterns of wood on the
mahogany table as we all lean inward to hear the recording better.

*"I believe Ares is planning something big. His army will
immediately double in size if he can cure the wolves who can't
shift. Combined with the power boost caused by the alignment of
the realms, the Shifters could tip the scales for Ares. Their population would drastically outmatch the Elementals. Mortal governments would fall, and Ares would finally rule Gaea. But Ares
needs the Elemental. His Mage is not strong enough. This
woman is the key, and he'll go to the ends of Gaea to find her.*

*"Follow the breadcrumb trail of the Zeta King, and your
search will deliver you to the Underworld. There you can stop
Ares and free the Shifters.*

*"Hermes, you have allies within the Shifter population that
don't want this future. You have no idea the torment they endure
or the tortures they bear if they go against him. There are good
people here, and they need our help. The world needs our help.*

*"Be careful whom you trust and know; wolves in sheep's
clothing are in your midst. Hopefully, I'll be alive to meet with
you tomorrow. But I know you'll do the right thing if I'm not."*

We sit silently for a moment after the recording stops with
a click; a melancholy cloud hangs heavy over the table. I push
my chair back, resting my elbows on my knees, and wipe my
hands down my face. The weight of the words from the
recording sinks into me, and my mind races. I feel like I'm in
the middle of a crossroads, directionless and waiting for the
crushing cars to barrel into me from all sides.

Achilles stares with unseeing eyes at the empty wall across from him. Callie looks down at her lap with her hand resting on Achilles' forearm. Rhea quickly wipes a tear rolling down her cheek and stands. Walking to the sliding glass doors that lead to a portico and view of the Commune's lake, she stares at the scenery.

Standing, I round the table and firmly squeeze my friend's shoulder. I know that far-off look. The Zeta Wolf's mention has triggered the memories of his sister's death. My touch snaps Achilles out of his trance, and he pats my hand with his own, nodding his head. An unspoken understanding of regret passes between us, and I join Rhea by the door.

"Let's get some air," I tell her, motioning to the portico doors with my head.

Even though it's a hot summer day, Rhea hugs herself as if to warm her cold skin. The wind catches her honey-colored locks, and they dance in the breeze as she squints her eyes in the bright morning sun. Turning away from her, I rest my forearms on the portico's railings and gaze at the sparkling lake. Deep blue waters rustle in the wind, and gleams of sunlight catch on the peeks of the small waves.

"This just got complicated," I say, counting eight birds skimming the water's surface as they fly past the lake.

"Why?"

"Aside from an impending war with the Shifters?" I release a breathy, forced chuckle as I rub the back of my neck. "A long time ago in the Viking Commune, rumors spread among mortals of a wolf unlike any other. It was huge with red fur and was attacking mortals—not just mortals found in the woods. It intelligently set traps or broke into their villages to hunt them.

The Elementals in the area searched, but could never find the wolf.

"Out of nowhere, a massive pack of giant wolves attacked the Viking Commune. The Elementals that lived there barely got out a call for help, and the other Communes arrived quickly, but it was too late. Everyone was dead.

"Achilles' twin sister, Freya, ran the Commune and sacrificed herself to save a group of mortals. The last thing Achilles saw as he fled with a group of children was the red wolf, the Zeta King, ripping out his sister's throat.

"Achilles has never forgotten the sight of that moment, and the screams of the mortals suffering haunt him.

"That was the first time I met Achilles and convinced him to return to the Grecian Commune at Delphi with me. Shortly after, he met Patroclus. Their mating bond was immediate, and we all became close friends." I chuckle, recalling our antics as we drove Atlas crazy with our unruliness.

"Like the three-headed Chimera, we moved as one on the battlefield. No one could defeat us. Callie was sailing the globe with Odysseus and Penelope, looking for the lost teleportation pads. But she returned about twenty years later, and the fated mate bond between Callie, Achilles, and Patroclus was complete. A truly rare matching of three beings but even more amazing as it was shared between a strong Wind Siren and two intense Flames." I shake my head in disbelief as the memory of their flaming hurricane comes to mind. A great raging beast of fire and wind, roaring through the ocean with their combined powers. It was a sight to behold.

"The fury they exacted on our enemies was legendary. The threesome held back Ares' naval fleet for three days while Athena gathered the Trojans for her renowned battle against the God of War." Rhea intently listens and hangs on my every word with fascination coating her gaze.

"Athena and her mate arrived with the Trojans. The battle was unfathomable as Elementals and Shifters collided. Ares had convinced fleets of mortals to join him. There was nothing left of them as they fought against elemental powers, but Ares didn't care. He only needed as many living bodies as possible to keep rushing to the front lines, charging at the Elementals to keep us using our powers and exhaust us."

"I thought Patroclus fought *against* the Trojans?" Rhea asks, tilting her head to the side. I look at the lake so I can answer. If I look into her eyes, the deep honey may lure me into her depths, and I might allow myself to drown in them. The memory of Patroclus' death has torn a hole in the caverns of my soul that will never heal, like so many wounds Ares has inflicted in this realm.

"Ares has a powerful Mind Mage, like Atlas. His name is Moros. He wormed into Patroclus's mind and turned him against us. Patroclus began setting our forces on fire; the Elementals we have lived and fought beside for centuries were screaming inside his flames. Then, the Moros turned Patroclus against Callie. And the Zeta Wolf joined Patroclus' side to go after her together, licking his teeth to sink them into Callie's throat, just like he did Achilles' sister, Freya.

"Atlas tried to push the Mind Mage out but was injured and fell unconscious. Patroclus was at the mercy of Moros, and Ares directed the Mage to break them—to cripple the powerful trio of mates forever."

Rhea gasps, and I can almost sense the images she is conjuring, thinking about the horrors of that scene. But nothing can amount to the reality of that terrible day.

"Ares threw a wooden spear. It pierced Patroclus through his head and Moros," I pause, struggling to form the heavy words. Rhea's gaze scorches with desperation to hear the rest while my eyes blur with tears of anger and sorrow. Tightening my jaw, I continue. "He had total control over him and was slowly tearing his mind apart. He was torturing Patroclus while forcing him to charge at Callie."

"But a wooden spear can't kill an Immortal," Rhea interjects, her wide eyes filling with dread.

"Correct. Only Adamantine Steele or Elemental powers can kill an Immortal," I swallow hard, forcing the knot down my throat. "Achilles had to do it. He screamed and roared the most gut-wrenching sound I've ever heard another person make as his Soul Fire killed Patroclus."

"No," Rhea whispers, tears falling from her golden eyes, and spilling over the tops of her hands wrapped around her mouth.

"You can feel the death of your fated mate. So, Callie and Achilles had to endure it. Not only did Achilles have to kill one of his mates, but he was causing immeasurable pain to the other."

17
Rhea

So, the God of War wants to use me like a pawn in his sadistic game of chess. Hearing Damien's voice on the recording and his theory about what Ares might be planning starts to form a picture in my mind. I am the woman they are searching for, and that is why Lupo's pack abducted me and wanted to provoke my powers. But something Lupo said as he was locking me in the metal coffin hangs around the back of my mind like an anchor tethering a boat to a dock.

"Don't worry, goddess; you performed perfectly. Sit tight while the cavalry comes to save you. I'll see you around, little one."

"Are you sure this is the plan, Alpha? We're supposed to release her?"

"You have a problem with the plan; take it up with Ares yourself."

"There are wolves in sheep's clothing," I mumble the words from Damien's recording to myself.

"What was that?" Atlas asks as we walk silently to his office for another attempt at my memories.

"Oh, I'm just thinking out loud."

Hermes' story of what Achilles and Callie endured at the

hands of Ares is a heavy weighted blanket hanging on my mind. The demented nature of Ares' commands and the blind following in which his army obeys him is something I can't comprehend—torturing an immortal and forcing them to maim and kill the people they love, all while a battle is raging. It's heart-wrenching to think about what these people have lived through.

The memories of my family's death have haunted me, but how much worse could things be? If the memories in my mind are false and the truth lurking in my mind is worse, I'm beginning to wonder if my mind will break in two when I learn the truth.

Callie bounds toward us, walking in the opposite direction with Terra, who is deep into an explanation about something and swinging her hands wildly as she talks. Her platinum hair is not in its usual high ponytail; it hangs in long ribbons of silky sunshine down her back. Callie waves at us, giving me an exaggerated wink when she passes like she knows a secret I don't. It pulls me out of my dark thoughts and makes me chuckle.

"How do you like the Commune so far?" Atlas asks to break our awkward silence. I've been lucky to avoid him for the most part since knocking him out, but I knew I would inevitably have to face my humiliation.

"It's amazing. I enjoy the portals, but they are a little confusing." I tuck my hair behind my ear, and Atlas pushes his glasses on his nose with his finger.

"Oh, I hate using the portals. A few hundred years ago, I was reading some new writings from an old friend, Dante. I got so distracted, I forgot to put in my coordinates and stood in a portal for twenty minutes reading." He laughs at the memory. "I much prefer walking."

Chewing on the inside of my lip, my nerves climb like vines up a trellis as we near his office. Preparing to open my mind again and feel his cold tendrils of power is enough to make me bolt back to my room and climb into bed, but I know this is necessary.

"I'd like to move into the Commune officially," I tell him, my tone turning unsure as I finish the sentence. I don't know how things work here exactly—if permission is needed or if space is available. It seems to be an open community, and if I'm going to be a constant target of Ares, I'll need their help and protection. And being around people like me, with powers, is all I've ever dreamed of. Knowing there are entire populations like me brings me so much hope.

"We would love to have you as a permanent resident. I'm sure we can secure you a new apartment by tomorrow."

"I probably also need to call my job and my aunt. She's planning on visiting me in a few weeks. Maybe I can make an excuse and push her off for a little while until we figure things out."

"I think that's a great idea." Atlas has a relaxed demeanor and speaks with a gentle tone.

My worries about the memory exercise are easing as I think about how caring he is. I'm sure he does not intend it to be uncomfortable, or maybe I am just extra sensitive to the feel of his powers. Whatever it is, I'm sure he wouldn't want me to feel this discomfort, so I ask him about the cold and burning sensation I feel when the white light scorches my vision.

"I had no idea it was like that for you." he exclaims, taken back by my description of the sensations. "I can certainly help with that." He smiles.

Arriving at his office, Athena is there and ready with her

monitors. I lie on the couch, and Atlas sits near my feet. Patting my hand, his touch warms my palm as the sensation of his power softly rolls up my arm, spreading across my shoulders and up my neck.

"Is the warmth better?" he asks with his gold-rimmed glasses slipping down his nose and his soft brown hair falling in front of his eyes.

I nod my head yes, thankful the sensation feels much more relaxing. "Thank you. This is much better."

Closing my eyes, I focus on the memory I avoid the most.

It's time to show Atlas how I killed my family.

THE ACCIDENT

L arge raindrops bounce off the top of the car with a plop. *It's a gloomy day as water-filled clouds spread across the sky and fog hangs low to the ground, encasing our car as we travel home. The bright and cheerful mood in the vehicle contrasts with the grey day outside.*

Dad drives us home while Mom sings along to 'I Got You, Babe' while holding hands in the front seat. She looks back at me with a smile, and I stop tracing bored shapes on the foggy window to smile back at her. My book sits on my lap, and my little brother is propped against his door, sleeping. His mouth sags open, and a fond smile slides across my face.

We are on our way home from my fourteenth birthday party, and he spent all his energy at the skating rink. Jason is only six, so he didn't know how to skate. He stuck to my side, holding my hand as I taught him.

I smile at the thought, but it fades as I remember he's about to die. And this is one of the last times I get to look at him.

The dream seems so real, for a moment, I forgot it is only a dream. Everything is so perfect, down to the last detail. Even the air freshener's vanilla scent and the leather seat's texture are exactly as I remember. My palm rubs down the seat's cold hide, and I place my hand back in my lap.

The dismal outside pulls on my mood, and my eyes follow a black crow sitting observantly on the branch of a tall pine tree. Its head turns, curiously tracking the movement of our car as we drive past. The fog outside makes my magic tingle in my fingertips, and I peek back at Mom to ensure she is not looking. She and Dad are engrossed in singing together, so I steal the moment to let my magic play.

This is the moment I regret, and I would give anything to change. Why did I have to be bored? Why didn't I wait until I was home, lock myself in my room, or sneak out to the field to let my magic out? Why now?

Turning my hand over, the tendrils of my powers weep out of my palm as cool, dark mist undulates in a happy dance, thankful to be free. I watch it twirl as the mist waterfalls off my hand, disappearing before landing on my pant leg. The swirls and curls of the dark haze always settle my busy mind, and after a long day of entertaining friends and family, my racing thoughts can finally stretch and be calm.

I turn the mist into shadows and make little horses with wings like the Pegasus I read about in my new book. The two black stallions prance on my lap, and I smile at their small forms.

A gasp jerks my head to the front of the car. Mom stares at the figures on my lap and shifts to meet my eyes. A chill cascades down my spine, knowing she saw my secret. My face burns with embarrassment and shame. I wipe sweaty palms down my blue jean pants, but my mist refuses to retreat and begins spilling out of my hands and legs, collecting on the car's floor. I swallow hard as it pools and spreads away from me.

"*Rhea, what is this?*" Her eyes are wide, and her voice is strained with disbelief.

"*Mom, I-I...*"

"*What's going on?*" Dad asks, rising in his seat to look in the rearview mirror. My brother's sleepy eyes pop open, and he wipes a line of drool from his chin.

"*Are we home?*" Jason asks, looking outside the car at the landscape still racing past us before looking back at me. Horror takes over his face when he spies the black mist rolling out of me, its wisps coating everyone like an icy blanket. He scrambles in his booster seat, raising his knees to his chest and pushing himself away from me.

"*Rhea, what is this?*" my dad exclaims.

"*Jason, it's okay.*" My panicked voice is a tone higher than usual. "*It won't hurt you.*"

"*What are you?*" His question stabs my heart, and the mist torrents out of me more. He thinks I'm a freak; this is exactly why I never told them. The car is full instantly, blocking all windows and casting the interior into smoky darkness. Vines made of shadow slither out from the fog and pool on the car's floor. Their thin branches climb my parents' legs and reach over the booster seat, coiling around my brother.

"*Rhea!*" Mom's tone snaps my guilty eyes to her, but I can't find her in the thick fog of my powers.

"*This is not me.*" I squeal as my chest constricts tightly. My magic has never been so unyielding, and I can't suck it back inside. My hands fumble against the door, trying to find the button to roll down the window and pull the mist out, but the windows are locked.

The vines thicken and squeeze tighter as they wind up my family's bodies. My Dad attempts to keep hold of the steering *wheel, but vines snap around his wrist, pulling his hands to his sides. My mother yelps and screams, pulling at the vines, but grabbing shadows is impossible, and her fingers pass through the translucent forms.*

"Mommy?" Jason calls from the backseat, and I reach for him to pull away the vines wrapping around his neck. I don't understand what is happening. I don't know how to stop it. I just wanted to play with my powers a little. Tears fall in unrelenting streams down my face, and my fingers are frozen cold as terror courses through my body, pulling tremors into my hands.

The gangling vines spread through the entire car, covering the sides and roof as they spread like a virus. Wrapping around my family's heads, their mouths are bound with layers of my shadows, unable to scream, suffocating as the vines invade their mouths and noses. Slithering into the recesses of their skulls, I see Jason's eyes roll back in his head as his back arches in agony.

No.

My parents also share the look of paralyzing pain as the vines enter their skulls, taking over their forms from the outside.

Pulling against my dad's headrest, I lean forward and reach for the steering wheel. The vines coil down his leg, wrapping around the gas pedal, and the car growls as it takes on more speed. Reaching the front, I can push the brake and stop the car. I can get the vines off them, and everything will be okay. They'll be okay.

"I'm so sorry, Mom!"

A thick vine slithers up my back and wraps around my waist, thrusting me back into my seat and wrapping over me like a seatbelt, bolting me to the car. The world slows down. The next few seconds pass like hours.

The tires scream along the road as the car's brake is applied fully, and the putrid smell of burning rubber invades my nose. My body jerks violently in response, and I lash out instinctively with my arm to hold on to the door handle and reach for my brother. Feeling the cold tendrils of the vines still coiling around him, I pull my hand away in disgust as chills rush up my arm.

Glass fractures into a million pieces and explodes around us. Inside the vehicle, a great wind whips in a violent spin. I shut my eyes tight and bring my head down to my knees, covering my ears with my hands. The black mist careens out of the open window, and I feel the weight of a hundred pounds lift off my chest as my family is freed of the vines that were suffocating them.

My elation is quickly diminished as they slump in their seats. White and clammy skin glistens as boils form in places where the vines thorns pierced their skin. A cloudy white film covers their eyes, which stare unseeing into an abyss of nothing. A scream rips from my throat as black tar begins oozing out of their eyes and dripping from their ears and nose.

They're dead. I killed them.

The car door at my side is ripped off its hinges, and I watch it bounce across the pavement. The car is spinning as if caught in a vortex, but a powerful churning air builds inside it too. I strain to grab onto my dad's seat and hold the headrest while my feet brace against the sides of the doorframe, serving as my anchors to keep me in the car.

The force of the spinning vehicle and cyclone of wind whipping in the center of the car pushes and pulls on me harder. My slick hands slowly lose the battle as the last of my fingers slide off the metal bar of the headrest. I'm ripped out of the car, leaving my dead family within.

No, let me die with them, please.

I beg my powers to take me back, but they act against me.

My body flies through the air, and I try curling myself into a ball before I hit the hard road, tumbling like a limp doll. With the jolt of the impact, all the breath in my body is pounded out of me at once. When I finally come to rest, my back pressed against the soft ground; I open my eyes to see the sky and trees above me spinning rapidly, my ears ringing with a steady high-pitch whistle.

I watch helplessly as the car slams into a large oak tree. A great fireball erupts, and the heat rolls over me as the force of the blast shoots outward. I expect to hear the crunching metal or the explosion's blast, but all I hear is a deafening silence.

As my vision blurs and fades, the flapping wings of a bird echo within my mind. Black mist billows heavily around me as if caressing me with soothing strokes. I let the darkness wrap around me as the large raindrops bounce off my face.

Without warning, I'm snapped back to my seat; like a movie wound back a few scenes, the memory of the event starts over.

I hear the rain plop on the window and momentarily look up from my book to watch it. I'm in the car with Mom and Dad. My little brother slumped against his door with his head back and mouth wide open, sleeping.

It makes me laugh.

Mom and Dad are in the front. Dad is driving.

... I know what happens next.

The accident plays again with the suffocating vines and burning rubber and smoke filling my nostrils. The cloud of black mist blocks my body in a blanket of darkness, with nothing else to see after the sound of the flapping wings.

"Please, not again," I beg my dream to wake up, but sleep keeps its hold on me.

After the third replay of the memory or dream, my body

soars into the sky as though the arm of a claw machine has clasped around me, and I'm waiting to be dropped into a bin like I'm nothing more than a prize stuffed animal.

My stomach rolls and grumbles at the force of the movement, and my lunch threatens to spill out of my stomach. I'm jolted until I face the ground a hundred feet below me. Vertigo shakes my vision as I float in the sky. The wind billows around me due to the stormy day and the altitude of my new vantage point.

Far beneath me, the movements of the accident and car occur in reverse like a VHS tape on rewind until an abrupt stop occurs, like the memory went back as far as it could and hit a wall, refusing to go further. I watch from above as the car drives forward, releases my black mist through broken windows, and crashes into an inferno.

Tears pour out of my eyes and are pulled away by the wind. I beg the universe to stop it. I beg myself not to play with my magic in the car, so I can stop the accident from happening. But it still happens despite my cries. Of course it does. This is only a dream—a memory.

I watch my body fly outside the car, encased in a whirl of wind, protecting me as I bounce along the gravel road. The casing of protective air bursts, and I watch my fourteen-year-old body slide until I come to rest. The billows of black mist arrive on cue and surround me.

From my perch in the air, I'm thrust downward. The distance to the earth below is quickly eaten up, and my arms react to protect my face before I hit the hard ground, but the impact never comes.

Everything is quiet in an instant and the air around me stills. Carefully opening my eyes, the stormy outside is replaced with a sterile hospital room. Hovering like a flying pixie, I stare down at my body in a hospital bed. Except this is not a child's fairytale. It's a child's nightmare. My nightmare.

Transfixed by the sight of myself, unblinking, I take in the details of my younger face. This girl seems at peace and doesn't know she will wake up soon and remember the worst event of her life. At this very moment, she may still dream of fantastical beasts and fairies. Soon they'll be night terrors, and she will be the monster that plagues them.

I know who comes in next, and I turn my head to the door, waiting for my aunt to walk through, but she doesn't. My stomach clutches again, and I take it as a warning that the memory is about to change. This time I'm prepared for another nauseating flow through the memories of time.

With a slam, I'm returned to the body of that little girl, standing by her mother's casket, the black dress still itchy against my skin. To the left is my father's casket, and to the right, the smallest of them is for my brother.

The funeral is depressing, as they always are. So many people are crying. Everyone is staring at me. No one knows what to say.

"We're so sorry for your loss."

"Do you need anything?"

"Yeah, I need my family back."

Another vice twists my stomach into a knot, and I'm ready for the memory change again. I'll go anywhere except back to the accident.

I'm in my room now, slammed onto a soft, bouncy surface. It was a foreign room back then. My aunt's guest room, sitting with my legs crossed in front of me on my new bed. My quilt, a gift from my mom for my birthday, made with souvenir shirts from my seasons of travel softball, covers the bed. I wrap it around me, inhaling her scent deeply. It still smells of her soft lavender perfume, and the fragrance seeps into my bones, relaxing me.

I only have a moment to look around the room before a frustrated force pulls my subconscious back to the car crash, and I begin to think I'm dying.

This will be my assigned ring of Dante's Inferno, destined to relive these days on a loop for all eternity. I lose track of myself, the difference between my current body and the body of the memory. Everything goes numb as I relive the most terrible day of my life. The vice pulling me to and fro pushes on my chest, wanting to go back farther, beyond the car accident to earlier days, but the fog wall is an impenetrable barrier.

The distant caw of a crow echoes through the tall pine trees. I shut my eyes tight and fold in on myself.

"I'm done."

I won't relive another memory. The trees shake, and the ground quivers in irritation as the dream growls its frustration into the grey sky.

"I said, I'm done."

19

Rhea

The pale-yellow ceiling spins like a carousel slowing down so riders can exit. It takes several attempts to open and close my eyes before my vision focuses and the room stills. Turning my head to the side, I find Atlas sweating and breathing hard. His forearms are resting on his knees, and he's removed his gold-rimmed glasses to rub his eyes. Athena is next to me with her fingers on my wrist, counting the pulse of my heart. My body is stiff as if I haven't moved for ages, but looking at the clock on the wall, only an hour has passed since we arrived.

"How do you feel?" Athena asks, looking over my face. My hands shake, and I'm still lying down.

"That was weird. It was a dream, but it was like, on a loop." I reply. "What happened, Atlas?"

"I was trying to guide you through the memories, to move around the fabricated edges of the fake memories so we could see what was on the other side, but they have been woven too tightly." he explains as Athena hands me a bottle of water.

"What does that mean?"

"You believe in the lie too much, so it's too deeply rooted."

I drop my head, and my chest constricts with disappointment in myself. Every time I cling to a ray of hope, it bursts into flames in my hand, and I'm constantly scalding myself with the anticipation of something I'll never have.

"We'll get there." Atlas places his hand on my shoulder with a reassuring squeeze.

The session must have been tiring for him as well. Athena studies the tablet, scrolling through the contents. My mouth drops when I realize it is a recording of the dream, and I see my nightmare play out on the screen.

"Oh my god." My eyes remain fixed on the screen. Athena notices my attention on the device and presses a button, making the screen turn dark.

"Rhea, we must study this and understand how your memories were manipulated."

I move my large round eyes to hers and nod in agreement as if I understand. But thinking about watching the horrors of that crash like a movie turns the taste in my mouth to acid.

"What I can tell you is you are no killer, Rhea. You did not do that." Athena's stare into my eyes is intense and full of conviction. I want to believe her. I want nothing more than to believe I didn't murder them, but that day changed my life. I've relived it so much it's etched onto my soul.

Applying my carefully constructed mask of indifference, I head to the portal. I'll pretend my world is not falling apart until I return to the seclusion of my little room and break down in peace.

"Thanks for trying. I will run by the library for a new stack of books before I head back to Callie's."

Atlas smiles. "I find much more comfort in a book's bindings than in a room full of people. Let me help you with the portal." He inputs the code for the library and closes the portal door with a wave. The lights immediately shut off when the door clicks shut, putting me in total darkness inside the portal.

I fumble for the handle and, finding it, attempt to push the door, but it doesn't budge. My heart beats quicker, and I bang on the door for help. I should have practiced using these more with someone with me. This is the second time I've had an issue operating the portals.

"Atlas! Athena! Can you hear me? I think the door is stuck!"

There is no answer.

"Hello?" My voice echoes oddly as if the space suddenly expanded beyond the small confines of the portal.

My breath is coming in and out quickly as my face heats with uncertainty. This is not supposed to happen.

"Can anyone hear me?"

Searching in the dark, with my arms are in front of me, I wave my hands around attempting to find anything to help me understand where I am. But the enclosure of the portal is no longer surrounding me. Stumbling into a dark void, I arrive at a large expanse. My body shakes as frigid air brushes against my skin. Thinking I see movement, I whirl left and right, searching. The movements remain in the corners of my visions, refusing to be seen.

My mind is dizzy without being able to decipher any sense of direction. Taking a deep breath through my nose, I blow it slowly through my mouth to calm my racing pulse.

I can figure this out.

I'm the most powerful Elemental Hermes has ever encountered. This is definitely something ethereal. If there is ever a time to use my abilities, it's when I'm accidentally stuck in a bottomless pit of nothing. Steadying myself with my breathing,

I roll my shoulders back, relaxing them and loosening the tension. Shaking my arms to the side, I ready myself and pull on the powers inside me.

At once, my surroundings lighten with the silver glow of my aura, shining like the only star in the vast expanse of outer space. Elated and smiling, I clap for myself, happy I called my aura out with such little effort. My applause echoes endlessly, bouncing on nothing and reverberating away from me until it fades into the dark.

Holding my palm out, orange and yellow flames dance around each other, shining warmly on my face. The heat surges down my arm and chases away the cold. Holding my arm behind me, I launch the flame into the dark. Bouncing across a thin layer of black water, a hundred ripples spread outward until the fireball bursts, sending yellow and orange embers to the sky. Like stars in the universe, they hang in the blackness above my head and go on forever.

Raising my arms above my head, two pillars of water follow my command and shoot into the sky. It rains down on me as bright blue orbs of burning light join the yellow and orange embers.

Wind.

Like a child waiting for its mother's call, a breeze eagerly rushes around my ankles and swirls up my body. I spin along with the wind as sparks of purple burst upward in a current that splatters the sky with violet starlight. Like a kaleidoscope has ruptured and spilled into the sky, the colors of my powers twinkle and burn above my head. Like standing in space among the stars, they reflect endlessly in the dark water at my feet. The beauty of the place takes away the haunting darkness, and with it, my fear.

As I think of my earth element, the familiar slow creep of black mist glides across the wet ground from behind me. I feel comforted with it here, but as a fresh breeze blows against my face, an ominous presence rides on the wind as a warning.

I feel the burn of eyes on me, and the hairs on my neck stand to attention when the growl of a beast crawls along my skin. Like a billion falling stars, the embers of my powers fall from the sky and sizzle as they land in the dark water, thrusting me into darkness again. My silver aura makes me a beacon against the black void for the creature approaching me.

My mist grows and billows protectively, and through the haze as the muzzle of a vast, grey wolf protrudes, its red aura reflected in its silver eyes. My legs freeze in fear as I stare back. The pounding of my heart is a booming drum as my breathing deepens. The wolf exposes its fangs, and the growl becomes a snarl.

I put my hand out in front of me as if to keep the beast at bay. My feet respond by taking slow steps away from the creeping wolf while the noises reverberate from its throat in a terrifying melody. *This must be a dream.*

Could I still be dreaming? The session with Atlas to work on my memories may still be going. Maybe we didn't finish, and he didn't put me in the portal. Perhaps I'm still lying on his couch being monitored by Athena.

Moving further into the fog, I sense something familiar behind me. A waft of lavender perfume dances around my nose, and somehow I'm sure the doorknob to my bedroom is near. Keeping my eyes on the wolf, I back up to it and fumble for the knob.

The wolf continues his ascent forward, faster now, and lowers himself down in preparation to leap. Holding my breath, I finally grasp the handle firmly and turn it. Seeing the muscles in the wolfs' legs tense under its fur, I wait no longer. Flinging the door open, I burst into the room, and slam it behind me. I push all my weight against the door, bracing for the impact of the wolf.

A powerful bang on the door jolts terror throughout my body, and a scream rips out of my throat. My hands fly to cover my mouth.

"You can't hide from me for all eternity!" A voice yells back at me. "I'll *always* find you."

Ares.

I know his voice as surely as I know mine. The voice, the presence from my night terrors, is here.

I back away from the door as if it were burning. The knob turns incessantly, and Ares' fists beat on the other side of the door. The human sounds transition back to the snarling of a beast.

A pause settles, and a quiet weight hangs over the strange room. Looking at the corners where the shadows collect, I see them rolling and undulating. This place is not real. It must be a dream. Looking closer, other artifacts from my teenage years are here, filling in the details of the memory. Approaching the side table with a small lamp, a stack of books, and an alarm clock, I wave my hand through the lamp. Its solid form becomes a translucent vapor that swirls as my hand passes through it before reforming again and appearing solid.

Amazing.

A howl echoes on the other side of the door, and I snap my head toward it. A barrage of howls and snarls join in chorus from afar. Howling, snarling, and scratching assault the room from every wall as dozens of wolves descend upon my small room of protection. The beating on the door resumes, and an overwhelming sense of helplessness squeezes my throat like a vice.

"This is your fate, Rhea. Stop *fighting!*" Ares spits the last word in his smoky voice, and ice runs through my veins.

I have to get out of here.

I don't understand what this place is; or how well it can keep standing up to the assault Ares is unleashing outside. The door and walls may not hold much longer. My chest tightens as my ragged breathing becomes shallow. I need to get myself back. The sounds boom around me, making it impossible to form a coherent thought. The cool metal of the sword necklace bounces against my chest. I clutch it like it's tethering me back to my mind.

Home.

As I think the word, ultra-cold power explodes within me, and my back arches as my arms flail outward. Beams of pure black shadow, so cold they burn, stream out of my center as a tidal wave of billowing dark mist, and fog rolls out of me. Unable to escape the surge of power, I hold on to it with every fiber of my being, screaming through clenched teeth as it swells out of me at blinding speed.

The wolf's howls and snarls are snuffed out in the snap of a finger. The room made of mist and smoke dissolves away, and I begin to fall. So slowly, I drop through a bottomless void. The darkness and shadows swallow me like a vacuum chamber where sound and wind do not exist.

The power surge has expended all my energy, and my arms have no strength to react and grasp for a savior. With nothing for my eyes to focus on, I lose all my senses as I fall through a veil of shadow out of this dream.

Slow at first, then rushing in all at once, the void of nothing turns to earth and sky. The silence of space is replaced with a crescendo of crickets singing across the hot summer night. The rough ground and damp grass rush up to meet me. Instead of the hard ground, I'm met with hands that reach out and grab me with a gentle firmness, encasing me in strong arms. The scent of sandalwood and spice grounds me back to reality, and I collapse against him.

Home. My mind repeats. *I'm home.*

"Rhea?" Hermes' voice fades in and reverberates throughout my mind, along with the distant flapping of wings that haunt the memories of my family's car accident.

Unstoppable shivering rattles my body as a frigid cold clings to me, stubbornly refusing to be washed away by the warm night. My eyes close of their own accord as the warm light of Hermes' aura fades.

"I found you. I'll always find you." he whispers in my ear as he holds me tighter.

Hermes

"**You need to warn the other Communes: a war with the Shifters is coming.**"

"And you need to remember your place, as Head of Security, is for this Commune and this Commune *only*." The Headmistress stands behind her white marble desk with her hands on each side, looking down her nose at me. Atlas puts his hand on my shoulder. My signal to drop it.

The Headmistress of our Commune is a joke—a laughingstock. I know Elementals with more integrity in their pinky fingers than she has in her entire immortal body. She always has a chip on her shoulder regarding me, all because of my mother.

My mother was Head of Security at Delphi, and Eris challenged her position and lost. Eris has never been able to live with the fact that she is not top tier. Now that I hold the title my mother once did, I'm a constant reminder of her failure.

But I have no intention of dropping this subject. If she won't act, I'll join another Commune that will. Turning on my heel, I storm out of her office, and push the double doors open with both hands; an echo bounces down the stark hallway as they bang loudly against the walls.

Bounding behind me, Atlas jogs to catch up with my

long strides. Taller than him by several inches, my pace always outmatches his, especially when I'm in such a heated mood.

"What are you going to do?" Atlas asks, breathless.

"You know exactly what I'm going to do."

I feel like I'm standing on the horizon's edge, and everything is about to tip upside down. Finding Damien murdered and Rhea's room broken into, hearing Damien refer to a missing Elemental and warn of a looming war with Ares... we need a break.

There is no doubt the wolves need Rhea. What I can't figure out is when Lupo had her, why would he release her? Maybe Lupo and his packs didn't have a facility to hold her. Binding her in three sets of Thaumium cuffs still didn't contain her, and that's unheard of. Or perhaps there is an underlying motive we can't see yet. We need to be cautious and increase our protection of her. None of us missed the warning at the close of the recording, either.

"There are wolves in sheep's clothing in your midst."

Spies must be planted within the Commune, perhaps all of the Communes have Elementals working for Ares. So, our group of trusted allies has shrunk.

Atlas insists on talking about my warning to Eris, but I need to cool down before I let my temper drive me. It's not a time to be irrational, but I have no intention of sitting back and waiting to see what happens. Atlas has known me my entire life and knows I need some time.

He retrieved Rhea to walk her to his office for their

memory session, whereas I need to be busy with things to take my mind off the anger.

Achilles, Callie, and I discuss increasing security and keeping our work within our small group. We must also ensure that one of us—Atlas or Athena—is always with Rhea. I know that will piss her off because she doesn't like being dependent on anyone, but she will have to learn to trust others and let people help.

Achilles took a few tactical teams to The Coat, increasing its protective range and adding additional wards. I plan on spending the rest of the day working on Rhea's new apartment, and the distraction was exactly what I needed. Callie and Terra went on a shopping spree for me and will return with things for a surprise.

Hoping she will want to stay here permanently, we got her a larger loft apartment than the smaller studio apartment she was in the first few days of her stay. Next door to Callie and Achilles, the open space of the kitchen and sitting room has a huge picture window overlooking the lake and tall twenty-foot ceilings. Five members of the tactical teams are nearly finished moving furniture and hanging pictures. The long portico has been set up with a glass table and chairs for lounging outside. Surrounded on two sides by a trellis, I asked one of the Commune members, Flora, a Life Elemental, for help with the greenery.

"What is something pretty that can grow up the trellis and has nice flowers?" I ask her. Botany is not my strong suit, but Flora lives for plants, and runs our greenhouse, overseeing all the crops grown for our food.

"Wisteria is nice." With a flourish of her hand, a small vine grows a few feet up the trellis, and bunches of hanging purple flowers spring up, surrounded by deep green leaves. "It's late in the season for wisteria, but I can make it bloom year-round if you like."

"That is perfect." The leaves and twisting branches, with their clusters of flowers, will provide a beautiful backdrop against the otherwise plain exterior wall. "Can you make it hang over in the corner? She likes to read a lot. So maybe some overhang for shade in that corner?"

Flora cuts her eyes at me, and a slow smile spreads. "Sure. I can do that."

"What is that look for?"

"You seem to know a lot about this woman." Flora shrugs innocently, still smiling. "That's all."

"She's Callie's friend."

"I bet she is." Flora's smile widens, and she pushes me off. "Get out of here. I got this."

Shaking my head and rolling my eyes, I leave Flora at the portico. Knowing her, she'll add other plants to make it look lush. I turn my attention to the loft for Rhea's surprise, and climb the wrought iron spiral staircase. This end of the Commune is more modern than the other parts, and living among mortals, I'm hedging my bets that Rhea will enjoy the exposed brick walls of this large loft and its more modern fixtures.

A circular window brings natural light into the loft, adding a unique design feature. Arranging the furniture and assembling the bookshelves, I finish just in time for Callie and Terra to return from Once Upon A Spine. Hearing the chime of the portal below, I peek over the iron railing and see Callie emerging from the portal along with Terra. Stacks of boxes filled with books accompany them.

"Easy as pie." Callie beams, picking up one of the boxes and heading to the stairs. "Mortals are so nice!"

"It was monstrous." Terra grumbles.

I chuckle at Callie's enthusiasm. She loves shopping; she's a total people person. Never meeting a stranger, she is comfortable anywhere and with anyone.

"You didn't have any trouble?" I ask.

"I just asked for the owner and explained whom I was shopping for. Mrs. Clark immediately knew who Rhea was and said she is always there." Callie picks up a brown beverage swirling in ice with white cream swirled around the top. "She even gave me an *iced coffee*. It's perfect!"

Shaking my head at the simple things Callie finds joy in, I grab a few boxes and sprint up the stairs and back down. Using my speed, I finish unloading the twelve boxes in the time Terra carries one.

"Show off," she mumbles with a huff. "Am I dismissed? Mortals are exhausting."

Callie laughs and waves her off. Terra is always in a gloomy mood, no matter our mission. We have learned to ignore it and accept that not everyone is a ray of sunshine like Callie.

Callie helps me unload the books onto the shelves, which are nearly packed by the time we finish. She explains the different types of books the store owner recommended based on what Rhea likes to read, and Callie had instructions to buy them all. Mortal money is such a primitive practice that has no value for Immortals, but we have electronic forms of their payment for occasions where we need to abide by their customs. Callie says the store owner went wide-eyed when she said she wanted to buy everything.

Standing back and looking at our handy work, the small

library we have created in Rhea's loft is perfect. The ceiling was painted this morning with a rich deep blue and fixed with gold foil stars and constellations, looking like a treasure map of the universe. Brass Turkish lamps cast a mosaic of colors on the wall as the golden light shines through the stained-glass openings. A wide rocking chair is perched in a corner, while floor cushions rest across the room. In the center is a writing desk with all the essentials she could need for her research and writing.

I can't help the smile on my face as I think about how she will react when she sees it. The books stand tall on their shelves, with their inked treasures waiting for Rhea within their pages. I envision her sitting sideways in the rocking chair with her legs hanging over the sides, a book in her hand, and the sun gleaming through the circular window behind her.

"You think she'll like it?" I ask Callie.

She smiles at me, grasps my waist in a hug, and squeezes me tightly. "She's going to love it."

To finish off the apartment, I extend my aura around the entirety of the space, filling all dark corners and every entry point with the glowing blue light of my aura to create a shield of protective light.

Every elemental power can create a shield of some form. Callie's Wind armor is called the Shield of Currents. Achilles' is called Flame Armor. Each element has an opposite which is its weakness. Wind and fire, for example, can either help or hurt each other. Callie's wind can fan Achilles' flames higher or blow them out. But only two elements are the exact antithesis of each other and can leave permanent shields of armor behind. Light and Dark Elementals.

No matter where I am in the world, I'll know if anyone

other than Rhea sets foot over my shield. And if the Dark Mage that's been hiding in the shadows breaks my shield, I'll know that too. And goddess help the Elemental that comes for her.

With our work in Rhea's new apartment finished, Callie and I meet Achilles in the cafeteria. It's busy for dinner, and the scent of grilled meats and fresh flatbread makes my stomach protest while waiting for the others. After dinner, we will bring Rhea back to the new apartment and discuss our research with Damien.

Atlas strolls into the cafeteria, chatting with Athena, but Rhea is not with them. Alarms ring in my head. Shooting up from my seat, I meet them as they walk down the rows of tables occupied by Commune members enjoying their dinner. Several eyes look at me with curiosity but return to their conversations quickly.

"Where is Rhea?" I ask in hushed tones. "We agreed to stay with her."

Atlas raises his eyebrows in recollection and turns his head to Athena, who looks equally shocked.

"Hermes, I'm sorry. We forgot. Her session was so amazing that we were transfixed with analyzing it immediately." Athena explains.

"She went to the library after our session," Atlas informs me.

Before I can take one step toward a portal, every warning surrounding the Commune blasts at once.

The Coat has been disengaged, and Shifters are within the Commune grounds.

The Commune erupts in a hailstorm of bodies running in all directions. Lower-level Elementals head to safety zones within the Commune. Off-duty tactical team members jump into action, either helping direct people or running off toward the gear room to suit up. We have seconds before the Shifters will reach the buildings, so time is of the essence. The wolves, once shifted, are very large and have heightened abilities. They'll certainly come here in wolf forms, and I bet they are here for one thing.

"Please tell me where you are." I send a silent prayer to the Fates, hoping Rhea is safe as I try to connect with her through telepathy.

"I've got the tac team; go find her," Achilles says, his eyes turning steel as he and Callie head to the grounds, jumping straight off the second-story portico onto the ground. Callie uses her wind element and carries herself higher on the currents to begin scouting the locations of the intruders from above. Achilles is a trail of flames as he takes off, speeding around the perimeter.

Like a streak of lightning across the sky, I run to the library as I extend my aura outward in all directions. I pick up all the souls of the Commune members—those fleeing and preparing for a fight. I grit my teeth as I sense Headmistress Eris crouched in the corner of her office, covering her ears with her hands. *Coward.* Sensors are positioned across the Commune and are using their powers to pick up the wolves. But I don't sense Rhea.

Casting my powers out further, I pick up the wolves. Sending Achilles and Callie a message through our mind connections, I tell them there are five wolves about half a mile east of Achilles' position. He and Callie head there with others from the tactical team.

"Come on. Where are you?" I send out the call through telepathy again, hoping maybe Rhea is somewhere shielding herself. Again, nothing. The teams and Commune have trained for such scenarios, but Rhea has not. My fear for her grows with each second.

She's been through so much already, alone as a child, and now abducted and thrown into a strange world with no memory of who she is. The desperation I feel each second I'm not with her drives my search for her harder and faster.

Pushing my aura to the farthest reaches, I extend it several more miles in all directions as I run as fast as light travels through the Commune and the grounds, searching for her.

Then I sense him about six miles away, resting atop a hill.

The Onyx Alpha and the man I plan to kill soon sits in human form, cutting a red apple with a pocketknife. A growl escapes my throat at the thought of him so casually spectating, sending his pack into harm's way. I pick up the image of him and his surroundings on the light beams, letting me see him clearly.

He knows I'm watching.

A menacing smile stretches across his face, and he turns his eyes up. If I were standing before him, we would be looking each other in the eye. But I know he can't see me. He's only feeling the reach of my power brush against him. With a nonchalant chuckle, he tosses the half-eaten apple to the ground and stands before turning and walking away.

"The wolves are leaving," Achilles reports. *"We're going to stay on them a bit longer."*

"Flint and I are restoring The Coat now, Hermes." Terra updates from their positions in the War Room.

I've got to find Rhea. She *has* to be here somewhere.

It's been four hours, and there's still no sign of Rhea. Achilles and I are in the War Room with some tactical teams. Checking the cameras a dozen times, the last time Rhea was seen, she walked into the portal in Atlas's office. Then the camera went dark for half a second. When the camera comes back up, the screen shows an empty portal. Standing in the War Room, we've called the entire tactical team to search, and they are covering the grounds in and out of The Coat and the Commune buildings.

Atlas is interviewing Commune members who were not accounted for during the attack to root out any accomplices. Callie stands on the rooftop of the Commune with currents of Wind flowing through every tree and under every rock, feeling for signs of Rhea. Sensors and Sonars are looking for traces of her presence, hiding or masked.

But there is no sign of her.

I stare at the monitors, playing over the evening as Commune members run to a shelter or their defense positions. We know the wolves breached the Commune several hours after she went missing. Someone inside the Commune is working with the wolves and helped them take down The Coat. A portion of Lupo's pack circled the outer perimeter while he watched from afar, and then they left. I close my eyes, and my shoulder blades sink as a thought barrels into my mind.

It was only a test.

Of course, it seems so obvious now. The wolves were only testing to see what our responses would be with a real attack. They didn't have time to cause any damage because The Coat was restored within two minutes, so they didn't attempt an assault. The purpose of tonight only served as a trial to see how quickly we can mobilize, maybe even see what our lower-level Elementals do during an assault. In an attack, they would be the most vulnerable.

Like the Shifter community, Elementals have a variety of strengths and weaknesses. Shifters rank their communities in order by the size of their wolf and challenge through combat. The biggest and best wolves become the Alpha of their pack, with a Beta who is their second in command. The ranks continue downward to the lowest level, Omega.

Elementals determine our ranking by the Elemental Test. It's an obstacle course for our physical prowess and coordination while staged attacks are launched by monitoring Elementals. The objective is to use your powers to defend yourself, and each time a course is completed, they take a harder one with stronger Elementals until they can go no further.

In an attack, our lower-ranking Elementals could not defend against the top ranks of Shifters. The Coat was taken down at a time when most members were congregating in a similar area. So, when the alarms sounded, most flooded the same secure zones, which could be a vulnerability. If the wolves target them, we could lose many Elementals, or Ares could gain a lot of new prisoners.

As I think about the wolf attack and the purpose of tonight, a warm, pulsing sensation in the center of my stomach steals my attention. The sword necklace around my neck begins to shudder against my chest as the topaz stone on the hilt of the charm glows blue. A gift given to me from my father long ago. I wear it daily, never taking it off—a twin of the necklace Callie regifted to Rhea two days ago.

"If you ever feel scared or alone, hold it and remember you're not."

My father's words ring through my mind as the pulse of the charm quickens to a vibration. My core reacts, tightening my abdomen as if a large surge of power is building, and I'm preparing to absorb it. Darting my eyes between the Elementals in the War Room, they seem oblivious to anything happening. They hover over monitors or whisper to each other, apparently unaware.

"What is it?" Achilles is at my side, noticing the shift in my demeanor.

"Don't you feel that?" I ask him, holding the necklace in the palm of my hand. Looking at it blankly, he shakes his head no.

"Go." he says quietly. "I've got things covered here. Go find her."

Closing my eyes and extending my aura, I let my powers guide me. Blind to the world, the glow of my abilities steer me through the Commune halls and out the door. Running like a lightning streak, I sense the familiar opening of a portal ahead, and the force pulling me intensifies. Pushing myself faster, I can feel her aura. Finally, the one soul in this realm I've wanted to sense for hours and she's finally returning.

Rhea.

It's not a portal of light, but of shadow and darkness as her body rushes to meet the ground. My powers ache to be near her, and my aura projects itself, pulling me to her. Jumping to greet her, I catch her in my arms and soften my landing.

Her body is as cold as ice, and her skin is pale blue with dark purple rings around her mouth and eyes as if locked in a freezer. Pulling her close, I breathe in the scent of berries and vanilla as if it's the very air I need to live. Heating my aura to warm her, I encase her in my arms and my powers. Thankful she is okay, but angry she was in harm's way again, I push back the growl that wants to escape from my chest and whisper my promise.

"I found you. I'll always find you."

21

Rhea

"Why do you always pass out? I think that's the real question we should be asking." Hermes' tone is gentle and on the cusp of teasing.

I'm cold, and he's walking through the woods in the pitch black of night. My body is nearly convulsing with chills from that strange place.

"Put me down. I can stand."

"Not a chance."

Ugh! He's carrying me like a doll, and the position leaves me little choice but to wrap my arms around his neck, putting my face dangerously close to his. Squirming in his arms, I wriggle my elbow between us and push against him, swinging my legs over his arm. Tipping myself out of his hold, it's much farther down than anticipated. I stumble while he curses at my sudden disruption.

"How tall are you anyway?" Even in the dark, I see a gleam in his eye before he answers.

"Six foot four." Brushing my hands down my pants to smooth them, I resume the trudge through the woods in the direction Hermes was heading. I roll my eyes in the dark and hope he can see me. Smug bastard probably loves being so big and makes it his entire personality. My mind instantly wants to wonder about the size of the rest of him and I immediately have to scold my train of thought. *Calm down girl.*

"Where are we going?" I change the subject to stop myself from thinking about grasping Hermes' wide shoulder while he picks me up, allowing me to wrap my legs around his six-foot, four-inch frame.

"You should probably see Athena."

"I'm fine. I'm just cold."

"What happened?" He pulls tenderly on my arm, making me stop and face him.

"I don't know. One second I was in the portal trying to go to the library, and the next second I was in outer space."

"What?"

"See for yourself." I hold out my hand, and he steps forward, taking it. My frigid fingers are so cold they burn against his warm skin. He shoots me a stern look before he wraps me in his warm blue light. Casting my eyes to the dark forest floor, I give him access to the memory with his Mirage ability while I mask the comforting satisfaction of feeling him around me. When Ares' muzzle protrudes from the misting fog, he cuts his eyes to me.

I can't explain how, but something in me recognized his power. A muscle memory buried inside knew him, even though I have never met him. Just like the other nights in my dreams when I saw him and was aware of who he is. It's without explanation, but part of what I intend to understand.

With the memory over, I sigh and shake my hands. The cacophony of howls in my memory makes my anxiety spike, and I swear I can hear the distant echo of a wolf even now.

Resuming the walk forward, I extend my aura outward and

am proud when it gleams easily again. The bright silver shining in the darkness hurts my eyes, and I squint and recoil. I chuckle my apologies and work on toning down the intensity. Focusing on my fire ability, my silver aura takes on a yellow-orange center as I heat myself.

"Getting better at that, I see," Hermes says, taking long strides beside me. The compliment makes me smile, but I push it away, remembering my status. *I'm just a job.*

"Thanks."

"Rhea, something happened while you were missing." His tone lacks its usual mockery, and dread stops me abruptly. I chew the corner of my lip, waiting for him to continue.

"Was anyone hurt?" My throat clamps, thinking about people I'm getting to know, and care about, getting hurt.

"No, it was just a test of our response. But it was Lupo."

The world dips, and my stomach drops to my knees. Stumbling on nothing, my feet nearly come out from under me. Hermes is quick, reaching out and taking my hand. The surge of quivers that transfers from his skin to mine where we touch forces me to choke back a cough. Pulling my hand away, I close my eyes, fighting against the tears that want to flood my cheeks.

These people are not safe because of me.

As we resume our trek back to the Commune, the pine needles and twigs crunch under our shoes disturbing the quiet forest of pine trees. My unfocused eyes roam the trail, and Lupo's words echo in my mind.

"Don't worry, goddess; you performed perfectly."

There is a motive behind capturing me, then letting me go. And a reason behind testing out the Commune's defenses. But what is it? Ares and the werewolves are playing a game with the Elementals and are using me as their pawn. I can't sit here waiting to be hunted by Lupo and his pack again. I can't be responsible for hurting people because I don't know how to use my powers.

My throat burns as I think of leaving. I want to tell Hermes that I'm going to sneak into the portal room and use it to take me back to my apartment. I'll pack a bag quickly. I have a car and money in savings. I can hide my powers again, locking them away, and stay on the move for a few weeks. Then I'll return when it's over, when the Equinox has passed, and they can't use me to multiply their army.

But the words stay a secret in my mind, stuck around my breaking heart. Finding a sense of understanding and belonging is all I have ever wanted my entire life. And now I've found it, I'm going to run away. But it will keep them safe from being hurt because of me.

Anxious to get this plan in motion, I look around, the lights of the Commune not yet visible. *This walk is taking forever.*

"Can't you teleport or something? You're Hermes." I huff as my foot slips down a smooth rock.

"Not exactly." he chuckles. "Though, I'd be happy to transport you more expeditiously if you like?" The playfulness has returned to his tone, and I roll my eyes. He is probably a big flirt with everyone. A playboy that knows he's hot and knows exactly what to say to women to make them pant over him.

"No thanks." I bite back.

I'm angrier now, spending the rest of the walk back in my head with thoughts of running away and Hermes' endless flirting. I stop at the wide stairs that lead up to the rear portico. I'm starving, but I need to pretend I'm going to sleep so I can sneak out. The Commune is quiet, so it must be well after midnight.

It would be the best time to move before everyone wakes up for their morning assignments.

"Rhea, thank goodness you're okay." Atlas greets us at the top of the stairs. "Let's have Athena check you out quickly." Leaving no room for debate, Atlas has a portal ready, delivering us to an open hall. Callie and Achilles are sitting on a bench, and Callie rushes to me with a hug. A knot forms in my stomach, knowing I will lie to her and leave. "Come sit, and we'll wait on Athena."

"What happened to you tonight?" The look in Atlas's eyes turns from warm to cold in a second, and it coats me in gooseflesh.

"I don't know." Keeping my tone even, my chest rises and falls, giving away my false bravado.

"Atlas, what is going on?" Hermes steps toward Atlas, and Callie lowers beside me on the bench. Achilles remains on her side, with his arms crossed over his chest. The tension in the hallway is rolling in like fog coating the morning dew. My eyes flick between Atlas and Hermes.

"I found the Elemental that took down The Coat for the Wolves," Atlas says coldly.

"Who?"

"Flora." He looks to Hermes, Callie, and Achilles for their reactions. Shock and confusion are painted on their faces as their eyes widen, and their mouths gape as they look inquisitively at each other. "Her vines crept up the tower and hit the switch to reset the system. They were too small for the cameras to detect, but I interviewed her."

"That doesn't make any sense. Flora and Zephyr are the two most gentle people in this realm." Callie argues. "This can't be right."

"How do you know she wasn't being controlled or forced to do it?"

"She made a hemlock potion to make herself forget the memories so the Sensors wouldn't be able to detect her. But just because she doesn't recall the memories doesn't mean I can't see them." Atlas removes his glasses and rubs one of his eyes with the back of his hand. His weariness shows in his bloodshot eyes.

"What is going to happen to her?" Callie asks, the blood draining from her face and leaving her ashen.

"She'll be sent to the Labyrinth." Sympathy coats his words as they pull tears from Callie's eyes. I read about the Labyrinth in a book from the Commune library. Two hundred angels from the realm of Hel were part of Chaos' army and helped him murder other Titans and take over realms. They were captured and imprisoned at the Labyrinth on the island of Crete. Shadow creatures that spill out of Elysium are given free rein inside the Labyrinth. Immortals are sentenced to time in the Labyrinth when they break the law or the Mortal Treaty— some for decades, others for centuries, even millennia. Everyone is eventually sentenced to the shadow realm when they finally give up their fight inside the twisting tunnels of the Labyrinth.

"Flora will never survive there. Isn't there anything you can do?"

"I'm afraid not. It's already done."

Hermes tilts his head to the side, his eyes narrowing at Atlas. "What else."

Atlas returns his glasses to his face and hesitates, keeping his eyes on Hermes as if a silent conversation is passing between them.

"She mentioned a name. Someone from long ago. Ares' daughter, Persephone."

Everyone gasps, and Callie looks at Achilles with questions in her eyes.

"The Battle of Thermopylae." he says quietly.

"Exactly." Atlas points his finger at Achilles whispered words.

"There is no record of Ares having a daughter," Hermes says, placing his hands on his hips. Confusion runs through my mind trying to piece together their conversation. Of course, I've heard the mythology of Persephone. Daughter of Zeus and Demeter and married to Hades in a weird outcome of events.

"Many truths were hidden when Ares destroyed the Library at Alexandria," Atlas explains.

"How do you know it was destroyed?" I ask.

"Because I was there, and I saw it burn." His look upon me is still detached, and an eerie foreboding makes the hairs on the back of my neck rise. "Ares' daughter, Persephone, is the only Elemental known to possess control over all four elements, other than you."

My world is getting smaller and on the verge of collapse. Could I be the daughter of the God of War? Could my real name be Persephone? That would mean the memories of my family are a lie—something I keep telling myself can't be true. All the years of memories can't be fake; there has to be something real in there. But Atlas said I believe the lies too much.

"Why didn't you tell us before?" Hermes' tone rises at the end of his question. Perhaps offended Atlas didn't share the information sooner.

"I didn't want to divulge what I knew until I was certain Rhea could be trusted," Atlas answered. "Ares and Hera had a daughter just after fleeing to Gaea. Hera fell ill within a few hours of arriving in the realm. Within a few days, she had a terrible delivery and died. She never even held her daughter."

"Then all the Elementals that were with child began miscarrying or dying. And no Elemental has been able to carry a child since we arrived here. Ares's daughter was the last Elemental born in this realm."

"Is that why Ares went insane?" Hermes asks coldly.

"I wouldn't say he went insane," Atlas says. "An obsession festered and boiled inside him, spreading like a disease; it consumed him. He blamed Chaos for making us flee here and wanted his revenge. And you know the rest of the story from there."

"What happened to his daughter?" I ask, cutting my eyes at Hermes as I pick my thumbnail nervously.

"We don't know. She went into exile with him. The last time we saw her fight was during the Battle of Thermopylae. We brought a massive army, and he had fewer fighters in comparison. But he had her, and they annihilated us. It took us hundreds of years to locate him again, but we never saw her after that."

"So, you believe I may be Ares's lost daughter? Wouldn't he have recognized me?" I ask, tears welling in my eyes. "What about my parents, my family?"

"I'm not sure," Atlas says, returning to his theory. "Maybe you are his daughter... and he knew it. Or perhaps he only made it seem like he was torturing you because he knew we'd save you and bring you here? It is a curious coincidence that Calypso seemed to get the worse of the beatings, don't you think?"

Callie stands firmly. "You're out of line."

"I don't like your implications, Atlas. You think she is working for Ares and using us?" Hermes asks defensively, putting himself between Atlas and me.

"I'm saying we don't know anything about her. She shows up out of the blue at the same location as you and distracts you; Callie follows her, and both are abducted. It would make sense if Ares were trying to infiltrate our Communes or use her to steal information."

I can't breathe. My chest feels like it weighs a thousand pounds, and the edges of my vision begin to darken. He thinks I'm a spy.

"What?" Hermes pushes closer, and Atlas takes a step back. "How can you honestly say that? You've gotten to know her. You've seen into her mind. Do you think she could be capable of being a spy? Lying to us like that?"

"I agree with Hermes." Achilles nods his head. "But H, you have to admit, there is logic in Atlas's thoughts."

The friends turn to face each other now. "Don't you dare." Achilles meets Hermes' gaze, unwavering.

"Hear me out. Maybe she doesn't know. What if Ares changed her memories and gave her new ones? She may have no idea. Atlas has been struggling to get past her repressed memories, right?"

A portlet chimes, and the door opens. Achilles and Hermes stare a moment longer before they step away from each other and turn. We all look to the portal expecting to see Athena.

"Great," Hermes mutters as the Headmistress and several of her guards march toward us.

A coldness seeps off this woman like an iceberg floating in the Arctic with no warmth for thousands of miles. Her hair hangs in a low, tight bun, and it seems she presses her mouth into a thin line so frequently they have permanently deflated into a perpetual frown. Her dark gaze looks me up and down with her sunken, wrinkled eyes that show her age. If Hermes and the others are tens of thousands of years old and look to be in their mid-twenties, I wonder how ancient she must be.

She points at me.

"Place her in custody."

"What?" I exclaim as two of her guards surround me, each taking an arm.

"Athena is dead." The Headmistress declares.

"I'm sorry, Hermes, but this is for your own good." Atlas raises his hand, and Hermes immediately drops to the ground, unconscious.

"Run." His voice rings in my mind as he falls.

22
Rhea

The guards pull my wrists hard, and metal locks click around me, each one making my shoulders flinch and my eyelids flutter—Thaumium collars and cuffs are affixed around my neck, wrists, waist, and ankles. The hallway flashes and turns into the dark caves reminding me of the wolves preparing Callie for her lashing with Lupo. The enchanted metal tugs my powers deep inside me. Accustomed to being locked away, they slide into their protective box without a fight and the sense of complete loss and emptiness makes me feel like an open cavern.

"What is happening here?" Achilles booms, rushing to Hermes' unconscious body and turning him over. Callie moves to her brother's side as well as they both work to sit him upright. He's limp and leans up against Achilles.

Two more guards enter and push them aside; pulling Hermes up by his arms, they drag him from the room in a set of his own cuffs. His head hangs low and lolls around roughly. The guards yank me out after him. Looking behind, I find Atlas holding Achilles back with his hand over Achilles chest. Callie appears calm, but the storm brewing in her eyes is filled with an unspoken promise. She nods at me just as she did in the caves. *Just survive.*

"Hey! It will be okay! I'll find out what is happening!" Atlas yells to me.

We're carried into a portal, and when the door reopens, the basement of the Commune is before us with its vast grey halls and corridors. Nothing of the grandeur and craftsmanship of the ancient structure above extends down here.

I recall the mundane room where I first woke up after my rescue. Athena is the first person I met, and her death is what is bringing me here again in a twisted turn of irony. Closing my eyes to the past few mornings when she took me to the lake to practice my aura control. The feeling of her golden warmth was like being wrapped in protective sunlight, and I'll never forget it.

The sense of blame is heavier than the four chains binding my powers. Hermes said no one was hurt tonight, but perhaps the Wolves had more than one goal. Maybe the disruption was only a distraction so someone could murder Athena.

With a harsh grip on my arms, the guards push me into a room while the others continue down the hall with Hermes. I fall forward, lose my balance, and slide across the floor. The door slams behind me, and a lock secures me inside. The empty room is cold with its cement floor and cinder block walls: no table, chairs, vents, or windows.

I search for my powers, but they have retreated deep into their box. Not even a splinter of magic is there. Nothing.

Sitting up, I inspect my arms that burn from the guard's rough handling, and my knee throbs from hitting the floor. I scoot against a wall and hug my knees into my chest. My insides are in a vice grip of turmoil, and my eyes burn with angry tears.

So many thoughts surge through my mind, and I shut my eyes tightly: flashes of the caves, Lupo, Damien's haunting corpse, the void with Ares, it's all too much. I rock back and forth, hugging my knees, pressing my eyes into them, and sobbing.

I have to get out of here.

A few minutes tick by, and sound in the hallway carries into the room as people pass, but no one enters. Rushed footsteps move along the hall outside, retreating from my holding room. I lay my head on my arms again, and my tears slowly stop. It's quiet again outside the room, and I begin to think of a plan. If I can remove one of these cuffs, I know I can break out of the others. I did my first day here. But uncertainty lingers within me. Should I go back for the others as well? If I leave, won't it make me look guilty?

Atlas believes I'm a planted spy and Ares' daughter, and now it seems I'm also suspected of causing Athena's death.

A cool breeze enters the room, soft and refreshing. I search for the source of the current, hoping I can yell into the vents for help, but I find nothing. The calm wind swirls gently around my arms, relieving the burning. It whistles as it churns around the room, whipping my hair.

I stand and back up to the rear of the room.

"Rhea," The wind whistles my name—no. Not the wind. Callie's voice runs over the wind. It's hypnotic, like a field of tall grass moving in a harmonious dance as the wind moves gently through it.

"Move away from the door." her soft voice sings to me.

Backing up as far as I can, I crouch down and cover my head with my cuffed hands. The collar around me neck and chest pinch at me and confine my breathing. The wind swirls intensely in the center of the room. A visible funnel forms, and growls. The vortex swirls around the door, and the hinges creak and groan from the force. The funnel shrinks in on itself, and the rotation intensifies. Finally, a snap occurs as the wind dies.

The door pushes open, and Callie emerges, breaking the hinges to free me from the room. She grabs the collar around my throat and runs a piece of metal across it. The collar falls away, and elation drums in my chest as my powers soar within me. Immediately, my anger surges, and the three cuffs around my hands, ankles, and waist drop away.

"Come on! We only have a few minutes." she exclaims with a quirk of her brow. I meet her at the door, squeezing through the small opening. She grabs my hand and helps pull me through.

"Where is Hermes?" I ask.

"We can't get him right now. Achilles will take care of that. We must get you out of here first." she says, running into a portal.

"I'm not leaving him!" I say steadfastly, not wanting to leave anyone behind.

"It's not an option, Rhea! You and I *have* to leave now. We only have a few minutes. Odysseus and Penelope are causing a distraction. Achilles will get my brother out, and they *will* meet with us, but we must go now."

Pursing my lips, I release a frustrated huff and reluctantly follow Callie, irritation etching hard lines across my brow as we run down the hall. I don't want to leave Hermes, but they are more experienced than I am.

The portal delivers us to a large tactical room. Similar to the room we used to prepare for our visit to Damien, this one houses heavy-duty vehicles like hummers, ATVs, and dirt bikes. All of them are matte black, and cages of equipment and weaponry line the room's perimeter. In the center is a large, round platform with a glowing blue disk.

A small matte black sports car sits on top with both doors open; the windows are tinted dark. This must be where they prepare for missions and transport their vehicles. I imagine Hermes and his teams of fighters gearing up and heading off to some dangerous assignments.

Achilles is at a console and rushes to Callie, embracing her. "Everything all right?" he asks, scanning over her with his eyes, looking for injuries. They have changed clothes and are wearing all-black tactical gear and boots—Callie's long, platinum hair is in a high ponytail.

"Yeah," she says breathlessly.

"What is going on?" I ask, joining them at the console.

"Callie will fill you in, but you two must leave. Another attack could be coming, this time for something worse. I'll go get Hermes, and we'll meet you." He holds her gaze and places his hands on each side of her face with tenderness. "Be careful."

He kisses her, and they lean their foreheads together for a moment. Releasing each other, Achilles looks at me and nods reassuringly.

"I'm sorry for what I said back there about you. I don't believe you are working with Ares."

I return his nod with my own.

"Let's go!" Callie says to me and takes off for the driver's side of the car. Before we can shut our doors, Atlas rounds the doorway and stops abruptly. He is breathless, and his clothes are soaking wet below the knee.

"I should have guessed." He bends over, putting his hands on his knees and breathing deeply. "You sure about this?" he asks Achilles with a stern look on his face.

Achilles nods in agreement. "Hermes is right about her, and we need to get her out of here."

With a pause, Atlas looks at the three of us before nodding in agreement. "Okay. I'll buy you a few more minutes if I can. They know she's gone, and the Sensors are looking for her."

"Thank you," Achilles says. And with that, Atlas turns and makes his exit.

Callie and Achilles give each other another look of adoration and unspoken reassurances. Then, she shuts the door and starts the engine of the car. Achilles focuses on the control panel in front of him, pushing buttons. The circular disk the vehicle is sitting on glows brightly, and there is a gentle hum as it powers up.

"I need you to help us with somewhere to go. The usual places we would go will be obvious, and it will take them longer to track us to a mortal location. Just think of a place and put your hand on this panel here." Callie points to a blue rectangular panel fixed in the car's center console.

"I just think about it, and the portal will take us there?" I ask. Callie nods her head.

I take a deep breath and think for a moment—Aunt Demi's. Having a visual of the house fixed in my mind, I place my hand on the panel. The glow of the round platform intensifies, and a zap sounds around us. It feels like being a bug and flying into a zapper, sizzling with cool, white light.

Instantly, it's night outside. The tactical room has vanished, and we're sitting on the dirt road that winds up to my aunt's house.

"Just up there." I point to the house. A few windows have warm light spilling out, and a small stream of white smoke escapes the chimney. It's Sunday night, so my aunt will be in town at the local rec center for Bingo. My heart pulls, wanting to hug her. Callie presses the gas pedal and drives us up the dirt road to the house, rocks splaying behind the car in her haste. Having reached the home, Callie exits the vehicle and looks around.

"Hold on before we go in." she says, holding her hand up. I pause, waiting, and hold my breath. The wind rises and rustles the nearby trees, swishing them back and forth with the movement. Callie closes her eyes and lifts her head as if she is listening. After a moment, the wind dies, and she opens her eyes.

"We're clear. There's no one here." Callie calls to me as she gets two bookbags from the backseat of the car, tossing one to me. Retrieving the hide-a-key from the flower bed, I unlock the door, and we enter.

"There is some gear in that bag for you. Change your clothes and get what you need from here. We'll only be here a few minutes while we wait for Achilles and Hermes."

Callie stomps up the stairs behind me as I go to my old room. Dumping the contents of the bookbag on the bed, there are tactical boots, belts, clothes that match Callie's, small weapons, and Damien's journal.

"Jesus," I exclaim. "Fill me in while I change. What is going on?" I change my clothes while Callie looks through the window, keeping an eye on the long dirt road that leads up to the house.

"Athena was murdered, burned from the inside out with Soul Fire. Her lab was trashed, and the recording of your session was gone. They think someone was robbing her office, and she walked in on them. It must have happened during the break-in when everyone was occupied with the wolves."

Sitting on the bed to lace the boots, a wave of sadness

238   REBEKAH SINCLAIR

washes over me. Athena has been amazing and kind since I first opened my eyes at the Commune. I can't believe such a wonderful person was killed in such a terrible manner. Set on fire until her immortal ichor burned.

Callie continues, pulling me from my sad thoughts. "And someone burned the box of Damien's research."

"Shit," I exclaim. "You had this on you?" I ask, holding up Damien's journal. Callie nods her head. Callie joins me to help fix the weapons around the clothing, strapping a small knife to my ankle, under my pants, and other small handheld weapons around my belt.

"How will they find us?" I ask, shifting things around the belt for more comfort. "Hermes and Achilles?"

Callie smiles at me. "Fated mate connection. Come on. We need to leave soon. Do you need anything else from here?" she asks, holding up the book bag to return a few items to it before handing it to me.

Looking around the room, I'm unsure what would be helpful, given the circumstances. My life before was not very exciting, and I didn't have an arsenal of weapons for such occasions. The poster of Angel Falls floods me with memories of Hermes: sitting in his lap a few days ago as he came into my mind to calm me. I look away quickly before Callie catches my red face. One of the books on my shelves shines out at me with its gold foil lettering glinting in the yellow light of my ceiling fan.

The Abduction of Persephone by Hades
By Daphne Helios

Throwing the journal in my bag, I grab the blue leather-bound book from my collection and add it. It's just mortal mythology, but with the mention of Ares's daughter, maybe something in the legend will be a clue.

"Okay, I'm ready. Now, tell me how Hermes and Achilles will find us." I demand again. Callie chuckles as she turns to leave the room and begins explaining over her shoulder as we exit the house.

"Achilles and I are fated mates. We can always find each other.

"How come he couldn't find you when we were abducted?"

"The Thaumium cuff blocks more than just our powers. He couldn't sense me, so Hermes had to try, and it took several hours before he finally found us. Except he found you, not me." Callie says, raising her eyebrows up and down in a teasing way. My throat catches, and my cheeks flush slightly. *I didn't know that.*

As we step out of the house, the sound of several vehicles in the distance grabs our attention, and we stop immediately, straining our ears to listen.

"That's not Hermes and Achilles," Callie says in a low tone. "They were meeting us on foot. We need to run."

"This way!" I start for the woods. "There's a clearing just through here, and we can hide." Callie nods and we take off in a hard sprint.

Callie is faster than I am and reaches the woods before me. She hurdles over a downed tree and crouches behind it, scanning the area, waiting for me to join her a few steps behind. There are no lights from the vehicles, but the sounds of the engines roar louder as they get closer.

"Let's go... quickly," Callie says in a breathy whisper. I nod, and we begin sprinting through the woods toward the clearing.

Jumping over rocks or stumbling over downed branches, the urgency to distance ourselves from the house is burning through me like wildfire. My heart beats so intensely that it feels like it's about to rupture from my chest at any second. My legs feel like lead as I drag them through the forest floor coated in a layer of dried pine needles.

A loud bang echoes in the night behind us. It's a small explosion. I can only assume the door to the house is being blown open, and I thank all the stars in the night sky that Aunt Demi is not home. They'll soon find we're not inside. It gives me the motivation needed to go faster.

A moment later, the echoing of voices returns behind us. My assumptions prove correct when I hear the word "*empty*" echo through the night. The clearing is just ahead, and I didn't expect it to be so bright. I had hoped for more coverage from the darkness. *It's a full moon.* It probably doesn't matter if wolves are hunting us; their predator eyesight is impeccable during any of the moon's cycles. The forest dims as if the goddess of the night has taken mercy over us and pushed clusters of puffy grey clouds over the moon.

God, Hermes. Please hurry.

The clearing in the woods opens and exposes a dark field before us. I push us to the other side, and we crouch behind fallen trees, panting heavily from our run through the woods. The anticipation of the approaching horde makes the stillness of the woods much more ominous. I hold my breath, hoping it will prevent them from finding us.

After a few minutes, dark figures begin materializing out of the shadows of the trees on the other side of the clearing, moving slowly and without noise. My heart beats louder, and I'm confident they'll be able to hear it like a bass drum. I count twelve people, but I suspect more are hiding in the woods.

They must know we are here.

The wind picks up, and Callie has a determined and fierce look on her beautiful face—such a solid contrast to the cheery and kind disposition she usually has.

"Cal? Rhea?" A familiar voice calls to us. Callie lets out a small gasp and looks at me.

"Flint." she mouths his name silently. I gasp in realization.

"It's okay, girls. We're not here to hurt you. We're here to help you escape. Come on out. It's safe." Flint calls out across the clearing. He's still scanning the area and doesn't know exactly where we are. After Flint's stunt in the closet, I wouldn't trust anything he has to say. Something about him doesn't sit well; if someone were a wolf in sheep's clothing, it would be him.

"Achilles and Hermes are here, behind us." Callie tells me, but the familiar knot in my abdomen pulls tight; I knew he was near before she spoke. "They'll be here in just a second."

My heart jolts, relieved, and chills run from my scalp down my spine, knowing Hermes is here. The pair of friends silently slide beside us within a second, joining our crouched position behind a fallen tree. It's eerie how quietly and proficiently they move with their imposing frames made of long limbs and lethal muscles.

Achilles puts his arm around Callie, and they exchange a quiet look. "We're okay." she says.

I look at Hermes, wanting so badly to leap into his arms and tell him how glad I am he's here, longing to press my lips to his and tell him I'm so happy he's safe. Instead, we make eye contact, and he nods once before returning his focus to the show of force in the clearing.

Just a job.

"It's Flint." Callie indicates with her eyes to the figure in the center of the slowly approaching group of people. They wear dark clothing like ours but also have black hooded masks. A low growl escapes Hermes' chest at the mention of Flint.

"How many?" Hermes asks.

"Twenty-five total. Fifteen are here, and another ten are working around the sides." Callie says plainly. "Two others are approaching the clearing now."

"We'll take care of them," Achilles says. "You two get out of here."

"What? No way! You can't take twenty-five people alone!" I exclaim quietly.

"Oh, that reminds me," Hermes says, pulling a small rod from his tactical pants and handing it to Callie.

"It's from Odysseus and Penelope. It's portal tech from their Commune to be safe." I notice he has a bloody bandage wrapped around his wrist.

"What happened? I ask, concerned.

"We have trackers in our wrists. I had to cut mine out. It took a few extra minutes, so I'm sorry we're late." He winks and his gaze flicks down at my mouth for a split second, making my stomach flip. I repeat the mantra in my mind. *I'm only a job, a protective duty, a shiny new penny that will soon be dull.* Don't read into these small feelings because it's just my desperation and hopefulness.

Glancing at Callie and Achilles' wrists, they have small bandages in the same spot. They have also cut out their trackers and abandoned their lives because of me. The notion only adds to my growing list of guilt. But I don't have time to dwell on the thought when a deep, gravelly voice rings through my mind, pulling a gasp from my throat.

"Rhea?"

"What is it?" Hermes says, scanning the clearing at the unmoving occupants.

"It's Ares. I can hear him." My body trembles as Ares' eyes flash in my mind from the moments in the darkness only an hour ago.

"I've missed you for so many years. Where have you been hiding all this time?" He echoes in my mind.

"Callie, find him." Hermes directs, his eyes darting quickly around the clearing. The wind rustles in a swirl around us, and the branches of the trees dance with Callie's power.

"He's not here." she whispers.

"He says he's missed me," I say, horrified. Hermes growls again, and his eyebrows furrow in anger.

"Like hell. Let's stick to the plan. He's not going to show his face here." Hermes says. There is movement in the clearing, and Flint removes his mask, revealing his face. Two more shadows emerge from the wooded trees. Someone is being pulled along and is struggling.

Horror strikes the pit of my stomach. One of the twins, Pain—the one I scorched in the face back in the caves—holds a woman tightly with his muscular arm around her neck as his eyes reflect white across the darkness.

"That's my Aunt."

"Rhea? I know you can hear me." Flint says across the clearing. "You know, deep down, you belong with us. Come to me."

With no control over my motor functions, I stand without thought. Flint immediately turns to me, a wicked smile creeps across his face. Disgust seeps through me at his expression, twisted with something unnatural—nothing like the flirty redhead back at the Commune. An unbearable force tugs within me, like a lasso tied around my waist, pulling me into the clearing against my will.

"Rhea!" Aunt Demi calls out to me, her eyes wide and scared. "What is going on?"

"No!" I exclaim, but the sound doesn't escape my mouth. I feel like a puppet on a string while a marionette controls me. My feet move independently, taking me closer to Flint.

"Shit! Stay down!" Hermes says to Achilles and Callie. Hermes stands, drawing Flint's gaze to him, and it turns murderous.

"Hey there, H. Hoped you would show up too." Flint's smile is downright evil and looks more like a snarl.

"Rhea, what's happening?" Hermes pleads. My mind wants to run to him, but my body is moving like a puppeteer is pulling the strings. Tension is building within me as my fear grows. My legs move, taking another uncontrollable step forward.

"Come home to us, Rhea. We've missed you." Ares' voice rings again. A shiver of revolt slides down my throat, threatening to make me vomit at the thought.

"Never!" I call back, hoping he'll hear me.

"You can't deny your fate. You'll only delay the inevitable. Succumb to it now and avoid bloodshed."

Another step forward.

"Rhea?" Hermes' voice sounds injured. There's pain in his tone; he's scared. Frightened I'm leaving of my own will? Afraid I'm choosing Flint over him? I pull against the invisible cord pulling me away from Hermes. The more I fight, the greater the force pulls against me. My foot moves again in another step toward the clearing.

I clench my fists and tighten my abdomen. The force is beginning to bubble, like it's boiling inside me. The pull increases, and a growl resonates in my mind as Ares's anger rises, but I hold myself in place.

"Rhea, think about your aunt. You don't want her to get hurt." Flint taunts me, his man still holding my aunt hostage around her neck.

I can't let them hurt her. If I'm an Immortal, there is no way she can be my real aunt. But that doesn't mean she didn't raise me. It doesn't stop me from loving her as my aunt and seeing her as my family. She is the one who held me after my family died, letting me cry for days and days while pulling me out into her garden and teaching me how to grow tomatoes. She made me love history and antiques as she took me shopping with her on weekends and let me keep all the money from her farmer's market for the honey candy I would sell.

She may not be my family by blood, but she'll be my family by choice.

"Rhea, please." she whimpers, but he squeezes his arm tighter around her neck, cutting her off.

"No," I command myself. *"I'll never go with you."*

Ares' scream reverberates through my brain, turning into a wolf's howl. The noise rings around my head, and the pressure roiling within me can no longer wait to be released. I gather all my strength and disgust toward Ares and compress it inside me until it forms a tight, swirling ball.

"I will kill her, Rhea." Flint's eyes darken, and I know he is telling the truth. The monster is revealed. Sweating, I fight against the pull, and the force within me trembles, trying to be released.

"MINE!" Ares screams.

"Never!" I yell defiantly through my mind to Ares. Flint nods at the man holding my aunt, and she is dragged away, back into the dark of the woods. She screams and kicks, her feet making tracks in the dirt. The turmoil grows as I desperately fight against the unnatural force pulling me toward Flint. I'm bound as if I were locked within a dozen Thaumium cuffs, tight as a mummy.

"No! Please!" Aunt Demi's frantic cry echoes through the clearing. "Rhe—"

A gunshot rings loud in my ears, and her voice cuts off instantly before she finishes screaming my name. My head snaps towards the flash of a muzzle in the woods as I stop my struggle and look.

The force inside me explodes, and my scream emanates from my soul, rising out of my throat across the clearing. I'm trembling uncontrollably, but it's not me. It's the ground beneath me quaking. The unbearable war inside me breaks loose like a dam, and my powerful black mist careens out of me. A resounding boom billows outward as the mist speeds across the clearing. Flint is struck with the power of the force and tumbles until he skids to a halt. The others in the clearing are blown back, slamming violently into trees or knocking into each other.

I collapse to the ground, turning to meet Hermes' eyes. "Hermes," I call his name weakly, stretching my arm out to him.

"Now!" he calls.

A gust of wind drives behind me as Callie stands and

commands her element to propel her into the clearing. Achilles blasts fire bolts behind him, following her into the clearing. They land beside each other and begin an assault with their elemental magic. Hermes drops to my side, picking me up in his arms and turning to run in the other direction.

"Help them," I say faintly.

He smiles wickedly. "They can handle themselves," he says, not stopping. "Surely you've heard of the Rage of Achilles? It's nothing compared to Callie when she gets pissed. And they just fucked with her best friend, so they're toast."

My head snaps to the clearing when he calls me her *best friend* and my heart warms with the sentiment. I clutch the sword necklace as the clearing glows orange under Achilles' fire. Callie has conjured a tornado surrounding the spot where Flint was standing. The wind is rolling around, whipping her gorgeous platinum hair that seems to almost glow in the night.

Achilles shoots a jet stream of flames by her side into the vortex, and they swirl, rising to the top. The air fuels Achilles' fire, intensifying the blaze into a terrifying sight. The gushing wind sounds like a locomotive barreling around the clearing. Flint's convoy of masked figures screams in their futile attempts to run away. There is no escaping Callie's wind.

She raises her arms, building her power into an apex, then slams her hands downward. The cyclone erupts into a dozen lightning bolts, striking everyone in the clearing as thunder booms across the sky. Giving their enemies no time to recover, Achilles spreads his arms outward, and the fire swirling within the cyclone roils downward like a rolling wave, setting the people within the clearing aflame. The combination of lightning and fire is a terrifying sight. The growling tornado deeply rumbles through the night, raging with Achilles' fire burning inside Callie's wrath.

I'm awestruck at their powers, having never seen anything like this before; watching them move together is incredible and beautiful. Every action is a compliment to the other. The small practice session Achilles and Flint held before seems like children practicing compared to this.

The clearing is no longer in view, hidden by the trees, and I clasp my arms around Hermes' neck tighter as he continues running. Satisfied no one has followed us, Hermes finally slows and sets me down on my feet. He's breathing heavily and keeps an arm around my waist. His eyes are scanning the woods for movement as I see and feel his light power pulse outward, searching farther than his basic senses can reach. He reaches into his pocket with his free hand and pulls out a small wand, just like the one he gave to Callie.

"Hold on to me," he says.

My arms are still around his shoulders, and I stand on my toes, trying to reach higher around his neck and hide my face against him with my eyes closed. He chuckles and tightens his hold around my waist.

"I've got you." he whispers into me.

Like the portal back at the Commune, the wand emits a solid blue glow. The noises and temperature within the woods we just inhabited are gone in a flash.

Instantly, my eyes are burning, trying to adjust to the bright sun's light—such a stark contrast to the night sky of the woods. I raise my hand to shield my eyes when a coil snaps around my wrist, yanking it back by my side. Another whip snaps around my other wrist, and my hands pull behind me.

What now?

"Damn it!" Hermes mutters under his breath, raising his hands in surrender. I look at him, panicked, seeing a coil of something wrapping tightly around his neck. My powers are sluggish inside me from expending them in the clearing just a few moments ago.

"Hey, Deuce. It's been a minute." His voice strains, and he forces a pained smile. Hermes doesn't appear alarmed as he innocently holds his hands out. Tears run from my eyes at the bright light, but I force them open, trying to see the danger and understand what is happening.

A woman steps from behind us and directly before Hermes, looking up defiantly at him with her piercing green eyes, almost glowing like emeralds with glimmering specks of yellow near their centers. She is not intimidated by him even though he is taller and significantly larger in size. Dark tattoos cover her caramel skin, climbing up her arms in intricate twists and letterings, beginning at her wrists and disappearing under her black tank top.

"You have some nerve showing up here. I'll assume you're here to repay your debt?" The woman says with a thick African accent.

Did we teleport to the other side of the world?

"Ummm... not exactly. We need your help." he replies, still grinning.

"Who is this?" the woman asks. She is motioning toward me with a nod of her head.

"This is Rhea. Ares is hunting her, and we need your expertise." Hermes answers.

The coils around my wrists unravel, and I'm free. Hermes is also free of the loop around his neck. The whips slink away from us, gliding back toward the woman, and I realize it's not whips but her hair. The serpentine tendrils retreat into a complex coil of braids at the top of her head.

Gold bands and stone beads adorn her braids, and a charm of a gold snake is wrapped around one of the thicker braids hanging near her face; a matching gold coil snake encases her bicep with two green jewels for eyes.

"Rhea, this is Deuce." Hermes looks at me, his smile returning. A wicked gleam flashes over his eyes. The woman extends her hand, and I cautiously take the welcoming gesture.

"Only this fool calls me Deuce." she teases. "You can call me Medusa."

Enjoy this bonus content!

23
Hermes

When Rhea met Medusa, the look on her face was **priceless.** Deuce and I have been friends for a long time. We've gotten each other out of many tight spots over the millennia, and she is the Head Mistress of an all-woman Commune in Kenya. With the potential of a war with the Shifters on our horizon, not only do we need her warriors and support in talking with other Commune leaders, but there is no one better in this realm to help train Rhea on her powers than Medusa.

"Penelope and Odysseus got here about ten minutes ago." she says as we walk to the portal that will bring us into her Commune.

"You knew I was coming, and that is how you welcomed me?"

"I'm still mad at you. You owe me a new bar for throwing a vampire through my last one." she says gruffly as we step onto the portal. Rhea and I join her, and the bright blue light delivers us inside her Commune.

"That leech had it coming." I tease Medusa with a wink, earning me a punch to the bicep.

"Come on; I've got some food in my office. I hear we need

to talk." Medusa leads the way through her Commune, and Rhea's head is on a pivot, looking at everything with wonder.

The Commune sits on the rocky side of Mount Kenya. Nestled directly in the mountain, the facade is an arced metal and glass enclosure with Medusa's trademark signet, the Black Mamba twisting around two carved pillars of basalt rock, framing the entrance to her largest community space. Inside, the hewn mountain walls and ceiling are high with warm yellow lighting, making the large interior seem cozy and welcoming. A massive mural along the left wall depicts Medusa and her immortal life's work, fighting against human trafficking.

The spread of food in her office immediately beckons me, and I all but pull myself and Rhea to the steaming platters as soon as we enter. Neither of us have eaten in nearly half a day, and Rhea looks like she could pass out any second. Penelope goes to Rhea, embracing her, asking if she's okay and whether she needs anything. Odysseus approaches and grasps my shoulder with a firm squeeze.

"Glad to see you are both okay. Callie and Achilles will be coming soon?"

Before I can answer, they round the doorway and enter Medusa's large office. Thankful for the sitting area—separate from her desk and wall of trophies—it provides us room to move without being on top of each other. Medusa's office dons a white motif with a classy and modern aesthetic, complimenting the traditional Kenyan touches. Sleek lighting and contemporary furniture contrast beautifully against the brightly colored clay masks and other tribal artifacts lining her wall.

Callie and Achilles are coated in sweat and soot from their

fight against the wolves. Rhea runs to Callie with an embrace and inspects her for injuries. Seeing their care for each other, my heart flares, and a small smile lines my face. As we gather in the room, the swirl of power from the Elementals blends and mingles with the friendships. Within, I search for Rhea's power, missing the feeling of her energy as it pulsates through her aura. Masking herself carefully, her powers must be tampered down, and I can't pick up on her.

"Flint got away," Callie reports.

"But I gave that scarred twin a new burn for the other side of his face." Achilles devilishly grins at Rhea. She ducks her head down at the floor, crafted of mountain rock and smoothed to a shine with faint etchings of coiled snakes, so small they are nearly imperceptible.

"My aunt?" Rhea asks with a small voice.

"They took her body. I'm sorry."

Callie bites the inside of her cheek and brings Rhea into another hug. She melts into it briefly before straightening her shoulders and wiping the tears from her eyes. Rhea nods in acknowledgment to Callie, either understanding what Callie is saying or telling Callie she is okay and still holding together.

Giving Rhea a moment, I walk with Medusa over to her desk.

"I'm sorry about Athena, Deuce," I tell her privately, looking around her office at the memorabilia on her built-ins— gifts from survivors she has helped.

Medusa looks down at the floor before answering. "Athena and I were a long time ago." Rhea snaps her attention to Medusa, surprised by her comment. The human lore about Medusa are the jealous doings of Eris and it's the main reason I hate that woman. Medusa and Athena suffered enough at the hands of Ares. Medusa didn't need Eris spreading her filthy lies as well.

"Doesn't matter. I'm sorry."

"So..." Medusa changes the subject, putting her black boots on her desk and crossing her ankles. "Eat and tell me what riffraff you are bringing to my doorstep this time. Why have you gathered us here, Hermes?" There's a knowing smile on her face at my fondness for mischief.

I explained meeting Damien, and Callie steps forward, pulling her cell phone from her bookbag. She was smart to scan all the loose documents and digitize the recording as a backup. None of us knew someone would destroy everything before we could dive into it properly.

Callie plays Damien's recording as Medusa, Penelope, and Odysseus lean forward and strain their ears to hear every syllable of the message. The three Elementals meeting here run two of the largest Communes in this realm. If war is indeed coming with Ares and the Shifters, they won't be able to stay out of it. Ares would eventually target their Communes, bringing the fight to them. If Eris is going to ignore the warning, I'll bring the other Communes in to help on my own.

"Man, can you imagine how off-balance this realm will be if Ares doubles his army?" Medusa shakes her head.

"Millions would die. Entire countries would be overrun, and the mortals would fall into war." Penelope rubs her hand nervously against her collarbone as she ticks off the list of items in jeopardy. Odysseus places his arm around her waist, pulling her into him.

"I have a wolf that owes me a favor." Medusa stands, pulling her phone from the back pocket of her black leather pants. "I'll set up a meeting and see what he knows about this."

"Oh yeah? And how does a Werewolf come to owe Medusa a favor?" I ask, amused to hear this. Our species are rarely friendly with each other.

"You owe me a favor when your sister is lost in a human trafficking ring, and I save her, regardless of her being a Lycan. The pup and her brother run a shop in Nairobi where I have some businesses. I'll have someone stop in. Do you know who the Elemental is they are looking for?"

Rhea stops in the middle of taking a large bite of grilled meat. Putting the food back on her plate, she raises her hand, a flush rising on her cheeks as she calls the room's attention to her. Medusa snaps her eyes to Rhea and gives her a thorough inspection from head to toe. Leaning forward in her chair, she rests her elbows on her knees and presses her hands together in front of her.

"Rhea may have had her memories changed, and Atlas has a theory she could be Ares' daughter," I tell everyone. This last part is news to Penelope and Odysseus, who lean into each other, exchanging whispers.

"That sounds like a job for the Oracle." Medusa's eyes gleam at me, knowing fully why I stay away from *her*.

"We've got three weeks until the equinox. I'm sure one of your Mind Mages can figure things out before then." I dismiss her suggestion, which makes Medusa chuckle and shake her head.

"Always so stubborn. But it's her choice." Medusa looks around me and speaks directly to Rhea. "You want to go see the Oracle, just let me know, and I'll make the arrangements." She gives Rhea a wink before rolling her eyes at me.

"I'm sorry, I don't have separate cottages for everyone." Medusa opens the door to one of the guest cottages for Rhea and I. "Next time you are going to show up with a horde of Elementals and life-shattering news of impending doom, give me a day or two heads up." She smiles with mockery in her tone, putting Rhea at ease. "We just rescued a large group of mortal girls from a trafficking ring in China, so we're tight on space." Her eyes darken, but she keeps the smile on her face.

"Oh my god," Rhea says in a breathy voice.

"There are no gods in those dark pits. Only weak men who designed a system to give them the illusion of power." Medusa faces the harsher cruelties of Ares' influence over the world. He's designed systems of feeding humans and Immortals into rings of torment. The gladiator arenas of the Roman Empire have been moved underground for the rich and powerful to feast on their demented fantasies. Medusa and her warriors find them and make sure they can't operate ever again. But each time they take down one facility, it seems like two more appear.

"How did you dispose of this batch of monsters?" I ask, knowing her pension for leaving behind stone remnants of her victories.

"You know how much I love to see the mortals dig up my rows of terracotta soldiers a few thousand years later." Her emerald eyes sparkle as Rhea's mouth gapes open.

Leaving us to clean up for the evening, some clothes have been prepared in the cottage along with some essentials. We'll get more things tomorrow for our stay since we didn't have time to prepare to leave the Atlanta Commune.

Rhea is still cleaning up in the bathroom attached to the

only bedroom in the cottage. Dressing the bare mattress with sheets and blankets, she exits the bathroom as I put the last pillows on the bed for her.

"Oh! Sorry," Rhea's eyes linger on my abdomen before she quickly averts her eyes, avoiding looking at me without my shirt. I would do anything to know what she's thinking and if her body is reacting to me as I am to her. A moment longer, she'll know exactly what effect she has on me.

"It's okay. I'm sleeping on the couch." My voice is a bit deeper than I intended. My mouth is practically salivating at the thought of tasting her. The thin pajamas she is wearing are challenging my resolve to avoid touching her, devouring her, and seeing what pretty noises she makes when she comes.

But I know she likely has a mate somewhere, destined to be her perfect partner and the balance to her Elemental powers. Getting involved with each other would only add unnecessary strain to an already terrible situation. Since the Fates left the rest of my immortality for suffering without my mate, I don't have to make it difficult on Rhea.

"Hermes, you're tired, and it's been a long day—even though I was in a black hole for most of it." she scoffs, trying to avoid eye contact. "I'll sleep out there."

"Well, if it makes you feel better, I have no problem sleeping in the bed with you," I smirk, taking the pillow and throwing it back on the bed. I lay down on my back with my hands behind my head and close my eyes. Rhea remains standing, still looking at me.

"Something I can help you with?" I purr, eyes still closed. I allow a sly smile to creep across my face. I can feel Rhea's gaze heating my core, and her irritation only makes me smile more.

"No thanks. I'll take the couch." She finally responds,

reaching for an extra pillow. I open my eyes and take the pillow from her hands, tossing it back onto the mattress.

"I'm just kidding; lighten up." I close my eyes again, still smiling a little. "But if you try to sleep on the couch, I'll throw you over my shoulder and bring you back here."

My stomach jolts at the thought, and I hear Rhea's sharp intake of breath.

Maybe she would enjoy that? I'll save that thought for my shower tomorrow morning.

Standing a few extra seconds to think about her options, she concedes and draws back the covers on the bed to climb in next to me. Having her so close is going to make this torture. I can imagine the feeling of her skin on my hand as I draw my palm over her ample curves, running down her smooth thighs and squeezing her into me. I have to stop my thoughts and turn my back toward her. She tenses as I move, still frozen on her side of the bed.

I sense a tension building as she lies behind me in the bed. But it's nothing to do with me. Something is bothering her. Turning to face her, I prop my head on my hand, and she keeps her gaze firmly locked on the ceiling above us.

"What's bothering you?"

Like a balloon deflating, she sinks further into the mattress and releases a breath of pent-up air. "I can't feel my powers. Since being in the clearing, they're gone."

"Rhea, you've been through an extraordinary chain of tragic events the last few days. Today was exhausting in every sense of the word: physically, emotionally, everything. You need some rest and answers to your questions. Medusa is the most amazing teacher and trains the realm's best warriors."

She finally looks at me briefly, but that one look could save a starving man in the desert. Her honey hair splayed across the pillow is a curtain of satin and I want to run my fingers through it.

Gods, it takes all my strength to stop from reaching across the short distance between us and pulling her face to mine. The feel of her soft lips would be sweeter than warm honey. If I let my mind wander further, I would pull her under me and wrap her in my arms. Like the moon protecting the earth, I would shield her from any pain or sorrow that may try to reach her.

"Were they partners?"

"Who?"

Her gentle voice pulls me from my thoughts, and I blink away the visions of her parted mouth open in ecstasy as I slip my fingers between her thighs. She chuckles as she turns toward me, propping her head on her hand and mirroring my position.

"Medusa and Athena."

"Yeah." For the next hour, I fascinate Rhea with the true tale of love, ripped away to nothing by Ares.

After Athena lost the Trojan War against Ares, Medusa turned herself in and pretended to pledge loyalty to him. She wanted to find out which Elementals were betraying us and putting Ares a step ahead. She wanted to know where his secret bases of operations were.

Ares found out and sent Medusa home. Athena disagreed with the plan to begin with and was happy when Medusa returned safely. But when they woke up the following day, Athena's memories had been manipulated. She believed Medusa forced herself on her, and their fated mate connection had been severed.

Athena stopped fighting after that and turned to healing.

Medusa went down a dark path of revenge for a while but eventually found her passion and saw the sunlight again.

Rhea hangs on my every word without moving. Her eyes widen and her mouth gapes throughout the story. Her eagerness to hear our history and her bewilderment is endearing. It's nice having someone to talk to after so many years of silence. I miss the days lying in bed with Juliette and talking the night away until sunrise. A part of me wants to think I can have this again.

But it's selfish of me to want Rhea. I had my fated mate, and we shared amazing lifetimes of love together before she died. Like Juliette and I, Rhea needs the freedom to find her mate and be happy.

Finishing the story, Rhea releases a large yawn and stretches onto her stomach. She hugs her pillow as her dark eyelashes sweep the tops of her cheeks.

"Try to relax and get some sleep. You'll be safe here."

The crowd in this little cottage stretches it beyond its limitations. Callie and Penelope spent the morning printing out the dozens of items that used to live in Damien's tattered box. Odysseus arrives with a laptop in the crook of his arm, and Achilles follows behind him. Medusa, Rhea, and I scoot the little table in the dining space to allow room for more chairs as everyone huddles around the cozy room.

"Damien said to follow the Zeta Wolf, and we took his hint literally. He said, 'Follow the breadcrumb trail.'" Odysseus begins, hooking his laptop up to a projector that shines on one end of the dining space.

"You think the Zeta was leaving behind intentional clues?" Rhea asks.

"Maybe," Odysseus answers. "Intentional or not, the best trail to follow is a money trail. It's so obviously traced in the mortal records."

"Odysseus and I looked into Lucas' finances, property, and anything that could tell us about his locations." Achilles takes over, walking up to the projected images and pointing to different places on a map with marker indications. "He's been off the grid for several months; we haven't found any trace of him, but Lucas does own several properties directly or through the dummy corporations run by his packs."

"Many of these dummy setups exist throughout the Americas, but one stands out. Lucas is the only one listed on the corporation and owns three properties." Achilles points to the map's three red markers in Mexico, Egypt, and China.

"Looks like Orion's Belt." Rhea chuckles under her breath. Odysseus and Achilles look at the map and then turn their heads to her. "What?" she asks, her shoulders dropping as she slumps down in her chair at the attention.

"Damien's recording. He mentioned an alignment to Orion, making this equinox more powerful." I answer. "What if the ritual will be at one of these locations, and Lucas owns a pack-house for each location?"

"That would narrow things down for us. We'll look more into these three locations." Achilles offers.

"Who is the Oracle?" Rhea asks.

I scoff, and Medusa chuckles. "The Oracle of Delphi. She's a powerful Dark Mage and Sonus Elemental." Medusa answers.

"Oh my god, the Oracle of Delphi!" Rhea's eyes widen as large as saucers in amazement. "What's her name?"

"Hecate. Hermes doesn't care for her, but don't let him dissuade you. If anyone in this realm can help you, it's her." Medusa kicks her feet up on the table and crosses her arms, sending me a challenging glare.

"She's a con woman, Deuce."

"I would call her an entrepreneur. You need to let the past go." Medusa waves her finger accusingly at me, then turns to Rhea. "Hecate is a Seer; she sits at the crossroads of fate and gives advice. What people do with her advice is up to them; they choose their path and go down it." Satisfied with her opposition to me, Medusa pretends to be bored by looking at her nails.

"The Oracle used to advise my father when he was a Commune leader. He sought her *advice* before meeting Ares, and then he was murdered. She could have at least kept him alive." Sitting back in my chair, I cross my arms over my chest. I'll never forgive her for letting him walk away that day, but if Rhea wants to meet Hecate, I'll support her.

"You know as well as I do her prophesies don't work like that. There is no way she could have known." Medusa places a hand of surrender on my knee, moving us past our disagreement and returning her attention to Rhea. "I'll set up a meeting with Hecate for you."

Rhea's spirit seems to come alive as the day wears on, and my pull toward her hums louder as nightfall looms ahead. It seems to be the time of day when I feel Rhea. Something about the darkness or the moonlight makes her glimmer and buzz with electricity.

The day drags on as we look eagerly into the documents and research from Damien. Sorting it into different categories and placing it in timeline order, our small group of six hunches together in that small dining room for nearly the entire day.

Breaking for dinner, we head to the dining hall. Rhea looks much more relaxed than when we arrived, but her head hangs low as we walk to the dining area.

"Hey, you okay?" I nudge her with my elbow, my hands stuffed in my pockets.

"I was just thinking about my aunt." she confesses as she wipes a tear away. I want to move closer to her and put my arm around her in comfort. I think about the surprise Callie and I worked on back in Atlanta for her—the library that would have made her light up with happiness, and she may never see it now. It feels like such a stupid thing to hold in regret, but I wish I could have shown it to her.

"I'm sorry." Silence walks with us the rest of the way to the dining hall. Nothing else needs to be said, and being among an audience, I know Rhea wants to rein her emotions back in before someone notices.

Dinner is hearty and delicious, filled with chatter and laughter in the dining hall. Grilled meats and vegetables sit alongside steaming stews and platters of rice and ugali. Medusa shows Rhea how to ball up the stiff cornmeal porridge and grab a clump of tender beef stewed in brown sauce and tender greens. Rhea melts into the bite of steaming food, and I savor the sight of her enjoying the simple pleasure.

"Hermes, I heard from my source in Nairobi. They are at the Commune gates and want to talk with us." Medusa tells me quietly, but not enough because Rhea's attention peeks as she turns toward us, listening.

"You want to meet a Werewolf?" I ask her, smiling as I know her eyes are about to widen.

"Are you serious?" she asks with a look of shock and interest, making me chuckle. "Are they... safe?" I grab her hand, standing along with Medusa to follow her out of the dining hall.

"No one in their right mind would think of double-crossing Medusa." I wink at her, and she bites back a smile.

"If they try anything, I'll turn them into a pillar of stone," Medusa says pointedly, making Rhea gasp.

"So, you can really *do* that, then?" We begin the short walk to the Commune portal, and Medusa explains her elemental power.

"I'm an Earth Elemental." Her braids uncoil from their intricate nest atop her head as she talks. "I move these stone beads in my hair and whip the shit out of people who get out of line." She feigns an attack at me and claps one of the braids on my calf.

"Come on!" Our banter and friendly teasing pulls giggles from Rhea, and the sound is like the trumpets of Hel, playing a symphony of glory from their great celebration halls.

"The body contains earthly minerals. I manipulate these and petrify the minerals, spreading them through every organic matter and fossilizing it to a solid block of stone."

Watching Rhea as she listens to Medusa, the thoughts behind her eyes must be full of color and vivid imagination. Amazed by Medusa's explanation, she launches into a series of questions that Medusa answers with pride, pushing her shoulders back as we reach the portal.

Twin platforms sit, one inside the Commune and one at the mountain base in the plain below for Commune comings and goings. Waiting for us on the plain is an impressively sized man and petite woman. The man wears a simple black suit and tie with a white shirt, fitting a businessperson in any metropolis. His bald head shines in the night against his ebony skin and he holds my gaze as we approach.

His sister wears the traditional cloth of Kenya, and her kanga dress is brightly colored with orange, yellow, green, and black shapes of all forms. The glow in the man's eyes indicates his wolf is lurking within him, but his companion has not yet turned her into a wolf. Her eyes don't reflect in the golden hour of sunset as she stands with an air of recency and delicate poise.

The aura coming off him is Alpha energy, but he from what Duece says, he became a Lone Wolf to protect his Lycan sister. Pity. He could make a lot of change for better if he lead a pack. Several of Deuce's warriors are standing on each side of them, but as these guests are in her debt, I doubt they will attempt anything.

"Kellan, thank you for coming." Medusa greets them as she puts her hand out to him. Kellan bows slightly before grasping her forearm as she grasps his. "Zara, nice to see you again." Medusa smiles at the young woman, and she also bows but flashes a giant smile at Medusa as they embrace with a hug.

"You know this is dangerous for us," Kellan says with a deep voice that matches his dark complexion.

"I wouldn't call on you if it weren't important," Medusa answers. "We need to know if you have heard of anything planned in the Americas for the Autumn Equinox."

Kellan glances down at Zara, and her smile fades as she shifts uncomfortably.

"They are looking for someone," Zara says. "The Maiden of the Triple Moon Goddesses." Rhea and I share a look of understanding that we both think Zara may be referring to her.

"Persephone? She is only a myth." Medusa dismisses.

"Legend, yes, but still real. Wouldn't you agree, Hermes?" Kellan says to me. My eyes narrow at him.

"Who is Persephone to the wolves?" I ask.

"Not the wolves—Ares. She is his daughter." Kellan's eyes dart to Rhea with his answer. Instinctively, I move in front of her and keep my gaze fiercely on Kellan. "Relax, Ferryman. Medusa has retained my loyalty for the past fifty years when she saved my sister. I would never move on someone under her protection."

"There is a legend among our kind that Ares created the wolves from his power, but the Maiden is a unique Light Elemental with the power of the moonlight." Zara breaks the tension with her explanation. "When we are of age, her magic calls our wolves out during the full moon of our packs. She's been missing for a long time, which has devastated the wolves."

I think about the vision Rhea shared of the cave and having her direct the moonlight into the box to tamper down her aura. That was only a Mirage but could she be capable of something like that in reality?

"How so?" I ask her.

"You may have noticed I have no wolf yet, even though I am beyond the age of maturity, and my wolf should have emerged when I was a young pup," Zara explains. "The Maiden disappeared around four centuries ago, and ever since she vanished, wolves have a harder time emerging without her presence. It's mostly affecting female wolves. But if a female wolf cannot transform, neither can her pups. Those of us who cannot transform are less desirable for mating. Who wants a wolf-less pup? So, the females that can shift into their wolves are bred for offspring like factories, often forced to bear the pups of multiple males."

"That's horrible," Rhea says quietly.

"Without the goddess, we're not sure how many more generations of wolves there will be before we're left to legend like the gods." Kellan finishes.

"That sounds like the missing piece of the puzzle Damien needed," I whisper to Rhea quietly.

"Why is Ares looking for the Maiden now after so long?" Medusa asks.

"Their family bond sparked to life twenty-four years ago. Ares threw a large party to celebrate her return, and the wolves have been helping Ares hunt her ever since. Ares is near desperate to find her now more than ever." Kellan tells her.

"The Autumn Equinox being the driving factor?" I ask.

"Indeed. Ares has a powerful and ancient Mage accompanying him to the equinox. Sometimes she successfully pulls the wolf spirit for a Shifter, maybe a small pack, but not nearly powerful enough to help all of us." Zara answers. "The goddess is the key since the power of transformation comes from her. They plan to find her and have a mass calling to pull all the wolves from those like me."

"Hermes," Rhea whispers. She doesn't need to finish the sentence. I know what she fears.

"Shhhhh. It will be okay." I say, pulling her into my arms and holding her tightly. Resting my cheek on the top of her head, she clutches at my shirt, pulling herself into me. Medusa looks at me curiously with a crooked smile on her face before turning back to Kellan and Zara.

"Thank you for the information. It's been very helpful." Medusa takes Kellan's hand again and then hugs Zara. I turn with Rhea, and we start toward the portal with Medusa following us.

"I won't lie to you, goddess," Zara calls after us. "I would give anything to have my wolf. You don't know how much we suffer being outcasts or bred like cattle. But the Mortals are worse. What they do in secret circles to someone like me... The Labyrinth would be a more pleasant alternative. Medusa saved me from that fate, and I'll be in her debt forever. We will not betray you to Ares."

"Thank you," Rhea says with a shuddering voice, holding back tears. Zara and Kellan exchange a look, speaking in that silent way only siblings can, and he affirms her promise with a nod.

The morning sun has not yet risen, and birds are beginning to sing a chorus outside the cottage window. Medusa is waiting outside when I open the door, and I'm curious about what she has planned today.

"Morning. I thought you would like to enjoy a beautiful Kenya sunrise." Her happy smile has a speck of sadness behind it, and we turn toward a path leading up the mountain. We walk silently for a moment, and I'm unsure what to say to someone so legendary.

"I reached out to Hecate, but she's not around right now. Sometimes she slips into the shadows for a few days but will return soon." Medusa finally breaks the silence, and I nod, looking down at my feet as we walk. "Hermes said you were having some concerns with your powers, and you were working with Athena?"

I smile, thinking of Athena's lovely demeanor and calming presence. I didn't know her long, but she was nurturing and helped me without hesitation. I'll never forget her. Hermes told me about Medusa and Athena, and my heart broke thinking how devastating that must be. Knowing your perfect soulmate was ripped away from you and having to live a life of eternity without them.

"She was helping me with my aura. At first, I couldn't control it at all. Now, I think I locked it away because it's gone."

"We'll see if we can get that working again. I have a feeling it's all up here." Medusa points a finger at her temple.

The hike up the mountain is pleasant and easy using a well-worn path. The people of the Commune frequently use this route, and it's a relaxed walk. Medusa turns us toward an alcove where there is an overhang. We sit in the chill of the morning, the light of dawn barely creeping over the horizon and turning the night sky into shades of green and yellow.

"We don't know where our abilities come from; they are just a part of us, as much as our eye color or height. But they are part of the world around us as well. Everything flows with energy, and the same cosmic dust that created this mountain also created you. Pulling your powers needs to come from within you just as much as it does the world around you. Close your eyes."

I do as Medusa instructs, closing my eyes and lifting my head to the sky as the sun kisses the horizon, saying 'good morning' to the mountain.

"As the sun rises, you can feel the energy of the night fade away and make room for the energy of the sun. They feel different. Suppose you think about the mood of nighttime compared to the mood of the day. It's the energy. Learn to feel it around you; feel your elements within that energy and move them to your will."

My forehead scrunches, trying to use my senses and feel the space around me. The night air at my back is cool, like the moon's white light. The crickets still sing loudly, and cold washes over me, making me shiver.

"Good. You feel it." Medusa says approvingly. "Now, put your hand down on the ground. Feel the minerals of the earth, moisture in the soil, cold rocks soon to be heated by the sun, seeds waiting to be blown by the wind to their beds to grow..."

I think about each of these, and my fingertips tingle while that cool chill runs down my arm.

"You feel something?"

"I think so."

"Wonderful. You can open your eyes now." The sky shifts colors by the moment and turns from deep blue and grey like night to orange and pink in the morning. "As you practice, meditate on your powers, feel them around you, feel for the energy in the air. Your powers will learn to react to the energy you sense, but it takes practice and patience. We don't try to rush the sun rising to hurry the day along, do we? No amount of coaxing or begging can pull it above the horizon any faster than it will happen. Why on earth would you rush yourself to learn powers so unique? Don't be so hard on yourself, okay?" Her smile is genuine, and she takes a deep breath, closing her eyes to the horizon and allowing the rising sun to fill her with the first rays of light.

Medusa is much different from her legend—in the obvious sense, she is not a Gorgon with the body of a snake—but in other ways as well. The angry monster sulking in a cave and petrifying anyone who dares to enter is not the crusader sitting beside me. She is confident, calm, calculating, and passionate about looking out for those who need her help. She is fierce and unapologetic. So many things I wish I could embody.

We sit silently as the sky is painted with the fiery colors of the sun. It truly is the most beautiful sunrise I've ever seen. Of course, I've never sat on top of a mountain in a beautiful country to watch the sunrise, so I may not have many examples to pull from. Medusa's words sink in as we sit. I know I've been pushing myself and adding unnecessary pressure. I'm just so afraid of disappointing everyone, afraid I'm not enough to stand up against an enemy they have fought and lost against for so many years.

But the thought of having people who understand me is worth all the world's treasures.

"We'll start with water," Medusa says as she circles me. "I think it's one of the easier elements: potent and versatile." The outdoor training arena is an ample, open space with a level dirt ground. Wooden fencing encircles the area, separating spectators from those inside.

A small group from the Commune is gathered on some wooden benches, bleached and worn by the Kenyan sun. Hermes sits on top of the fence, watching. A woman with deep chestnut hair and bright hazel eyes walks toward us. Her head-scarf frames her delicate face, but the ferocity in her eyes tells me she holds a strong force within her. It reminds me of Callie and her petite frame and sunshine personality, so underestimated until she rips you off your feet with a tornado. The woman approaches like a calm river before turning a bend and meeting powerful rapids.

"This is Anahita. Ana is a Freshwater Elemental." Her kind smile reaches up to her hazel eyes as she greets me. Extending her arm, deep brown swirls and curls of henna ink her skin. She waves her delicate fingers toward a thin stream of water running down a gully of the mountain.

"Close your eyes, please, and I'd like you to concentrate on the feeling of the water moving around you." Ana's voice is so serene, almost hypnotic. I follow her directions, holding one of my hands and closing my eyes. "Feel the energy of the water in the stream."

I do as Ana says, letting her hypnotic voice entrance me. "Feel the water running downhill; imagine the ripples." As she talks, I can feel the calm swell of my power stretching inside me like a cat after a slumber. There is a sluggishness, but still, it makes me hopeful. I focus on the coolness of the water and imagine it bubbling down the stream.

"Now, extend your hand toward the water—relaxed. Imagine a connection between the stream and your hand." I extend my arm and the internal rolling moves down through my arm toward my fingertips.

"When you feel ready, think about the water moving toward you. Focus on that connection and use it like a channel, directing the water to you." It's an odd sensation—a slimy almost, sludge-like consistency, meandering from my stomach to my arm. I push it further toward my fingertips, but there it stays, held back and unable to breach the stream beyond.

I push harder and feel it resist now. Like a recoil, the sensation goes back, fighting against a thin membrane that won't let my powers through. A gleam of sweat beads near my hairline as my brow furrows in concentration. With trembling hands, I try harder. I finally drop my arm and concede defeat, gasping for air.

"Let's try something else," Medusa says, looking at Hermes with a mischievous smile.

"I don't think I'm going to like this." he says, standing and cautiously making his way toward us. Medusa and Ana step off to the side, and she whispers into Ana's ear.

As Hermes approaches, Ana laughs with a sinister snicker, and my nerves spike.

"Your goal is to free him." she says plainly. "Ready?"

What?

Medusa and Hermes face each other like a pair of gunslingers in an old-fashioned duel. The stories of Medusa tell a tale of misery and revenge, depicting her as a snake-haired, soul-eating monster. The fighter before me makes it difficult to imagine such a myth can derive from her tall and strong form, but I soon realize how truth gives way to legend. The sound of rattlesnakes fills the arena; it is soft and distant at first, but it grows louder and more ominous.

Hermes shuffles his feet, changing his stance and turning his shoulders to reinforce himself but remains steadfast in her path.

Medusa's braids begin uncoiling themselves from her crown, shaking rapidly, mimicking the mannerisms of rattlesnakes. They emerge from her woven nest of braids like vipers untangling from their den, sneaking, and slithering along to attack their prey.

Hermes looks to his feet and quickens his breath, his nostrils flaring under tension. I look down; I see his shoes and legs slowly turning to stone as if he is becoming hardened, petrified rock, weathered by time. The formation creeps gradually up his legs toward his knees, and he struggles in vain to free himself.

Ana sashays around Hermes to stand behind him and lavishly waves her arm to the stream behind her. Another snake-like formation of water slithers along the ground towards Hermes. A nervousness builds as my mind races with what I can do to help. My stomach ties in a dozen knots, and I stand frozen.

The water formation slides along the dirt and corkscrews around Hermes' ankle. The petrification of his legs must prevent him from feeling the water because he doesn't react as both elements overtake him. A raging cloud of uncertainty forms inside me, threatening to spill outward in an uncontrollable avalanche of panic.

"Stop!" I plea. Neither woman relinquish their slow assaults, and Hermes remains steadfast in his focus on Medusa.

"Deuce, let's not get carried away." he warns with a concerned undertone in his voice.

"She should stop stalling and help you. It will become harder to breathe in a moment." she threatens, cocking her head to the side. Like lightning, one of her serpentine braids shoots out and winds around Hermes' neck, tightening around him. He grabs at the coil in a futile effort to loosen it as two more braids constrict his wrists and force them downward.

"I would take a deep breath if I were you," Medusa warns. Hermes does, just as the water column morphs into a sphere, encasing his head in a violent swirl.

"I don't know what to do!" I exclaim, running up to Hermes and looking for a way to help free him. Fear and panic are beginning to blind me as tears flood my eyes and a boiling sense of helplessness consumes me. I raise my hands to cover my ears and muffle the terrible sounds of Hermes' struggles and grunts, crushed under Medusa's tightening coils and Ana's suffocating water confinement. He's visibly in pain, suffocating. *Will they let him die?* Terror gives way to anger, and the battle inside me roars, wanting to break free but locked inside.

It's as if I'm trying to split myself in two, tearing off my flesh while it instantly heals. An eternity passes while I watch Hermes struggle; a guttural noise escapes him, forcing an agonizing crack within me. A deep chasm finally fractures with a thunderous boom. A violent wind billows outward from my abdomen, whistling with an ear-piercing shriek.

Medusa careens backward with her braids and limbs flailing uncontrollably in the sudden gale storm from me. Ana is knocked off her feet and swept away; the water she had been controlling disappears in a fine mist. She bounces clumsily along the ground, flailing for something to grab onto.

The force of the eruption throws my head and arms back, locking me in a bitter standoff with the unrestrained wind emitting from me. In an instant, the chasm shuts, extinguishing the loud noise promptly. The great wind vanishes as quickly as it arrives, and the loss causes me to drop to my knees, gasping for air to clear my blurred vision and regain my surroundings.

Hermes also drops to the ground, spitting and sputtering from the suffocating entrapment, now freed. The rocky exterior of his petrified skin has blown away, and a few final remnants are dissolving back to their natural state.

I lunge to him, tears streaming down my face and pain ripping through every fiber of my muscles from the sudden release of power I just discharged. Medusa and Ana slowly recover, soiled with dirt and water, dazed by the violence of the force. Ana adjusts her headscarf back in place as the bystanders also recover themselves. The onlookers stand and straighten their clothes, looking shocked.

"Are you okay?" I ask Hermes in a shaky voice.

"Rhea, that was amazing," Hermes says, raising his hands to each side of my face and cradling me. "I'm fine. They wouldn't hurt me." He reassures me softly, and tears stream down my face with more vigor.

"That, my friend, was sheer power. Truly impressive." Medusa says to me with a giant smile on her face. "I bet you could summon a hurricane if you wanted to." She turns to Hermes and pats him on the shoulder. "Let's consider your debt paid." He only huffs at her, shaking his head back and forth while she walks away, chuckling.

25 Hermes

Rhea feels perfect against me. Having her in the same bed has remedied my sleepless nights, filling my dreams with vivid images of the goddess who is overtaking my mind. Holding on tightly to the last tendrils of a perfect dream, I keep my eyes closed, still imagining Rhea's glorious curves nestled against me, with my arm thrown over her waist. Her soft, wavy hair splashes against the white pillow, filling my senses with her sweet fragrance.

It's pure bliss.

Awareness overtakes the dream, and my eyes fly open. I freeze, not breathing or daring to move a muscle, realizing her body is flush against me, and we are cuddling just as I imagined —the feel of her hip resting perfectly in the palm of my hand as her curves are burrowed into me makes it near impossible to form a coherent thought. The small sounds escaping her partially opened mouth, send surges of arousal through me. My mouth waters, wanting to nuzzle within the curve where her neck turns to her collarbone and evoke more of those moans.

Holding my breath, I ease away from her, ensuring I don't

disturb anything for fear of her waking. A small miracle happens when I stand fully, and she still sleeps. I sneak into the bathroom and exhale as I shut the door without waking her.

As I shower, I resolve to push my feelings for Rhea away and focus on her training. I'll drown myself in the research for Ares and his lair. Anything to keep my mind from flocking back to her.

I should ask Medusa for another cottage today to get some distance. The victims from China have been treated and moved on to more permanent locations for recovery; Medusa owns many factories where the women and children were taken. The women are given jobs with great pay, homes, medical care, and therapy. Their children are provided with education and clothing—new lives, safety, full bellies, and a means to stand independently.

We only need to get through the next two weeks. I can move on once we prevent the Equinox ritual and Rhea finds a Commune she wants to live at. Perhaps I'll join Aphrodite and her fleet of ships in the southern seas. Maybe I can be like Medusa and lock myself in a cave for a few millennia. Maybe when I finally emerge, I will be able to stop thinking about Rhea. With enough time, I could even forget her beautiful silver aura that calls to me like a lighthouse in a storm or how much I love the way the sunlight brings out the flecks of gold in her honey eyes.

I can do it. For her, I can.

Emerging from the shower, she's already gone. The bed has been neatly made, and the cottage is still warm from her enigmatic glow.

Seeing Rhea inside the training room, my resolve immediately wavers. The sun shining through the windows makes her eyes dance like a spring meadow full of yellow daffodils as the honey centers shine in the daylight. She's wearing hunter-green workout tights and a sports bra. Her curves fit wonderfully in the form-grabbing material, and I've never been more jealous of a pair of clothing than I am of those tights. A thin strip of her stomach and back are visible, already glistening in the morning heat. Her honey-brown hair bounces in a ponytail, and I imagine tugging it with my fist and pulling her face up to me so I can devour her lips.

Gods, how am I going to do this?

Stretching nearly murders my soul; seeing her bend and elongate throughout the routine and listening to the noises she makes nearly ends it all for me. Somehow, by the strength of the gods, I resist my impulses to take her up against the training room wall, and we get through the warm-up.

"That's not fair!" she exclaims as my bow staff strikes her upper arm.

"What do you mean fair? This is a fight. Everything is fair." I reply.

"No, it's not. You changed the sequence. I used the right block, but you made a different attack. You're cheating." She huffs at me.

She's a natural at sparring. Some muscle memory immediately kicked in as soon as she got out of her own head and let her instincts take over. Something within her has battled before, occasionally showing in her form and defenses.

"Rhea, you have to look at your opponent and be able to tell what they will do before they do it. It was obvious my attack would be coming from the opposite side. My stance was wrong; I had to change my grip and align my hips differently.

You would have countered if you had been paying attention to something other than my rock-hard abs."

Her face flushes. "I wasn't staring at you. You're being an ass!"

She stomps to the large windows that overlook the Kenya plain below. Crossing her arms over her chest, her brow is furrowed with frustration resting on her tight expression.

"What's bothering you?" I ask.

"I feel my powers trying to break free, but I just can't let them loose. I think Medusa knows, and she's getting frustrated with me. I just... I feel like I'm disappointing everyone." she explains.

"Hey, you're not disappointing anyone, okay?" I said, stepping closer to her. She turns toward me but refuses to meet my gaze.

"Look at me." I put my finger under her chin and encourage her stare upward. We're so close that our bodies are nearly touching, and I can feel the rise and fall of her breasts as her breathing picks up.

"Hermes, I'm all sweaty." she protests.

"You're changing the subject." I croon, moving closer to her, rubbing her arm where my bow struck her a moment ago. Every thought and promise I made to myself this morning dissolves as I look down at her beauty.

How am I ever going to stay away from her?

"Hermes..." she says breathless. I soak in the sight of her, looking at her with longing, the way I want to when we are alone in the cottage. My pulse quickens when she steps into me. Does she want this too? Does she burn for me every second of the day like I do for her?

"Can I ask about your fated mate?" she drops the quiet

question and it hits like a bomb. I didn't expect that, and my heart falters.

It's my turn to study the landscape of the plain below as I bite my cheek, thinking how to answer her best. Doubt circles me like a predator. I don't know if I'm ready to talk to Rhea about Juliette. How can I ever think about having a relationship with someone when the perfect woman lingers in my memories and still holds my heart? I'm the most selfish Elemental in this realm for the greed of wanting Rhea too, even knowing her mate is waiting somewhere to meet her.

"Is there something specific you would like to know? I don't talk about her much." I clear my throat and step back, putting distance between us and finding my breath again.

"I'm sorry, I'm just curious." she apologizes. Her head drops, and she looks down at her fingers twisting around each other. I don't want her to feel ashamed of her curiosity, but I also don't know if I can handle admitting I'm still in love with Juliette. Partly because I know it will hurt Rhea, but also because I know she'll stop looking at me, the way she was just a moment ago.

I want her to look at me that way forever and that makes me a greedy prick.

She looks so alone right now as she struggles inside herself. The desire to ask her question is fighting against whatever is holding her back. I want to take my hand and brush gently across her cheek. I want to feel her lean into my touch and close her eyes so I can press my lips against hers.

Our privacy is broken when the training room door opens, pulling us farther apart and snapping the moment's intensity. Callie enters the room smiling.

"Hey! Rhea, you about finished here?"

"She's all yours, Callie." I need to get out of here before I do something I'll regret. I don't help Rhea with her things because the second my skin touches hers, I know I'll pull her into me and give in to every vision that has been forcing its way to the forefront of my thoughts. I leave without looking back and with a knot in my throat.

I feel like Midas, except everything I touch turns to shit instead of gold. Everyone I thought was my family may not be my family, and they're all dead. I bottled up my powers for so many years that they don't work right, and now they're hiding from me. I'm being hunted by the most malicious villain of all time, and I'm so accustomed to being treated like crap by men that there may be a genuine one, but I can't tell because of my messed-up brain. *Why does my life have to be like this?*

If I could return to that void of outer space again and be alone with my powers and my books for the rest of eternity, I could get over the embarrassment I just suffered with Hermes. He's just so beautiful, and everything about him is perfect. I adore how his eyes gleam when he smiles, and his adorable dimples make me want to kiss his cheeks every time I see them. He's incredibly tall, and strong and he makes me feel utterly safe and secure when I'm near him. The way he cares for those around him, and his playful personality, makes me smile and laugh more than I ever have.

Everything about him exudes strength. I still think about how he scooped me up and *ran* through the woods like it was nothing. The feel of his breath and the movement of his muscles under his clothes made me yearn to feel his skin against mine.

This morning, I had such a vivid dream of him. Nestled behind me with my ass in his lap, his erection was hard against my back and pulsating for entry. He teased me with his mischievous fingers, running them along my hip and between my thighs as he nuzzled my neck. Tracing the edge of my panties with his fingers, I moaned as he finally slid them under the thin fabric, heading toward my wet center at a torturous pace.

I darted awake when I realized it was a dream and moaned out loud. I gave thanks to all the gods in existence that Hermes was already in the shower. I dressed quickly and bolted to training as fast as possible. Then, I saw him in the sparring room while I ran through stretches, enjoying how his shirt would fall forward for a glimpse of his firm body, coated in sweat.

But I screwed everything up when I mentioned his fated mate. I saw the shift in his eyes and the shutting of whatever door was possibly opening. When Callie interrupted us, he couldn't get away fast enough. He probably realized I have a childish school-girl crush and will feel uncomfortable around me, feeling obligated to protect me from Ares while trying not to be a jerk about rejecting me.

I know his main goal is to keep my abilities out of Ares's hands. Everything else is necessary to get along while we're forced to be near each other. But occasionally, I allow my mind to wander. I daydream about someone like Hermes, strong and kind, making me the center of their world for no other reason except for loving me. But then I stop before the sadness takes over—something like that will never be my life.

So, as Callie and I eat our lunch in the cottage, and the scent of Hermes fills the space, I pretend I don't have a gaping hole in my chest from his walking away today.

I flip through the printed pages taken from Damien's shoebox while Callie scours news reports of strange animal sightings attributed to increased Werewolf activity. Elementals and the Mortal Council control the messaging for the most part, but local news and social media sites are nearly impossible for them to sensor.

Having forgotten about Damien's journal, I retrieved it. The book has remained inside my bookbag, along with my blue leather-wrapped antique since we left my aunt's house. I don't even know why I brought that old book. My aunt took me antiquing shortly after the accident. I was so drawn to the book, and even when the shop owner said there was no key for the little lock, I still wanted it. Maybe like the mystery of my powers, I hoped to find a way to open the cover and finally know the story.

The pages of Damien's journal are brown with tea stains and showcase scribblings in all the page's margins as he filled in notes over the years. There must be two decades of information here, with small pictures and clippings from books occasionally pasted.

Finishing my lunch, I lean back in my chair and prop my feet on the table. Crossing one ankle over the other, my foot moves back and forth mindlessly while I focus on the pages. My mind goes in and out, thinking of Hermes and wondering if I should ask Medusa for a new cottage today. A piece of paper falls from the book and swishes to the ground.

The dark ink and old penmanship are visible through the thin, delicate paper, and the edges are scorched by fire. Keeping my thumb on the page of the journal, I lean down, retrieving the dropped parchment. Two phrases are written in the journal around where the scroll sat, folded, and waiting to be read. *"Taken from the Dark Mage."* and *"Salvaged Scroll from the Great Library at Alexandria."*

My face drops, and all the blood drains to my feet as I read the text.

The Forgotten Goddess
By: Hecate
There was a goddess of ancient lore,
Whose name and deeds they knew no more,
For she cast a spell upon herself,
That erased her from every mortal's shelf.
Her powers waned, and her temples fell,
As time moved on, she bid farewell,
For she wished to fade into history,
A forgotten goddess and timeless mystery.

I read the poem four times before I looked up at Callie with my mouth sagging open.

"What?" She jumps from her chair and rounds the table, knowing something profound must have been discovered. Still holding the fragile parchment between my fingers, Callie holds my wrist and reads the poem before slowly turning her eyes to me.

"Rhea." she breathes as she kneels by my side.

"I did this." My eyes are fixed on the table, but my vision blurs as I reflect on the poem's lines. Finally, I turn my widened eyes to Callie, blinking quickly as I attempt to form the words. "I did this... to *myself*."

"**B**last! Where in this realm could she be?**" Medusa slams her hand on her desk, cursing Hecate for remaining out of contact. Callie and I came to her with the poem penned by Hecate as soon as we found it. It must be referring to me. "She's never been out of touch this long."

"Could something be wrong?" I ask. I haven't met Hecate yet, but my eagerness to speak with her now that we found this poem makes my insides stir with urgency. If I did this to myself and messed up my memories, then maybe I can un-do it and return them.

Medusa looks at the shelves behind her at a silver hourglass. The ornate designs of the oblong glass sit on a pedestal. As I look at the black sand inside the mirror, I lean forward and narrow my eyes, not believing what I see. The sand flows upward into the top of the glass orb instead of downward.

"She is fine. She is just within the shadows." Medusa turns back as she answers, pinching the bridge of her nose with her fingers. "She's a Dark Mage from the shadow realm, Elysium. The sand in the glass flows upward when she is within the shadows. When she is within the light of the realm of Gaea, it flows downward."

"So, she has left this realm?" I ask, confused by the answer.

"Not really. No one can leave the realm. But the shadows of Elysium creep into every realm. Unable to be contained like an evasive vine, the shadows can never be removed from any realm. When Hecate is in the shadows, she is still in this realm, but connected through the darkness."

It's fascinating and scary to think about. A Mage of Darkness that deals in shadows.

"Let's get back to your training. I'll watch the sands and tell you when she has emerged."

We leave her office, walk to the adjacent building, and set into the mountain where the training facilities are. Callie holds the parchment, rereading it as we walk. My mind rushes back to the embarrassment of this morning, and my cheeks burn of their own accord. I'm thankful for the bright sun hiding my shame.

"I was wondering," I begin, twirling my fingers and trying to keep my tone casual and unrushed. "Are there any empty cottages? I'm sure Hermes would like some privacy from me."

Medusa keeps her head forward, placing her hands in her pockets as we walk. I cut my eyes to the ground in front of me.

"Um, no, not yet. Still occupied with the recent rescues, but I'll let the team know to come get you as soon as one opens up." She thins her lips in an inward smile and nods at me courteously. Returning the polite smile, I turn my eyes back to the ground and nip at the inside of my cheek, thinking about what excuse I can use to sleep on the living room couch.

I'm getting better at fighting each day. It's been a week since Hermes walked out of the training room, and I've only seen him in passing as he gave me a cordial nod of acknowledgement. With no open cottages, I planned to stay up late looking over Damien's research and give myself a reason to fall asleep on the couch. But Hermes didn't return to the cottage that night. As much as I dreaded being alone in the house with him, the emptiness that came without his presence nearly suffocated me.

But the next day, I woke up alone, leaning over the table of papers with a sore neck.

My training has now upgraded to include weapons, adding a new level of soreness to my poor muscles. Anahita and her sister, Avaley, started training me with different weapons and letting me test them. The spear and bow were odd in my hands, but I still hit the targets with them. I tried a few swords, but they were long and heavy and sat strangely in my grasp. I felt like I was on the verge of tipping forward the entire time I held the sword before me.

A pair of daggers hanging on the wall fit perfectly in my hands. Ana crafted long spears of water, sharp as metal, and we began moving through defenses. Slowly at first and then speeding up, the rhythm was nice and felt natural. Something about the movements and the feel of the daggers in my hands felt familiar. Ana let me set the pace faster until our weapons snapped through the air, and our faces dripped with sweat.

"My turn." Avaley stands on the other side of the training room with her longbow steady. Pulling the tight string back and positioning the bow in front of her, an arrow made of wind sits in her hand. The white, translucent currents of air tightly spin and form the arrow. Whistling at a high pitch, it screams at me as it flies through the space, directly at my chest. Using the dagger to knock the arrow aside before it can pierce me, the scream of another arrow follows immediately behind it.

The burn on my shoulders feels excellent. My tired limbs scream along with the arrows, but I love the feeling. Both sisters join in the session together. Avaley dashes through the arena and propels herself toward the tall ceiling, blasting arrows of wind at me from every angle. Ana engages me in close combat with her water spear. The sounds of wind-cutting and water splashing against the grunts from our straining bounce around the room as we take up every inch of the space. Ana hurls a spear at me from opposite sides of the room as Avaley shoots three arrows.

The practice has quieted my mind, and a natural rhythm has taken over my movements. Swiping the dagger behind me in an upward arc, I cut the three arrows with a single swipe. Catching the water spear with my hand, I use the momentum of its course, allowing it to spin me in a circle. Like a practiced dancer with years of training, my body seems to know what to do. Putting all my strength into the throw, I hurl the spear at Ana with a loud grunt.

Dizzy from the motion, my aim is off, but the spear cuts through the air, singing its high-pitch whistle. Opening the training room door, the spear is headed directly toward Hermes' face, but he reacts fast as lighting. Still holding the door open, he shifts his shoulder to the right and catches the spear with his other hand, narrowly avoiding it. Slowly, he turns his eyes to me and a lopsided smile forms on his face.

"Challenge accepted." Clenching his fist, the water spear ruptures, dripping down his hand as he saunters into the room.

I thought Hermes looked amazing in his all-black tactical gear but seeing him in fighting leathers sends me into another universe. Brown leather boots lace halfway up his calf, and the handles of two small knives stick out of the tops of each boot. Brown leather pants lay flat over the lines and curves of his muscular legs, and each thigh holsters a blade. A deep blue tunic, the color of his eyes, stretches across his biceps and sits under a light brown leather vest. A scabbard fixed to his back showcases the hilts of two swords crossed over his shoulders. Sliding one of the swords from the sheath, a bright blue light matching his aura glows from the blade.

My mouth is a desert as I take a position in the center of the room, my feet wide and knees bent. A dagger in each hand and my fingers grasped tightly around the handles. Hermes' entire demeanor changes and the mask of a lethal warrior slides over his face. Focused and determined, his eyes lock onto me for the first time in days and I feast on the feeling of him taking me in. Spinning the sword in a circle, he flips it, catching the hilt again and swinging it in an arc by his shoulder.

Show off.

"Oh! Fancy sword tricks. I'm so scared." I tease him, and it brings a dangerous gleam to his eyes. In truth, his deft movements of the sword are intimidating as he looks at me like prey he is about to devour. He has had centuries—no, much longer than that—to perfect the weapons in his hands. But maybe I have too. The poem I've memorized runs through my mind, and I remind myself. I did this and made myself forget. Perhaps I'm the predator, and he doesn't know he's being hunted.

Spinning the daggers in my palms, we near each other and circle the floor, keeping cautious and focused. The sight of the gleaming metal is more ominous than the weapons crafted of water and wind. I knew I wouldn't be injured if Anahita and Avaley's weapons hit me. While I know Hermes won't aim to harm me, the stakes seem higher.

The swing of the glowing blade slices through the air, and dipping my shoulder to the side, I push it away with the dagger.

Hermes' smile is devilish as he winks at me and says, "Let's dance."

The assault is brutal, but I keep pace. He spins and slides quickly, arching and slicing with his sword. The clang of our metal blades kissing each other rings across the room as we turn and sway away from each other's thrusts. With one slice, Hermes twists one of my daggers out of my hand, and it soars several feet behind me. Pushing me against the wall, he holds the wrist of my other hand, still clutching my dagger firmly over my head. His knee against my thigh keeps me locked in place, and he gently brings the tip of the sword to me, laying it carefully on my shoulder and dragging it down as his eyes burn through me. Our chests rise quickly, out of breath; with parted lips, we're only inches away from each other.

Fire sears within me at his nearness, and my powers react to him, not in defense or alarm but almost as if they want to play. His parted lips are so close to mine that it would only take a slight tilt of my head to taste him, to feel him groan against me as I run my free hand up his thigh and watch the desire take him over.

Clapping on the other side of the training room breaks the enchantment of the moment. Releasing me, he walks to my discarded dagger and picks it up. Flipping it in the air, he catches the blade in his hand and offers me the handle. Walking away, Medusa takes his place before me and grasps my shoulders. With her chin tucked into her chest, she looks at me through her lashes and speaks softly.

"What the fuck was that?"

"What?" I gape. That was the first time I had been in a sword fight, and I thought I did pretty well to hold out against him.

She turns her shoulder, still holding her hand on me, and looks back at Hermes. The point of his sword digs into the floor as he stands casually with one hand on the hilt, his other perched on his hip.

"Look at that sword. It glows with his power." She turns back to me and places both hands on my shoulders. "Where is your power?"

Cutting my eyes to the floor, I realize she is right.

"You think he's not funneling his speed and strength into the sword? He is. He's a Light Bearer. He is using his power to predict your movements, knowing where you will be before you get there. He *can* move at the speed of light, but he's not. So, make him."

Everything she says should have been evident to me. I was only fighting as myself. I need to fight as a goddess. I may not remember who she is, but I know a goddess is inside me. Medusa raises one of her eyebrows, cocking it upward at a sharp angle as she watches me think.

"That's it. Find it. Find the power inside." she encourages.

Rolling my shoulders back, I meet his gaze. Spinning one of my blades on my palm again, I unlock the door holding my powers back, and my aura flares to life around me. Gusting and gleaming in the training room, the silver tendrils of my aura whip around. Medusa backs away from the wall, taking a place beside Ana and Ava.

Walking toward him, I send a tendril of my aura and stroke it across his cheek. "Let's dance."

The smile spreading across his face is pure seduction, but the warrior's mask instantly takes over. Neither of us stalks around the other, but we both advance directly to each other. Propelled by my wind and fire, I burst forward as the streak of blue power pushes him toward me. Clashing in the center with my daggers forming a cross, I meet his blade and hold it. Our faces show our strain as we push against each other.

Pushing away from each other, we slide back several feet, each catching ourselves and righting our stances before we surge back into the fight. Spinning and slicing, the sound of our blades colliding rings across the room in another attempt to disarm each other. As the momentum of our power carries us past each other, I fling three blades of water, pushed by my wind behind me and they stick in the floor around his right foot.

Caught off guard by the conjured weapons, he looks down at the blades, then nods. Then we move again. Boosted by flames and wind, I surge forward with both arms behind me. Hermes turns to a streak of blue light, but I can still see the mass of his body within. His aura surges ahead like a wormhole he is rushing through, and I can see its route. I know where he will be at the end.

A split-second shift and I feign to the opposite side, making him change his course. He's moving too fast, and the distance is too short. He sees the mistake a moment too late. The earth crunches under my foot, creating a well for me to push against. Not expecting my change in direction, I use his momentum against him. Wielding my wind like a whip, I send a tendril of aura around his ankle. Pulling hard, he spins onto his back and falls. He loses his grasp on his sword with the impact, and it clamors to the ground, spinning away from him as it collides against the wall.

Using the whip like a tether, I pull myself to him with a single leap and land with one knee on his chest. My opposite foot is firmly on the floor by his head, and my dagger is pushed flush against his neck. Pride runs like lightning through my blood as I sit over him, panting from the exertion. His heavy eyes stay on me as he matches the pace of my breathing. The pulse in his neck races against my blade still at his throat.

Medusa jumps, pounding her fist in the air with elation at my victory. Hermes smiles widely, his dimples shining at me with satisfaction in his eyes. The lightning dies, and my blood rushes to my cheeks as I stand and back away, holding my hand out to help him up. I've never held power like that, not my magic, but the power to feel confident and strong. It felt amazing, and I wish I didn't feel ridiculous for having guilt over enjoying the sensation of being in control.

Hermes takes my offering and grasps his hand in mine, standing. Our bodies are close as he looks down at me with those burning blue eyes, bright with the thrill of our fight. Wetting his lips with his tongue, I fight to keep my eyes on his.

"*Very* good job." he says to me in a breathy deep tone before dropping my hand and walking to the side of the room. The words drive right to my core and heat me from within. Retrieving his blade, he reaches behind his head, puts it back in its scabbard, and leaves the training room.

Medusa takes me to her office for a congratulatory bottle of water. On the way, she dissects how I used his speed against him and waves her arms, excitedly mimicking my movements during the fight. Arriving at her office, she tosses me a water bottle and sits at her desk.

On top of it is the intricate silver hourglass and dark sand.

"She's back?" I exclaim, noticing the sands are falling downward now. Medusa smiles at my excitement.

"She is. She just got back and she wants to meet you tomorrow night." My shoulders drop in disappointment. I was hoping we would be able to meet right away. With the equinox only a week away, I feel like my time to figure things out is escaping faster than these grains of sand as they drop through the skinny neck of the hourglass. Medusa raises her hands in surrender.

"I pressed to meet today, but whatever she has been doing, she needs a day to rest before we meet."

Nodding my head in understanding, I take a hearty sip of water. Looking around the space, I notice a pile of folded clothes and a pair of Hermes shoes on a couch in the sitting room of Medusa's office. With a folded blanket under a pillow, I realize Hermes must be sleeping here to avoid returning to the cottage.

The disappointment that stabs at my heart pushes a knot into my throat. Heat rises up my neck, and I focus my breathing through my nose, trying to remain indifferent to Medusa. She continues, talking about our meeting with Hecate tomorrow.

"We'll meet her in her old home. It's well protected, and we can travel there through Odysseus and Penelope's nightclub. They've already prepared their security, and we will bring a detail of my guards, just in case."

"Okay, thanks for everything. I appreciate your help." Glancing again at Hermes' belongings, I excuse myself to get a shower before dinner. The excitement and adrenaline from today's session has left me, and my body's tired limbs and muscles are beginning to scream at me. Medusa sees me as I tear my eyes away from the clothes and stops me.

"Hey, you should know he loved her immensely." She is talking about Hermes' mate, Juliette. "He will always love her, and he believes he needs to punish himself for losing her." She smiles sadly as I nod, trying hard not to let the words pull the tears from my eyes. "Immortal men have had lifetimes to become as stubborn as they are. Just be patient with him."

The walk back to the cottage is somber as I think about Juliette and what she would have been like, what they would have looked like together, and if he thinks of her when he looks at me. Hugging my stomach, I bite my lip from the questions racing through my mind. I don't want the answers because I know I can't measure up to someone with a soul connection to Hermes. Their bond was rooted in the universe—nothing about me can hold a candle to that.

Once again, I let my mind create a fantasy that cannot come true and allowed it to distract me from what I need to do. Like the times before, I must be the one to break my heart and walk away. Hermes is a distraction, and I know either way, it's a dead-end road.

I wish things had gone differently in Atlanta. I wish Athena and my aunt were still alive and I had been able to sneak away that night. The events turned so quickly, and everything flipped on its end. But I'll have another chance tomorrow; this time, I won't let anything stop me.

Arriving at the cold and empty cottage, a smell of jasmine and honey greets me at the door. Through the dark bedroom, I can see flickering lights coming from the dimly lit bathroom.

"Hello?" I call out; the essence of my aura slithers through the home, checking for the presence of someone. Glad to know it's answering me again, I cautiously walk through the doorways and peer into the bathroom, finding dozens of candles flickering on all the surfaces.

A steaming bath sits full, tempting me with the allure of jasmine. Delicate white flower petals float on the surface, and a wicker basket on the corner of the tub catches my attention. Small glass vials with silver tops sit in the basket. One of the tubes full of bath salts and flower petals has a handwritten label, explaining they are for muscle pain. Opening one of the vials, the sweet floral scent greeting me fills my senses with instant relaxation.

I'm certainly not going waste this effort if someone prepared a bath for me. Soaking in a bathtub is one of my favorite ways to relax; the steam rolling off the surface waves me in. Stepping in, the waters wrap around every tight muscle and sore limb. Releasing the pain of training, the waters heal me. Resting my arms on the tub's edge and dipping my head back, I breathe in the vapor and melt into relaxation.

Taking in the candles and watching the dancing flames, a small stack of books grabs my eye. Looking at the titles, I release a bubble of laughter. Four books are sitting on a table showcasing titles with Hermes' name. The one on top is a Greek mythology romance novel with a chiseled, muscular man on the cover. A single daffodil sits under the book's cover, and I can't help the smile of disbelief that remains plastered on my face. Daffodils are my favorite flower. Opening the cover and taking the flower, I lift it to my nose as I notice a note handwritten with blue ink.

This one looks especially interesting.
~ H

Taking in the words on the first few pages, this book is filled with absolute filth, and I love it. Shaking my head and covering my eyes with my hand at the audacity of this man, I stifle a laugh. I love reading romance novels with total smut printed on the inside pages, but I'm not sure I can look Hermes in the eye again if he knew I read a romance book about him.

Enjoying the waters that seem enchanted to remain steaming hot, I read a few chapters of the book, envisioning *my* Hermes doing the devilish deeds printed on the pages to me. Sitting up and sloshing water on the floor, I realize that is what he was aiming for. Tossing the book back onto the table, I roll my eyes and drain the water from the tub.

Stretching my limbs, the stiffness of my body is completely gone, and I feel amazing. The salts must have contained some healing properties, and I take in the basket full of vials of salts with appreciation.

I'll have to remember to hide these in my bag for tomorrow.

Wrapping myself in a towel, I exit the bathroom with a billow of steam. A white box is on the bed, wrapped with a black stain bow, and another note sits on top next to another daffodil.

Will you do me the honor of having dinner with me tonight?
~ H

Chewing my lip, I don't know what to do. I don't want to add more pressure to an already complicated situation. But Hermes is probably waiting in the cottage, expecting me to have dinner with him. Do I reject him and break my heart, watching his disappointment and always wonder if it could have been different? Or do I take a chance and risk having my heart ripped out by him when he realizes I'm not worth the trouble? Sitting on the bed, I make a choice.

One night.

I'll allow myself one night to dream about being Juliette, wrapped in the arms of the man that loves her. I can pretend she is me and his feelings are mine. Then tomorrow, I'll leave. I'll carefully hold my heart as I rip it out because I know how to do it in a way I can survive. When I mend it back together, I will shove it deeper into the caverns of my chest so it's harder to find next time.

Taking the bookbag from the closet, I stuff two changes of clothes inside and the vials of bath salts around my blue-covered book from Aunt Demi's house. Stashing the bag under the bed, I turn to the gift box.

A simple black cocktail dress waits for me inside, and heat rushes up my face when I find black silk panties and a bra that is my perfect size. A pair of strappy black heels hug my feet snugly, accentuating the cut of my calf muscles as I turn in the full-length mirror, inspecting myself. The fabric slides against my skin as I run my hands down my waist and hips. The end of the dress rests above my knees.

Twisting and turning in the full-length mirror, the two weeks of traumatic events and warrior training have done something to my body. My soft tummy, still squishy, lays somewhat flat against the fitted dress. My curves are usually a point of contention with me, but they look smooth and almost inviting in the dim evening lighting.

I slip the sword necklace over my head on its long chain, settling just below my breasts: a lovely contrast against the dark fabric. It gleams at me as the black stone dances on the chain, and a pang rubs against my heart, pulling on my plan to leave tomorrow. I think of Callie and how much her friendship means to me. Leaving Hermes will mean leaving Callie as well. I squeeze the necklace and think of her words when she gave it to me.

"If you ever feel scared or alone, hold it and remember you're not."

Holding on to this thought, I push the pain down and shove it inside the box where I usually keep my powers and leave the bedroom to find Hermes.

Rhea

The cottage is quiet and empty. The sun is setting outside, and I inhale my appreciation for the onset of night, my favorite time of day. I think back to the sunrise with Medusa and feel for the shift in energy as the night air takes over from the sunlight.

The back door leading to the rear of the cottage is cracked open, and walking through it, I'm shocked at the incredible scenery in the rear garden. My breath catches in my throat at the luscious green space full of crawling vines and exotic flowers. It's been transformed into an enchanted garden, just like the memory in the field of my childhood.

A short, white fence encloses the area, and blooms of all colors and varieties dwell within it. Small glowing orbs of light float like hundreds of tiny fireflies, providing a warm romantic glow. Inspecting them further, I realize they are little glowing flames encased in a small glass bubbles, hovering all around the air above our heads.

It's magical.

In the garden's center is a white metal table and two chairs. The ornate design of the twisting vines of metal holds a large bouquet of daffodils, standing attentively in a vase. Casually leaning against the table is a very delicious and handsome Hermes, wearing black dress slacks and a white button-down shirt. The cuffs of his long sleeves are rolled just below his elbows, allowing me an uninterrupted view of his forearm muscles. I love how the muscles dance as he moves, and it's an effort to tear my gaze away from them.

The scorch of his eyes engulfs me and turns my insides into a swarm of butterflies. A familiar comfort settles over me with his presence, washing away my trepidation from the past few days of his absence.

Looking at him now, it's as if we have exchanged millions of glances and words over thousands of years, and my worry was for nothing. The heat of my desire for him floods my face, rushing up my throat, and making it difficult to speak. A very unflattering choke emerges, and I quickly clamp my mouth shut again.

He ascends toward me with his dimples on full display. His ocean eyes gleam as they wander up my body from my feet poised in the perfectly fitting heels and up my bare legs to the curves aided by the snug fitting dress. He rests his eyes on the sword necklace for a moment and fondly turns it over in his fingers with a smile before meeting my eyes.

"Rhea, you make me breathless." Chills run the length of my body at the intimacy of his words. "Come on. I bet you're starving." He says, taking my hands and leading me to the table.

"Hermes, this is amazing," I exclaim, taking in the garden's beauty as the sun sets in the sky. His smile widens with a boyish tenderness that is endearing. "I don't think I've ever seen anything so magical."

The dinner is fantastic, and we talk comfortably, enjoying the food and several glasses of wine. A rich blanket of darkness envelopes the garden, making the enchanted glass orbs of golden flames cast hypnotic dancing shadows around us. I can't help but watch them sway above us as the flames hypnotize me. Beyond them, the bright stars in the Kenyan night look like a billion diamonds have erupted across the night sky.

"So, the swords." I raise one of my eyebrows with an accusing look in my eyes. "Where are those from?"

Hermes grins lovingly at my mention of the swords. "They were a gift from my father," He pauses with his fork perched above his plate, a twinkle of mischief gleaming in his blue eyes. "Apollo."

My mouth gapes open, and I drop my fork on my plate with a loud clink. Hermes chuckles at me and wipes his mouth with his cloth napkin. "You're kidding me? Your dad is the Sun god?"

Hermes tells me of his father, a powerful Light Bearer—like himself but with a strong yellow aura like the sun. The big three: Apollo, Ares, and Atlas, close like brothers until Ares descended a dark path.

"Ares was my mentor and trained me to fight. When my father disagreed with his plans, Ares poisoned and challenged him as ruler of all Elementals." Hermes tells me the solemn story as we stand at the picket fence and soak in the velvety night sky.

"I could see something was wrong with my Dad, so I stepped in front of him with Apollo's sword, the Lord of Light, and my mother's sword, the Mistress of Darkness; I beat Ares." Standing behind me, his warm hand slides low on my hip, pulling my body into his. My body responds to his touch, melting into him as his spicy scent wraps around me. Sweeping my brown hair to one side, he plays with a long tendril of my wavy hair and his breath on my skin ignites my senses to an overwhelming sensitivity.

"Were he and your mother fated to each other?" I ask carefully to not let my questions lead to Juliette.

"He never found his fated mate, but he was quite fond of women... and men." He laughs. "My mother was a huntress and one of his highest-ranking warriors. They formed a friendship over archery, and a romance started, but it was never serious. I remember they used to spar quite often, and I thought they glided around each other like two birds flying around the clouds. They were both great parents. Since they weren't mates, it was more companionship for them both." He pauses momentarily, his eyes staring at nothing as he recalls childhood memories.

"My mom had a fling with William Shakespeare, you know?" he says, shifting the conversation and lightening the mood.

"For real?"

He chuckles at my surprise. "She was a fierce warrior but also an artist. She authored many books and poems for mortal libraries. You would have loved her. She loved living among the mortals and watching them enjoy the simplicity of their short lives. She spent her last few hundred years living among them. She always thought her mortal name was so clever. *Daphne Helios.*"

The name strikes me, and the familiarity tightens my shoulders.

"What is it?" Hermes tenses, alarmed by my reaction.

"What did you just say?" I ask, a bewildered look on my face.

"What? My mom's name? Daphne."

"Daphne Helios?" I repeat quietly, remembering why that name seems familiar. Realization strikes me, and I hurry into the cottage and pull the blue-bound book from my bookbag.

The Abduction of Persephone by Hades
By: Daphne Helios

Hermes doesn't say anything for a moment. He only looks at the book for a while before looking at me.

"How do you have this?" he asks.

"My aunt and I bought it in an antique store about ten years ago," I hand him the book, and he softly rubs the leather cover, running his fingers over the lettering. He turns the book over a few times and begins inspecting the lock.

"Have you read it?" he asks.

"No, it's locked, and we never could open it," I reply.

He assesses the lock further, squinting his eyes, and then looks around the room, searching for an object to unlock it. After looking around and thinking, his eyes rest on my necklace. A small smile creeps along his face, and he takes the charm in his hand.

"May I?" he asks flirtatiously, and I nod my head. My face flares red at his alluring voice.

He pulls me closer by the necklace's chain, keeping his eyes on mine. Finally, he looks away and sticks the sword down the length of the lock in a small hole made for the key.

With a tiny *click*, the lock snaps open.

The tiny click of the lock resounded so loudly in the quaint cottage. Holding the book's cover, unshackled, I'm eager to see what lies within. My wide eyes are drawn to my name, scrawled across the centuries-old page in my mother's handwriting, still as fresh as the day it was penned.

> *"To my son, Hermes.*
> *Only you can free her.*
> *But first, you must free yourself.*
> *Remember."*

I remain fascinated with the words my mother wrote hundreds of years before and feel Rhea's intent eyes watching me and reading my reactions. I hand her the book, and she holds it in her delicate hands with such tenderness, looking it over eagerly but with care.

"You found this in an antique store?" I ask, and Rhea nods in confirmation. "She used to take parts of our lives and turn them into fantastical tales for the mortals—stories of our battles and our powers told in ways they could understand. The mortals would sit around fires and celebration halls, hanging on her every word, entranced by her voice and the imagery she conjured. She was quite the storyteller." I recount the memory of the woman she was, and sorrow floods me with the grief of missing her.

"Will you read it to me?" Rhea asks me; her request is so tiny that it makes me smile fondly.

"Come on." I pull her across the cottage to the main room and build a fire in the quaint fireplace. Rhea retrieves our opened bottles of wine and glasses from the garden. I read to her well into the early morning as the faint light of a new day begins creeping over the horizon, bringing a soft pink hue to the sky.

Every morning, Zeus, the lord of light, escorts dawn to the horizon between realms. He waits to meet his love, Demeter, mistress of darkness, who is the escort of dusk. During the brief time between day and night, their love blooms in that small space between the horizons, and they bear a child of both their realms —Persephone.

She holds the sun's power to shape the earth and command fire. She has the moon's magic to call wind and move water. She is the sole keeper of life and death, light and dark.

Zeus and Demeter created the realm of Gaea for Persephone, born of both realms, to thrive where her parents could watch over her. As she grows and wanders the realm alone, she creates great masses of land and sea, bringing beautiful and abundant life to them both.

In time, Persephone grows into a young maiden. Loneliness and sadness consume her and the realm falls into shadow, and the beautiful life created from her heart begins to rot and wither.

Zeus and Demeter, saddened by their daughter's loneliness, ask the gods for a companion worthy of Persephone to bring back the spark to her happiness and restore the beautiful life of Gaea.

The gods offered her Hermes, Herald of the Gods, and Guide of the Underworld, as Hermes can live in all realms and would bring love to Persephone's heart.

But the lord of the Underworld, Hades, was jealous of Persephone's power over death and loathed the disgusting mortals. Hades devised a plan to capture Persephone and take her powers, so he poisoned Gaea with deceit and strife, bringing darkness to the mortals' hearts and disease to Gaea's lands.

Distressed by the suffering of their realm, Hermes flees to the divine realms for help from the gods. Hades deceived Persephone and lured her to her garden, tricking her into eating a poisoned pomegranate seed.

Persephone, weakened by the poison, is chained to an inverted mountain in the Underworld. Hades extracts her powers which he consumes for himself.

Hermes returns from the divine realms to find Persephone is gone, the mortals are in chaos, and Gaea is withering away. Hermes finds Persephone chained and weakened, her life and power feeding Hades.

The ensuing battle spills into both realms, bringing death and destruction. As the war rages and death devours the realms, Gaea becomes weaker while the Underworld grows stronger. With the help of the divine realms, Hermes can finally rescue Persephone, and by breaking her chains, her powers are restored. The mortals lend their strength to her, and Persephone defeats Hades.

The gods banish Hades to the barren realm of the Underworld, the dead of the great war its only inhabitants. The fissure is sealed forever, freeing the realm of Gaea to begin its rebirth.

Tired from her imprisonment and the great war, Persephone retreats into the sustainable recesses of Gaea to restore her strength and rest. Hermes, her faithful lover and companion, seals her within her bed chamber and vows to watch over her slumber until she is strong and able to return as the keeper of her realm.

I close the book, and Rhea is fast asleep. I return to the dedication page and look at my mother's inscription again, rubbing my hand fondly over her writing. I can nearly hear her voice and see her sparkling brown eyes as if she were here with me. The story is beautiful and tragic and makes me sad. It much reminds me of Rhea and Ares, and I wonder if some truths aren't hidden within the words.

Careful not to wake her, I carry her into the bedroom and remove her heels. Pulling the blanket over her, she tucks it under her chin with a satisfied sigh. Sitting beside her, I lean over and gently kiss her forehead. The overwhelming sense of wanting to protect her clashes with the need to let her go to figure out who she is. I wish I could take her to my private home on Mount Olympus and forget about the rest of the world—forget about Ares and the possibility of a war with the Shifters and wrap myself in everything that is Rhea.

A few days ago, when she asked about Juliette, I panicked and turned my back on her. I went to Medusa's office, I asked her for a spare cottage, and she turned me down. Storming out of her office, she followed me to the top of the mountain.

"Are you going to spend the rest of eternity moping about

and being miserable? Because I may have to rethink our friendship if that's what you are going to do."

It made me chuckle then, and I smile, remembering it now.

"How did you keep going after Athena was severed from you?" I turned my eyes from the sunset and looked at my friend. She grieved in the caves of this mountain for ten thousand years, a monster to her anger.

"You know as well as I do; I was no archangel for a while." She wouldn't look at me while we talked about Athena. She never can. "But knowing she was there, still aware of what I was doing, made a difference."

We sat for a while without speaking and watching the sky turn yellow, green, and blue. Rhea floated across my mind, entangled with thoughts of Juliette. They are so similar but different; they are each their own women. Both strong and talented, caring, and passionate about everyone but themselves.

Before Rhea, I used to think about what eternity with Juliette would be like if she were still alive. I used to lie in bed, staring at the ceiling with my hands behind my head, and daydream about a life that would never be. Now, I daydream, and it's Rhea I see.

I think about defeating Ares, restoring the portals to the other realms, and showing her the beauty in them. Watching her taste the sweet golden apples of Avalon or watching the herds of galloping Pegasus on Tartarus. I imagine her eyes lighting up with wonder and holding her next to me as she experiences it all.

"You know one thing?" Medusa interrupted my thoughts. "I never lost hope." She finally turned and looked me in the eye. "I used to hope we would figure out how to free Athena's mind of the false memories or figure out how to restore our bond. Sometimes I thought, with enough time, I could just make her love me again."

"And what about now?"

She tipped her head, looking back at the horizon. "We'll find each other again. I have all of eternity to wait. In this realm or another, I'm sure of it."

"I'm afraid I won't be able to protect her. The way I couldn't protect Juliette." I looked at my lap and picked at thread on my jeans, remembering the day my partner died.

"What if she doesn't need your protection? Maybe all she needs is someone to believe in her."

29

Rhea

I **miss my daily meditation with Athena.** It was a great way to unwind and stop a million voices in my mind, worrying about the Shifters, my powers, and everything else. It's still early morning, and Hermes sleeps next to me. Sneaking out of the cottage, a smile spreads across my face as I think about last night. I could slap myself for falling asleep, but even still, the evening made me feel great.

Never before has anyone put so much effort into me. The bath and stack of books with his snarky note, the flowers and the dinner, and the magical glow cast over the garden by the enchanted flames. It was almost enough to make me believe I deserve something like that all the time.

I hike up to the spot where Medusa and I watched the sunrise and sit on the ground with my legs crossed. I begin my meditation by thinking about Medusa's guidance to feel the different energies in my environment. It takes a few minutes, but my mind finally settles, and I envision the elements.

Standing, I position myself in the starting formation of the routine Athena and I would practice. As I move my body, I think of each element in the space around me, like particles of air, water, earth, and fire. I imagine them glittering and swirling around me in sparkling currents as they did in the dark space I accidentally went to.

Keeping my eyes closed as I glide through the meditation, cool and warm sensations waft around me, giving me goose-bumps as if tiny particles are tickling my skin. Remembering the beautiful Kenya sunrise, I imagine the sun peeking over the horizon and feel a burst of light radiate through me.

Finishing the routine with a respectful bow, I wish Athena was across from me. My heart feels heavy, but my mind feels lighter. A single tear rolls down my cheek, and as I open my eyes, the scene before me takes my breath away.

My aura, silver and iridescent, shimmers in the pink morning sun at least thirty feet around me in all directions. Tones of blue, green, and red glimmer within the silver as my aura pulsates with the beating of my heart.

It's beautiful.

I wish Athena could see this. I wish I could have shared this part of myself with my aunt before she was killed. Seeing the magnitude of my power field surging around me, it's the first time, maybe ever, I feel unafraid of it. The familiar tinge of my panic is nowhere to be found, even as I wait for it expectantly, I'm happy to feel in control of myself.

Turning to recede down the mountain, Hermes surprises me, standing in the middle of the trail with his hands on his hips, radiating a big smile almost as big as my aura.

"Rhea, that was amazing. You are the most incredible person I've ever met." His sentiments make me blush, and I dip my head down, embarrassed. "Feel like going on a field trip?"

My heart blooms with the offer, and I am nearly bouncing with excitement. "Of course!"

"You're just going to have to trust me," Hermes says,

walking up to me. He retrieves a small wand from his pocket, which I recognize as the device he used to teleport us here. Sadness creeps over my happy mood, thinking about my plan to leave tonight. Maybe I can sneak this away from Hermes and use it tonight to escape.

One day.

You gave yourself one day. Well, technically, the day is over later tonight. I still have a few more hours to pretend I'm someone desirable, so I push the feelings down, not wanting to spoil the surprise.

Hermes' sturdy arm wraps around me, his hand gripping my hip. I encircle his waist and feel his corded stomach tense under my touch. He leans close to my ear and whispers, "Close your eyes."

I smile widely, trying to imagine where we could be going. I don't know the range of these things, but it delivered us halfway around the globe in the blink of an eye before. He clicks the button on the portal device, and a bright blue light engulfs us. The new day's warmth is replaced by cool, moist air.

"You should open your eyes and look around."

We loosen our holds on each other, and opening my eyes, my breath catches in my throat, and an odd mix between a choke and a gasp escapes my mouth.

"I thought you should see it in person." He smiles at me, watching me take in the spectacle before me.

It's Angel Falls.

"Oh, Hermes!" I say in awe. My eyes widen, and I stare at the mountain before me with the immense waterfall tumbling thousands of feet into the pools below. I lean against his chest and take in his scent while committing the landscape to my memory. I never want to forget this sight or this feeling with Hermes—not for an eternity.

"I've always loved coming to this place." he says, breaking the silence. "I'll sometimes sit at the top and hang my legs over the edge. I think about what may be at the bottom of the pools. I'm always so tempted to jump in and go for a swim." He laughs, a beautiful sound he doesn't often emit, making me look up at him. A gleam of happiness reflects in his deep blue eyes while he stares at the falls. After a moment, he looks down at me.

"So beautiful," he whispers as his eyes take me in.

My doubt begins to surface, but I desperately kick it down, trying to drown it in the depths of myself. As the sun rises in Kenya, it's setting here, and the moment is perfect. The war inside me wages, and I tear myself to pieces, considering doing what is right or what I want. I should forget Hermes and focus on the wolves that want to hunt me, but the girl inside me who was never chosen wants Hermes so desperately. I may be willing to let him tear my heart in two because no matter my choice, I know both paths lead to destruction.

"Something has always confused me." He turns me toward him, and his lips that drive me mad with desire one moment and furious with his stubbornness the next are like a beacon, calling me to him. He responds, tightening his arms around my waist and pressing my body against his. "Icarus, it never made sense."

I chuckle, not expecting that. "Icarus?" Winding my arms around his neck, I lengthen my height and stand on my toes. My fingers thread into the silky tendrils of his deep brown locks.

"Yeah, the mortal's story of Icarus. He got his freedom and

used it to fly toward the sun, even though he knew it would kill him. I never understood it." He strokes my hair, pushing it behind my ear as it whips around in the breeze of the falls. "Until meeting you, Rhea."

My breasts rise and fall against him as my pulse quickens. His eyes darken as his pupils widen, looking into my soul with his gaze.

"I feel like I've been a prisoner for hundreds of years, and you've finally freed me. Even if someone told me it would kill me, I would fly to you as fast as I could if only to look into your eyes one last time."

Tilting his head, he slowly lowers his mouth to mine, stopping just before our lips touch. My head is dizzy in anticipation of him, and his spicy scent cocoons me in a blanket of comfort. So close, mere molecules of space separate us, and the hesitation erupts a burning urgency within the pit of my stomach.

"To taste you... one last time." he whispers the words, and they dance on my mouth. His soft lips part in a teasing brush against mine before I tighten my arms around his neck. He drives his lips onto mine like a starving man who needs the taste of me to survive.

Surging pleasure erupts through me when Hermes grabs me and pulls my body further into him. Taking my mouth, Hermes parts my lips with his tongue; the kiss deepens, and he expertly strokes my mouth with his deft movements. A million sparks erupt along my skin like a firework exploding in the sky, and my icy protective casing melts as I mold into him. The satisfaction of finally feeling him fuels my movements and eagerness to consume him.

His hands roam my body, leaving a trail of fire that warms the deep recesses of my soul and makes me writhe against him, wanting more. His hand travels down my back to grip my upper thigh and pulls me into his hardness.

A moan of satisfaction escapes me, causing Hermes to growl, and he abandons his assault on my mouth to trail kisses down my neck, gently biting into my collarbone. My head rolls back, and my mouth parts to release exclamations of the pleasure his touch is bringing me as I fist his dark hair with my hands. Now that he is finally touching me, the war within me pulls on its shackles, begging for freedom. Like the feeling before my powers shatter, pressure builds within me, wanting a release that can't be satisfied.

"Rhea." My name escapes his throat in a breathy whisper before he reclaims my mouth again, playing my tongue like a composer plays a symphony. He takes my face in his hands, and the kissing slows. We pull away and look into each other's eyes, panting.

"I've resisted the urge to kiss you since I first saw you in the bookstore." He kisses my neck, my cheek, the tip of my nose, and above my eye. A giggle bubbles up from within me as he peppers me with gentle pecks around my face.

"Well, I have to give you credit. This kiss will probably be the most amazing first kiss in history." I grab the belt loops of his pants and pull him into me, claiming his mouth again with mine briefly before pulling away. "Thank you for bringing me here," I whisper to him.

He kisses me softly; I let my tongue graze his lips in a gentle tease. A wave of satisfaction washes over when my actions wrench another growl from Hermes, followed by him pulling me eagerly into his body and capturing my mouth in another passionate kiss. I could stay here and let him consume every inch of my body under the night sky. The moment feels so right, like it was destined to happen this way.

Our mouths part and Hermes rests his forehead on mine. I hold my eyes closed a moment longer to relish the final lingering feelings where his lips joined mine and inhale his intoxicating fragrance. With a deep sigh of contentment, I open my eyes and meet his hungry gaze, still full of desire, as Hermes' phone chimes in his pocket. He releases a deep breath before he retrieves it and checks a text from Achilles.

"As much as I'd love to keep this going for the rest of eternity..." He smiles mischievously. "We have to get going soon." He leans down and places another kiss on my lips—the sweet gesture filling me with happiness. We turn, and he wraps his arm around me as we watch the falls a moment longer.

My one day was perfect. And now I must lock it all away and prepare to leave him behind with only this memory. The sun finished setting here, marking the finale of a love that will never have a chance to get started. And on the other side of the world, a handful of puzzle pieces are waiting for me to put together the mystery of my life.

"Ready?" he asks. Smiling, I nod. My lips are plump and warm, alive with more need to touch Hermes. He grabs my hand and pulls it to his mouth with a kiss. Retrieving the blue wand from a pocket, I take a deep breath, releasing it slowly before beginning the lies that will end in Hermes discovering I've left.

"Can I do it?"

He hands me the wand, unaware I'm going to keep it. We turn to the falls for one last look before I press the trigger, and we're surrounded again by a bright blue light.

Hermes

The afterburn of our kiss at the falls leaves a gentle smile on my face and a slight blush on Rhea's cheeks. I could throw Achilles off this mountain for texting me, but he said it was urgent. Returning to the cottage from the trail, Medusa, Callie, and Achilles are waiting for us in the garden. My heart falters when Rhea pulls her hand out of mine before we cross the threshold of the white gate. Medusa notices the small retreat and flicks her eyes at me as she stifles a knowing smile while I roll my eyes at my old friend.

"We have a problem," Achilles calls as we enter the gate. "The wolves have gone to the Underworld."

"Which wolves?" I ask. My brow crumples inward at the confusion of what he means.

"All of them."

Fuck.

"Kellen and Zara called early this morning." Medusa takes over the explanation. "They won't be able to help us anymore because Ares has called all the wolves to the Underground. Especially those who have not shifted. He's preparing for the equinox."

I look at Rhea and take a step closer to her without thinking. She is rubbing one of her arms like she's cold, and her eyebrows sit high on her forehead as she listens. I want to hold her but seeing that she pulled away from me a moment ago, I will give her space.

I don't want to say my thoughts out loud, but everyone is probably thinking the same thing; we may have to rethink our approach to keep Rhea safe. Ares has never made this drastic move with the Shifter population before, so something big is coming. Damien's theory is likely correct, and it's time to prepare for war.

"Ares must have a plan to come after Rhea again. If he's pulling all the wolves worldwide, he's getting ready." Everyone shakes their head in agreement at my statement, except Rhea. She stares at the ground with unfocused eyes.

"Should we contact Hecate and postpone the meeting?" Achilles suggests.

"No," Rhea answers quickly. "I'm meeting her tonight. If I'm going to have any chance against Ares, I need to know who I am; I need my memories."

Callie steps toward her and takes her arm inside her own. "I agree."

"Let's see if Hecate will come here, then," I add.

"Already tried," Medusa interjects, throwing a hand up and brushing off my suggestion. "She is adamant the meeting *must* occur at the Cave of Aid."

Gods, this woman gets under my skin.

"Penelope and Odysseus have gotten things ready for us. We need to dress to impress tonight and wait at their club. When Hecate is ready, we'll meet her at her cave. Hermes, we'll need Mirage to hide our identities." I nod in agreement as Medusa conveys the plans.

"Guards?" My expression is expectant as I tilt my head to the side and raise my eyebrows, but I know Medusa is taking the threat seriously.

"You wound me," she mocks with a smirk. "Only the best for the Ferryman."

Rhea and I share the book, penned by my mother, of Persephone's abduction. Callie and Rhea agree it's a loose parallel to our current conflict with Ares and decide to bring the book to Hecate tonight. Stuffing the poem inside, they put the book in Callie's purse for safekeeping.

The afternoon turns to dusk, and we head to the dining hall. Grilled meat and vegetables permeate the air in a delicious beacon that lifts everyone's tense spirits. Achilles and I boast to Medusa about our shooting range scores and feign loudly in disbelief when she confesses she outshot us. Anahita and her sister, Avaley, each choke on their drinks, spilling them as they laugh at our seemingly *low* scores. Callie locks her arm in Rhea's, and they chuckle at the spectacle we are making.

A pleasant warmth fills me as I suddenly realize this happy little family gathered around Rhea without her awareness, pulling her into the safety of our comradery. If Ares himself showed up right now, everyone here would be ready to put themselves in harm's way to keep her safe.

Pulling myself out of my vacancy, I lock eyes with Rhea. She gives me a coy half grin and inquisitively raises her eyebrows, as if asking what I'm thinking. It makes me chuckle, and I give her a flirtatious wink that makes her squirm.

Anticipation follows dinner, and we prepare to see Hecate. Callie insists on getting ready with Rhea because she shopped for the perfect outfits for tonight. This facade of going in through the nightclub adds an element of danger that can easily be avoided, and I don't feel good about it.

Music and laughter seep out from behind the closed door of our bedroom. Eventually, Callie emerges wearing a white shimmer mini dress with a diagonal strap over one shoulder, leading to a shallow cut back. The charm of her gold necklace —two olive branches symbolizing her two mates—swings as she spins, showing Achilles her outfit. She giggles when he pulls her into his lap, showering her with kisses.

My heart was not ready for the vision of Rhea in a satin, hunter-green dress, and it shatters me. It fits her form and curves perfectly with a cinch around her waist. A sinful slit up the side exposes her plump thigh as she strides over to me. The dress straps rest comfortably on her shoulders, holding up the draped neckline with a seductive hint of cleavage that bounces as she walks. Perched perfectly on green heels, the sexy straps hug her narrow ankles. The deep green dress brightens her honey hair and eyes as they burn through me.

I don't care if she took her hand away from me at the gate; no power in this realm, or any other, can stop me from worshipping the goddess before me. I pull her into me, possessing her mouth and running my hands down the smooth satin fabric of the dress. Continuing the curve of her back to the roundness of her bottom, I grip her firmly. Reluctantly, I pull away, and she flutters her beautiful eyelashes at me, looking like pure seduction.

"Rhea, you are devastating." My deep voice is breathless as I speak into her mouth.

"Are you sure we have to go out tonight?" she asks as her full lips curl into a wicked smile.

I chuckle and watch it roll down her body, sending a shiver

down the length of her. I move my mouth to nuzzle her neck and answer. My lips graze the skin of her neck as I speak.

"Don't tempt me because I have no willpower to say no to you at the moment."

"You two ready?" Achilles asks, clearing his throat.

"You guys go ahead, and I'll meet you at the portal." I call over to them, releasing my hold on Rhea. "I have to stash a few more weapons on me."

Callie stands by the door, looking pleased with her efforts. Rhea ducks her head in embarrassment but leaves the cottage with Callie and Achilles. After getting what I need, I jog up the path and catch the group as they arrive at the portal.

Medusa exudes power and confidence in a black snakeskin bodysuit with thigh-high boots. Her toned arms sport the tribal inking of her tattoos and serve as the perch for her favorite gold-coiled snake, wrapped in a tight hug around her bicep. The arm bangle was a gift from Athena long ago, and Medusa never takes it off.

I love going out with Medusa to nightclubs when she looks so terrifying. She usually puts some egotistical man in his place and then steals his date. This would be a fun evening if tonight was not a serious mission.

"About time!" she calls to us, eyeing Rhea's green dress. "Man, I would kill to be that dress right now. Rhea, you look amazing."

"Hey, stop flirting with my lady, Deuce." I tease her.

"Why? Worried she may leave you for me?" She winks at me, laughing, and steps onto the portal. I roll my eyes while Rhea chokes back a laugh at Medusa's heckling.

With everyone gathered, we step onto the platform. Medusa will be using her personal portal device so we can get directly in and out of the Commune without going to the plain below. Her Commune brings a lot of mortals through their gates, and the dual portals are a necessary safety measure. Just before the portal flashes, the anticipation of the evening brings a cold chill across my arm to my neck, prickling under my flesh, making me adjust myself in discomfort.

The enormous flash of light encases us, and the change of scenery to the booming nightclub could not be more dramatic against the silent and still Commune we just left. Reverberating electronic music pulsates behind two large double doors, and our guards immediately step off the platform to begin covering the area. I wrap an arm securely around Rhea's waist and grab low on her hip.

"Welcome to the Land of the Lotus Eaters," I say in her ear with a seductively foreboding look in my eyes.

Rhea's mouth drops open in disbelief as she looks around the interior, taking in all the great details of the extravagant decor. The nightclub is in the center of the Greek Isle of Kriti. Lotus extract in the food and drinks intoxicates the patrons, sustaining them for days with unending fun.

A haven for Immortals and filthy rich humans who delight in feeding a Vampire or being a lover to a Shifter. The decor is lush and velvet with rich jewel tones and gold accents. A lotus flower, split in two, makes up the large brass handles of two giant doors carved in an intricate scene of the infamous lotus-eaters.

Penelope and Odysseus approach through the double doors; the music suddenly blaring subsides again when the door closes behind them. Penelope dons a tight bondage-style leather dress with a strapless black corset tied tightly. Her hair is in a high, sleek ponytail looking like a whip.

Odysseus is sporting black pants with his shirt unbuttoned, nearly down to his beltline, revealing a toned chest and smooth lines of his fit abdomen. Rhea eyes them timidly, adjusting the straps of her dress, suddenly self-conscious of herself. She really doesn't know how envious all the stars in the sky must be of her beauty.

I'll have to work to change that.

"You look wonderful, Rhea; welcome!" Penelope says coolly, kissing both sides of Rhea's cheeks.

"Hecate is not quite ready to meet, so we need to stall up here for a bit," Odysseus calls out as he looks over our ensemble. Casting my power of Mirage, my aura distorts our faces for anyone who may see us tonight. Ares is innovative and strategic. He won't call all the Shifters and leave none in their territories. He likely has scouts out looking for Rhea at this very moment, so everyone must be cautious.

As we enter the club, the music is pounding; bodies are pulsating and surging like rolling waves of water, undulating back and forth with the winds and tides. Rhea's eyes are wide as she takes in the scene. The black lights of the club illuminate Immortal auras of all colors. She watches one man in particular as he caresses a woman's arm, licking her wrists as his eyes reflect silver in the darkness.

"Vampire!" I yell to her over the music. Her mouth drops open, and she snaps her head to me, shock in her big honey eyes.

"Is he going to bite her?"

I can't help but chuckle. "Probably. But it seems like that is exactly what she is hoping for from the looks of it." Rhea turns back to the couple as the Vampire feasts greedily between the woman's legs. She pierces her wrist with a silver talon that covers one of her fingernails, dripping blood down her center for her lover. With a bow in her back, the thumping music drowns out the sounds of her climax, and Rhea quickly diverts her eyes away.

Odysseus directs us to a private nook while we wait. Cocktails with high-end hors d'oeuvre seem to fabricate out of thin air.

"Just don't eat the sweets!" I caution Rhea.

"Why?"

"Because they are laced with a toxin," Odysseus takes one from a platter and winks at her. "It heightens the erotic feeling of the club and keeps you here for a few days. You won't want to leave, and you'll consume more of the lotus sweets. We'll have to pull you out by force in a week or two!" About to pop the small tart in his mouth, Penelope smacks it from his hand with a stern look.

"My love, what?" he exclaims in disbelief while Rhea and I chuckle at their interaction.

"We're working tonight." She shakes her head at him before shrugging her shoulders at Rhea.

Eyeing the security of the club and the support we brought with us, I feel like it's safe to take a moment to let Rhea enjoy the club. She's been through so much the past three weeks, and it'll do her good to blow off some steam for a few minutes.

Standing, I adjust the rolled-up sleeves on my black button-down shirt and hold my hand to her. "Let's dance." Her eyes narrow at my jab back to our sparring session. The thought of pinning her against the wall floats through my mind, and my eyes roam her body, thinking how amazing this dress would look bunched up around her ass.

"You feel like ending up on your back again, Hermes?" she teases as she takes my hand and stands.

Pulling her into me, I wrap my other arm around her waist and tuck myself into her. Taking her ear in my mouth for a small nip, she yelps at the surprise, drawing a smile on my face.

"If it also ends up with you on top of me, absolutely."

We rotate in and out of the dancefloor in different groups. Rhea is a great dancer, and we hold our gaze as if we're the only two people in the club. Her hips sway in a fascinating rhythm with the beat of the music, and her arms cast spells over me as she works her body to the song. Losing myself in the pulsating wake of her movements, I feel as if I'm floating on top of the water, lost in the enchantment she is casting, and I'm happy to let it drive me into her oblivion. I slide my hand across her midriff from behind and move in close, matching her movements with my hips. She turns her head to the side, giving me access to her neck.

A whisper invades our moment, and Rhea's body tenses under my touch.

"Bellissima."

A cold shiver of warning shoots down my entire body and rips me out of my haze.

"Ares," Rhea whispers with a tremor in her voice.

I spin around in a rush but find no one behind us as I cast my aura through the club, I search for him. "I heard him too."

"What is it?" Achilles is by my side in seconds, alert and scanning the crowd. My breathing has quickened, and my pulse is racing like two galloping horses to keep Rhea safe.

"Ares. He just talked to Rhea using telepathy." I answer him.

"Hecate is ready for you now," Odysseus reports with a detail of his guards behind me.

Achilles taps Callie and Medusa, snapping them out of their dance. I try to conceal my tense body from Rhea and put my arm around her protectively, steering us through the crowd.

Retrieving my phone from my pocket, I fire off a hasty text message to Atlas, asking him to call me in an hour. Locking the screen, I slide the phone back into my pocket.

"Penelope and I will stay here and keep an eye on things. My security will escort you to Hecate's. You can use the passageways." Odysseus and I exchange a firm handshake by grasping our wrists together.

Our small horde of Elemental warriors from the Kenya Commune and the club security form an impressive escort, and I'm glad to have them all with us. We're led around the back halls of the club, beyond the kitchens, and into a large, enclosed portal.

"What is Arkession Antron?" Rhea asks no one in particular as she reads the plaque inside the portal, promising our destination.

"It's the *Cave of Aid*. It's rumored to be the birthplace of Zeus by the mortals." Medusa chuckles, humored. "But it's just Hecate's... *fortress,* I guess. People have been coming to her here for years, wanting all kinds of things: remedies for illnesses, potions for love, fortune telling."

When the portal doors open, the scene before us is truly breathtaking. A grand facade is carved out of the rock fifty feet high, and the waves of the Mediterranean slam against large boulders behind us. Intricate scenes carved and painted into the cave walls of ancient Greece depict a great battle that morphs into a processional of peace and celebration. In the middle of the center of the massive mural is a set of enormous gold doors, and dual torches burn on each side. Rhea is enamored with the sight and takes in the surroundings in amazement.

Hecate stands by the entrance, ready to greet us, looking as if she is stuck in a time warp from ancient Greece. Her long, wiry black hair has a strip of grey framing her face. A braid crowns her head, and she's wearing a deep red silk chiton with a golden sash draped across her shoulder, cutting her hip on the other side.

"Welcome, Rhea. I'm glad to see you again," she says, smiling. Rhea's gaze flicks to me with a furrowed brow before looking back slowly at Hecate. "Come. I can't tell you everything, but hopefully, I can tell you something that will help your journey," she says, opening the door wide for us to enter.

The interior is vast and encased in stone. Our shoes echo across the cavernous space and high ceiling while we follow Hecate. A large fireplace casts dancing shadows that stretch along the cave floor while a large black dog rests in front. Logs half the size of trees are burning, and a brass bowl sits on a three-legged pedestal in front. A large black crow is perched on an impressive marble mantle, flapping its wings as we disturb the quiet space with our visit. It watches us with a knowing intelligence in its eyes. Rhea tracks the crow, watching it with a curious expression that I can't place.

Sitting in a chair with deep velvet upholstery is a shell of a woman, barely recognizable. Her once-tanned skin from time spent outdoors in her gardens is pale and pulled tight across her bones: chestnut brown hair, usually in silky ribbons of tight coils springing around her face now sits frazzled and dull on her head. Eyes once lively and dancing are now dark and hollow.

Flora.

Callie gasps when she recognizes her friend and rushes to her, kneeling in front of her and taking her face gently between her hands. Flora closes her sad eyes and weeps into Callie's touch. Standing next to the chair is Flora's partner, Zephyr. A benevolent pair, Flora and her power over life creates flowers and bountiful crops for harvest, and Zephyr, a Wind Elemental, carries the pollen and breeze to strengthen Flora's plants as the pair spend their time in the greenhouses and fields of the Commune.

I can't believe anyone can think Flora capable of betraying the people she loves and cares for. But her presence here begs the question of *how* because no one can escape The Labyrinth. Medusa and I seem to reach the same conclusion because we immediately shift our attention to Hecate.

"That is why you were in the shadows for so long." Medusa accuses with a pointed finger at Hecate. "You went to the Labyrinth and got her out?"

Hecate stands by her basin with her hands folded in front of her. With a smile and a bow, she dips her head at Medusa's conclusion.

"How?"

"I am the Architect, after all." Medusa and I look at each other with disbelief in our furrowed brows and raised shoulders. "The hard part is staying out of the watchful gaze of Archangel Michael. That man is a narcissist if I ever met one."

Hecate walks to the chair next to Flora and holds her hand to Rhea. Understanding the invitation, Rhea approaches as she picks at her thumbnail. Her eyes dart around the cave's interior, taking in all the details and trying to keep from staring at Hecate.

"Rhea, this is Flora, and she was falsely accused of a crime she did not commit. There was another traitor in the Commune that night orchestrating things."

Flint. The bastard revealed his true colors when he tracked Rhea at her aunt's cabin. I can't wait to give that piece of shit what he deserves.

"I would appreciate it if you could heal her." Hecate's eyes curve as she smiles expectantly at Rhea as if this is a challenge Hecate is posing intentionally. Ana is with us and is a Water Healer, but Rhea kneels next to Callie, taking one of Flora's hands.

Closing her eyes and breathing slowly through her nose, Rhea's silver aura tremors just above the surface of her skin before flaring to life around us. The minerals within the cave walls gleam and sparkle like glitter. Swirls of blue and yellow orbs twinkle in the space between Rhea and Flora. Rhea's skin begins to glow pale yellow until a ball of light passes from her into Flora.

Like being reanimated from the dead, Flora's dismal brown hair springs to life again in silky tendrils. Color and fullness return to her face and cheeks, and her eyes brighten and sparkle like the hope that arrives with spring when it chases away a long winter.

Letting her shoulders drop, and releasing a large puff of air, Rhea opens her eyes and inspects Flora, who looks down at Rhea with admiration glistening in her eyes. Zephyr releases a muddled sob disguised with a laugh as they cover their mouth, looking at Flora's returned health. Water healing is tending to wounds on the skin and within the body, like cuts and fractures. What is happening shouldn't be possible. Rhea restored Flora's *life*.

Ana steps forward from her place at the door, her mouth gaping open. "That was no water healing I've ever seen."

Hecate helps Rhea stand with pride in her eyes as she looks at Rhea. "Correct. That was Life healing." Every head in the room turns and looks at one another in amazement. With control over four elemental powers, Rhea's powers are incomprehensible, but Hecate suggests she also controls Life. *Five elemental powers.*

Could that be how Ares plans to use Rhea to pull the Shifters during the Equinox?

"Thank you for helping me," Flora says quietly to Rhea. "You must be the one I made the Wisteria for. Did you like it?"

"I'm sorry?"

I close my eyes to hide the regret. Flora doesn't know Rhea never got to see the apartment or the surprise. Leaning around Rhea so Flora can see me, I interject.

"Sadly, I never got to show it to her, Flo."

Rhea looks back at me with a look of puzzlement on her face.

Flora nods at me as Zephyr places their hand on Flora's shoulder, and leans down; they touch their foreheads together, closing their eyes and reveling in being reunited. Hecate tucks Rhea's hand into the crook of her arm and escorts her across the cave to her basin.

"Everyone sit, and I'll begin. Rhea, please join me at the table." The group follows her direction; Rhea sits at a small table, her eyes are back on the crow. She fidgets nervously, and I track her as she explores the cave, waiting for everyone to settle.

She finally notices Hecate's dog resting unassumingly by the fire. "What is that?" Rhea's voice is a mixture of horror and intrigue. Admittedly, it's not every day you see a dog made entirely of soot and shadow.

Hecate looks at her dog affectionately before answering. "Cerberus is a *Hellhound*. A gift from Lucifer's son." The dog stretches and rolls to his side, lying his head down to resume his slumber. Smoke and shadow roll off him in endless waves, but somehow the beast remains solid.

"You're kidding me. The devil is real too?"

Hecate chuckles. "I know you have many questions, but as I said, I cannot reveal everything. You have ensured that long before your visit today."

"Is that because of your poem "The Forgotten Goddess"?" Rhea asks as Callie reaches into her purse and retrieves the book containing the poem.

Rhea hands the poem to Hecate, keenly watching the parchment paper in Hecate's hand as if expecting it to do something at her touch. Leaning back in her chair, her shoulders drop when nothing happens. She wants answers so badly, and knowing Hecate, this will only leave her with more questions.

Closing the book, Rhea turns the cover to Hecate. "Hermes' mother wrote this story. Is it about me also?" Again, Hecate agrees with Rhea's assumption.

"So, Hades is a reference for Ares? And long ago, in our battle, I was gravely hurt?"

"Yes, young goddess."

"And I cast a spell to make the world forget about me?"

"I'm afraid so."

Rhea reflects on the answers as she looks at her lap and continues to pick at the skin around her nails. Sitting on the edge of the fireplace, the crow flaps its wings and pulls Rhea's attention. She looks at the bird, going to that far-off place in her mind that she goes when her eyes glaze over. Coming back to herself, she blinks quickly as she straightens her posture.

"What do you remember?" Hecate asks Rhea.

Tilting her head and looking deeply at Hecate, Rhea reflects for a while before answering.

"You were there, weren't you?" Rhea says, her chest rising quickly as she waits for the answer. Hecate closes her eyes and nods her head once. "At the car accident, you were there."

"I was."

"You are the woman I can never see at the end of my memories. They weren't my family, were they?"

"No." Hecate answers pointedly.

"Did I kill them?" She looks down at the stone floor with tears in her eyes. I start toward her, but Callie holds her hand up to me in a silent signal to stop. Her gaze is harsh, as if telling me Rhea needs to do this on her own. Thinking back to Deuce's words, she doesn't need me to protect her, only support her. I shift my shoulders, adjusting the weight between them.

"You did not kill them. That little girl was a mortal and would have died with her family that day," Hecate explains slowly, with steely eyes on Rhea. "At the exact moment of her death, your immortal soul inhabited her body."

"What does Ares want with me?"

"What all insecure men want. Power." Hecate is always nonchalant and brief with her answers. She often talks in riddles that leave you guessing. A trait that annoys me. "He wants to consume your abilities like a cannibal."

Rhea visibly shutters at the admission.

"I have dreams sometimes." Rhea's voice is quiet as she

fixates on the stone floor again. "Dreams of different times, and Ares is in them. He captures me." Rhea's words come out faster with Hecate's prodding her on to keep moving through her thoughts. "He captures me, and I remember him stabbing me–in the dreams. So... those are real memories before I die and come back to do it all over again, and no one knows because I cast a spell to make them all forget."

"Yes, my goddess." Hecate lowers her head, a look of regret etched in her eyes. "You are the great phoenix, Rhea, reincarnating in a karmic cycle until you defeat the hunter. You live and die, then rise again in a new life, and attempt to solve the riddle of your spell. In some of your lives, you are found by your allies; in others, your hunter has found you first." Her face drops, and a veil of sadness flows over her momentarily before she clears her throat. "Those lives are the hardest for me. Such a short time to get to know you before I grieve you again."

"How do I break the spell?"

"You split your immortality and your powers, hiding them within four objects of great meaning." Hecate pulls a deck of tarot cards, the edges rounded and tattered from their years of use. Flipping four cards over on her table, she reveals the ace of swords, the ace of cups, the ace of pentacles, and the ace of wands. "You must find the objects and fully restore your immortality and powers."

"If the family is not real, what about my Aunt Demi? Did she know what I was? Did she know I was not her niece? The wolves killed her because of me."

"My half-sister, Demeter—not your aunt. We both keep watch over you in your lives. She is not dead, but I believe the wolves have taken her captive."

"So, where did I come from before? Do I have a real family

out there somewhere?" Rhea's shaky voice is barely a whisper. Hecate reaches across the table and rubs Rhea's hair, momentarily resting her palm on Rhea's cheek. Endearment and love pass from Hecate to Rhea like a mother consoling her daughter.

"The answer to that mystery is hidden with the Great Library."

"Alexandria?" Rhea says in her high-pitched voice, showing her intrigue. "So, it is still here? It's not destroyed."

Hecate smiles widely with a gleam in her obsidian eyes. "You always did have a fondness for books, and you protected the Library under a great Mirage. If you find it, you'll get the answers to your question."

"How do you know these things when no one else does?" I ask.

"Many things hide in the shadows. Pieces of the truth that remain are tucked away in the dark corners of our minds. Places where Light cannot travel." There she goes with her riddles for answers. Balling my fists at my side, I thin my lips in irritation.

"You are part of this as well, Hermes." She smiles fondly, rubbing the blue leather-bound book. "You are bound to the journey of the goddess. The antidote to your release is within the book, and Rhea holds the key. Follow the inscription, and your journey will begin, as will hers."

She stands, scanning the group accompanying Rhea tonight, and smiling at us all.

"I wish I could tell you more, but I am bound. Good luck and goodbye." She bows, and a long silver necklace holding an ancient key with three circles at the top swings from her neck. I watch it dangle as my anger spills over.

"That's it?" I bark. "Cryptic messages with no help, just like your last advice for my father. Perfect."

"Hermes," Callie whispers.

"I knew this would be a waste." I turn on my heel and stomp through the great cave toward the enormous doors. When I reach them, I look back to see Rhea, still at the basin, looking at Hecate apologetically.

"Thank you," Rhea says politely. Hecate rounds the basin and takes Rhea in an embrace. Keeping her eyes on me, Hecate whispers into Rhea's ear. One more message of confusion, I'm sure, before she sends Rhea off to figure all this out on her own. As Rhea turns around, her body is rigid, and her face is white like alabaster.

31 Rhea

I t's an odd feeling, knowing I have a choice in whether I die tonight or not. Hecate said I had to know. She took me in an embrace and told me.

"You have a choice tonight. Stay, and you will meet your hunter. Leave, and you will die, and the cycle will start again. Hermes is not strong enough to do what he needs to do. He can't admit it, but he loves you too much to do what is necessary. Make your choice, but above all else, give him the key."

She places my sword necklace in my hand and closes my fist over it. Then, she puts the four tarot cards inside the blue leather book and hands it to me. Her eyes are strained as if she needs me to understand words she cannot say. I don't even know how she got the necklace off my neck.

A cold terror slowly seeps over my limbs and crawls around me in a suffocating caress. How did she know I was planning on leaving? While Callie and I were getting ready, Callie was in the bathroom fixing her hair, and I finished packing the bookbag and stashed it under the bed with the teleportation wand hiding inside.

He loves you too much.

Her words about Hermes bounce through me. How can

he love me when I don't even know who I am? I don't even know my real name. Rhea is the name of the girl who died before I stole her body.

This is all too much.

The cave starts spinning, and a high-pitched ring in my ears drowns out the low tones of everyone's murmurs. According to Hecate, I have lived a hundred lives. Lifetimes through the rise and fall of kingdoms, loving and dying over again. I wonder how many ways Ares has killed me. Have I even died on my own before, or have all of my deaths been at his hands?

Maybe I shouldn't remember. The pain of it all would be too much to stomach. The weight of my thoughts bears down on me like a thousand pounds.

I'm hardly aware Hermes is near. His cologne surrounds me like a hug, and I realize how cold my body is turning. The tips of my fingers tingle from the chill that will soon spread up my hands. I turn to face Hermes, trying to focus on him. He's upset, grabbing Hecate's arm.

"I told her what she needed to hear." Hecate's voice echoes around the cave chamber as she answers Hermes' question.

"Hey. You okay?" Hermes asks me. The warmth of his hand fights off the cold compressing over me, and I lean into him. Closing my eyes, I take in his scent, the feel of his hard body against me. He's like a safe harbor in a storm, and I squeeze my eyes tighter as I understand what Hecate means.

Hermes is not strong enough to do what he needs to do.

He needs to let me go, but he can't.

My eyes roam up his chest, hovering over the dimples on each side of his mouth that I'm so fond of before reaching the deep blue depths of his eyes. Slowly, the great thumping in my head softens, helping me focus on the cave's interior room.

With both hands resting firmly on him, I can feel his aura roiling with frustration and anger, but also care and hopelessness and something else—something I cannot pick out. A part of him, locked away like a secret wanting so badly to be told.

The antidote to your release is within the book, and Rhea holds the key.

My throat opens, allowing air to enter my lungs as more of the messages from tonight absorb inside me. My spell has become a prison for him. For everyone. I've trapped them all, and I can feel that piece of him that's been locked up.

Hours ago, I wanted Hermes to make me feel like the woman he loved–the goddess that took his heart when Ares killed her. But that woman *was* me, and I was her. A different body, but the soul of the woman he loves. It's why I can feel him before he enters the room. It's why I fell into his arms while trapped in that dark space and wanted to return home.

Searching that deep chasm within me where I lock away my powers, I want to find the connection that I remember from my dreams. I was locked in a cage on the night of the battle between the valleys. In the dream, I pulled on that tether and sent my hopes down the bond, only to feel them disappear into an endless void.

I can feel it now within me, fishing out the connection of our souls among the swirl of my powers. Like the dream, the other end of the line that should be connected to him hangs slack. Ares has taken this from us, too.

Perhaps it's why I keep failing life after life. Ares knew we would chase this severed connection that died long ago, hoping it could be brought back to life. But like Medusa and Athena, the love that could be between Hermes and me has already been murdered by the man that haunts my soul and hunts my powers.

When I finally look at Hermes' face, the thought of him remaining trapped, confined, and suffering because of Ares' obsession rips through me like a cannonball bursting through the walls of a castle. He's watched me repeatedly die and hurt so much, hanging onto a hopeless dream.

Stay, and you will meet your hunter. Leave, and you will die, and the cycle will start again.

If he knew what Hecate said, he would probably want to hide me away and keep me from either fate. Hermes would probably be okay with existing for all time as a living prison, constantly running from a monster. But I'm not.

I'm done hiding from Ares and dying at his hand for all of eternity; I'm done feeling too scared I might become a victim. I'll find the Library of Alexandria and learn about its secrets, how I came to be, and the truth of my name. I'll break this curse of a spell I cast on myself. If Hermes and I have no chance of love, at least I can free him of more lifetimes of torment.

I want to tell him goodbye. I want to give him something that can end it all for him and release him from the obligation of following me, from trying to protect me from an inevitable conclusion.

But the words won't come out.

I collide with him, desperate to feel him, crushing my mouth to his. Hermes pulls my body flush with his and we meld together as one being. A deep recess within me begins swirling like two dragons trapped together, stirring and clawing to free themselves. Pulling away, my breathing is heavy but returning. My lips tingle from our passion. I stare at him, wanting to burn the image of his beautiful face in my mind, so in the moments of my solitude, his face is all I will see. I can remember that moment at the waterfall where I was the one girl in the universe he wanted.

I close my eyes and take a deep breath to steady myself. I need to be brave and strong. I'll do this, but I can't do it scared. I don't want Hermes to see me afraid; when he thinks about why I left, I want him to know it was for the right reason. When I open my eyes again, I don't feel as shaky, and I breathe normally.

"I'm ready to go," I say out loud.

With the book in my hand, I hide the necklace. It feels odd letting it go. It's been like a shield I could hide behind when feeling alone the past few weeks. The feeling of it on my neck was reassuring and gave me comfort. Now with it in my hand, I feel a cold vulnerability where its warmth should be.

If Hecate is right and this is the key to something else still needing to be unlocked, I know Callie will return it to Hermes. I deliver the book back inside her purse, the necklace dropping secretly with it. Callie has been such a great friend through everything. I've never really connected with anyone or allowed myself to trust people, but with Callie, it was such a natural friendship.

My heart was so cold after my family died, but it's finally warming with the relationships I've found. I want to burst into tears and cling to them all, devastated to let them go too soon—I'm broken thinking about the struggles they may have endured in my past lives, and torn knowing it's not over yet and there could be more pain in their futures because of me.

I'll add this to my thoughts as I search for the answers to break the spell and set them all free. On the cold nights when it all seems hopeless, knowing whom I'm doing this for and the pain I'll be saving them from will keep me going.

"Rhea? Are you okay?" Callie asks me.

Smiling with sad resolve in my eyes, I answer. "Let's go."

Our train of guards, with their stoic expressions, flood out of the cave and into the portal. Medusa leads them and barks orders for vigilance as we make the short track back to her Commune. Hecate's cave is protected by Dark Shield, so teleporting by light power doesn't work here. We'll return to the Land of the Lotus-Eaters and teleport from there.

Flora and Zephyr will stay with Hecate in hiding and find a new location for them to live. Since Flora is supposed to be imprisoned in the Labyrinth for the next two thousand years, they'll have to live in exile like mortals. If they are caught, they'll both be killed by Adamantine Steele.

Maybe I can fix this too.

As the doors to the portal close, I share one last look with Hecate, my mind determined, my jaw firm, and my shoulders pushed back in the confidence of my choice. I hold her stare, and an approving smile is the last thing I see, as if she knows what course I've chosen and she is telling me to go for it.

The booming nightclub assaults our senses as we walk through the side halls and back to the portal platform. Penelope looks at me with a smile that quickly fades. The worry is etched in the lines of her eyes as she and Odysseus tell us goodbye. My hands can't stop fidgeting as I feel the pressing need to distance myself from Hermes, Callie, and the others. The longer I'm with them, the more danger they are in. Hermes slides his cell phone back into his pocket and takes my hand, giving me a small squeeze of reassurance.

Biting my lip, I hold myself from shaking my leg and

showing my anxiety. When we return to the Commune, everyone will want to discuss Hecate's message. I can take advantage of the excitement, excuse myself to the bathroom, and then leave with the portal wand. I can be back in Atlanta, in my car, and heading to the open road before they know I'm gone.

Medusa readies her teleportation device, and Odysseus gives Hermes a nod of confidence as the blue light flashes around us to return us to the Kenyan Commune. The breeze that greets us carries in the songs of crickets singing in the tall grass.

This is not right.

We were supposed to arrive directly in the Commune, but we arrived at the plain below. The vast expanse of the flat grassy field fades into pure darkness. I can feel them. A mass of beings blanketed with obscurity lurk toward us, and the tiny hairs at the nape of my neck stand to attention.

Werewolves.

One by one, pairs of reflective eyes shine back at us in the darkness of the flat expanse of land. They've come for me.

Muffled voices waft around me as everyone talks over each other, but I can't focus on anything except the fur and fangs before us. Prowling on all fours, the bodies of the wolves look like a large undulating mass within the shadows.

"There have to be forty or fifty of them against our twenty. We won't last long out here." I tell our small group. "They're here for me." I hold my hand out to Medusa and ask for her teleportation wand. "Just let me leave, and they'll leave too."

"Not a chance," Medusa shakes her head at me. "We don't go down so easily, and we don't just abandon the people we care about. Avaley will run to the Commune for help, and we can hold out against them long enough."

Achilles and Callie walk several feet in front of us, standing ten feet apart and facing Ares' small army. The other warriors join them, forming a line of defense. Behind them is the great Kenya mountain, and upon it, the unsuspecting Commune with new rescues freshly saved from another gladiator arena.

"Hermes," I turn and face him, touching his chest to keep him from joining them. "This is stupid. There is no reason for these people to die because of me."

He wraps a large hand around mine and holds it as he looks at me with longing eyes. A ripple of blue light shines against his back, and the black straps of my bookbag and the hilts of his two swords reveal themselves. From his pocket, he hands me the portal wand that I kept after we left Angel Falls.

"I was looking for my wand, just in case we needed it tonight, and found your bug-out bag." He slips the strap off his shoulder and slides it up my arm. "I would never hold you back from doing what you must do." Fixing the other strap on my shoulder, he brings his hand to my cheek, and I close my eyes, leaning into his touch. The knot in my throat is too large to swallow as I look up at him blankly, not knowing what to say.

He knew.

He knew I was going to leave, and he brought my bag with him, hiding it and his swords with his Mirage because he loves me; not because I'm just a job.

"Hermes," I choke out his name from the tears swelling in my eyes.

"Shhh." He silences me with a kiss, softly pressing his warm lips to mine and holding me in his touch. "Don't you see? Not even death is strong enough to keep us apart. We have found each other a hundred times, and I'll find you a hundred more. Across every lifetime, in any realm, my soul belongs to no one else but you."

He touches his forehead to mine and closes his eyes. The pained furrow in his brow relaxes, and his tight shoulders drop. With a large exhale, he stands to his full height and gazes down at me.

"My Mirage will make you invisible, and I will project an image of you next to me to make them think you are still here. I'll buy you as much time as I can." He releases my hand and takes a step back.

His blue aura glows over me and pulls a mirror image of my body. Translucent to my eyes, a Mirage projection of myself stands next to him, taking solid form as he makes it walk to the line with the others. To the wolves looking on, it would seem I'm planning to fight with the other Elementals, while he's actually shielding me so I can leave.

Blinking with tear-filled eyes, I stare at him, unable to speak about what he is doing. He's going to let me go. My chest rises sharply as a tightness grips me from the inside. *Say it.* I beg myself to say the words that are stuck in my throat.

Tell him you love him before you leave.

Squeezing my eyes tight, I feel his retreating form as the warmth of his aura leaves me without a word of goodbye.

He stands with our warriors in a line. Ana is at the ready with a long spear of water. Avaley stands a step behind her sister with whipping air currents forming her trusted bow and arrow. Medusa has her braids unfurled, and the echo of their rattles is an ominous promise to the unwelcome visitors.

Hermes' back to me feels like a tall, looming wall of rejection, and I can't look at him. The light projection beside him tears my heart, and my body wants to go to him. But I will myself to remain still. *I have to leave.* Callie stands with Achilles, wind whipping the long ribbons of her platinum hair as Achilles' hands hold two balls of molten flames. Smoke billows off his shoulders as a warning of the fire inside him.

The darkness of the plain masks Ares' forces as they creep closer and begin materializing in the moonlight. My breath catches as their sheer size is overwhelming to my senses. They are massive and could easily wrap their jaws around a human torso, not to mention that their paws are larger than my head. Their sharp claws will easily shred anything crossing their path.

As the growls and snarls bounce off the grassy plain, the wolves continue their silent trek toward us. And then I see him. The one wolf that terrifies me the most. Lupo. His orange eyes are locked onto the light projection Hermes is casting. If wolves could smile, I would swear Lupo is wearing a sinister grin as he licks his razor-sharp fangs.

With a chill of fear running up my spine, my hand squeezes around the barrel of the portal wand. My thumb rests on the button as I think of my destination.

Avaley stands, her posture taught and straight. Pulling the invisible bow up toward the night sky, her arm strains as a translucent bowstring pulls back tightly, held in place with anticipation.

The distance of a football field separates the two groups of warriors when Avaley releases her arrow of wind, whistling through the night. The snarling and growling of the wolves vibrate my chest as they howl into the cool air.

With my thumb on the trigger and holding my breath, I push the button as tears stream down my face.

Since Juliette was lost to me, I felt this emptiness within. A cavity inside from something plucked out of me, stolen away, leaving me void. When Rhea and I are together, I can feel that space resonate and stir, longing to be filled with something—something only Rhea can give me. Because she is Juliette; they are the same soul residing in different bodies—my true mate. Somewhere deep inside, I know this is true.

My heart sank when I found her bag with my portal wand and several pairs of clothes. I finally gave up my stubborn battle with feeling worthy of love again, but I didn't act fast enough. Rhea needed me to be sure of her, and I wasn't. I wasn't sure of myself, but she wants to leave even after last night, the waterfall this morning, and me sharing my feelings for her. She needed more. She deserves more.

Just because I feel the connection there, buried deep inside me and longing for my mate, doesn't mean she feels it too. And so, she hid the portal wand and intended to leave. Maybe not tonight, but soon.

Tucking the device into her hand and stepping away from her is the hardest thing I've ever done, aside from watching the life drain from Juliette's eyes—her eyes. Rhea takes a deep breath her eyelids drop, hiding their beautiful honey-amber hues from me as I take my place in line with the others, breaking my own heart with each step.

"Damn, there's a lot of them," Achilles says to no one in particular.

Callie and Achilles are to my right; Medusa and her warriors are to my left. The projection of Rhea is by my side, animated under my power.

"What happened to the portal, Deuce?" I call to her, taking a deep breath and ignoring the burning urge to run back to Rhea.

"The Commune portal must be disabled, so it delivered us here to the portal on the plain."

"We're sticking to the plan," Looking at Avaley and giving her a nod, she releases the first arrow into the night, shrieking across the sky. "No one die."

Looking behind me as a great howl rips the still night, Rhea opens her eyes as tears spill over the edges of her brown lashes and roll down her freckled cheeks—the pad of her thumb toys with the trigger of the device.

And then she's gone.

The blue light flashes around her, and she vanishes. She'll reappear somewhere else in the realm and go into hiding. Rhea is intelligent and strong; gods, she has more power than I could ever imagine. But she doesn't remember the world of the Immortals.

Despite what she thinks, we need each other. But if she believes this is the best course of action tonight, I'll spend as much time as I can tearing each of these wolves apart and give her as much of a head start as possible. And when we're done, I'll spend the rest of eternity proving that I love her.

Medusa and three of her warriors step forward and cast their arms wide. With flexed fingers and determination blazing in their eyes, they pull up a mound of earth between the wolves and our position. The quaking mass of the moving earth causes us to shift and lose our balance as we shuffle on our feet to remain standing.

Medusa's green eyes dilate to near black as she turns the unearthed dirt and minerals to hard rock. Twenty feet high and two hundred feet long, the wolves will have to work to pull it down or run around it, and it will buy us a few extra minutes.

"Avaley, run to the Commune and get help," Medusa tells her Wind Siren and the Second Commander of her forces turns on her heel, powered by her winds; she is ready to surge up the mountain. With a missed step, she falters.

"We have company." she says in a dark tone.

Medusa pivots behind us, and I cast my aura outward in all directions.

Damn.

Sixty wolves and ten Elementals are approaching the earthen wall, and twenty-five wolves are behind us, creeping down the mountain with fanged snouts. Searching further with my powers, I pick out the Elementals accompanying the wolves to determine their powers. Most are Flames with a few Earth and Wind Elementals. A slow sense of dread climbs up my spine as I sense a large pocket of darkness in the center.

"They've brought a Dark Mage," I call out, recalling the day in the alley that set all this in motion; the Sensors also detected a Dark Mage there. I'm guessing this is the same one.

Hecate would come in handy right about now.

A low bellow hums from the other side of the earthen wall, and power collides with the dirt on a continuous attack. A powerful force is hitting the center of the structure. The stone veneer is being eaten away as the middle section of the wall quakes. Small rocks and clumps of brown dirt begin to fall to the ground below. The wolves will soon have an opening.

Pinching my eyes tightly closed, I push my aura outward again. It's the Dark Mage.

At that moment, the center of the wall bursts, and a beam of pure dark energy shoots directly at Medusa as she stands in the center of the line, facing the wolves behind us. Turning my feet in her direction, I shoot myself in front of her and brace for the impact of the column of darkness. With my knees bent and my front shoulder dropped, I project a Light Shield across the line of our warriors.

The Dark Beam, neutralized by my Light, lets off a haunting sound like a baritone scream. Straining against the power, I push back, adding more force to the shield, and roaring against the intensity. *This mage is powerful.*

The Dark Mage drops their attack as if turning off a light switch. My chest heaves and sweat drips down the center of my spine from the effort as I peer at our blockade. The wall is crumbled in the middle, about twenty feet wide, and the dark energy has eaten away the ends. With a great howl, a wave of fur and fire ascends upon us through the opening.

"Earth Mages, keep rebuilding the wall all you can and make it a choke point," I call, pulling the swords from the cross-shaped scabbard at my back and holding each in my hands. Half of us break out of line and run into the onslaught. The Earth Elementals narrow the opening and turn the dirt to soft mud. The massive paws of the Shifters sink and slide in the slippery mud.

Callie shoots a funnel of Cutting Wind directly through the middle, slicing five Shifters in two. The top halves of their bodies slide off as the lower halves tumble and fall over themselves. Achilles and two of Medusa's Flames hurl fireballs, sending thousands of embers flying in all directions as they burst upon the wolves that rush through the opening.

Ana hurls her long spears through the heads of the wolves, and their large bodies thump to the ground and slide several feet before coming to rest. She has taken out two Elementals that ran through the opening, impaling them through the heart with a single spear. Their bodies on the water spear shoot backward with the force of the throw. As the water spear pierces the ground, it ruptures, and the two Elementals fall to the ground, dead.

Three fireballs have been launched toward us from the other side of the barricade. The Elementals that accompany the wolves are launching their counterattack. Callie sends bursts of air to the fireballs as they arc over the wall, dispelling them and raining cinders above our heads.

With the center of the wall still narrowed, our warriors are holding their own for now, but we can't stay here much longer. Some Shifters have grown impatient and decided to run to the ends of the wall, and Avaley takes them out with her air arrows, pivoting on one knee to each end.

Medusa has her back to me and focuses her petrification on the wolves descending from the mountain. As Avaley takes out the Shifters at the ends of the wall, she pivots behind her and aids Medusa, shooting arrows of wind at the wolves behind, then shifting back to the wall.

Several Alphas are here tonight, and one walks through the wall's opening, stepping on the bodies of the fallen wolves to avoid getting his paws dirty in the mud. His tongue licks greedily around his snout, readying himself for a meal.

Lupo, the Onyx Alpha, stalks the plain, looking for Rhea. The projection I'm casting of her still mimics her mannerisms and appears to be observing the battle. Leaving the projection, I set out on a path of death, cutting and slicing Shifters on my way to Lupo.

My sharpened blades of Adamantine Steele cut quickly through the muscles of the Shifters' bodies. The Lord of Light's enchanted blade burns blue in my hand, powered by my aura and the etched runes; my speed is faster, my aim is true, and my strikes are stronger. The wolves yelp and snarl as my sword drives through their bodies, leaving them in pieces.

Achilles roars to my right as he burns through a pack of wolves. Sharp as knives, his flames slice through the Shifters just as my swords do, and we move into the growing sea of beasts, leaving their bodies split and spilling their ichor into the Kenyan soil.

Callie, propelled by her wind, flies low to the ground, wrapping her arms around the necks of Shifters. The crack of their bones echoes into the night as she flings their bodies to disappear over the wall and grabs another.

"Lupo!" My voice bounces off the wall, coming back to me. The beast's large head snaps to me, and orange eyes narrow like darts. He accepts my challenge. Returning my swords to their homes, I place my hands in my pockets and take a casual stance. The key to this wolf's death will involve cutting his ego before my swords take his head.

Lupo lowers his haunches before he leaps at me. He's

angry. I put my weapons away, not seeing him as enough of a threat to wield them. As his great body soars through the air, I wait. The speed of light is always within me, and I hold until the last possible second to slide out of his path.

Landing behind me, he skids from momentum, turning to face me and taking another running lunge. Like a figure skater on ice, I move around the grassy field, turning and ducking the lunges and swipes of Lupo's giant paws. With my hands in my pockets and a coy grin, he's nearly trembling with anger.

Lifting his muzzle to the sky, he releases a howl, and six wolves immediately turn their course and head for me. Stretching my neck to each side and rolling my shoulders back, I ready myself for their attacks.

Moving as one large body, their wolf telepathy lets them communicate together. Lupo stalks the perimeter as they lunge for me. Massive fangs dripping with saliva hope to land their mark, but I leave them disappointed. Coming for me in pairs or trios, the flash of my sword is the only movement their eyes track as I decapitate each of them.

Curling lips release a growl from Lupo's throat as I flick the ichor of his pack off the tip of my sword and return it to its scabbard.

Mythology says I am the Guide of the Underworld and escort souls to Charon: the Ferryman who takes fairs across the River Styx. But mythology often gets things wrong, twisting over the sands of time. Stories change. I don't bring souls to the Ferryman; I *am* the Ferryman. Named for my victories in battle, I've sent countless souls by the boatload to their next realm. And Lupo will be the next soul to pay my fare.

I don't know what happened. The portal never flashed. Pushing the button again, I'm immobile, frozen, and locked in place. The wand drops from my hand. I can't blink or breathe; I'm still standing on the plain.

Medusa and her warriors create a long mound along the earth like a wall, but I can't hear anything inside this soundless chamber. As the wall climbs higher and higher, pulling from the dirt of the plain, I watch the line of my friends balance themselves against the vibrations they must be feeling, but nothing is reaching the inside of the strange atmosphere I'm surrounded by.

Avaley turns to run in this direction, and my heart flares that she'll see me, but she doesn't. Medusa snaps her head back and looks right through me at whatever threat is approaching from behind. Fighting and straining, it's like being locked inside a dozen Thaumium cuffs and collars. My body feels like a barren wasteland devoid of my aura, powers, and senses.

"Mmmmmm." A man's deep voice crawls up my spine and worms into my mind. If I could move, my entire body would shiver and recoil from the thick oily feel of his voice. "So much power here."

He rolls his letters like a snake slithering its tongue and licking the air as he talks. Like a great claw has been squeezing my windpipe closed, the grip around me loosens enough to allow me to breathe. Taking in a large sniff of air through my nose, I search the plain for the source of the Elemental holding me.

"Let me go!" I bark through my mind.

His chuckle reverberates around me in all directions, like I'm trapped in a bubble.

"In time. The show is just getting started." My stomach curdles at his words, and I want to vomit, but I can't even gag locked in these unseen shackles.

The newly formed wall cracks and crumbles in the center as a large column of blackness barrels through it. Hermes' Light counters the darkness, and then chaos ensues. Fireballs and weapons of fire, water, and wind are propelled toward the wolves, and Elementals funnel through the hole in the wall.

"Who are you?" At least my mind still works.

"Ah, how rude of me; my name is Moros." The voice slithers through me.

The name is familiar, and I search my memories to recall where I saw it. In my mind's eye, I see the titles of the books I scoured through the Commune library.

"Sadly, I won't get to play with you today, perhaps later." The implications this vile *creature* conjures flash a wave of heat through my body.

Watching the scene ahead of me, the hot nausea is replaced by chilling fear as I watch Lupo step over the dead wolves and into the fray. *I have to get out of here.* Sweat flows down my back, and my thumb twitches. I try to hold back the burst of joy at the tiny movement, so as not to alert my captor, but I'll need a lot more than that to break out of his power.

Moros. Still thinking of the name repeatedly, I try to hide the feeling slowly returning to my digits. I scour my mind for the origin of the name. *I've heard this name recently.*

Lupo's shoulders roll as he prowls across the field to Hermes. Stashing his weapons, Hermes puts his hands in his pockets and shifts his weight onto one leg, casually waiting for Lupo's attack. And then he lunges. Fifteen feet or more away, the beast lowers his front half to the ground, and as his muscles ripple under dark fur, he bounds into the air.

The atmosphere within my confined bubble rolls, and I'm turned around so quickly I can't see Hermes as he battles Lupo.

"*No!*" I yell in my mind, straining and pushing against the tight, invisible vines wrapped around me.

"Let's watch back here for a bit." Moros' slime-coated words trickle across my neck. I can feel the sensation of a phantom hand, cold and clammy with sweat, grabbing my cheeks and holding my head forward, preventing me from looking behind me at Hermes.

"*Turn me back!*" I push hard against the force binding me, but it only tightens as I fight. My body on the outside remains still as the internal battle with these elemental powers rage inside me, fighting to take back control as it squeezes the air from my lungs as the power coils around, constricting everything from moving.

Medusa stands before me, her back to me and holding off two dozen wolves. Her carefully placed crown of braids is uncoiled, and their lengths sway with serpentine movements. Whipping and striking like lightning, she fights against the wolves, throwing several of them in different directions at once while she takes on two with direct combat. Further up the mountain, stone figures of three wolves with their snarls frozen on Shifted forms adorn the landscape as new permanent sculptures to the Kenya mountain.

"Oh, look. She's getting company." Moros turns my body a fraction to the left. Straining my eyes further, I try to find Hermes, but Moros knows what I want and denies me. He fixes my gaze on six wolves prowling toward Medusa as if directing my eyes straight ahead.

She remains focused on the fight at hand, viciously battling the wolves. Both arms are coated in petrified rock as she has turned her own flesh to stone. Tearing a front leg off a Shifters body, she shoves it through its mouth and it bursts out of the back of the wolfs skull.

"Turn around." I try to tell her with telepathy, but I feel my power rebounding against the space, preventing me from communicating with them. The agony of watching this battle helplessly is tearing at my soul. They think I've left and believe they are giving me an advantage by distracting this small army of Shifters.

The wolves trail her. Crouched low like lions stalking a gazelle through tall grass, they wade across the plain toward her. Like a faint breath of air, a wisp of my power stirs inside my entrapment. I watch the wolves as I quietly coax the stirrings of my magic out like threading a needle, I breach the bubble surrounding me. Moros's grip is focused on my center and neck, forcing me to watch. He's not paying attention to all of me, and his power is receding from my fingertips ever so slowly.

If I could only remember who he is. I could recall his power and escape this confinement.

He doesn't notice I've gotten through his enclosure, and I can feel the distant thuds of the battle outside the soundproof chamber. Moving the little strand of wind faster, I wrap my power around the wolves like a rope.

You will not touch her. If I could speak, I would grit the word through my teeth. The wolves halt, and one yelps at the sensation of my power encasing them. It's enough to get Medusa's attention to the threat sneaking up on her.

"Tsk, tsk." Moros clicks his tongue at me. "That is a very sneaky goddess." The surge of his power engulfs me as he finally feels my breach. My spine stiffens as a blinding pain scours my mind. A white-hot light replaces my vision as pain burns through me. Releasing me from his hold on my mind, my body, still in his grasp, goes slack.

The feeling is a lot like Atlas looking at my memories. Maybe he is a Mind Mage too.

"Okay, we can stop playing around." His whisper is soggy in my ear, and I fight again in vain. "Send in the boy." Moros' call rings through my mind, and I know he's communicating with someone else.

Within the bubble of my confinement, a whirlpool of darkness and shadow swirls, spinning open and closing again. Through the dark portal, Flint steps out only feet away from me. With his hands in his pockets, his messy red hair stands on end like wild flames, and his brown eyes gleam at me.

"Oh, Rhea," His eyes take me in like I'm a prize he's won at auction. "That dress is doing it for me." Running his tongue across his lips, he saunters to me while he lets his eyes invade my body freely. Taking his hands from his pockets, he rubs them together as he nears me.

Beyond him, I see Medusa fighting the pack of wolves. Hunching down, she raises both hands as the muscles in her arms tremor. She's going to petrify the lot of them. After cutting several of them down, only ten wolves remain in her relentless combat. From the corners of my vision, I see the wolf's steps falter as she turns their paws to stone first. The veneer spreads up their bodies and takes them over from outside. Leaving the soft tissue of their organs for last, they remain alive through the fossilization of their bodies.

Their heads twist and turn as they raise their snouts. The soundless chamber doesn't allow their cries to enter, but I can imagine them. The wolves fight against it until nothing is left but their eyes, looking around for one last ray of hope before they glaze over to stone for eternity. Finished with the pack of dead wolves, she turns and runs out of my view. Sweat courses down her head as her braids dance and sway with her strong strides.

Flint stands mere inches from me. The toes of his shoes touch mine. I can't move my head up to look at him, still frozen in the clutches of Moros. So, I'm forced to stare at his chest as he looms over me.

"Keep her *just* like this," he croons to Moros. "I like them–*submissive*." He leans down, whispering the word in my ear. My nostrils flare, the only sign of my anger aside from the burn in my cheeks. He takes his forefinger and runs it along the draped hem of my dress, tracing a line gently on my skin over the mounds of my breasts. "Mmmmm." he purrs as his path dips down my cleavage before finishing the trek to the other side of my chest.

His hand slams across my cheek and mouth as he back-hands me. A tickle of warm blood travels slowly down my chin from the corner of my mouth. My eyes blur, and my cheek pulsates with my pounding heart. Grasping my biceps with a crushing hold, Flint flings me around, pulling my body flush against his. The taste of copper curdles in my mouth when I feel his erection against my back. The sick fuck is aroused right now. He's disgusting.

Pushing his nose into my hair, he takes a fist full of my long waves and yanks my head back, turning my locked gaze to the dark sky. Tears run out of the corners of my eyes as his free hand slides along the smooth fabric of the dress, finding the slit that rests high on my leg. Grasping the thin material in his hand, he rips the bottom of the deep green dress, exposing nearly all of my bare legs to the cool Kenya night air.

"*No.*"

Inside, my body is quaking in anger and fear. How much farther will he go? How do I stop this? Invisible from everyone I care about, Flint may be free to take anything he desires from me, frozen under the control of Moros. My body trembles at the thought.

Flint begins stepping backward, pulling me along with him, my heels scraping over the grassy plain as he wrenches me into the remnants of Medusa's fury. He positions himself on a flattened ledge and tilts my head down so I can finally see the battle scene below. Blinking away the tears from my eyes, I scan frantically, looking for Hermes and the others.

The swinging blue blade grabs my gaze quickly, and the relief that floods me sends a wave of my aura pulsating out of me, absorbed within the confines of the bubble. As it takes in my aura, it ripples like the aftershock of throwing a rock into still waters. If I can do it harder, I can break this forcefield.

Hermes is bleeding from scratches along his neck and forearms. His shirt has been torn, and a long gash covers half his chest. Lupo's head rests separately from his body as smoke lifts from his fur like he was burned. My eyes dart quickly through the moving bodies, finding Callie and Achilles. Their vortex of wind and flame surge beyond the earthen wall that is largely still intact.

Callie soars with her currents, feet first into the dirt wall; using it like a springboard, she surges off it toward an Elemental. With her hands pressed together, her winds propel her, and she pierces the chest cavity of the immortal man she is fighting. Spinning in a circle, she keeps hold of the man, hurls his body over her shoulder, and slams him into the ground, creating a divot with the impact of his body.

With her hands coated glossy red with blood, she tosses the immortal's heart into the ground next to him. Surveying the field as she wipes her brow with her forearm, she soars off toward Achilles.

"Moros, you feel like finishing off your little trio?" Flint's voice is loud inside this vacuum chamber, and his words echo around my mind.

That's it.

Moros is the Mind Mage that causes Patroclus' death. I heard Hermes say his name when he told me the story on the balcony. Despite the confines around me, my trembling body nearly vibrates in Flint's grasp. What if he uses me against them all? *What if he makes me kill them?* The roll of my aura pulses again, and the confinement quakes under my power.

I can't. I can't be responsible for their deaths.

"I would love to add to my collection, but we have orders to follow." Moros answers. Flicking my eyes across the field, I sense him. Like a dark stain of cancer polluting the earthen wall, Moros sits on the top, swinging his legs without care.

Moros tips his head at me, and the hollow black orbs for eyes pierce me with ominous knowing of their plan. He looks as slippery as he sounds, with oily black hair flattened to his head and contrasting his snow-white skin, almost sickly pale.

Hermes said only Atlas was a stronger Mind Mage than Moros, but his power can't be limitless. He's preventing everyone from seeing and sensing Flint and me, preventing me from moving, while also hiding his presence atop the wall. Hermes would have perceived him otherwise.

What are they working toward? *They need something.* They could have easily left with me immediately and no one would have been the wiser.

"Let's get on with it. The girl is smart." Moros tells Flint.

"A body with these curves, the brain of a scholar, and the mouth of a bitch." Gripping my chin under his hand, he forces my head back and smashes his lips onto mine, forcing his greasy tongue into my mouth. "I don't have much use for the brain, but I have many plans for this mouth."

"Quit playing and get on with it." Moros stops him, and the assault to my face is over. Tears spill from my eyes, and I remain nothing more than a puppet sitting on Flint's lap, controlled like he is my marionette.

Like the Mirage Hermes is casting of me, a projection of Flint walks through me, stepping in front of where we are hidden under Moros' blanket of invisibility. Where Hermes' projection is his beautiful, brilliant light, this projection of Flint begins as shadow and smoke. Still translucent from our vantage point, I can still see through the figure to the field below. I sense the presence of someone else to my left and another to my right; though locked to movement, I can't see who it is.

"Let's get finished and get her to Ares."

If I weren't frozen under Moros' power, the woman's voice next to me would have stopped me dead in my tracks. My eyes widen, and my chest heaves as my body breaks out into a sweat.

Aunt Demi.

The Onyx Alpha is pissed. I removed part of his pack in seconds and returned my swords to my back. Feigning boredom, I pretend to yawn, and he trembles with anger. I didn't mean to laugh in his face, but he's making this too easy for me.

"Okay, okay. I'm sorry." I pretend to apologize. "Let's fight for real now." Pulling a small throwing knife concealed in my belt, I widen my stance and crouch for his attack. He comes at me with everything he has. Fuming at my taunts, he's sloppy. The small Adamantine blade is coated in Oleander toxin; each small slice into his flesh slows his heart, yet he's too seething to know it.

Still darting around his attacks, I drive the blade through his flesh and slide out of his path too fast for him to track. Shifting his stance with a split-second reaction, he finally catches me off-guard and lands two swipes, one across my chest and the other on my arm.

He keeps driving toward me: lunging, swiping, and snapping as I land shallow cuts into his dark pelt. The images of Rhea, beaten and broken, flood my mind. My sister was whipped by his hand. I have no intention of making his death quick.

My assault increases, and I push more strength behind my blades. I leave him no time to recover as I wage a hailstorm of attacks. Finally pulling my sword from its home, the blue blade glows as I slice into him faster. The blur of my movements looks like streaks of light as my sword swings true, and I hit my mark repeatedly.

He kicks his powerful legs backward, knocking my sword from my hands and sending me ten feet in the air and landing on my back. My sword slides across the plain, resting at Achilles' feet.

I run toward Achilles, and he hurls my sword at me.

"Stop playing with your food." he yells to me.

I jump to reach the handle and launch myself, stretching my hand out for my sword. Connecting with the handle, I spin my body around and swing it in an arc as I move.

The great Alpha jumps behind me, hoping to end our fight with my neck in his mouth. But it's my power that cuts through his throat. Channeling my Light energy through the topaz stone, it shoots a beam of Absolute Light like a laser. Slicing through his neck like a hot knife through butter, I hit the ground in a crouch with my sword out at my side. Lupo's head rolls to a stop by my foot. The orange glow of his murderous eyes fades to pale yellow as the bloody ichor of his immortality darkens the soil of the plain.

The packs can feel his death, making them falter. *The second son of Ares is dead.* They lift their heads and howl at his loss. I scan the fray for the Zeta, King of Shifters. According to the pack hierarchy, he can command them all. If I get him to surrender, perhaps this fight can end. He's been missing for months, but I can't imagine an attack like this without his presence. Scanning the field, my eyes dart from wolf to wolf, looking for him.

I finally spot him near the tree line, sitting with more than a dozen wolves watching the battle. The size of him is unreal. Alphas are the most prominent and strongest of the Shifter packs, but this wolf makes even Lupo look like a juvenile. He has to be ten feet tall, standing on all fours. Gritting my teeth at the coward who stands by and watches his packs die, I take a step toward him before the fiery red hair of a traitor catches my attention.

An endless parade of wolves step in front of me with snarling fangs and reflective eyes. Rolling my neck and gripping my sword tightly, I begin my ascent toward the mountainside, where Flint stands alone on a ledge; the wolves' bodies drop to the field in my wake as I slice through them with my sword and light. Like the Zeta, he only watches, refusing to add his weak powers into the mix, and seems content with his smug smile to supervise.

Casting my aura out, I focus on the fights around me as I approach Flint. The Zeta sitting by the tree line makes me nervous. *What are they waiting for?*

"Reinforcements are coming." Medusa's voice rings out, "The Commune portal is nearly working again."

"We need more than reinforcements, Deuce." I nod my head to the trees, and she sees the Zeta.

"Avaley, get to the Commune. We need Delphi to send their warriors." Medusa's command echoes across the plain.

Avaley and her sister, Anahita, fight with the skill and precision of assassins. Keeping their backs to each other, they shoot arrows and throw daggers, but wolves are closing in on them. The circle of wolves tightens their formation and descends slowly upon the sisters.

Sensing the urgency, Avaley takes three bounding leaps toward Ana. Bracing her sister's foot in her hands, Ana boosts her upward. Propelled by her winds, Avaley flips high in the air as she arches over the wolves. Her arms splayed wide, she looks like a diver performing a perfect swan dive. But on her descent to the ground, aiming toward the mountain to use her wind speed to run for help, a wolf runs; jumping off the back of another Shifter, it soars into her from the side. The wolf's large muzzle engulfs her neck and nearly half her head.

Slamming her body to the ground, the wolf takes the life of the young Wind Siren.

Her older sister, Anahita, releases a guttural scream of agony into the night. Her power and aura rush from her, thrusting ice blades three feet long in all directions. Wolves duck or are impaled through various parts of their body by her grief. I throw up a Light Sheild to protect my side from impalement and they sizzle within the hot blue light of my power.

She drops to the ground, falling to her knees. With shaking limbs, Ana places her hands on the sides of what remains of her sister's face. Seeing the delicate headscarf has fallen on the ground, Ana gently places it back over Avaley's head, covering her hair.

Turning to Flint with anger in her hazel eyes, she stands with wild revenge burning in her gaze. Flint has his eyes locked on Ana, laughing until he doubles over, covering his stomach and pointing at her sister's dead body. The state of rage consuming her causes her entire body to shake with violent tremors. Oddly, the remaining wolves around her snarl and huff at her feet but leave her alone and unharmed next to the mutilated body of her little sister.

"Your sister's debt is paid." With that, a portal flashes near her, and a young woman's beaten, dirtied body drops to the ground. Ana crawls to her with wracking sobs echoing across the field.

Medusa's attention snaps to her General. With a gaping mouth and slumped shoulders, she is in disbelief at their betrayal.

"I'm sorry, Medusa," Ana says with a quivering chin. The beaten woman and Ana huddle over the body of their dead sister as the horror of the plain continues around them.

"The great Hermes!" Flint yells across the plain. "Getting tired already?"

"We'll see how tired I am when I meet you on the mountain."

Twenty more wolves are fighting a dozen Elemental warriors and another twenty are pawing across the plain from the other side of the earthen wall. The Dark Mage is working against the wall again, opening up a large middle section and allowing more wolves through. Callie and Achilles keep their attacks focused on the other side of the wall and the wolves approaching as we fight, the wolves arriving on our side.

Two of Medusa's Earth Mages are working together to churn the earth at the point of entry. Like a blender, the dirt and mud roil together and suck down the wolves that attempt to cross—burying them deep within the earth to claw their way out. Several wolves have scaled the dirt wall and, breaching the top of it, and they descend upon the Elementals.

"We need to get out of here," I yell across the field as our small group dwindles like a candle flame, slowly burning into nothing but a stream of white smoke.

The wolves jump off the top of the earthen wall, ripping the two women apart limb by limb. Continuing their earthen work until the very end, they fight until the last of their ichor drenches the ground, pulling five Shifters into the earth with them.

"Where is your little vixen, Hermes?" Flint calls to me. "My father would like a word with her."

My attention snaps to Flint. *Father.* Is he Ares' son, his true son? A monstrous snarl stretches across his face at my reaction.

Armed with my swords, my strength and speed push me through the bodies of fur and claws, slashing and stabbing them. Our small group is working ourselves to the middle so we can teleport out of the plain. If we can return to Odysseus and Penelope, we can bring reinforcements back and protect the Kenya Commune.

"It's no matter, Hermes. I already have her."

"He's goading you, Hermes. Don't listen to him." Callie calls back as she and Achilles have moved into position behind me.

Flint's head rolls back as he laughs at Callie's reassurances.

"Where else do you think she would go? She knows nothing of this world." he calls out with his voice to the plain. "She's nothing more than a predictable mortal with too much power. Of course, she would go back to her apartment." He rubs his hands together and paces two steps back and forth. "The Zeta was ready for her to appear from her little portal."

"He's lying," Medusa calls out.

"Am I?"

Rhea wouldn't go directly home. Surely, she would be

more cautious... but the Zeta Wolf's presence with his pack sitting at the edge of the plain doesn't fit. Why didn't I talk to her before we left about her leaving? I was so sure I would be wrong and misread the situation. *Why didn't I just talk to her?*

"And as soon as I watch the wolves tear your throats out, I'll go back to the Underworld to mount your little *bitch* and take everything I want from her."

My resolve breaks open like a dam, and my power surges through me like flood waters bursting from behind its walls.

Blue domes of light scatter across the ground as pockets of Medusa's Elemental warriors from the Kenya Commune teleport to the plain, providing us cover and jumping in the fray with the Shifters.

The Zeta King's massive paws thud across the plain as his long-striding gait brings him closer and closer to me. His pack follows his charge as he releases a great roar into the night. The wolves encircling us turn their heads to him, attentive to whatever command he conveys through their Shifter-telepathy.

Charging back my arm, with my fingers wrapped tightly around the hilt, the Lord of Light soars through the distance between us, aiming for Flint's heart.

"Hermes! No!" Atlas arrives with one of the recent groups of reinforcements. The horrid expression in his wild eyes follows the path of the sword to the place where Flint is standing, and time slows to a near halt as I watch my sword slice into the sternum of my victim.

"**You have a choice tonight.** *Stay, and you will meet your hunter. Leave, and you will die, and the cycle will start again. Hermes is not strong enough to do what he needs to do while you remain with him. He can't admit it, but he loves you too much to do what is necessary. Make your choice and give him the key.*"

Hecate's words ring through my mind as I watch Hermes light up with an ultra-violent burst of his power, fueled by Flint's taunting words. Locked in this confinement by Moros, held by the disgusting hands of Flint as he snarls and laughs at the impact his Dark Mirage is inflicting on Hermes, my powers inside thrum and surge, fighting against Moros. He is weakening. He can't keep up all the illusions *and* hold me back.

My silver aura reverberates around the tense atmosphere concealing my presence, and it quakes and shivers as my powers attack it. Moros's oily grasp is slipping, but he tightens his ropes of energy around me, squeezing the life from me.

Life.

The power of Life Hecate said I have in her caves when I healed Flora floats into my mind like a dandelion seed. The sensation of sunshine passed from me to Flora as I pushed my healing powers into her. I could feel life returning to her, replenishing all that was depleted.

If he intends to squeeze the life from me, I will siphon it out of him. Instead of pushing my power outward, I feel the threads of his power cutting around my body in tight coils. It's thick like sludge, and I pull it into me, taking his strength and aura.

He senses it immediately, and I can taste his panic. His powers spasm as I drain him. Like brown fog billowing low to the ground, his dirtied aura leaves his body and travels across the plain into the bubble of my prison. Desperate to pull his powers back, he tries to release me, but I refuse to let him go.

His power and aura swirl around my feet, twirling upward and blending with the silver pillars of my magic, dancing and twisting around the space. Moros' life force is powering me while he tries to maintain the illusion he's cast over this battle, but he's withering away.

He's still speaking to Hermes through the dark mirage of Flint, convincing him the Zeta King already has me in possession. The mention of his name draws my attention to the edge of the plain where a monster sits. Twice the size of every other wolf, he waits.

And then just as quickly as a shifting wind, everything changes at once.

Hermes rears his arm back, his great glowing sword ready to sail at his command.

The Zeta Wolf and his packs begin to descend into the plain.

A dozen portals of light open up, releasing fearsome warriors from Medusa's Commune. Atlas, Penelope, and

Odysseus, dressed in their fighting leathers and armed with weapons, emerge from various portals.

Hermes releases the sword, and its tip stares directly at me as it travels on the light of blue aura to my center.

"This will only hurt a moment, goddess." The real Flint says into my ear, tightening his grip around my neck.

I drain the last of life from Moros and feel his shriveled form disintegrate into dust. With his death, the illusion over everyone's minds drops, as does his hold on me. The atmosphere of my confinement bursts, and the dark mirage of Flint fades away.

Free, I raise my hand toward the oncoming sword as the metal blade slices through my flesh tenderly, with Hermes looking into my eyes.

Realizing that it was all a lie freezes him as his sword runs through me.

Hermes

I fall to my knees as my sword drives into the woman I love. Her dress is tattered and her bloodied face is streaked with black mascara showing the streams of her tears. An illusion that coated the battlefield crumbles, revealing the truth. The gargled gasp pushed from her throat echoes across the plain, and I drop to my knees, unable to remain standing.

A great wind rises from the plain and sucks all the air inward like a great vacuum toward the footpath of the mountain. With a pained expression locked on her face, her arms are cast wide, and her back is arched in a dramatic bow as the great winds from across the earth absorb into her. Visibly whipping across the plain, pulling dust and debris toward her, the roar of the wind is deafening. Everyone, Elemental and Shifter, strain against the force and attempt to keep their footing. Some tumble and flip across the plain before they grasp the dirt and grass to root them. Flint struggles to remain upright as the power roils around him, failing to keep a hold on Rhea.

The gushing wind stops, and a tremendous clap like lightning pops across the plain. A sonic boom erupts into the night as Rhea's aura rushes across the ground with blinding speed. Every living being is blown back by force. Achilles desperately reaches for Callie as she throws a Shield of Currents in front of her, pushing against the force threatening to blow her away; she reaches behind her, grasping for her mate. The Zeta King, only twenty feet away, hunches down, lowering his great shoulders while his red fur billows with the violence of the surge. Two wolves cower behind him, using his body to guard them against the power.

Lying low on the ground, I clutch the clumps of grass as I slide back. My chest feels like it is ripping open, as if my blade is slicing through me as well. The burning and tearing pull a scream from my throat as the pulsing aura billows with the force of a tornado.

Blinding light streams in great ripples from Rhea. Her aura throbs beautiful silver, like starlight itself pumping like a heart; her aura is cast into the night and travels fast beyond the horizon.

As her aura and power surges around us, memories rush into our minds. Elementals fall to the ground, clutching their heads and screaming against the pain—thousands of years of her memories are thrust into our consciousness. The Shifters drop to their sides, whimpering and twitching, locked in their Shifted state as the visions stream into them.

We see the memories of her mortal lifetimes and hear the voices she spoke with as we feel each of her deaths.

A cloud of darkness swells around her, and two wings of black smoke and silver aura emerge from her back like the great wings of a phoenix. Her body remains locked in the throws of the power escaping her as she rises in the air, lifted by the force of her .

Living and dying hundreds of times, we hear her names spoken. I've found her in most of them and loved her in all of them. My Juliette, with her hazel eyes and coffee-colored hair, looks back at me as she withered on the Adamantine spear of Ares; Queen Guinevere, with her flowing gown and strawberry hair waving in the wind, was abducted and drained of her powers on a hangman's noose before she was decapitated; the red-haired Cleopatra, standing tall at the top of the great Sphinx and serving as General for Medusa, was impaled on a Shifter's claws during the Great Exodus of Egypt; a golden apple poisoned Eve, the great mother and shepherd of mortals, as she dropped dead in our garden.

Dozens of faces and names echo across the plain as the cries of her deaths surround us. The agony is ripped from everyone as Elementals scream and Shifters yowl. Moments feel like hours until, finally, we see her.

The woman I fell in love with at the dawn of time and the edge of the horizon between realms. Raven hair as black as the Void and silver eyes that hold the light of a thousand stars looks back at me in my memory.

Night personified, fighting Ares, she flew through the realm on the phoenix's wings, billowing her power across the sky; she seemed to bring night across the horizon as her raven hair flowed behind her. She is the keeper of my soul and the savior of the realm.

Nyx.

As the waves subside, my head lolls to the side. With hazy vision, I see her form drop to the ground. The clatter of my sword clashes against the rocks of the mountain as it falls from her chest. Weakened, I fight against my limbs to cooperate.

I have to get to her.

Blinking away the clouds that cover my eyes, I try to focus as Flint crawls to her. Rolling from my back to my front, I push myself upright, stumbling on my feet while unable to clear the fog covering my sight. Shaking my head, I try to steady myself and call upon my power, but it's unresponsive. Spent by the battle and exhausted by Rhea's aura.

Nyx's aura.

Two women behind Flint edge to Rhea's body sprawled on the ground, oozing dark red blood across the deep green of her dress. Narrowing my eyes and tripping over my ragged steps, I stumble, falling back to the ground.

Lifeless honey eyes stare unseeing across the plain. My chest contracts and my heart rips seeing her lying there. The weight of hundreds of deaths is a volatile mass in my stomach that I push down as I fight to stand back up.

A dark-haired woman nears Flint, touching him as he pulls Rhea's body onto him. My power stirs inside me, seeing him touch her body. With pursed lips, I search inside for my abilities and feel the cool sparks of light. Looking back at Rhea, the second woman rights herself and kneels by Flint and the dark-haired woman.

Terra.

My nostrils flare as her eyes cut into me with hatred. *She betrayed us.*

The small fractions of my power charge and collide against each other as the storm brews within me to get Rhea's body out of Flint's grasp.

Terra places her hands on the shoulders of Flint and the woman.

No.

My vision turns white hot with rage, and I unleash a scream of pain and anger; the earth beneath me tremors and quakes. The very mountain of Kenya quivers under my rage as a chasm in the earth cracks at my feet. Lighting clashes around me as I feel a great beast within me, creeping, looking for a way out—my fury longing to devour Flint whole.

The ground beneath them swirls as Terra's earth power turns the dirt to quicksand.

My power is like molten lava leaking into me from the crater in my soul, ripped by the cut of Rhea's wound. In an instant, I flash forward with a great blue light surrounding me to the spot where Rhea and Flint just stood. But I'm too late. The ground is solid again, and they're gone.

She's gone.

Hermes

The seconds after she disappeared in the clutches of Flint, I turned to the Zeta. Still Shifted, the great beast looks back at me with deep brown and green eyes. With a nod, he lifts his muzzle to the sky and howls. All the wolfs on the plain respond, and their cries bounce around the night.

Walking to the location of Lupo's body on the plain, the Zeta sits as his pack surrounds him. An Elemental, bloodied and limping, approaches, and the rich purple light of their portal wand covers the pack of wolves, taking Lupo's body with them.

Defeated and frozen by shock, no one speaks as what remains of our small force looks blankly around the demolished plain that oozes ichor from the death of many Immortals. Of our twenty fighters, only Callie, Achilles, Medusa, and Ana remain with me.

Our tiny cottage reeks of her sweet scent, like honey and berries, and I can't go inside. I can't bear the cold rooms that would have filled with the warmth of her presence and the bright shine of her smile. Every crevasse of my body is full of dried blood and dirt. My chest feels gaped open with my heart hanging outside my body.

The feeling of the sword leaving my hands to sail through the air is emblazoned on my palms like a scar. I keep rubbing them together like I can make it go away. The sound of the sword cutting into her keeps playing through my ears like a broken record. I put my head in my hands again and let the sobs flow from me freely.

Why did I throw the sword?

A small click of the garden gate tells me someone is here. I don't care who it is. Hopefully, it's someone here to kill me too. I'll gladly surrender and let them, so I don't have to live another life without her.

"Hermes?" Hecate's voice is low and cautious. And for a good reason too. I stand and face her, my face burning with rage. I lunge at her, but shadows encase my ankles and wrists like chains holding me in place. Her Hellhound materializes from the darkness instantly, accompanied by more hounds that undulate from the shadows and swirl attentively around her. Burning embers glow behind their eye sockets in the darkness.

"Careful, Ferryman. My children do not take kindly to someone threatening their mother."

"What did you say to her tonight?"

"That she had a choice."

"Why did you send her to her death? Why do you send everyone I love to die?" Tears pour down my face, and I fall to my knees. The shadows release me, and I beat my fists on the ground.

"It was still her choice. She let the events play out; she could have told you or surrendered to them. She chose this path, and now we must go down it with her." Hecate, still roiling with cold shadows that permeate from the ground, approaches me. Kneeling, she places her hand on my back.

"I killed her," I whisper the truth as I beg the night to swallow me into the darkness so I can join her in the Void. A ragged breath enters my lungs, and my lip quivers as I accept my actions.

"You set her free. The first of her immortality was returned to her tonight, locked within the runes of your sword. Hermes, you are the one true mate of the Goddess of Darkness. There was no one else she could trust more than you." Her voice echoes and bounces around the garden as if the surrounding shadows speak and whisper Hecate's words. "She will not die on this night."

I snap my head up from the ground.

"That's right, Hermes. She will survive, but she remains in grave danger. Ares now possesses the strongest Elemental that has ever existed and intends to use her to set the world on fire before he consumes her. We must stop him, and you have the key."

In a blink, Hecate is gone; dissolved into a swirl of Shadow. Sitting back on my heels, my shoulders drop, and I lower my head, closing my eyes.

I sit in the garden until sunrise chewing over Hecate's words. Atlas joined me for a while, knowing there was nothing to say; he just took up space next to me, letting me wallow in my guilt. With a clasp on my shoulder, he left to return to the Atlanta Commune and convince Eris of the ensuing war.

My eyes are heavy and swollen from my grief. In only five days, the equinox will be upon us.

"Hermes?" Callie's small voice calls to me from behind and startles me in the quiet garden, lost deep in my thoughts. She's crying too. I wipe my eyes and sit up to look at her.

Her puffy red eyes and red-tipped nose tell me she's been

crying for a while. She's so petite and slender, but her strength is incredible. She's always calm and rational. So many times, she has gotten us out of messy situations when we go on a mission and all hell breaks loose. She always keeps a level head and doesn't let emotions get in the way of the task. Callie usually has such a look of faith and determination in her aqua eyes. But not now. Right now, she looks so small and unsure.

She rushes into my arms, hugging me tightly.

"Oh, H," she wails. "I'm so sorry!"

"Shhhhh," I soothe her. "I know."

We stand like this for a few minutes until her tears slow, and her grip around my waist loosens. Achilles has entered the garden, quietly waiting by the gate. As Callie raises her head, I let her go, and she wipes her eyes. Achilles walks over, pulling a handkerchief from his pocket for her.

"You okay?" he asks me.

"I'll answer that question later," My reply is dry. Achilles puts his arm around Callie, and she leans her head on him.

Callie has her purse on her shoulder; retrieving it from the plain, she opens it, pulling Rhea's book out. Her face is curious as she returns her hand inside to retrieve something else. Callie pulls out Rhea's sword necklace and holds it in her hand. Her eyes turn sad, and a new tear rolls down one of her cheeks.

"I guess she put the necklace in my purse?" she says, handing the book and necklace over to me. I hold the chain in my hand, and the matching one around my neck feels cold, as if it knows the owner of its twin can no longer wear it.

I take Rhea's necklace and insert the tiny sword into the locket of the book. The latch clicks, and I open the cover, looking again at the inscription in my mother's handwriting.

"To my son, Hermes
Only you can free her.
But first, you must free yourself.
Remember."

I don't understand why my mother wrote this book, why she penned a dedication to me with such a cryptic message, and why the book was so compelling to Rhea. Several memories of the painful deaths of my mate flash behind my eyes. Hecate's words play in my mind.

"You have the key."

I stare at the book for several minutes, turning it over and thinking about what we must be missing. Something on the spine of the book glimmers and catches my eye. Gold leaf pressed into the letters and impressions; it gives the book a regal design against the dark blue leather. But something else reflects, brighter than the rest of the gold adorning the book as I shift it around in the moonlight.

A tiny hole in the book's spine, large enough for the point of the small sword that unlocks the cover.

My pulse quickening, I stick the sword charm into the hole. Like before, a tiny click of a lock releases. The soft sound resonates around us in the garden as Callie and Achilles lean in. A section of the spine pops open to reveal a hidden compartment. Inside is a tiny vial of black liquid. A cork top is coated in black wax and holds the impression of three moons.

The seal of the Triple Moon Goddess.

I remove the vial from its hidden compartment and hold it to the light. A small parchment is tied around the neck of the vial with a thin gold chain. Carefully turning the parchment over in my hand, I see a simple phrase is handwritten...

"Find me."

EPILOGUE

It's a lovely day in Avalon, a realm of mist and twilight. It's mid-day, so the full moon is high in the sky, lighting our path. I walk with my court guards, Hypnos, and Mor. They are a stoic pair, not much for conversation, which I don't mind today as I'm exhausted and in a brooding mood. We walk to Pandora's Cave to investigate the report from the Lady of the Lake.

"She says someone went through the portal?"

"Yes, Prince Regent." Hypnos is always so formal, even though we've been best friends, nearly brothers, for almost twenty ages.

"When are you going to call me by my name?" I huff, pinching the bridge of my nose. The small hike is already exhausting me.

"Your strength is fading faster these days," Mor says in her usual dismissive demeanor. She rarely shows emotion; we've only seen her smile once in the ten ages.

"I have strength enough to visit the caves."

The rest of the walk is quiet. Arriving at the dormant portal, the Lady of the Lake rises from the dark waters at the edges of the cave. She only exposes the top of her head and black eyes, leaving the rest of herself in her familiar aquatic home. The pale blue scales of her flesh glisten in the moonlight, and she looks at the portal. I've never understood how her communication works, but without speaking, her intentions are always received. I respectfully bow to her, and she returns the small gesture.

"Someone has used the portal between Avalon and Gaea twice." I give them her message. "Both times, they visited The Void."

"The Void? Truly?" Hypnos is surprised. "Could it be the goddess?"

"We'll soon find out. If they used it twice, they'd surely use it again soon." I stare at the portal, dreaming of the day it's operable again. "Mor, watch the portal and capture anything that passes through it. And I mean *anything*." Mor nods and sits on a boulder, staring at the portal. She'll remain here until she can fulfill my order.

"Hypnos, help me back to the castle and see if you can speak with Hecate in her dreams."

"As you command, Prince Regent." I give him a stern look with his formal response. "Yes, Orion." he corrects himself.

"Avalon will answer the call of the goddess when she awakens. Let's be ready."

Thank you so much for reading. If you enjoyed this story, please leave a review.

Up next up in The Forgotten Goddess series is The Unforgotten Flame, a Forgotten Goddess novella.

Acknowledgements

After a decade of struggling to put the ideas of this story into words, it is with immense gratitude but also an odd sense of wonder that I am taking time to write acknowledgements today.

When I first woke up from a dream thinking, *that would be a cool idea for a book*, I never thought I would actually go on to write that story. I am overwhelmed with emotion and pride in myself as I hold the finished product in my hands and see my name in print as an author.

First and foremost, I want to thank my kids who supported me through the ups and downs of this journey. Listening to me rattle off ideas and being patient while I took time from our life to type feverishly over my keyboard for months and months has gotten me to this point. Their unwavering belief in me kept me going, even when I doubted myself.

I would like to express my sincere gratitude to Suzy Vadori for her exceptional guidance throughout the development process of this book. Suzy's professional insight, and unwavering support helped shape this work into its final form.

Thank you, Suzy, for your invaluable contribution to this

book. Your professionalism, insight, and dedication have made all the difference.

Importantly a hearty thank you to every member of #Booktok. The community of people sharing their love of reading and writing is truly inspiring and gave me a place to belong after several years of floating around in the dark on my own. Without you, this book would not exist.

Finally, I want to thank the readers who will take the time to engage with this work. I hope that it will inspire, or entertain you in some way. It is a dream come true to be able to share this story with you after so many years of imagining this moment.

Thank you to everyone who played a role in bringing this book to life. Your support means more to me than words can express.

Rebekah Sinclair
Writes

To stay informed on my upcoming releases, book signing events, and more, visit my website and sign up for my newsletter.

www.rebekahsinclairwrites.com

If you'd like to chat with other readers, join the Rebekah Sinclair Writes discord!

CAST OF CHARACTERS

WARNING

Contains spoilers. If you have not finished reading the book, it is highly recommended you turn back now. Seriously, you don't have anything to prove to anyone.

Like the post-credit scene after our favorite movies, come back when you are finished and enjoy some illustrations and other details about the characters featured in this story.

Don't say I didn't warn you.

Rhea

As with every lifetime before, the passing of the goddess was swift and unexpected, but this time something was different.

A memory carried on the winds of her passing circled the realm and something was awakened.

Hermes

His heart was a compass that always pointed towards her, and
though the journey may be long and arduous, he will never
stop searching for the one who holds the key to his soul.

Memories of Patroclus flood our minds carried in by the winds, and take us back to the moments we shared together.

He will forever be our flame that burns brightly in our hearts and illuminates our darkest days.

Terra

No one knows why her heart was a locked door, but her
betrayal will leave scars that time cannot heal.

Unapologetic, she was a true wolf in sheep's clothing, who
reveled in the chaos she wrought and cared not for the
shattered trust in her wake.

Damien

He did not deserve to die in such a cruel and unjust manner.
He was a man of great courage and kindness.

We will continue his mission, because he believed in us, even
with the differences and strife that separate our kinds, he still
had faith.

Lupo

While some may mourn the passing of this man, in truth it is
the world that should breathe a sigh of relief. For he was a dark
and twisted soul, a purveyor of pain and suffering, who left a
trail of destruction in his wake.

Though death may bring an end to his physical presence, his
legacy of cruelty and malice will not be easily forgotten.

Atlas

I have seen the rise and fall of many empires throughout history, and troubling signs are on the horizon.

The winds of change are blowing, and with them come the seeds of conflict and upheaval. We must prepare ourselves for the storm that is to come.

Athena

Athena, goddess of wisdom and warfare, met her end not on
the field of battle but in a moment of treachery and deceit.

Her death was a shock to all who revered her, for she was a
symbol of strength and resilience.
Yet, even in her final moments, she remained steadfast, refusing
to give in to the darkness that had befallen her.

May her memory live on as a testament to the courage and
wisdom that she embodied.

Eris

I refuse to believe that the world is headed towards dark times. There may be challenges ahead, but we have weathered storms before and we will do so again.

Flint

This is going to be fun.

Odysseus & Penelope

Our hearts ache for our family who are going through such a
difficult time.

We may not be able to take away their pain, but we can offer
our love and support to help them through it.

Together, we will get through this, and emerge on the other
side stronger and more resilient than ever before.

The love and unity of family is a powerful force that can
overcome even the greatest of darkness.

Bridget

The storm clouds gather on the horizon, and I fear that what lies ahead may be even more difficult than what we have already faced.

We must brace ourselves for what is to come, for the winds of change will soon be upon us.

But even as I steel myself for the trials ahead, I cannot shake the feeling that something far more ominous looms in the distance, a threat that we cannot yet comprehend.

Flora & Zephyr

Though fate had cruelly torn us apart, we clung to the hope that one day we would be reunited, that we could pick up where we left off and make up for lost time.

For true love endures even the greatest of hardships, and in the end, it will always find a way to bring us back to where we belong

Demeter

There is nothing heavy about the weight of my betrayal. I only hope that someday, everyone will understand why I did what I did.

For sometimes, in the pursuit of a higher purpose, we must make sacrifices that test our moral compass and challenge our sense of right and wrong.

Medusa

Though time and distance had conspired to keep us apart, my love for her remained as strong as ever.

Even as I watched from afar, my heart ached for her, and I longed to hold her in my arms once more.

And yet, fate was cruel, and when news of her passing reached me, another part of me had died with her.

For though we may be separated for now, I know that our love is eternal, and that it will endure when we meet in our next lives.

Until I see you again, my love.

Anahita & Avaley

The dark path that we were forced to take was not one that we chose willingly.

We never wanted to betray someone that we respected and admired, but the circumstances of the situation left us with no other choice.

I hope that someday Medusa will understand.

Zara & Kellan

As we stand here on the edge of change, uncertain of what the future holds, we are reminded of the bond that has always held us together.

We will face this difficult time ahead together, as we always have, drawing strength from each other and holding fast to the hope that the future will be kind to us.

Hecate

The journey that has begun is but the first step on a long and difficult road, one that will put courage, wisdom, and strength to the test.

There will be many challenges, and difficult choices along the way. But know this: the path is one that has been foretold, and none of us are alone in this journey.

Printed in Great Britain
by Amazon